THE DAWN OF LOVE

Rick, carrying the crying child, made his way to the curb, and Linda followed. The child's mother rushed forward and grabbed the little boy.

Rick looked around and saw Linda. She looked into his eyes.

"I saw," said Linda. "I saw the whole thing. You were the only one to do anything. You saved his life!"

"You're ... so *beautiful*!" Rick said.

"You're the one who's beautiful," Linda heard herself say. "You're a beautiful person."

It was as if a light had come on, as if the sun had come out, in the middle of the drenching rain. She could tell by his look that he didn't believe what she had said—and then, by his look, that he did believe.

He leaned forward and kissed her, gently. Nobody noticed when they went off together, arm in arm.

But Where Is Love

Marguerite Kloepfer

AVON
PUBLISHERS OF BARD, CAMELOT AND DISCUS BOOKS

BUT WHERE IS LOVE is an original publication of Avon Books. This work has never before appeared in book form.

AVON BOOKS
A division of
The Hearst Corporation
959 Eighth Avenue
New York, New York 10019

First Avon Printing, February, 1980

AVON TRADEMARK REG. U.S. PAT. OFF. AND IN
OTHER COUNTRIES, MARCA REGISTRADA, HECHO EN
U.S.A.

Printed in the U.S.A.

To Lynn

I wish to express my appreciation to Leonardo Bercovici, author, screenwriter, and teacher of "The Novel and Human Behavior" at UCLA, and to Kathryn Vought, Associate Editor of Avon Books, for their help and encouragement.

MARGUERITE KLOEPFER

ONE

At the time Linda Allenby and Rick Dublin met, which was on a Friday in October of 1972 on the UCLA campus, Linda already knew what she wanted out of life, and it had nothing to do with men. She was in the process of shaking loose from what she considered a parental strait jacket. Linda desperately prized freedom.

Rick, on the other hand, was on the make. Linda's radar told her this, even as she watched Rick and Kemp Conway saunter in feigned nonchalance toward the NOW booth which was set up on the lawn across from Royce Hall.

Delcie Green, Linda's co-worker in the booth, quivered in excitement.

"Look what's coming," Delcie managed to murmur out of the corner of her mouth. "Robert Redford and Steve McQueen!"

"Don't be earthy," said Linda. Sometimes she wondered what Delcie was doing in the women's movement.

"Only twice as big and twice as handsome," breathed Delcie.

Linda glanced at her friend with an incredulity mixed with affection. Delcie inclined toward plumpness. She wore her hair in the new style, with short, tight curls which made her head look like a ball of feathers. Her nose, though small, had a sharp, decisive curve, and her mouth, also small, appeared to be in a perpetual pucker. Delcie affected large, round, tinted glasses, behind which one could barely perceive the heavy-lidded eyes which gave her a continual sleepy demeanor.

"Why are they coming to the NOW booth?" Delcie persisted. "Maybe they've lost their way?"

"If they have, it's a put-on," said Linda. She didn't know why, but her own arms were prickling with goose flesh, though the afternoon was warm. She had a queasy premonition of trouble. Even on an enlightened campus such as

UCLA the women's movement still drew its share of hecklers. Linda sat up, stiff-backed, and looked at the two men with what she hoped was a cool, detached expression.

"Hel-lo!" said Kemp, the Steve McQueen type.

Delcie was right. They were twice as tall and—

"Hello," said Linda reluctantly, speaking only because her mother had drilled politeness into her since babyhood. She was at a loss to recognize her own voice. She sounded like a robot.

"Hel-lo!" chimed Delcie. Her eyes widened.

The second man, Rick Dublin, who was broad-shouldered and rugged and bore a faint resemblance to Robert Redford, said nothing. He simply stared at Linda as if mesmerized.

"What are you chicks selling?" Kemp began.

"We're not selling anything," Linda replied coldly.

"Don't tell me you're giving it away!" said Kemp. He guffawed at his own joke.

Linda noticed Rick didn't laugh. In fact he seemed to be observing Kemp as if he were watching a play, a play with which he was not entirely sympathetic.

"We're explaining the women's movement," said Delcie, in the sweet, birdlike tone she reserved for special occasions. "We're trying to reach every person on campus."

"That right?" said Kemp in a blasé tone. He towered above the table, teetering from heel to toe, and gazed at Linda. Actually, Linda realized, he was sizing up her breasts. She wished now that the shirt, a faded blue cotton knit, wasn't so tight. She almost longed for the old, confining protection of a bra, which she had given up when she joined the women's movement.

"We have a quota," said Delcie. "We're supposed to talk to fifty people a day."

"That right?" Kemp repeated.

Linda jumped to a conclusion—that Kemp sounded like an imbecile.

"Only the quota's too high," Delcie rattled on. "Most people aren't that interested in Women's Lib."

"Now hold on," said Kemp. "Don't tell me a couple of cute chicks like you are Women's Libbers?"

The arrogance, the insufferable self-assurance of the man was more than Linda could stomach.

"He did it again," she said, not to Kemp but to Delcie, spacing her words in a low, precise tone.

"Did what?" said Kemp. "I did something? What did I do?"

"You called her a chick," said Delcie.

"I called her a chick? But she is a chick!"

"In the movement," Delcie explained patiently, "women are not chicks. We are not sex objects. We are persons."

"Chick, person, what the hell," said Kemp, floundering.

Curiously, Linda observed that Rick appeared to be cheered by his friend's discomfiture. He himself seemed to be searching for something to say. He cleared his throat.

"All I want to know," Kemp bumbled on, "is why a couple of classy foxes like you are sitting here killing time on a beautiful day like today . . ."

"That reminds me," Rick interrupted. He seemed anxious to make a contribution to the conversation. "You know what they call a mailman?"

Oh no, thought Linda. Not that old dead horse! Anger seeped through her like the heat from a gulp of brandy.

"Would you mind leaving?" she said aloud. She tossed her hair—which was blonde and shimmering—back over her shoulders. Unbidden and unwanted, the thought popped into her head that it was lucky she had washed her hair the night before. Equally unwanted was the knowledge that her blue T-shirt made her eyes seem an even deeper blue. "We have work to do."

"But Linda," said Delcie, "this *is* our work! This is what we're supposed to be doing! Explaining!"

"A person person!" said Rick, triumphantly.

"Don't waste your breath," Linda said to Delcie. "You might as well try to peddle popsicles to penguins."

Her glance swept over and past the men, consigning them to oblivion. Kemp shifted to a new ploy.

"Hold on, pardner!" he drawled. Linda groaned inwardly. First the dead horse, now the old Texas cowboy routine! Delcie giggled. Kemp barreled ahead like a bulldozer. "Do you chicks—I mean girls . . ."

"Persons," prompted Delcie.

". . . persons like football?"

Rick shot Kemp a lethal glance.

"I love football!" gurgled Delcie.

"What is it?" said Linda.

It was the ultimate put-down, and she experienced a fleeting pang of remorse. The old Linda would never have said that. This was the new Linda, who knew she had to be assertive. However, she need not have worried. Kemp had the hide of a rhino. With a grandiose swoop, his right hand raised an imaginary football aloft. He waited to be recognized. Delcie took the bait. Her eyes lit up, behind the tinted lenses.

"The *Daily Bruin*! Your picture was in the *Daily Bruin*! You're on the football team!"

"Give the girl an A."

"You're famous!" squealed Delcie. "Big stars! You're—you're Kempie Conover . . ."

"Conway."

"Conway! That's it! And you play . . ."

"End. Number sixty."

"And he . . ." Delcie's jaw dropped. "He's Big Rick!"

"Now we're getting somewhere," said Rick. He moved closer to the NOW table, and seemingly by chance rested his palm on a stack of pamphlets. In another moment his fingers would accidentally brush against Linda's. Linda pulled her hand away, as if she'd just noticed a rattlesnake.

"Big Rick Dublin!" breathed Delcie. "I can't believe it!"

"What's to believe?" said Linda. "You were expecting Godzilla?"

"But Big Rick!" bubbled Delcie.

Incredibly, Linda heard herself snort.

"I don't care if he's Big Rick or Little Rick or In Between Rick."

Why was she acting this way? Why was she being deliberately rude? The words simply popped out. She started stacking the pamphlets out of Rick's way to mask her confusion.

Kemp was impervious.

"The way I see it . . ." Kemp began in a confidential tone, obviously launching a well-rehearsed gambit, ". . . the game of football possesses a certain mystique."

"Mystique!" Linda couldn't help herself. "I'll tell you what I think of football! It's gross!"

Big Rick suddenly became alert. He stood with his feet

apart, as if braced for an onslaught of the Trojan line. "Why do you say that?" he asked in a reasonable tone.

"It's an idiotic waste of time and money! Grown men committing mayhem for possession of a little ball—appropriately enough, a pig skin!"

Kemp tried to interrupt, but Linda waved him down.

"How much does the university spend on football? Thousands! Hundreds of thousands! All that recruiting, the traveling, the uniforms! What a waste!"

"It's a sport!" protested Rick.

"It's so archaic!" said Linda. "It's like bullfights! It's like the gladiators! It's like the Christians and the lions!"

"It's exercise," Rick offered lamely.

"You could get the same thing running around the block! Meanwhile, how much is spent on physical education for women?"

Rick was taken aback.

"I haven't the foggiest."

"You see!" triumphed Linda. "It's never entered your mind! Take it from me, it's not as much. Not by a tenth, a hundredth, a thousandth! It's another instance of blatant discrimination!"

"They're starting a new policy," said Kemp. "They're letting girls go out for track."

"It's about time!" said Linda. "They'll beat the pants off the men!" Delcie giggled again. To offset this, Linda looked more severe. "They ought to do away with all sexist sports!" she declared.

"But you couldn't do away with football . . ." began Rick.

"Why not?" said Linda. "Give me one good reason. They could take all the money they'd save and give it to starving women and children in Bangladesh or somewhere, where it would do some good!"

The men looked at her as if she were crazy.

"You wouldn't want women playing football," said Kemp.

"Why not?" demanded Linda. She glanced at Delcie for support. Delcie was always a Rock of Gibraltar at the NOW meetings.

"Yes, why not?" said Delcie uncertainly. She sounded as if she didn't really want to know.

"Why . . ." said Rick, "they'd be liable to get hurt."

"There shouldn't be any difference!"

"There can't help but be a difference," said Rick.

"—With all your—uh—appendages!" put in Kemp. "*Vive la différence!*"

Linda felt the blood rush to her cheeks. She was furious.

"Sexist allusions," she said coldly, "are in the worst possible taste!"

"*Un momento!*" put in Rick. "My buddy here didn't mean to insult you ch—"

"Persons!" amended Delcie.

". . . persons! If he said—"

"I didn't say!" said Kemp.

"He implied!" countered Linda.

"If he implied you were sexy, he meant it as a compliment!"

"A compliment!" Linda's voice rose almost to a shriek. "Are you oblivious to the sheer, unmitigated gall of his attitude? His attitude, and, I might add, yours?"

"No!" said Rick. "I mean, yes! What's so sheer and unmitigated about it?"

"The idea," said Linda fiercely, "that it's a compliment to think of a girl as sexy!"

"It isn't?" said Rick in frank surprise.

"It is not!" hissed Linda. Delcie shook her head, but with less conviction. "You're treating us as if we were chattels—as if we were slaves on the auction block!"

"Lady," protested Kemp, "you're putting words in my mouth!"

The noise of the discussion had caught the attention of strolling students, and a circle of onlookers had assembled, unobserved by the four participants.

"It makes me so mad!" Linda's voice rose. She couldn't have stopped if she'd tried. Here it was, on the line, everything she was fighting for, everything she believed in. "Why can't we be valued for what we *really* are—not for how we look, but for what we know, and think, and feel? For what we can *do*?"

A burst of applause erupted from the spectators. Linda was breathing rapidly. She felt feverish. She scooped the pamphlets and papers into a raffia bag.

"Now you're playing my song, baby!" leered Kemp. "What can you do? Give us a chance to find out!"

The suggestion and all it implied hit like a cannon ball. The fickle crowd, which a moment before had been cheering Linda, burst into ribald laughter. Linda felt her face flush with humiliation. In her twenty-one years she never remembered being as angry as she was this instant. Tears welled in her eyes. She struggled to regain control. Certainly she wasn't going to give these clods the satisfaction of seeing her cry. She pulled herself to her full five feet seven, determined to rise above the insinuation.

"Women can do anything!" she declared hoarsely. "Anything men can do—"

"But not alone," reminded Kemp, wagging his head. "It takes two to tango."

"Ooh, you're so stupid!" Linda burst out in frustration. "You're missing the whole point."

"Yeah?" said Rick. He, too, had warmed to the fray. "Then tell me one thing—how does Women's Lib jibe with love?"

He caught her off guard. She hadn't expected this, certainly not from Rick.

"Love?" she echoed blankly. "The women's movement has nothing to do with love!" She groped for words. "The two aren't even related!"

For a split second the four adversaries stood, the girls facing the men across the NOW table. Then in sudden resolution Linda snatched up the raffia bag.

"Let's go!" she snapped to Delcie, and strode off through the crowd.

Delcie spread her hands in a gesture of helplessness.

"Well—see you guys around," she said.

Linda was halfway down the walk when Delcie caught up to her.

"Why did you have to leave so early? We were supposed to stay there till five."

"If you don't know, I can't explain."

"But Sadie said—"

"To heck with Sadie."

"I don't know why you had to jump all over them. You pulled out just as we were starting to make progress."

"Progress!" Linda was still seething. "You might as well try to explain the quantum theory of physics to a couple of orangutans."

"But they . . ." Delcie swallowed. "I thought those guys were kind of cute."

"Delcie!" Linda was shocked. "Those guys, as you call them, typify the worst variety of MCP's."

"Male chauvinist pigs? But they only—"

"Only put you down, put me down, put down every woman on this campus!"

"Linda, I don't think they meant—"

"That's the most vicious prejudice of all—when they don't even know they have it! It shows it's been ingrained for centuries."

"Now you're sounding like Sadie."

"I'm sounding like myself! I know what I'm fighting for—"

"Yeah," said Delcie, "a great new world."

"That's right! Where every female is free to function as a productive, valuable, autonomous—"

"As Sadie would say, her own person!" Delcie was slipping back into the groove.

"—free to make the most of any talent or ability she might be born with—"

A smile crossed Delcie's face.

"Free to play football?"

"Yes! If she's hefty enough and wants to do it. Why shouldn't she? It's blind stupid creeps like those gorillas who are standing in the way!"

"Right on!" Delcie shifted her books to the other arm. Then she looked perplexed. "Only I still can't see why you got so uptight."

"Why?" Linda glared at her in frustration. "Because—because they made me so mad!"

It wasn't a very good answer. They had entered their residence hall, and Linda waved good-by to Delcie without further comment. She was still rabidly angry, and she didn't know why.

TWO

Linda Allenby had an obsession about freedom. She had tried several times to explain this to Delcie. A month earlier when Linda had transferred as a senior to UCLA, she'd run across Delcie at a NOW meeting. When it developed neither of them knew anyone else, their friendship seemed natural, though they had little in common save loneliness. On the subject of freedom Delcie usually rejoined, "But you are free!" to which Linda vehemently replied, "I am, I am, and I intend to stay that way!" However, deep inside her she knew that—so far—she was only half free. She couldn't explain to Delcie what she didn't quite understand herself.

Linda had revolted from her parents, she had made the big break from her establishment background. After all, she was a member of the generation of revolt, but she was a late bloomer. For almost a decade her contemporaries had chanted, marched, prostrated themselves before government buildings, been dragged feet first from deans' offices, burned banks, spray-painted churches with four-letter words. Linda had been like the timid surfer who sits astride her surfboard, a quarter mile out to sea, watching the great swells roll past, each time deciding to go, then at the last minute changing her mind, pulling back, waiting for the next one.

Yet now, here she was at UCLA, not at Mills where her mother Margaret Allenby was on the board of trustees. Here she was, wearing jeans and tennies and a faded T-shirt without a bra, studying human behavior, not Renaissance painting. Here she was, even involved with a group of activists. She had cut the cord. The catch was, her parents didn't know it yet. Her parents didn't know anything was wrong, or needed revolting against.

Linda was torn. She loved her parents. Whenever she experienced feelings of revolt they were accompanied by

9

outpourings of guilt, so that the two became inseparable in her nervous system, and anything to do with one instantly triggered the other.

She had begun to feel trapped in her early teens. Year by year the panic had worsened, accompanied by the sensation of not being able to breathe, of smothering in a great, billowing feather bed of cotton candy. She hated herself for being ungrateful and disloyal. She dreaded crossing her parents; she feared their displeasure and retribution. Yet deep inside she had felt the stirrings of something which for lack of a better term she had labeled her "possible." She could do something, be somebody! But what? She had to find the answer. She had to stretch her wings and fly. Now that she had taken the first steps, she knew she must go through with the break, or forever lose the chance to be herself.

Twenty-six years ago, the marriage of Margaret and Robert Allenby had been the social event of the season. The couple was perfectly suited. Inherited money abounded on both sides. In addition, Robert, recently returned from a captaincy in World War II (which he spent behind a desk in the supply corps), was executive vice-president of a growing plastics corporation. The newlyweds truly desired children, but they were surprised and later concerned when, after a year's time, none came. After much discussion and indecision, they decided to seek professional advice.

At first the doctor told them to wait, then he told them they were too anxious, then said to stop thinking about it, adding that being up-tight could cause an unfavorable chemical imbalance in either or both partners.

"Relax!" he advised at the end of every visit. "Go on a second honeymoon. Go to Hawaii! Lie under the tropical moon and think about love!"

After the Allenbys had been home from Hawaii for two months and were sure nothing had come of it, the doctor referred Margaret to Dr. Baumfield, a gynecologist. She went through a series of tests and painful examinations, which revealed the presence of two tumors in her uterus. This news plunged the young couple into despair.

The growths were certain to be malignant, and their removal might sterilize Margaret, or worse still, prove fatal. Their anxiety before the operation drew them closer and they made constant protestations of devotion. When the preliminary D and C had been performed and the tumors removed, a rush biopsy certified them benign. It was as if Margaret had returned from the tomb. Robert brought her a dozen American Beauty roses every day she was in the hospital.

After Margaret's convalescence and a subsequent battery of tests extending over six weeks, Dr. Baumfield told her he could detect no physical reason why she should not conceive. He suggested the Allenbys try again, and they did, diligently and earnestly, morning and night during the "fertile periods," to no avail. The doctor suggested a sperm count on Robert might be in order, and gave them specific instructions on how to obtain the specimen. The condom containing the precious semen was immediately sealed and placed in the cleavage between Margaret's breasts, where it was held in place by her brassiere in order to maintain precise body temperature until she could get it to the laboratory, which had been alerted to expect her.

As she drove along the freeway, the pungent odor wafting from her blouse filled her with a mixture of hope and foreboding. If Robert proved to be sterile, she felt the whole purpose would have gone out of living, for she knew she could never love nor marry anyone else, and Robert had declared adamantly he would not consent to an adoption. He wanted a child, but he wanted his own child. He stated unequivocally he could never bring himself to love a child who had been sired by someone else.

The next day, in his expensive office on Wilshire Boulevard, Dr. Baumfield told Margaret that Robert's semen did contain live sperm, but the count was low. Margaret's eyes filled with tears of relief. There was hope, the doctor went on, but the mathematical probabilities were poor. He suggested the Allenbys try the dog position, and showed Margaret some photographs which in another time and place she would have ranked as pornographic. Now she was too intent on her obsession with motherhood to quibble, and memorized the angles, front and back.

Achieved after much maneuvering, the dog position proved stimulating for Robert, but excessively painful to Margaret. She clenched her teeth and endured it the best way she could, lying to Robert that she thought it was fun.

Immediately afterwards, as per Dr. Baumfield's instructions, she contorted herself into the uncomfortable knee-chest position, and maintained it for half an hour.

From that time forth, for years, this was the pattern of the Allenbys' sexual experience. Dr. Baumfield administered a variety of vitamins, shots and douches. The laboratory ran a fresh sperm count every three months, but it continued to show a paucity of viable spermatozoa. There was nothing to do, Dr. Baumfield said, but go on trying.

Every month when Margaret's period started she complained that the curse was well named. She tried not to think of babies, but found she could think of nothing else. She took to haunting the infants' department of Bullock's Pasadena and I. Magnin, exclaiming over ruffled toddler dresses and navy sailor suits for baby boys. Her preoccupation became a passion, a longing to hold a child, to nurse it, to kiss it and fondle it and feel the soft baby cheek against her own. She languished and became ill. To everyone's horror, the doctor discovered she had a diseased right ovary. Before she could protest, she was scheduled for surgery and the ovary was removed.

Although the surgeon tried to reassure the couple, pointing out that the remaining ovary was functioning normally, Margaret fell prey to an unshakable conviction that her chances of becoming pregnant had been radically reduced. She fell into a deep depression, which Robert gradually came to share. It was then, clutching at straws to save their sanity, that they bought the house in San Marino.

La Hacienda, as they later called it, was intended for a family of at least twelve. It had five bedrooms plus the maid's quarters, nine baths counting the two in the cabaña by the pool, and a forty-by-twenty-five-foot living room. Margaret turned her attention and skill to decorating, concentrating on a room at a time, and achieved a result which her friends declared to be professional. The by-product no one had anticipated was that she became pregnant.

At first the Allenbys were too dazed to believe it could

be true. When all the tests proved positive they were blissful. Their joy, which was constant, was soon tempered with anxiety. Margaret kept spotting, and Dr. Baumfield stated it was a chancy pregnancy at best. He ordered her to bed for the next nine months. Two dictionaries were placed on the floor under the foot of her bed so that she lay at a perpetual slant, head downward. Even so, she started to miscarry twice, and was rushed to the hospital by ambulance.

About this time both the Allenbys and the doctor began to worry that the fetus, which nature seemed determined to abort, was in some measure defective, and the child would be retarded or deformed.

When, at the end of a grueling thirty-hour labor, the baby, a girl, arrived perfect in all respects, the Allenbys considered it nothing short of a miracle. So profound was their emotional experience that although until then neither had been religious, they prayed aloud together, Robert kneeling beside Margaret's hospital bed, thanking God for the wondrous gift.

Before she left the hospital Dr. Baumfield told Margaret she could have no more children, and when the baby was four months old she underwent a complete hysterectomy.

More than anything on God's earth the Allenbys had wanted children. After five heartsick years of yearning, their wish had been miraculously granted, with one perfect child, but only one. There would be no more. It was little wonder that from that moment on, for the rest of their lives, for the Allenbys the sun rose and set on their daughter Linda.

Linda was shielded from germs, from accidents, from coarse language and undesirable companions as if she were the child of a fabled Eastern potentate. Margaret and Robert read every volume on infant care and child psychology in print. They were determined Linda should not be spoiled, and following the books, disciplined her lovingly yet firmly. They had few problems, as she was a remarkably easy child to train. As she grew into girlhood, Linda's manners were a continual source of delight to the Allenbys' friends, many of whom were childless couples. Wherever the family went, the child's beauty occasioned spontaneous exclamations from strangers.

Linda attended Marlborough, a private girls' school, and in addition was tutored in piano, ballet, tennis, riding, swimming, and French. Summers she traveled with her parents. She graduated fifth in her class from Marlborough, and the following September entered Mills, her mother's alma mater. During Thanksgiving vacation of her freshman year she was presented at one of the charity debutante balls, and when Linda sank into the deep debutante curtsy, and then rose to circle the room on the arm of her father, Margaret felt the tears streaming down her cheeks.

The next night, when they took her to the plane at Burbank to fly back to Mills, Margaret found she was crying again.

"Mother," said Linda, kissing her. "What is it? Is something the matter?"

Margaret shook her head and laughed, trying to mask the tears. "It's just that you're so pretty, and so good. You'll never know how happy you've made your father and me!"

"That's right," said Robert, his arm around Linda's shoulders. Robert was not one to display his emotions, but all three felt this to be a rare, intimate moment. "We're proud of you, daughter. You've become everything we hoped for, and more."

From the Allenbys' point of view, Linda's first two years at college proceeded without incident. She received the A's and B's which Margaret and Robert had come to expect. She phoned her parents frequently, and on her vacations seemed as glad to see them as they were to see her. Her junior year was spent in Florence, Italy, under a carefully supervised program for American university students abroad. There she haunted the *Palazzo Pitti* and the *Galleria Degli Uffizi*. When she flew home in late August, her parents met her at Los Angeles International Airport. They had scarcely retrieved her bags from the luggage carrousel when Linda announced she was not returning to Mills, but intended to spend her fourth year at the University of California at Los Angeles, not half an hour from home.

"You can't mean it!" Margaret Allenby said, her impeccably coifed hair forming a silver frame for her youthful features. Her voice was low and well modulated.

Robert joined in. "I don't think that's entirely wise, daughter."

"Dear," said Margaret, "that would mean you wouldn't graduate from Mills!"

"UCLA's too big," her father said. "Besides, it's too late to apply."

They were dumbfounded when they learned Linda had applied in March, been accepted, and had her credits transferred, all by mail.

"But why?" they kept saying. "Why on earth would you want to change?"

Linda couldn't enlighten them, not because she didn't want to, but because she didn't really know. Nevertheless, she was adamant in her resolve. In the end they capitulated. They had run out of arguments, they were doting parents; and this was the first major request Linda had ever made of them.

Even in her own mind, Linda could not come up with a clear-cut explanation. The reason was visceral: she had felt instinctively that she must extricate herself or perish. During her first days on the university campus, wearing jeans and old tennies, letting her long blond hair hang loose, Linda drank deeply of her freedom. She found it a heady intoxicant. She at first eschewed friendships or even acquaintanceships; she cut short the overtures of the sororities and she insisted on a private room at the dorm. (She would have liked her own apartment, but on that point her mother had stood firm.) She changed her major from Renaissance painting to sociology and, like a thirsty sponge, her mind soaked up a profusion of unfamiliar dogmas. She attended lectures on Yoga, Bahai, and Hare Krishna. She marched in rallies for the farmworkers, and when the Soviet Ambassador came to town she cut classes in order that she might parade in front of his hotel holding up a sign which read "Free the Jews."

She kept reminding herself that she must be her own person, and in the end that was her undoing. In the process of the fight for her freedom she had become a crusader, and what is a crusader without a cause?

One evening soon after school started, Linda wandered

into a seminar on Women's Rights at which Betty Friedan was the speaker. Linda had entered the auditorium a free spirit; she emerged no longer in possession of her soul. She had stumbled across her religion and, as sometimes happens, had experienced instant conversion. She was that rarity of which evangelists dream, the convert who metamorphoses into an impassioned disciple and goes out to save the world.

Communications between the Allenbys and their daughter, which had been excellent when Linda was at Mills four hundred miles away, suddenly dwindled to nothing. Linda would forget to telephone. She had declined to have a private phone installed in her room, insisting it was an unnecessary expense. Robert had been particularly proud of her frugality. But he and Margaret soon found that if Linda failed to phone them, it was virtually impossible to call her. The head resident of the dorm had an office with a telephone, but she was never there. Linda had given Margaret the number of the dorm pay phone, which was on the first floor. (Linda's room was on the third.) When Margaret dialed the number, the pay phone either rang endlessly or was answered by a passing student, always someone who had never heard of Linda or who was late to class and couldn't take the time to run up and see if Linda was in. Once when Margaret did manage to reach her on the phone, Linda explained that her change in major meant she was taking nineteen units and spent most of her time in the reference library.

At the beginning of the semester when they'd helped Linda move into the dorm, Margaret had told Robert that the change had one advantage: the university was so close that Linda would be able to run home on weekends. This was not to be. Linda couldn't run home without a car. The Allenbys had sold Linda's car when she went to Florence; now she refused to let them buy her a new one. Automobiles pollute, she told her father, and anyway, a car would be nothing but a big fat nuisance at UCLA, given the parking situation.

Thus, because they rarely talked to Linda, and saw her even less frequently, the Allenbys became unashamedly homesick for their child. The rub was that for twenty-one years the lives of Robert and Margaret had revolved around their daughter. Through her they had relived babyhood, childhood, early and late teens, savoring every nuance of the experience a second time around. It had not occurred to them to develop other interests, or to prepare themselves for a break. They had not even foreseen that ultimately a break would occur.

One Saturday on impulse the Allenbys drove on the freeways to Westwood, thinking they would surprise their daughter. Linda was not in the reference library, nor was she in her room. Her parents questioned various students, stopping them at random, but no one knew her. The office of the dorm resident was locked; the dorm itself was practically deserted. No one seemed in charge; comings and goings went unchronicled. At length they gave up.

"This place is totally unsupervised," fretted Margaret, waiting while Robert opened the car door for her.

Robert went around and settled himself in the driver's seat, fastening both safety belts before he spoke.

"You're making a mountain out of a molehill," he told his wife. "She is twenty-one."

"I know she's twenty-one," Margaret said, touching up her silver hair in the mirror on the reverse of the sun visor, "but that doesn't mean we have to stop being concerned! I expect we'll be concerned about Linda as long as we live!"

THREE

Trivial as it might have appeared to the casual onlooker, the interchange between Linda and Delcie, and Rick and Kemp, was a Happening in the mind of one of the participants, Rick Dublin. In a way, the meeting of Rick and Linda (for that was how he thought of it, with Kemp and Delcie in minor, superfluous roles) came as no surprise. Rick was psyched up for it, overpsyched. If it hadn't happened then it would have happened some other place, some other time, but soon; if it hadn't been Linda it would have been some other girl. Next to football, all Rick thought about was women. Yet he had never had a woman.

This fact continued to amaze Rick's roommate, M. Kemper Conway. Kemp constantly needled Rick. Kemp's taunts may not have been malicious; after all, he did say that he only had Rick's interests at heart. Nevertheless, underneath the placid surface of Rick's even temperament the barbs festered.

"Big Rick!" Kemp would deride, reading the latest accolade in the *Daily Bruin*. "If they only knew!"

"If who only knew what?"

"If they only knew!" Kemp would repeat piously, with a slightly different inflection, shaking his head.

The argument had become rote. Everything had been said and resaid; nothing new could be added on either side; the positions of each party remained what they had been at the beginning. Now they were at the point where they could leave out great chunks of the dialogue and each come in on cue.

"I didn't say you were a pansy . . ."

"Goddam it, you implied it!"

"I only said it's not natural for . . ."

"Oh for chrissakes, will you get off my back?"

By the time they got this far, Rick was up-tight. He could feel the muscles of his arms, thighs, and palms stiffen almost to the point of locking. Even the roof of his mouth took on a starchy, puckered quality.

Their dorm room exacerbated his distress. Ignoring residence hall regulations, Kemp had plastered the four walls and ceiling with a collection of erotica: larger-than-life photo posters from adult book stores, with a few Miss Octobers and Miss Aprils interspersed for variety. Kemp was a sex maniac by his own definition, and he never let Rick forget it.

"It's so easy," was his stock phrase; all discussions inevitably led to that. "You don't know what you're missing."

"Can it," was what Rick mumbled, if he mumbled anything. He pretended to be studying, his attention riveted to the printed page, but his face flushed russet.

Rick Dublin and Kemper Conway played shoulder to shoulder as defensive linesmen. Rick, six four, two hundred and fifty-seven pounds, was tackle number 74. Kemper, six three, and weighing two hundred and forty-one, was number 60. He played end. Both were popular with their teammates, and both were considered fierce on the playing field. The similarity ended there.

Rick had been raised by his mother, who had died of overwork and emphysema when he was a freshman. He was in college on a football scholarship which paid books, tuition, board and room. He worked at the gym, dispensing towels and equipment, for two dollars an hour. Kemp was the product of an affluent home. His parents had divorced when he was twelve. His mother had remarried and moved to New York. His father, a successful architect, lived in a chrome and glass ocean-front apartment at Newport Beach which had been featured in the Home section of the Sunday *Times* under the caption "Bachelor Shangri La." Kemp's father and mother had both been through analysis and emerged—as they went their separate ways—with one shining precept: sex was not a no-no, but a yes-yes.

"Good old S-E-X," Kemp would intone, spelling it out, licking his lips. "That's where it's at, baby, and that's all it's at."

Rick was in no position to argue. It stood to reason, he told himself, that Kemp was right. Why else were people constructed the way they were?

The war in Vietnam dragged on, corroding the expectations of the young. The current student body had neither ideals nor religion, and the prevalence of the pill had released any lingering inhibitions.

For Kemp, women were placed on earth for one purpose—to be enjoyed. Kemp was like an aficionado of chocolate ice cream who found himself in a room where hundreds of scoops were dished out and waiting to be gobbled up before they could melt. He flogged himself with a kind of frenetic urgency, continually seeking different women, untried experiences, fearful he might die or grow old before he had slept with every girl on campus, always wanting more, more, more.

Paradoxically, the idea of a permanent, or even a temporary, liaison with a girl was unthinkable. Women were paramount in Kemp's lifestyle, but they were disposable. Any conversation he had with a girl was directed toward one goal: to score. The possibility of feminine companionship unconnected with sex, or of a friendship with a girl based on an intellectual give and take, was inimical to his nature.

Kemp saw himself as a free-roving, irresistible man-about-town, the kind who appeared on the commercials for Brut and Hagar slacks, a forever-young, forever-potent Don Juan for whom the satisfaction of cravings, including all variations of sensation, provided the single justification for living.

He told Rick sex was like good Scotch—it was impossible to get too much—and Rick accepted this precept at face value. With no conscious decision on his part, Rick allowed Kemp's philosophy to become his own. The conversion exposed his hang-up, which he had heretofore recognized but ignored. Rick was afraid of girls.

"For chrissakes *why?*" demanded Kemp, after he'd wormed Rick's secret out of him.

Rick had been embarrassed.

"No reason."

"Big Rick Dublin! Better not let the SC line-up get wind of that! Big Rick Dublin! Scared of girls!"

"Not scared, exactly."

"What, then?"

"They make me nervous."

Kemp had rolled his eyes expressively.

"This I have to see. The terror of the Bruin defense, and girls make him nervous."

"Will you shut up?"

"No, I won't shut up. This is important."

"I said shut up, damn it!"

"It's *your* life we're talking about. If you want to be an all right, regular stud . . ."

Rick had felt a warm flush creep up his neck.

"Why do they make you nervous?"

"Come off it!"

"I'm asking a civil question."

"I don't *know* why."

"It's the most ridiculous thing I ever heard. Here Mother Nature has peopled the earth with thousands of gorgeous chicks . . ."

"Gorgeous—where?"

Kemp brushed this off.

"Gorgeous and not-so-gorgeous, they're all the same under the sheets. Anyway, they exist, in droves, and for what purpose?"

"What?"

"To provide comfort and solace to guys like you and me. To ease our tensions."

"Oh yeah?" In spite of himself, Rick had been intrigued.

"That's right, old buddy. That's their function. They're glad to do it."

"Yeah?"

"Hell, yes. They have tensions, too."

Rick had gone back to his books, but his imagination was awakened.

"I don't believe it."

"Believe it. They fall all over themselves to get into bed with you. All you have to do is give them the eye."

During the next week Rick had tried giving the girls in his principles of education class the eye. They looked at him as if he had suddenly erupted with measles. He became more nervous than before. He found he couldn't talk to a girl without slurring his speech, and in some cases, stuttering. He imagined he looked like an epileptic on the verge of a seizure.

He decided to drop the whole business, but Kemp wouldn't let him.

"You've got to loosen up."

"I told you. I'm not interested."

"That's a lot of b.s."

"Listen, will you lay off?"

"I will not lay off. You keep on the way you're going and you'll end up a goddam queer."

At this point Rick held himself in check, with an effort.

"Can't you see I'm doing this for your own good?"

"Yeah. You bet."

"I'm trying to help you. Some day you'll thank me."

"Fat chance."

"Some day you'll thank me on bended knee."

Kemp brought girls to their room. He tried to get everybody high on beer and grass. Rick sat on the edge of his bunk, up-tight and embarrassed. The girls giggled, their conversation dwindling into gibberish. They sat one on either side of Kemp, crowding close. Rick appraised them from across the room, wondering what they were like, what it would be like.

"Don't be stand-offish," said Kemp. "Loosen up!"

"Come over," said one of the girls. "Tell me about yourself."

She started toward him, weaving slightly.

Rick stood up in terror.

"Excuse me!" He spit out the words, trying not to stutter. "I just remembered something I have to see about!"

He bolted through the door before she could lay a hand on him. He went to the gym and worked out on the bars until he was positive the girls would be gone.

"Christ almighty," complained Kemp, foggily. The room was layered with smoke. "Why didn't you tell me you were going to split?"

"I had to see about something," said Rick.

"You missed a great performance," Kemp assured him, drifting toward unconsciousness, "on the part of all concerned . . ."

By the Friday in question, after weeks of wrangling, Rick and Kemp had arrived at a compromise of sorts.

Rick would give it a whirl. He would try one more time. He would make an honest effort. He wouldn't chicken out at the first brush-off. For his part, Kemp agreed not to crowd him too close. He would accompany him, strictly for purposes of moral support. He might enter the conversation to make the pick-up appear casual and unstudied, but he was precluded from any positive action. The choice, the proposition, was to be left to Rick's discretion.

Rick returned to the dorm after lunch and shaved again, examining his appearance with anxiety. His face emerged from the lather a series of broad, amiable planes, devoid either of distinguishing traits or disfigurements. He remembered the time the anthropology instructor, a thin, nervous Ph.D. candidate, had publicly credited Rick with Croatian ancestry because of his square jaw, thick neck and massive skull. In the next breath he hastened to add that the classification entailed nothing personal. Rick had shrugged it off. Kemp had told him he might be part Finnish or Russian because of his light gray eyes and sand-colored hair. Up to now it hadn't seemed important. This day Rick looked at himself critically, trying to think how he would appear to a girl, striving to conjure up a girl's point of view. He might as easily have tried to put himself in the mind of an auk or an aardvark. He had no more idea of what went on in her mind than an android from another planet.

When he got back to the room Kemp was there, studiously combing his hair, trying to achieve the dry look.

"All set?"

Rick put on a clean faded-denim shirt. He looked in the mirror over Kemp's shoulder, adjusting the collar. He wished he hadn't let Kemp pressure him into this wild goose chase.

"If I weren't so damn big," he said. He thought of how he would appear to a girl—a hulking giant.

"Forget it," said Kemp, clapping him on the shoulder. "Chicks like 'em big. Believe me, I know."

Unconvinced, Rick allowed himself to be ushered out to begin the hunt.

* * *

Although many students had departed for the weekend, numerous others strolled the walks or stood or sat in the courtyards, all nameless, faceless, and anonymous. Rick had moved among them for four years as he would have moved through a grove of trees; never stopping to talk to an individual tree, to learn if it were male or female, if it were capable of bearing fruit or could but produce flowers, if its roots were imbedded deep in the earth, if it thirsted, if it trusted the wind riffling through its leaves.

Now Rick focused on one person after another. This produced a strange effect on his consciousness, like a movie where the frame is momentarily frozen on a scene the director wishes to impress upon the viewer; the action resumes in a normal fashion, then again the frame is frozen, then action once more resumes, and so on and so forth. He perceived that each being had his own separate uniqueness, the blacks various shades of black, from burnished charcoal to the color of light tea; the anglos various shades of white, from unbaked pastry to strong tea; the chicanos jet-haired with quizzical expressions; the American Indians managing to look stoic and worried simultaneously; the East Indians inscrutable; the Orientals assured and self-important, the Japanese more intense than the Chinese or the Thais. Yet all had something in common, the cult of denim, leather thongs and the Afro hairdo. They were young, and yet they appeared to be mature. They had sampled everything as children and now the corners of their mouths hinted at disillusionment, as if they demanded "Is this all there is?" and felt cheated because there was no more.

"See anything you like?" said Kemp. His glance ran over, through, and around the crowds like that of an auctioneer at a cattle round-up.

Rick tried to concentrate on the business in hand. The first objective was to single out girls. For the most part they appeared to be a scruffy lot, most of them wearing suede boots and old jeans. He thought of the picture of Miss October on the ceiling above his bed.

"Not exactly," he said.

"Beggars can't be choosers," Kemp reminded him. "You gotta keep in mind this is your first time."

"Look," said Rick, "let's get one thing straight. All I'm

going to do is say hello, maybe, and then take it from there. If she's interested."

"Relax," said Kemp.

"Which she very well may not be."

"I said, relax."

"The chances are ten to one nothing's going to come of it."

"It sure as hell won't if you keep on with that defeatist attitude."

"I just don't want you getting your hopes up too high."

"My hopes! You seem to forget, buddy boy, we're doing this for you."

"In that case let's call the whole thing off right now."

Rick turned to go, but Kemp grabbed his arm.

"Oh no you don't! Don't think you can get off the hook that easy!"

They scuffled, like puppies romping in the sunshine. The passersby watched them without really noticing them, for they were all engrossed in their own thoughts.

After a time the horseplay stopped and Rick and Kemp resumed their Odyssey. Later, Rick would remember wandering across the half shaded lawn, kicking aimlessly at the dried leaves and finally coming upon the table with the banner above it, nailed to a wooden frame.

NOW
WOMEN OF THE WORLD, UNITE!

He would vaguely recall noticing Delcie, the short plump broad who looked like an owl. Then, he'd looked at Linda. After that, everything was blurred.

In a series of flashes, Rick would continue to see Linda, sitting stiff-backed and glacial, the ice queen, her hair streaming down her back like yellow-white, liquid sunshine. He would see Linda standing, gesturing wildly, a rosy spot of anger slowly spreading outward from the crest of each high cheekbone. He would see Linda's eyes, crackling with fury, blue as Crater Lake on a midsummer morning.

Rick could remember the abrupt moment when everything was over. Linda had pushed her way through the crowd; her owl-like friend, after some hesitation, had followed her in retreat. Rick and Kemp were left standing, looking after them like fools.

"There goes one kooky dame," Kemp said, struggling to regain his self-esteem and to bolster his ego. "She's a fireball, but she's a number one grade A kook."

Rick had said nothing. Linda might be a kook, he told himself, but she was the most gorgeous kook he had ever seen in his life.

FOUR

Although they used NOW literature, the movement, of which Linda became a part, had no official connection with the National Organization for Women or any other formal group.

"But who decides things?" said Linda. All her life had been structured. "Who plans your campaigns?"

"No one," said Aggie Jackson, a volatile black woman. "We just does our own thing."

"We see what needs to be done." Sadie Blankenhazen spoke with precision. "We do it."

"We believe," breathed Jody Jordan. Her tone was reverent.

Unknown to herself, Linda had been searching for someting to believe *in*. She swallowed the total package in one indiscriminate gulp. In large part Linda's conversion was due to the spell cast by Sadie Blankenhazen. To outsiders, Sadie appeared commonplace, a tall, thin, horsey girl with acne. To the chosen few, Sadie was a messiah. When Sadie spoke, her listeners somehow knew she spoke the truth. When Sadie voiced an attitude, her followers seized it as gospel to guide them in a dirty, rotten world. A politician, Sadie reigned by manipulating her followers. She would pit them against each other by appealing to their prejudices, fears and infatuations.

In the beginning, still celebrating her revolt from her parents, Linda had been attracted by the formlessness of the group. Nonetheless, she was flattered when Sadie suggested she drop over one Friday after dinner. Sadie and Aggie shared an off-campus apartment, furnished with rattan and posters. Some few of the inner, inner circle had been invited for supper and were finishing pizza and dago red; others kept arriving till the rooms were crowded with girls lounging on the furniture and the floor, all talking at once. Linda listened open-mouthed, recognizing four-letter

27

words she'd seen only in print. Beliefs were hammered home, and those "out there" who might think differently were alluded to with pity.

Linda was sure not one of the assemblage had an inkling of the Allenbys' wealth or prestige, yet everyone seemed eager to talk to her. "They like me for myself!" she marveled. It was intoxicating. Except for her family, Linda had never felt herself a part of anything. She had never made close friends—and despaired of this deficiency in her own personality. Moreover, every acquaintance she had known had been cynical, bored, disinterested and uninvolved. Here, the excitement of the movement crackled through the conversations like electricity. Linda sensed the others' blind devotion to the cause, and felt a thrill of solidarity. A joint was passed around the room. When it reached Linda she hesitated, repelled by the acrid odor, horrified at what her parents would think. Then she shut her eyes and took a deep, determined pull.

A giddy, euphoric feeling washed over her. She wanted to laugh and cry at the same time because everything was suddenly so beautiful. She looked about her and saw affectionate smiles mirroring her own sentiments. This is where I belong, she whispered, this is what I've been searching for. This is it!

At that moment Sadie Blankenhazen's voice, low and intense, pervaded the rooms, shutting off separate conversations like spigots.

"We've been criticized for hating men," Sadie began, her brooding eyes locking first with those of one follower, then with those of the next. "But I say to you, how can we not hate men? How can we not feel for our sisters, one-half the human species, one-half the people on this globe, who have been bullied and coerced and exploited—by men!"

Her eyes locked wtih Linda's and held her hypnotized. Linda felt her own lips part in a smile of approval.

"Yes!" Linda heard herself murmur. "You're so right!"

Sadie Blankenhazen was a dynamic leader—brilliant and decisive—able to sway her followers with unequivocal logic. Sadie's beliefs became their beliefs.

Sadie hated men.

Until she was six, Sadie's childhood had been pleasant. Her father was George Blankenhazen, an energetic, florid businessman in his early thirties, who mixed himself a martini the minute he came through the door, then bee-lined it out to the kitchen where Lou Ann, Sadie's mother, was cooking dinner. George would come up behind Lou Ann and put his arms around her, grabbing a breast in each hand.

"How's about it, baby?" George would say, nuzzling his nose into the back of her neck.

"George Blankenhazen!" Lou Ann would scream. "Not in front of the child!"

Sadie took care to remain out of the way, as invisible as possible, but she didn't miss a thing. She herself adored her father. Although he spent so much time away on busi-ness, he was hearty and good-natured when he was home. He called Sadie "Baby" too. He would slip her a pepper-mint Life Saver, which she would hold in her mouth, letting it melt slowly on her tongue, while they played "horsie," George crossing one knee over the other and dandling the child on his wing-tip shoe.

After the divorce, Sadie tried to cling to these memo-ries, but Lou Ann was both cunning and vindictive. Time and again she swept through her child's mind without search warrant, ferreting out every wisp of sentiment for George Blankenhazen and destroying it forever.

Sadie would never forget the day her mother found out. She heard her mother scream, then heard her cry. Sadie left her doll house and ran through the apartment to the entry, where her mother stood, waving a letter. Sadie was precocious; besides, the note was printed.

If you want to know where Lover Boy goes on business, she spelled out, *try the Blue Bell Motel. A Friend.*

"The bastard!" Lou Ann screamed. "The two-timing bastard!"

Sadie began to howl because her mother was howling, and for five minutes they stood together, caterwauling in the hall. After that, Lou Ann was moved to action. She went on crying, sniffing and blowing her nose, while she pulled out the phone book and looked in the yellow pages, paying no attention to Sadie, who was firing a steady stream of questions in between sobs.

"What's the matter? Mommie? What's the matter?"

"That goddam S O B!"

"Who, mommie? Who?"

"Your two-timing father, that's who!"

"You mean daddy?"

"You're damn right I mean your daddy. Only he won't be your daddy much longer!"

Sadie started to cry afresh.

"Has something happened to my daddy?"

"Not yet, but something's going to!"

The dialogue was interrupted because Lou Ann dialed information. After numerous tries and a caustic exchange with the operator, she located a Blue Bell Motel in Long Beach.

Sadie had stopped crying in order to listen.

"You're sure there's no George Blankenhazen registered?" Her mother slapped the phone on the cradle. "Don't suppose he'd be such a fool as to use his right name!"

Now that she no longer needed to listen, Sadie started to cry again.

"What's going to happen to my daddy?"

A malevolent expression hardened Lou Ann's pretty features. Ever afterward, Sadie was to remember that moment with horror. It was like watching the queen turn into the wicked witch.

"He's going to wish he'd never been born," Lou Ann said slowly, spitting out each word.

For a child steeped in television, there was no mistaking her meaning. Sadie started to scream.

"Don't!" she cried. "Don't kill my daddy! Don't kill my daddy!"

She was hysterical, but Lou Ann was too engrossed in her own trauma to notice.

"I'm not going to kill your precious daddy!" she snapped. "I'm going to crucify him! Get your coat!"

Sadie would never forget the ride to Long Beach, her mother smoking and burning her finger on the lighter, then swooping off onto the wrong freeways, or having to pull into one service station after another to ask directions. They arrived at the Blue Bell in the late afternoon. By this time Lou Ann's nerves were frayed past the breaking point. Sadie had been told that if she made one more sound her mother would open the car door and push her out on the street, and the child believed her. Sadie managed to control her whimpering by clamping her teeth and lips together, but the reflex of the long, violent siege of crying continued to shake her thin frame in periodic shudders.

Sadie was ordered to stay in the car while her mother went into the office. When Lou Ann came back her face was contorted in an expression of malice and venom which was to become her permanent mask.

"Damn lying bastard!" she said. "Wouldn't tell me a goddam thing."

Since up to now Lou Ann had characterized herself to her child as a lady, and had put soap on Sadie's tongue for saying some of those very words, the changeover in language only accentuated the catastrophic nature of the situation in the little girl's mind.

"But that won't make a hell of a lot of difference," Lou Ann went on, more to herself than to Sadie. "I can outsmart George Blankenhazen any day of the week!"

She parked the car between a pyracantha bush and a giant yellow trash bin which had City of Long Beach stenciled on it in black. By turning around on the seat and looking out the back window they were able to observe all the comings and goings of the Blue Bell Motel. Sadie became tired and hungry and needed to go to the bathroom, but the minute she opened her mouth her mother barked "Shut up!" like the crack of a pistol. At last their vigil was rewarded. Sadie saw her father's blue Thunderbird pull up to the office. Her father got out, went into the office, then returned to the car and drove out of sight. Someone sat beside him in the front seat.

Breathing heavily, Lou Ann managed to start her own car after two or three false tries, and wheeled around the corner of the two-story L-shaped building in time to see George following a woman into a ground floor unit. Lou Ann parked a distance away.

"Are we going to go and see Daddy?" said Sadie. She had started shivering and wanted to go home.

"You're damn tooting we're going to see him!" said Lou Ann. "Only we got to give the bastard time to get his clothes off!"

They waited, without speaking, in the car. It was getting dark.

"Come on!" said Lou Ann abruptly, opening the car door.

Sadie was scared.

"I don't want to go."

"I said come on! I want you to see with your own eyes what heels men are! I want you to see and never forget it!"

Sadie was on the point of sniffling.

"And shut up!" Lou Ann said savagely.

It was a nightmare, and the child was caught in the middle of it. They walked along the sidewalk, and Lou Ann knocked at the door.

"Who is it?"

Sadie recognized her father's voice. Then, mystified, she saw Lou Ann cover her mouth with a handkerchief.

"Manager," said Lou Ann, her voice muffled. "Towels."

"Oh hell," came George's voice. After a while the door opened. He was snapping his boxer shorts. Quickly Lou Ann stepped into the room, pulling the frightened child with her. The spread was off one of the beds. A young red-headed woman sat on the blanket, stark naked.

"Lou Ann!" shouted Sadie's father. Even in the midst of the crisis situation Sadie noticed he didn't call her mother Baby. "What the hell are you doing here?"

"Looking for you!" hissed Lou Ann. She was so overwrought her cheeks puffed and her eyes seemed ready to pop from their sockets. "Looking for you, so I can show your poor innocent little child what a dirty rotten swine she had for a father!"

"Now see here, Lou . . ."

"Don't you now see here me! I'm going to make you pay, George Blankenhazen. I'm going to squeeze the balls off you!"

"Lou Ann, for God's sake!"

"I'm going to take you for every last penny you own!" screamed Sadie's mother. "And you can put that in your pipe and smoke it!"

True to her threats, Lou Ann did exactly that. She hired

Jerry Hawley, the best divorce lawyer in LA. The legal battle raged for a year. Little Sadie was coached for her court appearance by Mr. Hawley and, more intensively, by her mother. She learned it was important to shade the truth in order to get the best of someone—someone she had recently loved and now was supposed to hate. The atmosphere of the apartment, now shared only by Lou Ann and Sadie, was redolent with hate. Lou Ann had been a housewife; she became a professional hater.

The betrayal by her husband, with its put-down of Lou Ann as a woman, was more than Sadie's mother could handle. Her reaction was to strike back, again and again and again. She was obsessed by her divorce case and thought and talked of nothing else for a year. When it was resolved and she won, she couldn't turn the hate off. She was locked into a pattern of loathing, of brooding, of venomous rancor toward *that man*.

The court had awarded George reasonable visitation rights to see his daughter, but when he telephoned once to suggest he had some tickets to the Icecapades and would like to take Sadie, Lou Ann rewarded him with a stream of invective, implying he was immoral, unfit to consort with children, and she'd see Sadie in hell before she'd let the poor innocent child associate with George and that whore.

Lou Ann was in the wrong. Ed Paine, George's lawyer, told him that.

"She hasn't a leg to stand on," said Ed. "You were given visitation rights. We can get a court order forcing her to let you take the kid. 'Course, it will cost you."

George grunted. He'd already been fleeced of everything he owned, and forced to pay both lawyers' fees in the bargain. His monthly support payments kept him strapped, and he was sick to death of Lou Ann's tirades.

"Forget it," he said. "I only wanted to take the kid to a matinee, not underwrite the national debt."

Years later Sadie, her own psyche corroded by Lou Ann's cancerous hate, thought of her father with resentment. What hurt most was that George had given up so easily. He never tried to see her again.

After the divorce was final, Lou Ann had everything she had set out to get—the big settlement, the support payments, sole custody of Sadie—but Lou Ann wasn't satisfied to let things drop. She'd telephone George at work and tell him what a no-good rat he was until he gave the switchboard operator strict orders never again to put his ex-wife through. She'd call him at his apartment until he got an unlisted number. After that, since by now she'd alienated all her friends, Lou Ann fell back on Sadie, assaulting the child with a wailing monologue of hate every waking moment. In a subtle way Lou Ann's vilifications undermined the little girl's self-respect. That man was a cheat, a liar, a sneak. That man was her father. Whenever Sadie misbehaved, Lou Ann proclaimed she took after her father. If she broke anything, she was clumsy like her father. If she misunderstood, she was stupid like her father.

As time went by, Lou Ann's diatribes enlarged from that man to include all men. Whatever went wrong in the world, Lou Ann had one stock explanation: men. By the time Sadie was in seventh grade, word got around that her old lady was off her rocker regarding anybody male. Boys avoided Sadie as if she were a carrier of the plague. Stung to the quick, Sadie retaliated in kind. "Who needs the creeps?" became her slogan. She was now five foot ten, weighed a hundred and three pounds, and her face constantly erupted in pimples. But Sadie was destined to become a leader. She possessed George's initiative and spirit, plus Lou Ann's obsessive endurance. She had survived the white-hot crucible of no-holds-barred divorce, and had come through scarred, but hard, tough, and ruthless. Since circumstances had removed men from her orbit, Sadie became a leader of women. She was elected president of Girls' Club, Girls' League, Girls' Athletic Association, and finally high school student body president by a margin of twenty-three votes. The boys never could figure what anybody saw in Sadie, but she was popular with the girls.

As years passed and Lou Ann became a recluse, nurturing the fungus of her hatred in the darkened apartment, Sadie became stronger, craving light, people and action. The balance of power shifted from mother to daughter, but their lives remained irrevocably intertwined, both committed to battle against the eternal enemy, men.

FIVE

Kemp Conway had spent the weekend at Newport Beach with his father and returned with a brick red sunburn.

"That girl . . ." Rick burst out, as soon as Kemp shut the door behind him and set down his bag.

"What girl?"

"That girl. The one we were talking to Friday."

"I don't remember any girl," said Kemp irritably.

"You know, the one who was gung ho on Women's Lib."

"Oh, her." Kemp was indifferent. He took off his dark glasses and tried to assess the damage to the back of his neck by looking in the mirror over his shoulder.

"I wonder who she is?"

"Who cares?"

Rick sat down facing his roommate.

"I can't make you out. All year you've been pestering the bejesus out of me. Get a girl! How's your love life? All that crap."

Kemp looked at Rick curiously. Kemp had spent the weekend talking to, listening to and doing things with several dozen people at one time or another. It was hard for him to zero in to Rick's problems, or even to think what they might be. On the other hand, with the exception of two sessions of handball with Darter Evans, the team's quarterback, Rick had spoken to no one since Kemp had gone. He had spent the two days brooding about Linda.

"So?" was the best Kemp could think of to say.

"So now you're turned off on the whole subject!"

"Aren't you coming on a trifle heavy?"

"I'm not coming on any way at all! I was voicing a simple, perfectly legitimate thought."

"You lost me," said Kemp. "What was that thought again?"

"I said, there must be some way to find out who that girl is."

"Forget her."

"Why forget her?"

"She's a dog."

"She is not a dog!" blazed Rick.

"Cool it!" said Kemp. "It's not as if she's anybody you know!"

"Calling her a dog is uncalled for."

"You asked me."

"You saw what she looked like."

"She's a dog in spirit."

"That's a rotten way to put it."

"It's true."

Kemp went down the hall to borrow some Un-Burn. When he returned, Rick took up the old bone.

"Why didn't we think to find out her last name."

"We didn't think to find out her first name."

"Yes we did. It's Linda."

"How d' you know?"

"Can't you remember, when her friend said, 'Linda, this is our work'?"

"I'd forgotten."

Kemp handed Rick the aerosol can and peeled off his T-shirt. His torso was the color of tomatoes.

"Man, you bought it!"

"Yeah," said Kemp gloomily.

Rick began to spray the mist over his friend's back.

"Can you imagine?" said Rick.

"I went surfing."

"I'm not talking about your cruddy back."

"Could be the last time this season if it turns cold."

"Can you imagine being that dedicated?"

"The waves were up to ten feet."

"Oh yeah?" Rick was deflected from his track, but only for a moment. "Can you imagine considering some cause your work?"

"No, I can't," said Kemp crossly. "A little lower."

"Linda," said Rick. His tone had an unfamiliar quality of awe. "I think that's my favorite girl's name."

"Cut out the crap and get on with the spraying!"

"I wonder how many Lindas there are on campus."

"You want me to tell you?" said Kempie. He shrugged out of his pants and started spraying his lobster-hued legs. "There're twenty-nine thousand students in the student body, right?"

"Give or take a couple."

"Give or take a couple. Of those, half have to be girls, right?"

"Right."

"Making fourteen thousand five hundred females. Out of those, at least one out of every twenty is named Linda."

"That many?"

"It's the commonest girl's name today. That makes five Lindas to a hundred, minimum, or a total of seven hundred and twenty-five."

Rick whistled.

"So how am I going to find her?"

"Listen," said Kemp, grasping Rick's shoulders in exasperation and giving him a shake, "you don't want to find her, her or that friend of hers who looks like an owl. Those are a couple of spaced-out dames that you need like you need a hole in the head."

"Kempie, baby, she had such a super bod! She's gorgeous!"

Kemp looked his friend squarely in the eye.

"If you'd been in circulation, you could see that is part of what's wrong. Sure, she looks okay. She could be a cover girl with no sweat." Kemp nodded sagely, the authority in such matters. "A girl with her face and tits should have it made—should be—oh, you know . . ."

"No, I don't know." Rick's voice was edgy.

"Well, hell, a bunny like that should be relaxed and all together. So what's the matter with her? Why is she so uptight about all this Women's Lib stuff?"

"Oh, come off it, Kemp, that's just her—"

"Why did she get so hot and bothered the minute we hove into sight?"

"But she's beautiful!"

"Beautiful! There's nothing beautiful about a broad who runs out of breath describing how crass you are. Take my word for it, forget her!"

Rick looked unhappy. Kemp went down the hall to the soda dispenser and came back with a couple of cans of

Seven Up. He pulled out the tabs methodically and offered a can to Rick.

"There are thousands of gorgeous chicks on this campus. Give any one of them a word of encouragement and she'll think you are God's gift to women."

Rick's expression deteriorated.

"Son," said Kemp in fatherly tone, "I'm only trying to point out there are lots of fish in the sea."

Rick glared at him.

"Man," he said, "you really bug me, you know that? First you blow hot, then you blow cold."

"I'm telling you what any five-year-old child could see for himself. That girl's a zombie."

"She is not!"

"I've got one big piece of advice," said Kemp. "Forget her!"

He might as well have told the sun to forget rising in the morning, or the moon to forget pulling the tides. As any jock on the scrimmage offense could have told him, once Big Rick was set on a course, there was no turning him back.

SIX

The movement numbered thirty girls from a wide spectrum of backgrounds.

Next to Sadie, the most forceful figure was Aggie Jackson, a beautiful black woman with a thin, elegant figure and a carriage that suggested royalty. Linda visualized Aggie moving, sensuously as a panther, along the fashion runway at the Beverly Wilshire, trailing a full-length chinchilla. Instead, Aggie wore tight jeans, low on the hip, and a calico print blouse tied in front to show her bare midriff. Aggie was bright, but was struggling to make passing grades because of the gaps in her earlier education. The girls in the movement took turns tutoring her in an effort to pull her through.

Though the two were as opposite as night and day, Linda was attracted to Aggie, particularly by her voice, a vibrant contralto, and her smile, which cast aside pretense and shone from Aggie's heart.

Aggie's hatred of men was as outspoken as Sadie's. Once when the girls were stuffing envelopes, Aggie deplored the awkwardness of the middle finger on her left hand, which Linda noted for the first time was unnaturally stiff.

"That no-account LeRoy," said Aggie with passion. "All my life it's going to get in my way!"

"Who're you talking about?" said Jody Jordan.

"LeRoy. Seeing's how he was the one who broke it!"

"What a terrible accident," said Linda, sympathetic.

Aggie looked directly at Linda.

"Twarn't no accident. He did it on purpose."

Linda stared, horrified, at Aggie's hand. Aggie's fingers were long, and delicately shaped, the fingers of a patrician.

"You can't mean . . ." Linda faltered.

"I do mean," said Aggie. "Held me down and bent it back till it snapped."

"Who was LeRoy?" said Delcie in an awed tone.

"Her mother's boy friend," said Sadie brusquely. "One of them."

"But why?" said Linda. She couldn't believe what she was hearing.

"So's I wouldn't snitch to my old lady. He knew if she knew he was making it with me she'd boot him out and he'd lose his free meal ticket."

"Gosh!" said Jody, assimilating the import of what Aggie was saying, "You mean he . . . with you . . ."

"He wasn't no different than the others. My old lady always had to have herself a man. And she always picked a loser."

"But . . ." Linda was trying to put the pieces together into something that made sense in the light of her own experience. "If they—with you—didn't your mother care?"

"Never happened when she was home," said Aggie. "Those buggers were not only mean, man, they were crafty. One of us kids would snitch and my mom would say, 'LeRoy couldn't have done a bad thing like that, nohow, could you, LeRoy?' "

"The wonder was, Ag didn't get pregnant!" said Sadie grimly.

"I did oncet," admitted Aggie. "But Belle, my girlfriend, fixed me up. She filched a dee-vice from her aunt."

"You mean she performed an abortion?" said Delcie.

"Right there on her mom's kitchen table. Man, did it hurt! Trouble was, Belle didn't know what the hell she was doing. She just shoved that rusty old dee-vice up my cunt and . . ."

Linda glanced down at her own hands, clasped so tightly the knuckles showed white.

"Blood!" Aggie was saying. "I like to never seen so much blood! Ran out on the table and dripped down in a puddle on the floor. Belle, she tried to sop it up with a dish rag . . ."

Delcie and Linda walked back to the dorm together, each immersed in her own thoughts. Linda tried to visualize what her mother's reaction would have been to Aggie's grisly tale—horror? Revulsion? She remembered her mother working on the committee for this or that charity ball, to "help those less fortunate"—Margaret Allenby's stock phrase. Linda realized with a jolt that her mother's interest in "those people" was valid only if they stayed at arm's length. If Margaret knew her daughter was palling around with someone like Aggie Jackson, she'd have a stroke.

At the same time, Linda was struck by the fact that Aggie had related the whole monstrous tale so calmly—as if it were day-to-day routine.

"What must the rest of her life have been like!" she observed aloud.

"At least she has guts," said Delcie. "She got out of there."

"How did she and Sadie come to room together?"

Delcie gave her a look of surprise.

"Don't tell me you don't know?"

"Know what?"

"They're more than friends, as in just good. They're gay."

"Oh," said Linda, weakly.

Her old WASP values flooded over her. Not only did she imagine what her mother would say, she could hear her father's outrage. No daughter of mine is going to get mixed up with any lesbians! Do I make myself perfectly clear?

"Perfectly," Linda said.

"What?" said Delcie.

"I mean . . ." Linda was embarrassed. "No, I didn't know."

"It's their own business," said Delcie, cheerful and matter of fact.

"Of course."

"It's their lifestyle. I believe every person should do her own thing."

"I do too," said Linda, striving for conviction.

"And you can see how they got to be that way, both of them."

"Yes."

"After what's happened, neither one could be anything else."

"No."

"Besides," Delcie warmed to her subject. "They're both wonderful persons. They're both sincere."

They were wonderful, Linda thought. Sadie was a remarkable individual. So was Aggie.

"I think sincerity's more important than anything!" stated Delcie.

"It is," agreed Linda. Inwardly, she struggled to make order out of chaos; out of her crumbling values. Actually, she asked herself, how sincere was she?

SEVEN

Off and on, Kemp Conway went home to Newport to spend a bachelor's weekend with his father. Rick Dublin didn't go to *his* father because he had no idea where—or who—his father was. He didn't go home because he had no home to go to. After his mother died in November of his freshman year, Rick listed the residence hall as his university address, and in the place below marked "permanent address," he painstakingly printed "Same." There was no sense in thinking of 39-D, the apartment in Temple City, as home because Rick himself had cleared that out the week after the funeral and sold the furniture. By now, 39-D had probably been occupied by four or five different sets of tenants.

As a rule, Rick exercised Spartan control over his thoughts, expunging what he classified as "baby stuff," but sometimes, before he knew what he was doing, he found himself wondering who lived in 39-D, how their furniture was arranged, how their lives were arranged. Would they be race track people, a jockey and his girlfriend, or perhaps a couple of gay hairdressers? They might be two girls rooming together and going to secretarial school. Of all the possibilities, Rick hoped it was a family with a boy. He liked to think of a boy doing pushups on the floor in his old room, or lying in bed, looking out the windows at the night light over the carports, dreaming of making the Temple City Rams' first team.

Sometimes Rick allowed himself the luxury of reminiscing about his mother, trying not to let it hurt too badly. Dot Dublin had been a faded high-strung blonde who bleached her own hair and slept in curlers. Still a young woman when Rick was born, she aged quickly from overwork, and became excessively thin, her once-pretty features sharpened by responsibility. Rick remembered the time his mother had ordered a giant sheet of pressed cork and had it delivered from the lumber yard. Together she and he had lugged it up the two flights of stairs and nailed it to the wall over Rick's bed. Rick had worried for fear the manager would hear the pounding on his precious walls and come storming up, demanding to know what the hell they thought they were doing. However, he hadn't voiced his apprehension because his mother had seemed so pleased with her extravagance.

"You have to have a place to put up your clippings," she told him.

At that time there had been all of two clippings, both one-line mentions in paragraphs about the high school Rams, one in the *Temple City Times* and one buried in the grocery section of the *Pasadena Star News*.

"Oh, come on, Mom, you're making a fuss over nothing. They're not that important."

"What are you talking about, they're not important!" It was one of the few times he had seen her fired up. "They are important, to me! And they're important to you!" They were, but he was too embarrassed to admit it. "Be proud of what you are, Rick." Funny, how he could hear her saying that, standing back, the hammer in her thin hand. He thought of it as a directive, a sort of guidepost in his life. "There'll be more, Rick. Lots more. I know it."

He wished she could have read Jim Murray, top sports columnist for the *Los Angeles Times*, the time the entire column was about Big Rick, or could have seen the program for the UCLA-Oregon game, with Rick's picture, in color, spread over the cover. But his mom had had her money's worth out of the cork board. It had been plastered with clippings and photos before Rick got out of high school. When he'd cleared out the apartment, Rick had taken them all down, and packed them in a shirt box. They were there now, under the tangle of socks in his drawer. He'd left the cork board on the wall in 39-D, in case the room might someday house another all-time Temple City Ram.

Rick's memories were compartmentalized in his mind, behind separate little doors in his head. He likened it to the multicolored wall in a TV program called Laugh-In, which had unlimited doors popping open and shut at random. Sometimes in Rick's memory a door would burst open when he least expected it, and he would find himself staring into his past, reliving a forgotten sequence, experiencing afresh a pain or pleasure, smelling the fragrances or the smells, hearing the background noises of traffic or hard rock.

Rick's rule of thumb was to keep his memories sealed off. He believed in the present, and tried to live one day at a time. Some doors he had triple locked and vowed never to open, but he knew they were there, and he knew what was behind them.

Similarly, he refused to recognize certain feelings which made him feel unworthy of himself as an adult; if they persisted, he masked them as something else. As much as Kemp got on his nerves, Rick hated to see him leave, even for a weekend. He never would admit it, but he dreaded being left alone.

The earliest thing Rick remembered was standing on a chair by the front window at the baby sitter's, peering out at the half-twilight, half-dark—it must have been winter—waiting for his mother to come from work. At the end of the day the other kids would be gone; he was always the last to be picked up. He sensed Mrs. Mulroony's impatience to be rid of him; her own children, home from school, were hungry and clamoring for her attention. She was tired after a long, nerve-wracking day.

"Maybe your mom's forgotten you."

Even now he could hear her voice, with its faint Irish brogue; he knew now that she was joking, or thought she was joking, and that she meant no harm.

The Mulroony children took up the ritual.

"Maybe your mom's been in an accident on the freeway, and smashed up her car."

"Maybe she got in an accident at the factory, in all that machinery."

"Maybe she's been hurt, bad."

"Maybe she's been killed!"

He could feel again the desperate wave of panic that washed over him.

"Now you kids, stop teasing the poor little tyke."

It didn't help for Mrs. Mulroony to intervene. She had started the ball rolling, they all knew that.

"Maybe she's run off with somebody else!"

That was the worst of all, the terror of being abandoned, of being left alone. Ricky would cling to the chairback, fighting the tears, the dread, determined not to cry. Even then, he knew that big boys were brave. Big boys didn't cry.

Rick's relief when his mother arrived, exhausted from her long day at her factory job, the inevitable cigarette between her nicotine-stained thumb and forefinger, was overpowering.

The exchange between his mother and Mrs. Mulroony was brief and stylized.

"Has he been a good boy?"

"Good as gold and twice as handsome."

"Get your things, Rick." He was already standing beside her, his jacket on and buttoned, stuffed panda in hand. "We're late," and then, "Thanks!"

"Thanks to you, Dot. 'Bye, Rick."

"See you tomorrow."

" 'Bye."

Sometimes, if she were extra tired, his mom left out the thanks. The exchange was meaningless. She and Mrs. Mulroony each provided something the other wanted: Mrs. Mulroony a service, his mother, the money to pay for it. Beyond that, they had nothing to say to one another.

A young child, like an animal, has no perception of time. For Rick the next hour, or it may have been two hours, were the high points of the day.

His mother drove the freeways with a nervous aggression born of necessity, clenching the steering wheel as if the battered Ambassador were plunging ahead through darkest Africa. She and she alone was responsible for the survival of the two of them in this dangerous and hostile environment. She flicked her cigarette without taking her eyes from the road; sometimes she missed the tray and the ash fell on the rubber mat. Clutching his panda, Ricky stood on the seat beside her, as close to her frail form as he could without disturbing her driving. It was a time of togetherness against the world.

Their conversation was limited.

"So you were a good boy today."

"Uh-huh."

"You're always a good boy. You're the best boy in the world."

Or, it might be, "What'd you do all day at Mrs. Mulroony's?"

"Played."

"That's good."

It wasn't the words, after all. It was the sound, the inflection, the approval, the mutual dependence.

His mother was all right. She hadn't been in a wreck, as Dennis Mulroony had said. She hadn't run off with somebody else. Rick was suffused with gratitude.

Often on week nights, they dined on cornflakes and cold milk because his mother was too tired to fix anything else. Dot Dublin devoted all her strength to being a parent, but she never made any pretense of trying to be both mother and father to Rick, or of being anything other than a woman. She was fragile and she was feminine. After she had bathed Rick and put him to bed she would soak herself in a hot bath, scented with White Gardenia bath oil—her one luxury—while Ricky listened for the occasional splash that reassured him she hadn't fallen asleep and drowned.

In those days they slept together, for they lived in a cramped studio apartment, and Rick's mother went to bed as soon as she finished her bath. She was always tired—he suspected now that she had been anemic—besides, they had to get up at five-thirty. She would hold him close, and he could feel her heart beating through the thin nylon tricot of her nightie. He was used to the smell of his mother; the tobacco breath, the Listerine mouthwash which didn't kill the tobacco breath, the White Gardenia cologne which neither masked the tobacco nor the Listerine—the total combination a not unpleasant odor, which became associated in Rick's mind with security. The last thing his mother would say, before they dropped off to sleep, was, "Whose boy are you?" and he would answer drowsily, "Yours."

The day children at Mrs. Mulroony's belonged to single mothers who worked. Mrs. Mulroony herself was divorced, and Rick was past four before he first grasped the idea of a father; it began with watching television.

It was late on a rainy afternoon; the Mulroony children were home from school, and everybody was inside, watching an old comedy. Rick was an active child with a short attention span, but for once he got the drift of the story, partly because the older kids kept ordering him to sit down and shut up.

"But who is that man?"

"He's their father."

"Whose father?"

"*Their* father, you dope."

"Dennis . . ."

"Shut up and watch!"

"Why is that man in their house?"

"I told you. He lives with them."

"Why does he live with them?"

"Don't you know nothing? Their father is married to their mother."

"What does married—"

"Listen, you want me to give you a fat lip?"

Rick had no father image. He had seen no pattern for the role of a husband.

He asked his mother.

"Why don't I have a father?"

Dot, already pale, became visibly paler. She pushed aside her half-finished cornflakes, and lit a cigarette.

"I was wondering when you'd ask me that."

He went on eating; she went on smoking.

"Mom?"

Dot sighed.

"Some children do, and some don't. You don't."

He waited.

"Mommie?"

"What?"

"What does married mean?"

"That's enough, Rick. I don't want to talk about it."

He flinched at her tone. He had displeased her, he didn't know how. Subtly, without either of them realizing it, the words married and father had taken on labels. Married meant unworkable and unhappy; father meant the bad guy.

It had not been until the next year, in kindergarten, that one of Rick's older and stronger classmates took him aside and instructed him in the facts of life. Rick had known about the difference between boys and girls; his friend, whose name was Eddie Hawes, explained graphically and in exact detail why.

Rick accepted the story with fascination.

"You mean that's what has to happen before everybody's born?"

"That's right."

"Everybody?"

"Yup. Everybody has a mother."

"Yeah."

"And a father. He's the stud."

"What's that?"

"That's what we're going to be. To make a baby you have to have both."

For two or three days Rick put off asking his mother. Then his curiosity got the better of him.

"Mom, do I have a father?"

He caught her unawares, but she rallied.

"No, you don't have a father. You know that."

"But did I have a father? One time?"

Her hand shook so that the coffee slopped over into the saucer. She took a paper napkin and placed it in the saucer, under the cup. Rick watched the brown liquid soak into the yellow napkin, making a pale, sunburst-shaped stain in various shades of ecru.

"Yes you did, Ricky. One time."

"But where is he?"

"I don't know."

"Where did he go?"

"I don't know that, either. I wish I did, that's all I have to say."

It took him the better part of two years to wrest the story from her, piecemeal, a crumb at a time.

Rick had had a father. His father, like him, was named Rick Dublin. Father and mother had been married, and then Rick was born—but one day before Ricky was a year old—his father had disappeared.

Rick became excited when he heard that.

"Maybe somebody killed him! Maybe a bad guy pulled

his gun on him and said, 'Hold it right there, buddy!' and then drilled him in the back."

His mother shook her head.

"I thought that too, at first. I almost went to the police."

"Why didn't you go to the police? Mom? Mom, you've got to tell me! Why didn't you?"

His mother hesitated, then spoke in a rusty whisper, the words, so long unsaid, rasping out separately, one after the other.

"I found out as how he'd packed his clothes the night before, and put them in the car. He'd planned it, planned the whole thing. Cleaned out everything he owned, lock, stock and barrel, and most of my stuff to boot. I had just been too much of a dumb bunny to notice."

This revelation had come at breakfast time, and Rick listened thoughtfully.

"But didn't he—didn't he say where he was going?"

His mother shook her head.

"Didn't even say good-by, just took off."

"Where did he go?"

Subconsciously, he was surprised she didn't cut the discussion off, as she had so many times before. It was as if at last, her defenses worn down, she was relieved to have her shame out in the open. For shame it was, in some secret, inexplicable way they both felt. She had failed—she had failed as a woman, or he wouldn't have gone.

"Where did he go? Who knows? I always thought he got clear away, went to another state, maybe another country."

"Why did you think that? Mom?"

His mother shrugged, tiredly.

"No reason. He might not have gone ten miles. He might still be in Los Angeles."

Ricky became excited.

"He might still be right here in Temple City! Maybe we could find him! Maybe we could get him to come home and live with us!"

His mother lit a cigarette, not noticing one was already burning in the ash tray.

"I don't think that would be such a good idea," she told her son. "The fact of the matter is, we hadn't been getting along worth a damn."

After that they rarely discussed Rick's father, but Rick thought about him a lot. Sometimes he tried to sense what it would be like if his father were there in the apartment, living with them—what would his father say to his mother, or his mother say to his father, but it was impossible. He had no real family relationship to observe, only the *I Love Lucy* show on television, and that didn't seem real. Sometimes Rick imagined his father hadn't left them, but that he'd only gone to get a new job so he could come back and surprise Rick and Dot with lots of money, or that his father had been killed or kidnapped before he could make it home. Sometimes Rick imagined that his father had been in an accident on the freeway and had been wandering about for eleven years with amnesia, but then he regained his memory and came to find them, bringing money and toys and treating them to a day at Disneyland.

But always, Rick brought himself up sharp, back from the fantasy to the hard, cruel facts: there had been something about the relationship between his mom and dad which his dad found insupportable, and his solution to the problem was to split.

Once, Rick had asked what his father looked like. His mother admitted that she had owned a photograph, but that she'd been so mad when Rick's father left, she'd torn the picture into little bits and thrown the pieces away.

"I'm sorry, Ricky," she told him. "I should have realized you might want to see it some day. But you were only a baby, and I guess I wasn't thinking."

"But I mean . . . well, you can remember, can't you?"

"He was an ordinary guy, same as anybody else."

"But he must have looked like something! How exactly did he look? Mom, you can remember something, can't you?"

His mother shrugged.

"He was big."

Ricky had zeroed in on this like a Geiger counter. He didn't know it, but he was groping for an image, a pattern, something to tie himself to.

"Big? How big was he?"

"Bigger and stronger than me!"

"He'd have to be bigger'n you! You're a girl!"

His mother was silent.

"I mean, how tall was he? Like, was he six feet? Mr. Weston is six feet. Was my dad six feet?"

"Yes, I reckon he was. Maybe more than that."

It was the one point of reference Rick had. After that he ate diligently, worked out on the bars at the playground at school, and even lay straight on his back at night, stretching his toes down into the cool, smooth, untouched places between the sheets (they had moved by this time, and he had his own bedroom)—in order to grow. His father had been a big man, and Rick would be a big man, too.

As the years went by, his father, never more than a silhouette, a shadow, figured less and less in their thoughts. His abandonment of his wife and child was a happenstance that receded into the past. Rick's mother never evinced resentment that she alone had been left with the financial burden of rearing the child; on the contrary, as far as she was concerned, the sun rose and set in her Ricky. He was the mainstay of her life.

She never remarried, and Rick never knew whether or not she had gone to the trouble of obtaining a divorce. What was more unusual, though as a child Rick didn't realize it, she never dated, all the time Rick was growing up.

She had had it with men, was her stock reply to Melba DeLaney, a divorcee who lived next door in the new apartment building. She had had it with men, which meant she had had it with sex. Melba, on the other hand, was ever on the prowl for a boyfriend. She found a new one every week, but as Melba put it, there was always a joker in the woodpile. Evenings, the two women sat at the kitchen table, drinking coffee and smoking, while Rick did his homework. Melba would urge Dot to go with her to a little bar on Las Tunas named Joe's Place.

"Why not? Give me one decent reason."

"Not interested."

"Christ, will you listen to that? I'm telling you, Dot, it's not your ordinary pub. They're a better class of people—professional types, you know what I mean? The kind your mother would want you to meet."

"My mother's dead."

"If she were living."

"You go. Tell me about it."

"It's a crime. A good-looking girl like you, not even thirty."

"I'll be thirty next month."

"You don't look it."

"I don't want to leave Ricky."

"That's a lot of b.s. Ricky's ten going on eleven. He could stay by himself for an hour. Couldn't you, Ricky?"

"Sure, mom. Go ahead."

"I told you, I don't want to. I'm tired and I want to get some rest."

Melba inevitably closed out the conversation with the classic observation, "Once burned, twice shy," and went off to Joe's Place by herself. The next night she would be over again to relate her bad luck in drawing another joker. Hunched over his homework, Rick listened to the two grown-ups' views of sex—his mother's, full of disdain, and Melba's, full of disappointment.

Rick's mother was perennially tired. She never caught up, she never got enough rest. In an indefinable way, that may have been the key to Rick's unfailing good behavior, in a decade when his contemporaries were in open revolt. His mom never complained, but Rick knew she was working beyond her physical capacity, and that she was doing it for him. He tried to make things easier. Naturally good-natured, he carried out the simple requests she made of him without question.

"You don't realize how lucky you are," Melba told his mother a dozen times a week, brandishing a newspaper for proof. "Look at this, will you? Kids set fire to the administration building, kids picked up on dope, kids breaking and entering . . ."

"It's terrible."

"You've got a regular jewel . . ."

"I know," said Dot, her face softening into a smile. Rick was her one vanity.

" 'Course, we wouldn't want him to get a big head!" Melba looked archly in Rick's direction. "But between you and me and the board fence, he'll be a prize for some girl. Let's hope she has enough sense to realize it!"

* * *

In the beginning, when Rick had started kindergarten, he'd walked to Mrs. Mulroony's after school. In second grade, however, he announced to his mother he was too big to go to a baby sitter's, and demanded a key to the apartment. After that, he was on his own for hours out of every day. He took to staying at the school grounds, working out on the rings and bars, or pestering the big kids to let him in the game.

He discovered the name of the game: Winning.

The game, played unsupervised, on the field of Emerson Elementary, every day after school, was a microcosm of everything Rick was to encounter later in life. It varied with the seasons. In the fall it was flag football, in the winter, work-up basketball, in the spring rounders baseball, but at all times it maintained a universality: it was tough, fierce and bitter; a bloody battle which barely stopped short of mayhem. The cast of players remained the same, each with his own savage individuality, his streak of cruelty, his ruthless strategy, his thirst for victory, no matter what the cost. The game had no room for sissies.

"Don't play with those bullies!" was Dot's first reaction. She had come home and found him in his darkened room, his face muffled in his pillow, sobbing, even though big boys didn't cry. "Rick . . ."

He was too shaken to talk.

"If they're going to beat the hell out of you like that, don't . . ."

He sat up then, and looked at her, his face woefully tear-stained.

"You don't understand, mom. I have to play with them."

She hadn't understood—up to then.

"Only they're all . . . they're all . . ."

"They're all what?"

Her thin hand lying lightly on his shoulder, was a healing caress. He stopped crying, but he still gasped for breath.

"They're better players . . . better 'n I am."

His mother knelt on the floor, and took his hands in hers.

"You can be as good as they are. All it takes is hard work." He listened. She was the authority on hard work. "All it takes is practice, doing the same thing over, and over, a million times."

* * *

There was no doubt that that had been a turning point in Rick's life, although his emergence as an athlete took not weeks, but years. From the beginning, the necessary ingredients were present: he was coordinated, muscularly sound, above average size and weight. He faced ferocious competition on which to hone his skills. Most important, he was obsessed with a determination that drove him to practice every spare minute of his life. He had the will to win.

After class and the all-important game after school, Rick spent his hours alone tossing the football, jogging the playing field, dribbling, shooting baskets, batting a tennis ball against the wall and doing sit-ups, knee-bends and sprints. His hands grew. They grew cradling a ball, fingertipping a ball out of space and holding on to it, throwing a ball with a curve, a twist, a drop; a little English.

When Rick reached junior high, his world exploded in a proliferation of new experiences, sensations, reactions, which left him at once bewildered and supercharged. He had entered the realm of organized athletics; for the next ten years he would eat, sleep and breathe nothing else.

There was, for example, the head-on clash between Coach Robinson, a martinet, and the motley, gangling rabble of seventh grade mavericks fresh off the range, who for years had made their own rules and never heard of discipline. There was the power struggle between the dudes from Emerson, Wilson and Jefferson Elementaries, in addition to the sub-factions of anglos, chicanos, and blacks.

There was the thundering rush to the showers and the cold foot vat of disinfectant. There was, too, the hiss of boiling water, the clouds of steam, the stench of tennis shoes, green soap, mildew and sweat. The clang of locker doors and the hollow reverberations of shouts of laughter bounced off the cement walls. There was the bustle—the calisthenics—(*in-out*! *up-down*!), and the stretch of unused muscles and the cramps. Then came the charley horse, the running till your chest bursts, the pumping of your knees like pistons and the plunge into the cold pool.

And last, the splash, the whistle, the rules, the hard slap of body against body and the blood pumping through your head and neck; the heart pounding against your rib cage.

All right you guys! Who's next, you guys? Get a hustle on! Shake a leg! Next! Next! Go! Go! Go!

There was the competition and the tryouts; the jockeying for position and the jealousy; the politics and the final burst of power; the choice, the winner, the loser, the exhilaration and finally the retribution.

There was the entity of the team, the bond of the team, the loyalty of the team, the back-up, the oneness, the dependence, the concentrated push, the feeling of power, the thrust, the magic of unity.

There were the plays, the diagrams, the blackboards; the squeak of chalk, the numbers, the signals; the strategy and the memorization, the repetition, and the flubs. All right, you guys! All right, you stupid jerks! All right, you blockheads! Again! Again! Again!

There was the reverence for the coach, the hypnotic quality of his exhortations translated into movement and coordination, into nerve triggering sinew, sinew lifting bone, bone propelling muscle, muscles contracting, squeezing, thrusting, pushing, forcing. There was the determination to do, to get in there, to die, to win!

And then, like a blast from Olympus, like thunder, hurricane, volcano; like adrenaline, whisky, tobacco, cocaine; there was the roar of the crowd.

GO! GO! GO! GO!
CHARGE! CHARGE!

Always, Rick was on the crest of the wave, in the forefront of the attack.

He entered junior high an outstanding athlete; he entered high school a star. During his four years with the Temple City Rams he shattered every record in every sport.

The school lionized him; the girls' pep club parlayed him into their number one hero; he became a living legend, immortalized by cheers, chants, songs. Yet he was painfully shy off the playing field. In class he managed to sit in the back corner, flanked by a buffer zone of teammates.

He moved through the hall at the center of a phalanx of friends. Girls wouldn't believe him when he said he didn't have a phone; they thought it was unlisted and he was playing hard to get. Whatever the season, he practiced late, then drove to Arcadia and worked in a drug store until ten. Sports filled his life; there was room for nothing else.

Rick maintained a B average in high school. The Bruin coach at UCLA recruited him personally, treating Rick to the same VIP rush he accorded Darter Evans, the Alabama Ace, top high school passer in the nation. When notification of Rick's four-year scholarship came in the mail, together with the papers to be filled out and sent back, Dot Dublin burst out crying.

"I'm glad," she managed to say, rummaging for a Kleenex. She never allowed herself to cry, and now she struggled to get her emotions in check. She put her arm around him—as far as it would go—and rested her head on his chest. "I couldn't see how we were going to swing it, even with you working. But now, everything's taken care of. You're all set!"

Later, Rick was to look back and remember his mother's words, wondering if somehow she could have known. But at the time he gave her a reassuring hug, and then started to fill out the forms.

EIGHT

In spite of Kemp's warning, Rick subconsciously was searching, combing the crowds, wherever there were people —in the halls, the lecture auds, the walkways and stairways and in the snack bar areas. Time and again he spotted a sheaf of blond hair and rushed forward, only to have the girl turn out to be someone else. It was no use. Whether he was awake or asleep, her image floated before him, eyes flashing, hair shining in the sun, her T-shirt and jeans clinging to her glorious body, every curve, every muscle signaling vitality, health, pulsating aliveness.

Then, one afternoon, he found her. The NOW table was back in business, and Linda and her owl-like friend sat behind it, big as life, as if nothing had happened. Unfortunately, Rick was with Kemp at the time.

"There she is!" It burst from him: Balboa sighting the Pacific, Noah welcoming the returning dove.

"Hold on a minute, pardner," said Kemp.

"Don't you get it? It's Linda!"

Kemp grabbed his arm.

"We are not," he said firmly, "going over there to be made fools of."

Kemp, still peeling, was not at his best.

"Speak for yourself," said Rick, shrugging off his grasp. He bounded toward the table, with Kemp tagging behind.

"Hi!" The *Daily Bruin* to the contrary, the word grudge didn't exist in Big Rick's vocabulary. "How are you ch—persons today?"

He was met with steely silence.

"We're . . . fine," said Delcie uncertainly. "How're you . . . persons?"

"We're right in there," Rick assured her, his eyes feasting on Linda. "How would you like to come over to the snack bar and we'll buy you a Coke?"

"We just came on duty," said Linda crisply. "Besides,

such a transaction is repugnant to the tenets of the movement."

"Come again?"

"It would put us in a subservient position."

Rick's forehead wrinkled.

"She means," said Delcie, "we'd be in your debt."

"That's bad?"

Delcie's head bobbed solemnly. Linda looked past them. Kemp took hold of Rick's elbow, as if it were a football he'd received in a reverse handoff.

"Let's split."

"Split? We barely got here."

"Perhaps you had better go," said Delcie, without seeming to mean it. "We shouldn't be seen fraternizing with the enemy."

"The enemy?" complained Rick. "You sound as if you were in the middle of a war."

"We are," said Linda. "So are you."

"You haven't noticed it yet," Delcie added in explanation, "up to now."

"Who said we were your enemies?" Rick strove for reason. "You got an enemies list, or something?"

"We don't need a list," said Linda sweetly, "but if we had one, you'd be on it."

Each time Linda spoke, Rick was knocked out by her mellifluent voice.

"Why would we?"

"Because you're men, that's why."

"Whoa, Nellie!" Kemp degenerated into his cowboy routine. "If that isn't the silliest answer I ever heard in my life!"

"It's true." Linda was dispassionate, almost clinical.

"I suppose every man alive, in the whole world, is your enemy."

"You're beginning to get the picture!" exulted Delcie.

It was too much for Kemp.

"Rick, for crying out loud, these are a couple of kooky dames!"

He had forgotten his friend's staying power. It was the quality in Big Rick which the line coach had valued most.

"Tell me one thing," said Rick, ignoring Kemp. "One

thing. That's all I ask. When did we get to be your enemies?"

"Prehistorically," said Linda, without batting an eye. "Before the dawn of civilization."

At this, Rick seemed to have trouble swallowing, but he kept his cool.

"Would you mind telling us exactly how this happened?" He sat down on the edge of the table, which creaked ominously.

"Please," said Linda, as if she were speaking to a two-year-old. "This is a table. It is not to sit on."

"Sorry." Rick reddened and stood up. He faced her. "I still want to know."

"It was simple," said Linda, "Like every other exploitation, man was stronger. If he wanted a woman, he bashed her over the head with a club and dragged her off."

"Originally," said Delcie, as if she were speaking a part in a pageant, "women were considered superior beings . . ."

"As they are," put in Linda.

"As they are," said Delcie, "because they gave birth."

"But the discovery of man's role in conception and birth changed all that."

Rick was listening, in spite of himself.

"You mean," said Kemp, "after they caught on to the connection . . ." He snickered.

The girls paid no attention.

"Exactly. Man, being the selfish, egotistical brute that he is . . ."

Kemp turned to leave, but Rick held up his hand.

"He wanted to make sure he and he alone was the father of the child. So he locked his woman up in a cave. That restriction of her freedom came to be called marriage."

"I thought all you birds wanted marriage," said Kemp.

Linda ignored him.

"Those persons who were restricted, who were easily identified because of a marked visible difference . . ."

"*Vive la différence!*"

Linda looked pained. She remembered Kemp saying exactly that once before.

". . . Women became inferior, supplementary beings," Linda continued.

Delcie nodded, her expression owl-like.

"Women were given work men did not wish to do. Women became the source of unpaid, or underpaid labor."

"Women were considered possessions."

"It's the oldest, most flagrant, most widespread violation of human rights in the history of the planet."

"Worse than slavery," put in Delcie.

"Slavery! It is slavery! You have denigrated, desecrated, excoriated . . ."

"I told you they were nuts," said Kemp.

"Your friend," continued Linda, as if Kemp were not present, "is a perfect example of what I'm talking about. Notice the patronizing manner in which he refers to us?"

"That's old Kempie spouting off to hear the sound of his own voice," said Rick. "You can't go by anything he says."

"Rick!" said Kemp in exasperation.

Rick leaned forward. He seemed impervious to insult.

"I haven't noticed any cavemen lately, going around with clubs," he pointed out. "So what are you so up-tight about?"

"Civilization has made superficial changes," conceded Linda, "but the basic position remains the same. The conqueror and the vanquished. The dominator and the dominated. Take right now, what will be happening to members of my class after graduation . . . I happen to be a senior . . ."

"You're a senior?" Rick grasped at the straw. "What a coincidence. I happen to be a senior, too . . ."

"Suppose we have two students," went on Linda, "with a degree in Business Administration, one a man, and one a woman. They apply for a job at the same company. The company hires the man and gives him the title of Young Executive. The first thing they ask the girl is, 'Can you type?' "

"What's so bad about that?" said Kemp.

A strand of white-gold hair had fallen over Linda's eye, and she brushed it back impatiently.

"It isn't *fair*, that's what's bad!" she said fiercely. "It stinks! Picture a dentist's office. Who's the dentist, pulling down fifty thou net? A man. Who's the helper, holding the tray of instruments, and making a hundred fifty a week, before deductions? I don't need to tell you!"

"Why do they call ships 'she'?" Delcie interposed, ominously.

"Have you ever seen a commercial of a man, waxing a floor?"

"Why do they give girls' names to storms?"

"Do you know out of thirty-two department heads in the City of Los Angeles, two are women?"

"Why is it that ninety-five per cent of presidents, governors, senators, representatives, mayors, the people in charge, are *men*?"

"I suppose you could do better!" challenged Kemp.

"Suppose? I know!" said Linda hotly. "You men have ruined everything, with your greed and power struggle and . . . and . . . contempt for humanity!"

"Methinks the lady doth protest too much," said Kemp.

"Just what would you do?" said Rick.

"Yeah, tell us," said Kemp, "if women ruled the world?"

Linda was on her feet. Her blue eyes sparkled, and she looked into the distance.

"We wouldn't have war," she said, "because the soldiers are our children, don't you see? We'd have food, plenty of food, with milk and orange juice for the babies."

Delcie stood smartly at attention beside her.

"And vitamins," said Delcie.

"Vitamins," Linda agreed. "We'd dredge the rivers, and make everybody stop dumping waste. Right now. Period."

"Smog," prompted Delcie.

"We'd insist on filters. We'd insist on car pools."

"The factories could clean up or shut down."

"We'd have flowers," said Linda, "flowers everywhere. And trees."

"You're nuts, nuts, nuts!" said Kemp.

"How can you say that!" blazed Linda.

"Because it can never come true!" said Rick.

"You're having a pipe dream!" said Kemp.

"It could! It could!" screamed Linda and Delcie in concert.

"No way!" shouted Kemp. "Men won't vote for you! Women won't vote for you either!"

"They will!" shrieked the girls. "They will! Women are fifty-three per cent of the population! All we have to do is get the message across! Then you'll see!"

At the end of the altercation Kemp stalked away in hauteur and disgust, dragging Rick behind him. Linda, flushed from the heat of battle, stacked and restacked the pamphlets as if readying a fortress for the next assault. Before they turned the corner of Rolfe Hall, Rick managed to look over his shoulder, and caught sight of Linda, her stance still militant, her eyes ablaze. No doubt about it, when she was mad she was more gorgeous than ever! He was turned on—worse, he was mesmerized, hypnotized. And he still didn't know Linda's last name!

NINE

When Linda came home for four days at Thanksgiving, the Allenbys had no inkling that she had been transposed into a different being. Outwardly she appeared the same, perhaps a trifle more tanned. Her hair seemed to blow more, drifting away from her shoulders at the slightest current of air. The transmutation might have gone unnoticed altogether had it not been for the incidents of the turkey, the tennis game and the shoe shine.

Linda had heard her mother tell the story of the turkey a dozen times if she had heard it once. It had become a family classic, something that belonged with an Allenby Thanksgiving in the same way that the tin angel from Guadalajara and the red velvet fireplace socks were brought out each year for the Allenby Christmas.

Although Margaret had household help three days a week, over the years she had become a gourmet cook. This year she had prepared the Thanksgiving dinner herself, and had invited the Prestons and the Fenwicks to be their guests. The Prestons were Linda's godparents. Both couples were childless, long-time friends who had shared the delight and beauty of Linda since her babyhood.

The cocktail hour had been a pleasant overture to dinner, which was served on the buffet, enhanced by Margaret's silver chafing dishes and Spode china. When everyone had settled at the table and Robert had intoned grace, it seemed the most natural thing in the world for Margaret to tell the story of the turkey.

"This always reminds me of a Thanksgiving years ago, soon after we were married. Robert's company was having a party for all the employees—not only executives, but everybody, factory workers, maintenance men . . ."

"Not everybody," corrected Robert. "Just the people from the main plant."

"So anyway," went on Margaret, underscoring syllables

in her inconsequential fashion, "Robert insisted we go. He
was so conscientious, a young executive and so forth . . ."

"I didn't insist," said Robert.

"Well however it was, we went. There were thousands of
people there . . ."

"Hundreds."

"Hundreds, and they were having a raffle to raise money
for something."

"They were raising money to build up the Pension
Fund," said Robert.

"Yes," said Margaret. "At any rate, they had four or
five girls—they said they were employees—dressed in
Playboy Bunny-type costumes, going around selling tickets.
Actually, it wasn't too appropriate for Thanksgiving! It
seemed more like Easter." Margaret paused here, as she
always did, for her audience to chuckle. "So anyway,
Robert bought a whole string of tickets, though I can't
imagine why . . ."

"I wanted to help out the cause," said Robert virtuously.

"He gave half of them to me," went on Margaret,
"though I told him I wouldn't win. I said, 'I've never won
a thing in my entire life!' But then, when they called the
winning number . . ."

"When they called the number," Robert interrupted
smoothly, "she just stood there. I knew from the last three
digits it had to be one of ours, so I said, 'Check your numbers,' and sure enough."

"And so then I . . ."

"So then she screamed . . ."

"I didn't really scream . . ."

"Yes you did. You've forgotten. She held up the ticket
and tried to get through the crowd to the stage . . ."

"I couldn't believe it," said Margaret. "I kept saying . . ."

"She kept saying, 'I won, I won.' "

"And then I finally . . ."

"Then she finally got up to the stage and they told her
she'd won the grand prize."

"I was so thrilled, but . . ."

"She didn't have any idea what the prize was. And then
a fellow came out from the wings, carrying a live turkey,
and plunked it right into her arms!"

"Yes," said Margaret, "he . . ."

"You've never seen anyone so surprised!" Robert was laughing aloud. "There she stood, her mouth hanging open, holding this enormous live turkey!"

"It almost bit me," said Margaret.

Linda helped her mother clear the table, and rinsed the plates for the dishwasher while Margaret cut the pie.

"Why do you let him do that to you?" Linda asked abruptly.

Margaret looked at her, surprised.

"'Daddy'—said Linda. "Why do you let him cut in on you like that?"

"Like what?"

"Like you know what," said Linda. "Just as you were getting to the punch line, he took over. It's your story."

"You're imagining things," her mother told her, appearing aloof and composed as she always did.

"Do you know the meaning of the word chauvinism?"

Margaret looked at her blankly.

"You're an intelligent, educated woman," pursued Linda.

"Of course, dear, and I do wish you'd stayed on at Mills . . ."

"So why do you let daddy do that to you?"

"Darling, what are you talking about? Do what?"

"Dominate you. Manipulate you. Keep you under his thumb!"

Margaret's expression remained unchanged, as if Linda had rattled off some words in a foreign tongue. She handed Linda the silver coffee pot.

"Here, dear," she said. "See if anyone wants more coffee."

The Allenbys belonged to the Fernleaf Country Club, and Robert had reserved a court for early Saturday morning, so that he and Linda could play tennis. They invited Margaret to join them, but Margaret said she wanted to re-pot her geraniums, and made almost too much of a point of urging the two of them to go by themselves.

"I haven't kept my game up," she said not once, but

several times. "So why don't you two go and have a good time? My goodness, you haven't played tennis together for years!"

When they returned, Linda semed fresh as a daisy and ran out on the pool deck to play with Djalmar, the family German shepherd, but Robert went into the library, turned on the TV, and slumped down in his leather chair without bothering to shower or change. Margaret looked in from the patio, her garden gloves crusted with planter mix.

"How did the game go?"

"She beat me," said Robert. He reached for the remote control and changed channels. "Four sets."

"My gracious, no wonder you're exhausted."

"Six love, six love, six love, and six love."

"You must have been off your game."

"No," said Robert, "I was not. I was in top form. But that girl . . ." He glanced out through the Arcadia doors. They could see Linda throwing a sponge ball for Djalmar. "She played like a maniac."

"Linda?"

Robert changed channels again. Every station had cartoons.

"She seemed so competitive." His tone was almost plaintive. "She wanted to beat me."

"It's a game," pointed out Margaret. "You're supposed to try to win."

"Not that hard," said Robert.

The shoe shine episode occurred later in the afternoon. Robert had gone to sleep watching the football game. Linda wandered out to the kitchen and found her mother applying black shoe polish to a pair of Robert's shoes. Eight additional men's shoes, stretched on shoe trees, were lined up on the kitchen table, which was covered with newspapers.

"Mother!" said Linda. "May I ask what you think you're doing?"

Margaret was one of those persons who are eternally poised.

"I'm polishing shoes," she said.

"I can see that!" said Linda impatiently. "Why don't you let him polish his own shoes?"

"Now dear," said Margaret, "your father works hard all week."

"That's a lot of bull," said Linda. Her mother looked at her, startled. "I mean," said Linda, "he seemed to have plenty of energy for tennis! So why should you . . ."

"Marcie's been washing the woodwork in the east bedroom," said her mother, uttering one of her famous non sequiturs. "I insisted she do the priscillas by hand because they're too fragile to go in the machine."

"That's not the point," said Linda. "He's making you . . ."

"He's not making me do anything," said Margaret, giving a final buff and holding the shoe at arm's length for appraisal. Even shining shoes she looked elegant. "He doesn't know I'm doing it."

"No, but you know," said Linda, "and I know. You're demeaning yourself by . . ."

"It's my own idea," said Margaret. "I don't have anything else particular to do. I want to do it."

"But why? When he's perfectly capable of . . ."

"It's something I can do for him," said Margaret. "I like to do things for him."

"Mother," said Linda, and her tone held an element of pity, "you are not with it. You really are not with it."

"That's part of marriage," said Margaret equably. She took off her gloves. Her manicure was flawless.

"If that's marriage," said Linda, "count me out."

"Cissy Leighton's parents have announced her engagement," said Margaret irrelevantly, placing the shoes on a tray to carry upstairs to Robert's dressing room.

"Well goodie for them," said Linda. "Personally, I think marriage stinks."

Her mother looked shocked.

"Now, dear, you don't—"

"I do! I never want to get married! Never!"

"Of course you don't now, but when Mr. Right . . ."

"Mr. Right!" Linda made no effort to hide her exasperation. "I'm not going to let some self-centered male push me around! I'm not going to be a doormat! I'm going to do something with my life—make it count!"

"That reminds me," said Margaret, lapsing into another non sequitur. "We must get you something more feminine to wear."

Linda bridled.

"Why exactly do you use that word?"

"Pretty," interpolated her mother. "The Prestons told me their nephew from Harvard is coming out for Christmas."

"I don't want anything pretty," said Linda, thrusting her hands into the pockets of her jeans. "I have no intention of becoming a sex object!"

Later that evening Linda insisted on being driven back to the dorm, though originally she had planned to stay through the weekend. Sunday night on the eleven o'clock news Margaret saw a film strip of some women parading in the rain in front of the Century Plaza Hotel, carrying signs urging the governor to abolish pay toilets. One of the demonstrators had long blonde hair, but by the time Margaret had wakened Robert to look, the news had changed to the football scores.

TEN

After what Rick thought of as the great caveman debate, which had ended with Linda and Delcie voicing the hope that they would never see either Rick or Kemp again, in a thousand years or ten thousand, it was difficult for Rick to put things in perspective. It was the middle of the football season, which meant that football occupied every moment of every day. Every first string player harbored dreams of being drafted by the pros. The team was under tremendous pressure from the students, the alumni and the coach. The Bruins had to win. It was up to Darter Evans to rifle a pass to Stu Jenks in the end zone, or snake his way through the enemy defense on a quarterback keep. The Bruins had to win, but that was impossible if their opponents scored. It was up to Big Rick to hold the enemy, to push them back, to bottle them up and force them to kick. No matter how tough, how rough, how dirty the enemy played, or how hard they hit, it was up to Big Rick to hold them. It was a fearsome responsibility and no one let Rick forget it, not for a minute.

It was a most inconvenient time to fall in love.

For one thing, Rick didn't sleep. All his life he had dropped off the instant he hit the sack. Now he couldn't get to sleep no matter how he tried. He would lie awake, tossing and turning, too big for the narrow bed, while the springs creaked and groaned, the sheet twisted into a rope and the blanket slid to the floor. The pillow lost its slip. Across the room Kemp snored, unaware of Rick's feverish dreams.

Rick constantly saw Linda. Everywhere he looked, there she was, her image superimposed over the blackboard, goal post, locker door. If he closed his eyes to ward out the apparition, he continued to see her, wearing the tight T-shirt and faded jeans, her sunlit hair streaming past her shoulders, her eyes defiant and blue, blazing with disdain.

She had scorned him. He couldn't get that out of his mind. Admittedly, Rick's peripheries of experience were not extensive, but he was used to being accepted as a person. In grade school he hit it off well enough with the boys on the playing field. Teachers and coaches were pleased with his performance; often whichever team he played on elected him captain.

From the time Rick was in the fifth grade, girls had pestered the life out of him. They passed him notes containing a variety of suggestions; they wrote his name with spray paint on the building's walls and steps, and, according to rumor, inside the stalls in the girls' lavatory. They stayed every night to watch him shoot baskets or play soft ball; they badgered him for his phone number. Although Rick had been too busy with sports, and too shy to pay much attention to girls, he had never until now had any reason to think they disliked him.

The irksome part was that Linda's put-down was for the quality he most valued in himself—his maleness. That was the essence of what he was and that was what she despised.

Equally baffling, he couldn't eat. He'd go to the training table hungry, but when food came he lost his appetite. The guys flipped for his dessert.

"Man, I think you got something wrong," said Darter Evans. "Like maybe a tapeworm."

"Nah," said Kemp. "He's sick in the head."

"Like what?" said Darter.

"Like's he's depressed about this old lady who's got part of her upstairs missing."

Rick lunged for Kemp, who was sitting across from him. Knives, forks, spoons, glasses of milk and plates of roast beef, potatoes and gravy crashed to the floor before two men got a hammer lock on Rick and forced him to his seat.

"I don't know why you're making a federal case," complained Kemp, picking up his chair, which was splintered. "She was madder at me than she was at you!"

By now, Rick knew her name, Linda Allenby. He found himself saying it in his mind, an incantation. The syllables reminded him of music. He wished he could play the guitar and sing. He wanted to write a song about Linda. He wanted to channel the churning, shapeless feelings inside of him into a ballad. He imagined himself singing it softly, shaping his lips to conform with the syllables, his fingers sliding over the frets of the guitar. He wished he could write poetry. He had no means of expression. He felt tongue-tied and uncouth. He brooded.

Kemp lost all patience.

"This dame is bad news," he told Rick fifty times if he told him once. "She's disasterville!"

Rick didn't reply. He had fallen into the habit of not speaking, sometimes for hours at a time. He moved in pantomime, going through the motions of living.

"She got to you," Kemp said, shaking his head. "Look! It is crucial you pull out of this! It's like you're in a deep depression, you know? What you need is a shrink!"

Rick didn't make the effort to reply.

"I'm serious," said Kemp. "My old man went to one right here in Beverly Hills. Helped him a lot."

Rick said nothing.

"How about I call and make an appointment?"

Rick shook his head.

"Wouldn't do any good. All I want to do is see her."

He found out where her residence hall was and took to standing across the street, leaning against a light post. He saw her come in and go out. It didn't help.

"You know what I heard?" said Kemp. "They're talking about you. You keep this up, they're going to send for the men in the white coats."

"Bull," said Rick.

"Any time," began Kemp, "I'd let a fat-assed broad . . ."

He was not prepared for the attack. They crashed to the floor. Rick's thumbs dug into Kemp's throat, shutting off air.

"Take it back," Rick hissed, wheezing to get his own breath.

"All right." Kemp mouthed the words because of the pressure on his glottis. "Uncle!" Rick released his grip. "Goddamn it!" Kemp got up and brushed himself off with an aggrieved air. "Man, you have bought it! We got to get you well!"

Rick lay on his back on the bed, and put his arm over his eyes.

"Sorry," he said. He could still see Linda. He turned over on his stomach.

"Why don't you call her?" said Kemp, looking in the mirror, examining the marks on his throat.

"She doesn't have a phone."

"Then talk to her in person. Wait till she comes out of the dorm."

"She says get lost or she'll call the cops."

"You want me to try?"

Rick reared up off the bed.

"Forget it," said Kemp hastily. "She's not my type, anyhow."

Rick didn't reply.

"So there must be some way. Everybody has an Achilles heel," said Kemp.

"Not Linda. She's untouchable."

"Herself, maybe. But how about something she cares about . . . or somebody. How about her fat friend?"

"Delcie?"

"The one who looks like an owl."

"Nah."

"Think about it." Kemp became excited, pleased at his own acumen. "You get to Delcie, wear down her defenses, soften her up . . ."

"Knock it off."

"No!" said Kemp. He paced around the room. "That's the way to go! You get Delcie on your side!"

Rick snorted.

"Delcie hates men. She hates men more than Linda does."

Kemp sat down facing him, straddling a chair.

"You know," he said with great deliberation, "I have a hunch that's all a put-on. I have a hunch Delcie could be crazy about a man, given a modicum of encouragement."

Rick's expression was skeptical, but he was listening.

". . . I have a hunch Delcie could be putty in the right hands."

"Not mine," Rick huffed.

"No," agreed Kemp, "but maybe somebody else's. Maybe mine."

"Yours!"

Kemp shrugged.

"Why not? And then, after we got to be friendly, I could get her to work on Linda . . . for you!"

Rick hooted.

"That has to be the most hare-brained scheme of all time. If Linda's not your type, Delcie sure as hell isn't."

"I am aware of that, old buddy," said Kemp with a magnanimous gesture. "I am willing to close my eyes. What are friends for?"

Rick grunted, but his eyes had taken on a spark of interest.

"You'll never pull it off," he said. "Not in a million years."

ELEVEN

A little after noon on a foggy day in early December, Kemp Conway fell into step beside Linda and Delcie.

"Hi!" Kemp said. His voice was honeyed.

Delcie looked up, recognized him, and became flustered.

"Hi!" She pronounced it high-a.

Linda didn't speak.

"So where you been keeping yourself?" Kemp continued. "Long time no see."

It was a small item, a minuscule item, the difference between singular and plural, self instead of selves, but it made the difference. All three were aware of it, and each knew, subtly, the rules had been changed. It was a new ball game.

"I haven't seen you, either," said Delcie.

Her friend was behaving like a fool, Linda thought. If Kemp hadn't seen Delcie, it stood to reason Delcie wouldn't have seen Kemp.

"Stop acting like an idiot!" Linda said under her breath.

Delcie didn't hear her. Delcie rattled on, a mile a minute.

"We've been busy," Delcie said, "getting out a mailing for NOW, even though we're not affiliated . . ."

"That right?" said Kemp. He sounded interested.

"The National Organization for Women. That's what the N-O-W stands for . . ."

Delcie was talking so fast her eye glasses fogged. In her excitement her walk had turned into a half-trot. She looked up at Kemp.

". . . So how have you been?"

"Oh me, I've been fine, fine."

"You've been keeping busy?"

Total, thought Linda, total insanity. She longed to take Delcie and shake her.

"I'm hung up on a class," Kemp said. "Geology."

"You're not going to believe this—" Delcie almost

75

hopped in her excitement "—but I took that same class last spring!"

"You're putting me on!"

"No, actually! Small world department!"

Linda felt baffled. She was being excluded from the conversation. Not that she wanted it. She had deliberately not spoken to Kemp, she'd meant it as a snub, but still . . .

". . . and when he gave us a spot quiz, I blew it."

"Not to worry. I still have all my notes."

"You had lunch yet? We could stop by for a burger."

"I'd love it," gurgled Delcie.

They had come to a crossroads. Delcie handed Linda the box of tracts.

"You don't mind, do you?" She took it for granted.

"Delcie, we're supposed . . ."

The couple drifted away, down the brick walk.

"See ya," said Kemp. It was the first word he'd spoken to Linda that day.

"So what's with it?" said Rick. "You made contact?"

"I promise," said Kemp. "I deliver."

"You saw her?"

"Bought her lunch."

"So what's happening?"

"Like I told you. She's a pushover."

"Come on, man!"

"She's putty. Putty in the hands of a master."

"But what did she say? Did she say she'd talk to Linda?"

"Listen, old buddy, you can't rush into these things like a bulldozer in a china shop. You gotta use a little finesse."

"She didn't say anything."

"She will. When I ask her. I gotta soften her up."

Rick was plunged into gloom. He shoved his hands in his pockets.

"We did mention your name."

"Great."

"Takes time," said Kemp philosophically. "Everything takes time. Besides, you know that geology class? I think that's the place to up my GPA."

TWELVE

Linda's friendship with Delcie was not so much out of choice as out of physical expediency. Delcie was part of the movement; Delcie lived in the same residence hall; Delcie was simply there, someone to talk to. However, during December Linda was so busy studying for finals for her nineteen units she didn't particularly notice that she'd scarcely seen Delcie all month.

The first Saturday after Linda returned from Christmas vacation, Delcie poked her head through the door.

"You going over to Sadie's?"

"I'd planned to."

"So'm I. About ten?"

"Quarter of."

"Stop by my room. I have something to show you."

Delcie looked different, Linda mused. Delcie's hair was changed—one of those new blow cuts, with a light permanent to give it body. More than that, she'd had it frosted. Linda was nonplused. She had never thought Delcie would cop out to the opposition.

Delcie met Linda at the door and drew her inside. She was wearing a sweater and skirt.

Linda was too surprised to be polite.

"I didn't know you owned one!"

"What?"

"A skirt."

"I didn't. I bought it." Delcie whirled around. The eight gore skirt spun out like a parasol. "Kemp says I have good legs."

Linda couldn't believe what she was hearing.

"Notice anything different?"

"A lot of things."

What things, exactly? There was something about Delcie's eyes—a luminosity, a gaiety; something about her mouth, no longer self-righteous, but piquant and expectant. Delcie looked pretty.

"I've lost ten pounds!" Delcie boasted.

Since October Linda had suffered through Delcie's monologues on diet. Small wedge of iceberg lettuce seasoned with lemon juice, no dressing. Scant half cup of cottage cheese. It was all rhetoric. Nothing worked. Now ten pounds!

"Terrific," said Linda uncertainly.

"Look around you," said Delcie.

Later, Linda couldn't imagine why the effect hadn't bowled her over when she entered the room. The walls were papered with Kemp Conway: Kemp on the starting line-up, Kemp making a flying tackle, Kemp trying to intercept a pass. Some pictures were newspaper clippings, some were posters, larger than life.

"Like it?" Delcie was more than eager. She was overbearing.

"It's . . ." Linda was at a loss for words. "It's . . . They're all . . . But where did you . . ."

"Went to the newspaper offices." Delcie was triumphant. "Went through the microfilm. Bought up back issues."

"The posters . . ."

"No sweat. You can have anything made into a poster. Look at this one. Doesn't he look mean?"

Kemp stared at them from a crouch. His teeth were clenched, his shoulders grotesque under their pads.

Linda shuddered.

"Let's go," she said abruptly.

"You'd never guess he was a pussycat," said Delcie. "Would you?"

"No," said Linda.

"I wish we had more time," said Delcie. "I have a lot more pictures I didn't have room to put up."

During the walk to Sadie's she talked non-stop. It was Kemp this and Kemp that, Kemp says or Kemp thinks. Linda listened, open-mouthed. The word sophomoric ran through her mind like a lyric, but what good would that do? You couldn't say to your friend, don't you think you're being sophomoric—especially if you couldn't wedge a word in edgewise.

Throughout the recital Linda sensed once again the uneasiness which had plagued her for a month. It was not that she wanted Kemp Conway. Lord knows, she couldn't stand him. Delcie was welcome to him, lock, stock and barrel.

But wasn't it funny—not funny ha-ha but funny peculiar—that Kemp had ignored Linda and made a play for Delcie? From the time she was born, the Allenbys had been determined not to spoil Linda. Handsome is as handsome does was her mother's stock phrase. Yet it is impossible for a woman to be pretty and not know it. Heads turn, eyes follow, an indefinable current, swift as a swallow's shadow, passes through the crowd. All this Linda had taken for granted.

Her preoccupation with the emancipation of women had elevated her consciousness to what she considered a loftier intellectual plane.

Now she felt vaguely uneasy. Was it possible she had lost her looks? Was it possible Delcie was now more attractive than she—Delcie, who had always looked like an owl? Linda turned and stared full on at her chattering friend. In point of fact Delcie no longer resembled an owl, not in the least.

"Your glasses!" blurted Linda. "You told me you can't see without them!"

"Contacts!" cried Delcie, triumphantly. "I thought you'd never notice!"

Aggie had made coffee and Sadie had run over to the Sweet Shop for baby Danish. They had card tables set up and the address lists were evenly divided, but all anyone wanted to do was talk about Delcie. The arrival of Delcie herself occasioned a momentary hiatus—an embarrassment which hung in the air like a toy balloon, and then popped.

"Say it isn't so!" Jody quipped.

"I don't know what you're talking about." Delcie was on the defensive.

"Somebody said you'd flipped out . . . over some guy."

"Oh that!" Delcie tried to act nonchalant. It didn't come off. "I have been seeing a certain someone, lately."

They jumped on her like chicks, pecking at one of their number who had suddenly become vulnerable, an open sore showing among the feathers.

Sadie went around the room pouring refills, her movements stylized and jerky, the lines on her face caricatures of discontent.

"I hope you know what you're doing," Sadie said. "I hope you remember where your first loyalty lies."

"My goodness," said Delcie. Her eyes, which had always been gray, were now blue. Linda realized she had colored contacts. "Just because a person is interested in women's rights doesn't mean she has to go into a nunnery or something. I mean, I thought that was the whole idea, to be a total person."

"Watch out he doesn't total you!" said Aggie.

"I thought everybody was supposed to realize her full potential."

"Don't forget," Sadie said. She tasted her coffee as if it were vinegar. "Don't forget, men are animals."

"You make me sick!" flared Delcie. "Hasn't any of you ever heard of love, good old-fashioned love?"

"I don't believe in fairy tales," said Sadie.

"I'll buy it," said Carol, "as long as it's on your terms."

"It's all right," conceded Rhoda, "provided you love 'em and leave 'em."

"Don't let him use you," cautioned Aggie. "That's all I got to say."

"What's sauce for the goose," admitted Jody, taking another Danish. "But don't let it develop into anything permanent. A one-night stand is okay."

"Oh, but I want it to be more than that!" Delcie was too excited to sit down. "I want it to be permanent! I want it to go on for ever and ever!"

"Listen to her," pitied Sadie.

"Don't let him use you," said Aggie again. "He'll use you and throw you over."

"Men are after only one thing," said Sadie.

"I'm a big girl," retorted Delcie. "I can handle it."

"Be sure you can, now!" said Aggie. "That's all I got to say."

"Besides, he hasn't . . . we haven't . . . our relationship is on an intellectual plane . . ."

"No kidding!"

"It's just that . . . when he touches me . . ." Involuntarily, Delcie shivered. Her eyes were alight with stars.

Sadie set down the pot and turned toward her, deliberately.

"You know," she began, "there's something we ought to tell you for your own good."

Delcie looked at Sadie, suddenly hypnotized. The crossfire of comments dwindled and stopped. Only Sadie's voice persisted, penetrating as a prairie wind.

"It doesn't make sense," said Sadie. "Here he is, an important jock, big man on campus, football star, man most likely, all that crap."

Delcie moistened her lips with the tip of her tongue. It was obvious she didn't want to hear what Sadie was about to say. It was obvious she was trying not to look self-conscious, without success.

". . . Women fighting over him," Sadie continued. "Sorority types. Gals with money . . ."

"So?" Delcie tossed her head, with the new cut.

". . . money," said Sadie, "and the figure, and the looks . . ."

"So!"

"So why you?"

"Why me?" Delcie was taken aback. "Why not me?"

"I just told you. You're scarcely his type."

"Opposites attract!"

"It doesn't wash."

"It happened!" Delcie said fiercely. "I didn't chase after him. He came after me."

"So you could pull him through geology?"

"Before that! He didn't even know I'd taken it!"

"Want to bet?"

Delcie turned on Sadie. The hypnotic spell snapped.

"He likes me for me!" she said fiercely.

"Don't bank on it."

Tears seeped into Delcie's eyes, clouding the contacts.

"You're hateful!" she blazed.

"I'm only telling you this for your own good," said Sadie.

"Bull!" screamed Delcie. She was trying not to cry, but her voice cracked. "You're jealous, that's what it is!"

"Jealous!" Sadie threw her head back and laughed, the high, mocking, Sadie laugh, the laugh which impelled Sadie's followers to join in. "Jealous! My dear, how little do you know of what you speak!"

THIRTEEN

When Linda wakened the next morning it was raining—a slow, steady downpour. The thought crossed her mind that she might go to church, though she had purposely not gone to church since coming to UCLA, part of her break with tradition. However, she was conscious of the fact that this day was Sunday. Somewhere, just out of reach, hovered the memory of contentment she had once felt in church, the sense that everything was proceeding according to blueprint in an ordered world. She had a feeling of need—of a need to be comforted, and instinctively she turned to the church to find that comfort.

With no clear direction she dressed for church in an old Davidow suit left from her days at Mills, and the raincoat which had seen her through the Florentine winter, and started forth, a scarf over her hair. She walked aimlessly toward the village, changing her mind a dozen times. She didn't know where there was an Episcopal church or any church. Since she had been in Westwood, she had vaguely noticed churches all over the place, but where was the Episcopal Church? Her parents insisted on high church. High church, low church, would that make a difference? She had loved going to the Catholic church, to Mass in Florence but that was before she became a pragmatist, a realist, an existentialist, before she learned to look at things in the true light of what they were.

In the end, she didn't find a church at all, but slogged on in the rain, trying to make sense out of the contradictory feelings which churned inside her.

What had happened to the sureness she had found in her new creed? Where was she headed for? After all, she was a senior. Soon she would have to make some kind of choice, take some definite direction. What was her "possible"—what could she be? Again she asked herself—as she had done so frequently the past year—What do I want

83

most? and again she voiced the stock reply, I want to be free! but for some reason the answer now had lost some of its potency.

Who am I, really? she heard herself demand next, aloud. Ah, that was the heart of the problem—if she could figure that one out, everything else would fall into place! What was this mass of protoplasm called Linda Allenby, this contraption of bones overlaid with muscles, actuated by nerves, pushed and pulled by sinews, packaged in skin; this entity that thought and breathed and suffered and hoped and worried? *Why* exactly was she worrying now— why was she so upset?

The answer to the last question, though for a time Linda refused to admit it, was that she was no longer attractive as a woman. Why else had Kemp zeroed in on Delcie— even at a time when Delcie still looked owlish—and ignored Linda? Why? The reason was obvious. He preferred Delcie.

Linda tried to banish this attack of self-doubt as childish and unworthy. What difference did it make? After all, she cared nothing about men. Men were clods, clumsy and bumbling and intellectually inferior. All any man cared about was manipulating a woman into having sex. Yet even as Linda parroted Sadie's slogans, she felt a gnawing sense of disquietude. As if she were listening to a taped play-back, she could hear herself, shouting those same shibboleths, standing behind the NOW table, putting Rick and Kemp in their places. *Methinks the lady doth protest too much*, Kemp had observed. Was that true? Was she, Linda, too loud, too vocal? I don't know why you had to jump all over them, Delcie had complained. Linda experienced a sickening self-insight. She had been overbearing, rude, mean—why? Was it a shell, a defense thrown up because she was afraid of men? Was it because through her teens she had never dated, had always been secluded, secretly had been terrified by boys? Was it because now that she was twenty-one she felt embarrassed and inadequate and secretly feared she couldn't compete?

No! Linda tossed her head back so that the raindrops pelted her face. What rubbish! But her attack of inferiority now became replaced, tenfold, by jealousy.

The idea that she might be jealous of Delcie—plump,

naive, well-intentioned little Delcie—was so ridiculous
Linda laughed aloud, but the feeling, embedded deep in
her viscera, didn't go away. That was how she felt, no
matter what she thought. Thinking and feeling were, she
perceived helplessly, two different things.

She passed a trio of male students hurrying in the rain.
They glanced at her impersonally, without evincing a
glimmer of interest. She was stung to the quick. What had
happened to her? What had she done to herself?

Her thoughts reverted to Delcie. She didn't want to
think of her but she remembered Delcie as she had been
yesterday morning, whirling about, showing off the new
skirt, her blow cut, the contacts, her new figure. There had
been something tremendously appealing about Delcie, that
only Linda had sensed, something sweet, unsullied . . .

Delcie had fallen in love. Delcie the crusader had become the story-book princess.

Delcie had believed in love, and by believing had become beautiful—and, in direct sequence, Delcie's Women's
Lib friends had pounced on her and torn her to bits.

At the corner Linda waited for the light to change. The
intersection was flooded, and water soaked over her shoes.

It wasn't right! Anger rose in Linda's throat like phlegm.
What did Sadie mean, where your first loyalty lies? Delcie
had been loyal. No one had been more loyal, more responsible, more dedicated. Always the girls in the movement could count on Delcie, dependable Delcie, Delcie
the soldier.

Now, for no reason, they had decimated her.

Why?

Linda tried to think. Everyone couldn't be like Sadie
and Aggie. Linda insisted to herself she still believed in
equal rights—but what exactly did that all add up to?
Equal rights meant equality. Wouldn't that mean equality
about love? There were many kinds of love. Linda had
prejudged and condemned her parents, knowing they
would be intolerant toward Sadie's kind of love. She was
dismayed to find that Sadie was equally intolerant with
Delcie.

Linda sloshed on, the rain beating against her face.
Despite the downpour the sidewalks were crowded, people
coming and going, each with a purpose. Linda slowed.

She, too, had a purpose. She mustn't lose sight of her purpose. She was part of the movement, the movement for equality. Yet a notion kept playing back—love, any kind of love, wasn't a crime.

Why should people be condemned for love? Wasn't love what everything was about?

Linda couldn't understand Sadie, Sadie whom Linda had revered, brilliant Sadie, Sadie the intellectual. How could Sadie, the leader, turn on Delcie and mow Delcie to the ground?

Again a flood of guilt and self-doubts attacked. Where was she, Linda, while the pillorying took place? Had she sprung to her friend's defense? No. Tongue-tied, she allowed it to happen, her silence her assent.

It was in this context of self-accusation that Linda glanced across the busy street and recognized Rick Dublin, striding in the driving rain, his shoulders hunched, his hands in his pockets. Her heart gave a queer flip, as if she were plunging in an elevator and hadn't caught her breath. What was Rick doing out in this downpour? Linda waited for the traffic light, staring idly at the autos and pedestrians without seeing any of them—then gave an involuntary cry. A little boy, no more than three, had left the curb and waddled out into the middle of the intersection. The light changed, and traffic bore down upon him. Linda watched, paralyzed.

It happened too fast to sort out. A tall, burly figure darted from the opposite curb, bounded before the cars, scooped up the child in the last instant of time, and shoved him aside before the first car plowed into the rescuer himself. It was Rick! Rick had been hit! He was down! Linda was deafened by the crash, the crunch of tearing metal and smashed glass as the cars behind rear-ended. Not knowing what she was doing, Linda stepped off the curb into the swirling water. The intersection was jammed with cars and shouting pedestrians.

Before she could push her way through, Rick had scrambled to his feet. He picked up the child. He stood in the rain, holding the child in his arms. The little boy was howling.

The car which had hit Rick, a lightweight MG, had

spun off to the side and escaped the multiple collision it had caused. Now its driver walked back to Rick.

"You hurt, fella?"

"No," said Rick. Linda noticed that Rick's pants were torn, but he seemed to be all right. "You barely clipped me."

"Hear that, everybody?" said the driver. He walked back to the MG and drove off.

An argument had erupted among the drivers of the three cars which had rear-ended one another, and now the pedestrians joined in. Rick, carrying the crying child, made his way to the curb, and Linda followed.

"Don't cry, little guy," she heard Rick say.

The child's mother, who appeared to be in her last month of pregnancy, ran out of the drugstore on the corner.

"Michael!" She rushed forward and took the child. Linda expected a protestation of love, of gratitude, of thankfulness that the child's life had been spared. The mother set the crying child on his feet and slapped his bottom. "I told you to stay by mommie! I told you not to run off!" Hadn't she heard? Hadn't she seen? The mother swatted the child again. "And that's for talking to strangers!" They left, the mother dragging the boy by the hand, the boy still crying.

Rick looked around, and saw Linda. He did not appear surprised. How strong he was, Linda marveled. How tall! Why had she never noticed Rick's eyes—steadfast eyes, clear gray. She looked directly into them.

"Linda," said Rick, the water running off his hair, making rivulets down his face.

"I saw," said Linda. "I saw the whole thing." He was embarrassed. Had she embarrassed him? She hadn't meant to. "You were the only one to do anything. You thought so fast! The rest of us just stood there!"

"Linda—" Rick said.

"You saved his life!"

He wasn't listening to her.

"You're . . . so *beautiful*!" Rick said.

"You're the one who's beautiful," Linda heard herself say. "You're a beautiful person."

It was as if a light had come on, as if the sun had come out, in the middle of the drenching rain. She could tell by his look that he didn't believe she had said what she had—and then, by his look, that he did believe.

He leaned forward and kissed her, gently, on her wet forehead. Because it was Westwood nobody paid attention. Nobody noticed when they went off together, arm in arm.

FOURTEEN

They lay on the bed in Linda's room.

Rick was stretched out in a trance, barely breathing. Linda rested lightly beside him, at once conscious and semi-conscious, delirious with joy. Ecstasy, welling from deep in her abdomen, in the secret center of her being, radiated through her skin, her limbs, her fingers and toes, transporting her, so that she floated, so that she no longer was an entity but became one with the air.

The room was quiet, the silence which follows nuclear explosion. The shock was past, the flash brighter than suns, the roar which shattered eardrums, the heat which fused metal—all had come and gone. Now it was breathlessly still, as molecules, dust motes, layers of hot and cold settled in place. Yet in Linda's mind fireworks continued, bursts of orange, scarlet, yellow and magenta, obliterating the geometrical dimensions of the room with their celebration, so that there was no ceiling, no air vent, no door jamb, only the successive paroxysms of color in endless space.

Her heart pounded. She could hear the pulse in her temple, against the sheet, bump, bump, bump, too fast, too loud. Her skin tingled with myriads of electrical pin pricks, on-off, here-there, faster than she could sense.

This was it! Her life, beginning with roller skates and Pablum, had culminated in this holocaust of desire and fulfillment. This was why she had come into being, this was why she *was*! Every second of her growing, of her searching, had been sweeping her toward this incandescent instant. After a lifetime of curiosity, of wonder, she knew the answer.

Gradually Linda accepted the feeling of this unaccustomed, incredible happiness; the marvel of hitherto unknown well-being continued to permeate her every cell. She had done it! She had actually done it! She couldn't believe she could have let down the barriers she had so carefully constructed of concrete and steel for twenty-one years, so easily.

Her amazement was supplanted by a heady contentment, a sense of pleasure with herself. She had come of age! She was a woman! At last she knew! At last she was living; she who had doomed herself to a sterile isolation, to spinning out her life span in an ivory tower—at last she was truly free!

She was dumbfounded at how fast it had happened. Looking back, she could see it had been inevitable from the moment Rick started up the steps to the dorm beside her, or perhaps from the moment she had spotted Rick across the intersection, even, perhaps, from the moment she had started on her quest in the rain, wearing the Davidow suit. Out of the corner of her eye she could see the Davidow in two heaps on the floor, the skirt a circle where she had dropped it and stepped out, a butterfly leaving the chrysalis. The thought emerged that perhaps it had been inevitable from the moment she had first met Rick. A fresh wave of desire engulfed her, reducing sinew and flesh to agar. She turned her head to look at Rick. He slept.

How gentle he was in repose, he who moments before had been a wild man, a force that neither propriety nor intellect could have dissuaded from the swelling tide that had engulfed them both. She savored the sweetness of his expression, the classicism of his features. Her eye traced the planes of his forehead, cheeks and chin, so still they seemed hewn from marble; passed lightly over the hair, coarse and straight, the color of beach sand; inspected the brows, stiff as hedgerows, lighter than the hair; glanced at the closed lids ending in thick stubby lashes, at the mouth, shockingly vulnerable. Linda was seized by an inchoate longing to kiss that mouth, to cure whatever sadness, whatever disappointment it might have. She raised her head in order to do so, propping herself on one elbow, but even as she gazed her passion dissipated itself into a feeling of tenderness, which flowed from her to her lover, enveloping him, gathering him forever close to her.

She shifted her weight, moving slightly lest she fall off, for he took up most of the narrow bed. She didn't want to waken him. She felt bereft. Why didn't he wake up? How strange, that she would feel lonely, she who had been alone all of her life, yet now felt so close to this other being, so dependent upon him for sustenance and warmth she could not bear to be parted even by the veil of sleep. Why did she feel this way? The thought whirled around in her mind, immediately joined by its twin: could he feel that way about her?

Why did he sleep so soundly? Was that part of it? There were so many things she didn't know. She experienced a surge of frustration with her mother, for not having told her. As quickly, this was replaced by a mingling of pity and condescension, the superiority one generation feels for its immediate predecessor. There must be a lot of things her mother didn't tell her because her mother didn't know. Margaret Allenby had lived her life in a vacuum; that was never more apparent than now.

Was he all right?

Linda wanted to put her arm across him, yet she was reluctant to disturb him, her hesitation stemming from a lifetime of respecting others' privacies. His chest was covered with coarse, curly hair the color of straw. Why was the hair on his head straight and the hair on his chest curly? The chest hair was thick and luxuriant, like fur. She longed to run her fingers through it. She imagined grabbing fistfuls with both hands and pulling, hard.

"It was so different!"

In surprise, she heard her own voice, pronouncing words in a tone of wonderment, her subconscious intruding on her semiconscious. That was sex! What had she expected, from the movies, the paperbacks? Something, certainly. She realized she had never pinpointed the image. She had been given to vague fantasies, mostly of some faceless person holding her close, kissing her.

"How square!" She spoke aloud again, in self-derision. Rick slept on. How strange, in this day and age, that she had reached the age of twenty-one, and, even in her fantasies, had gone no further than that! He must think her a prude! Lily white, naive. Inexperienced. Did he know? He must know. Men can always tell. She'd heard that. No, she must have read it somewhere. She hoped Rick didn't know. In the same instant, she resolved to tell him.

For some reason it seemed mandatory that she bare her

soul to this stranger. This struck her as inexplicable. She had always been a private person. Why did she feel this way now?

Rick's mouth was partly open, yet he slept silently. Linda thought of her father, who snored outrageously. She remembered the few times she'd had occasion to tiptoe into her father's room while he was asleep. Her father's snores had been like a wind machine. Maybe that was why her parents slept in separate bedrooms.

Linda seized on this hypothesis as if it were the missing piece in a jigsaw puzzle. She remembered when she'd come for Thanksgiving, her first year at Mills, and learned of the new arrangement. It was almost as if they'd waited until she was grown and gone, and then decided they no longer needed to keep up the pretense. She'd asked her mother a direct question and received an indirect answer, in her mother's cultivated, exaggerated voice, an answer which added up to nothing. Margaret Allenby was good at that. But was she good in bed?

Linda smiled, in spite of herself. She could not conjure up an image of her parents doing what she had just done. Her parents were proper. They never swore. Her parents were correct. They never told off-color stories. For off-color, translate sexy. Sex was a topic which never surfaced in the Allenby house. Her mother never talked about such things. It was understood that nice people didn't. Her mother was a perfect lady. She'd always said she wanted Linda to be a lady too.

Unbidden, Linda's pulse quickened, so that she could feel it pounding behind her eyes. The exhilaration of daring, the combination of bravado and terror of the lawbreaker surged through her as if she had gulped a stiff shot of whisky. She thought of what her parents' horror and disapproval would be, if they only knew. Her response to this disturbing stimulus was swift and effective, for it was a device she had used before. Her parents were never going to know because she was never going to tell them. Lock, stock and barrel, she shut them out of her mind.

Rick opened his eyes. He turned to face Linda, his expression lightening as he saw her.

"Hi!"

"Hi!" His lips parted in a grin of bewilderment. "Did I go to sleep?"

"Did you ever!"

"Sorry about that." He closed his eyes. His smile broadened. "Oh God," he murmured. "It happened!" Abruptly, he looked at her. "Linda?"

"Yes?"

"You all right?"

"You seemed to think so."

"Well, all right!"

She didn't reply.

"No, I mean seriously."

"What?"

"I didn't hurt you?"

"Well . . ."

"I did!" His eyes clouded in contrition. "I'm sorry. I wouldn't have . . . I mean, I didn't mean . . ."

Linda giggled. "You did mean."

"Yeah. Yeah, I guess I did." He laid a hand on her shoulder. It felt immense and burning on her bare flesh. "You . . . you're not . . . I mean, are you sorry?"

Linda shook her head. "I'm glad."

"You are?" His grin exploded in incredulity. "You liked it?"

"I loved it!"

"Oh, man." His hand shook with emotion. "You see, the fact is . . . Well, the way it turned out . . . Well, the fact was, I didn't know what the hell I was doing . . ."

He stopped. He looked into her eyes, pleading for reassurance.

"You did all right."

The tautness of his facial muscles slackened. "Oh, man!" he said, after a time. They lay motionless, staring solemnly at one another. "Your skin. It's so soft." He slid his hand along her back. "It feels like rose petals."

"Whatever they feel like."

"I know what they feel like. That's what you're like." His mouth contorted with the effort of voicing unfamiliar thoughts in unfamiliar words. "Like a flower of some kind."

"What kind?"

"A rose. That's my favorite kind."

"Mine too."

They rested. It seemed natural they should agree upon everything. His expression tightened.

"God, I didn't mean to hurt you . . ."

"It's all right."

"I mean is it . . . I mean how . . ."

"You're so big . . ."

She could tell by his look she couldn't have said a nicer thing. He propped himself on one elbow, to gaze down upon her.

"Bigger than . . . I mean, how about other guys?"

"What other guys?"

"Any other guys. I mean, guys you've known."

She put her hand up around his thick neck and drew him to her. She kissed him, long and sweetly. She could feel his great heart, pounding through the walls of his chest and hers. At last she released him. He continued to look at her, hypnotized.

"There haven't been that many."

"How many?"

"Not any."

His forehead wrinkled with the effort of believing. "But a girl like you . . ."

"Like me. Like how?"

"You're so goddammed beautiful."

She shook her head. "That was a first."

He burst out laughing. "Man-oh-man-oh-man!" He slapped his hands together, a thunderclap of exultation. Then he gathered her close to him so that she felt the matted curly hair of his chest engraving its convolutions into the sensitive skin of her breasts. He nestled his cheek against her forehead. "Want to know something, baby?" he said at last, so softly she could barely hear him. "It was the first time for me, too."

A surge of remorse swept through her. How could she have put him down? Ever? What kind of a monster was she?

"I was waiting," he whispered, "in some goddammed crazy way I was waiting. Even before I knew you, even before I saw you . . . because I knew, because I hoped . . ." She hardly breathed, she was so intently listening. "The guys, they used to ride me. Kemp, you know, he was the worst. But I kept . . . And then, oh God, after I saw you, there wasn't any question . . ."

They lay quiet, in the shelter of one another. Linda could hear the rain on the window, the thrum of the blower as the thermostat kicked on, a high-pitched laugh echoing in the stairwell.

"Oh man!" yelled Rick, thrusting her from him, springing to his feet, jumping over the bed, on to it, off it, like a giant jackrabbit, "Oh, man! We gotta get some food! Am I hungry! I'm so hungry I could eat a horse!"

FIFTEEN

"I'm not that stupid."

She heard herself say it to herself, the next morning, the day after, Day One, as it were, of her life. Forever, she knew, memories would be divided by that point: Before, and After.

Actually, she thought of herself as a with-it person. With-it, and, she was forced to add, sexy. She reached her hands behind her head, raising her hair in sheaves, turning this way and that before the mirror, a model being snapped for a centerfold in *Playboy*. She remembered the time she'd found a *Playboy* in the bottom of her father's armoire, under the piles of folded boxer shorts.

She'd always thought her breasts too small. She twisted to show them in silhouette, laughing in tantalizing manner at the camera over one bare shoulder. Little had she known their potency! They'd driven Rick out of his skull!

Ah . . . Rick!

With no warning, she experienced that jelly feeling behind her knees, in the blades of her shoulders, in the sinew of her wrists, everywhere. She trembled, helpless. She was a baby, a tiny baby. She was his.

She couldn't wait.

The day stretched, endless and bleak till she would see him.

But before then, she had things to do. Classes, but besides classes . . .

After all, she wasn't born yesterday.

She was brisk, getting dressed, hurrying out of the dorm, her feet thistle-light in her Keds.

It was the How that bothered her. Not that it was anything she couldn't figure, an intelligent girl. The health center was out. The university kept records. Everything was on a computer. They'd have to know her name. It

would be on file. Her name. The request. If her parents
ever . . .

They wouldn't, of course. There'd be no reason. She was
twenty-one, an adult. Records would be confidential . . .
you'd think. But, still . . .

After anthropology, she walked to a pharmacy in Westwood. She scrutinized the drug shelves, affecting nonchalance. Exactly what was she looking for? A small box?
A brown glass bottle? Fragments of sentences replayed in
her inner ear. Now that the pill is readily available . . . In
this day and age there's no excuse . . .

"Can I help you, miss?"

Jolted to reality, Linda managed a nervous smile. The
clerk was a woman, thank heaven, but middle-aged. Would
she disapprove? She must have kids come in all the time,
girls, asking the same thing.

"I . . . ah . . . yes . . . ah, do you carry birth control
pills?"

"Yes, we do."

Linda exhaled in relief. She was halfway home: "Fine. I
mean, I'll take some."

"Do you have your prescription?"

Later, Linda was to bless the woman for the face-saving
pronoun, your, but at the time she dissolved in confusion.

"No . . . I mean, I mean, do you have to have? I mean,
I thought you could get, just buy them?"

The woman was staring at her. It was impossible to tell
what she was thinking. Surely it couldn't be pity. What did
she know? More likely she was jealous.

"It's the law."

Linda retreated. How ridiculous. Law indeed! She borrowed a phrase from Aggie. Bunch of b.s. When they sent
the pill wholesale to developing nations, to the third world
. . . and here, of all places, in super-enlightened Westwood
Village, they had a law! Linda stll felt her face burning with
embarrassment.

"Boy," she muttered under her breath, "am I naive!"

Why hadn't she known they had a law? That was the
trouble—she'd led such a sheltered life, sheltered from
everything. She wished that just once at some time or other
her mother could have come out of her shell and frankly

discussed sex with her. Linda sighed. Frankness wasn't one of Margaret Allenby's strong points.

Aggie. Aggie was the kind of person Linda could ask. But it wouldn't do any good. Aggie wouldn't be taking the pill!

Linda forced herself to enter another drugstore, changed two dollars to dimes, and started calling gynecologists from the phone booth. Half an hour later she emerged, disillusioned. Nobody wanted her as a patient, not today. She thought of Doctor Dixon, the Allenby family physician in Pasadena. All she'd have to do was phone, and Mrs. Blakesley would work her in this afternoon. What's the matter, Linda? Not your asthma again?

But suppose . . .

Dr. Dixon had always been so buddy-buddy with her folks. Suppose Dr. Dixon ran into her parents some night at Fernleaf Country Club. She could imagine him lowering his voice. Very confidential, you understand, but there's something I think you people should know. At least if she were my daughter . . .

Planned Parenthood! The phrase burst upon her like a crack of thunder. How come she hadn't thought of it earlier? Planned Parenthood was a staple of the women's movement, the phrase guaranteed to take the wind out of the opposition's sails. She was so excited she misdialed twice before she got the right number.

Yes, yes, yes. The voice was simultaneously sympathetic and impersonal. Exactly right, coming up with all the right answers. A doctor will see you, he'll take your social and medical history, pelvic examination, Pap smear, T. C., gonorrhea check, breast exam, blood pressure . . . There was no hint of moralizing. None. All matter of fact. Happened all the time.

"And then?"

"Then what?"

"Will he give me the pill?"

"He'll decide, on the basis of the tests, what the best method will be for you . . ."

"But I really want the pill."

"Could be an IUD, or condom and foam."

"What?"

"Condom and foam."

"Oh," whispered Linda. She cursed her mother for not telling, for not knowing, for being the way she was. There was a lapse of silence. "Well then, when? I mean, could I see him this afternoon?"

"Our clinics are booked until Thursday," said the voice. "At six-thirty."

"P.M.?" said Linda inanely. She spelled her name. She walked back to the campus in a trance.

"You told me your father's a doctor," she said to Janet, a girl in her advanced social behavior class she'd never much liked.

"That's right."

Linda took a gulp of air, swallowing her pride. "Is there any way, I mean, it's asking a lot, but do you think you could get him to see me? Today? I mean, it's awfully short notice."

"What's the matter?" said Janet. "Is something wrong?"

"No, not really," said Linda. She smiled wanly and took another gulp of pride. "I . . . I want a prescription for the pill."

"He's in Europe," said Janet.

"Oh." Linda felt cornered.

"But the pill . . . hell . . . you mean you've never been on the pill?"

Linda shook her head. She might as well have undressed in public.

"No big deal," said Janet. "He gets them by the gross, as samples. Stop by my·room and I'll give you a year's supply!"

SIXTEEN

They hungered for one another.

They devoured one another.

They were alone together, isolated in a university of thousands.

They investigated the recesses of one another's personalities with the fervor of explorers. Apart, they functioned as hitherto in their day-to-day life, behaving with reasonable normalcy, but they did it by rote. All that counted was the time in each other's company; the rest was drudgery, merely to be gotten through.

When it came to sex they were insatiable, and when not making love they rested in each other's arms, content to feel the assurance of breath and heartbeat, of warm skin upon skin, of fragrances and odors intermingled. Occasionally, when there was nothing else to do, they talked. When they talked, they held nothing back. They forgot to listen to their own voices.

"I never thought I'd fall in love," Linda told Rick.

For answer, Rick kissed Linda.

"I mean," explained Linda, "I really had a very strong feeling about this. I was sure . . . I was so sure it was not for me . . ." Her voice trailed off. "I mean, you have to understand how I felt about men. It was a funny way."

"How funny?"

"Not funny ha-ha. It was . . . I was so down on men, in every shape or form."

Unconsciously, Rick sighed.

"I know," said Linda. "I'm the first to agree. It was bitchy. I was a bitch."

"You're not a bitch."

"I said I was." He kissed her to shut her up. After a while Linda went on. "That's why I'm trying to figure out . . . It was crazy, when you get right down to it. I hated men. I was afraid of every man. And yet . . . yet . . . underneath, I thought about nothing else. Men, men, men. All the time."

For answer, Rick placed one giant hand over her left breast, cupping it tenderly.

"It was like two opposites," she said, watching him, "warring inside me. I guess it could have been that deep down I was a romantic. Our whole culture throws it at us. You know what I'm trying to say? Boy gets girl. Fairy prince and all that."

"All what?" said Rick, cupping the other breast.

"They lived happily every after. Every song, every movie. Love, love, falling in love. Even toothpaste."

"Toothpaste?"

"How's your love life? Even my Barbie doll."

"What was that?"

"She was a teen-age sexpot, but I didn't know it at the time. She had a boy friend, Ken. He came to see her."

"What did he do?"

"He didn't do anything. They were dolls, for heaven's sake. My mother bought me every outfit. She must have spent a fortune."

"You know what? I'd call you a sexpot."

"You know what? I'd call you a . . ."

After another while it seemed time to get back to talk.

"So in a way, down underneath about a hundred layers, that was what I wanted out of life. I wanted to fall in love, to find somebody, the right somebody, somebody I could love . . . somebody who would love me. I was searching, searching all the time, every hour, every minute."

"It's funny," Rick said, kissing little places in her hair.

"I don't think it's funny."

"It's funny, what you're saying. Because I was, too."

"You were what?"

"Searching. The way you said. Looking. Hoping."

"But I'm trying to understand the other part," Linda said later, when they were walking to McDonald's. "I never admitted, even to myself, even for one instant, that that was what I wanted. Why?"

"I don't know."

"I think it was because when I got to be a big, grown-up

girl I knew it didn't exist. Love. It was a fairy tale." She had to run two or three steps to keep up with him. "It was as if I'd built up some kind of a calcium shell around myself, to keep myself from believing. Who needs it? That's what I said."

"Oh yeah?"

"That's what Sadie and all of them said."

Rick put his arm around her. They strode along together.

"Everyone knows there isn't a Santa Claus," said Linda.

"Not everybody."

"What about you?"

"I never gave up."

"That's because you're you. You're trusting. I'm more cynical." They had to stand in line. "In fact," Linda went on, "we were discussing that in my behavior class."

"Do you want a Big Mac?"

"No, a cheeseburger."

"Two Big Macs and a cheeseburger."

"No, I'll take a Big Mac after all."

"Make that three Big Macs, Mac."

"Inability to form a lasting relationship," Linda said. "It's a syndrome. It's the hallmark of our generation—that's what Dr. Neucliffe told us. Nobody really cares about anybody—because nobody lets himself care. Or herself," she added as an afterthought.

They were in the booth. Their eyes met.

"I'm glad you like onions," Rick said.

"Out of necessity. I'm glad you're trusting."

"Out of necessity."

She gazed at him, memorizing his blunt honest face. "I still don't know why I was so uptight."

"Forget it."

"I didn't dare let myself get involved."

He only chewed, watching her, half smiling.

"I was afraid I might get hurt, that's what it was! I was afraid to let myself go."

"And then you took the plunge."

"That was what was so fantastic! I'd thought I was so smart. I was wrong. They're all wrong, with their statistics and their trends. There really is a Santa Claus!"

"You know it," said Rick, still smiling, still chewing slowly, still watching her. "Ho ho ho!"

They were so different.

It was a challenge to synchronize natures so opposite, but they went about it with enthusiasm.

One night they ate at Mario's.

"What are you going to have?"

"A salad and ah . . . just a salad."

"I thought you said you were hungry."

"I'm starved, but mother . . ."

"One salad, one spaghetti, one pizza," Rick told the waiter. "Large, with everything on it. And a half liter of wine."

"You know I don't drink."

"Wine isn't drinking. It's eating Italian."

Linda toyed with her greens.

"You ought to order vegetables," she told him.

"Hate 'em."

"But you won't grow up to be big and strong."

Rick took a mouthful of pizza. "I'll manage."

"You know what I've always wanted to do?"

"No."

"You'll think I'm nuts. I've always wanted to eat spaghetti a string at a time, not cut it, just suck it up."

Rick stared at her. "You have to be out of your tree."

"I told you!"

"Better have some wine, first."

"I don't know . . . it's so public."

"We don't know any of these jokers."

"Will you, too?"

"No holds barred."

Linda giggled. "You mean it's going to be a race?"

"Drink up. You gotta grease the track. On your mark, get set, go!"

"No cutting!" "No laughing, either!" They dissolved in laughter. Fifteen! Seventeen! Truce! Drink! You look so weird! No weirder than you! You took two at once! That's cheating! They laughed so hard they could scarcely raise their forks. The waiter materialized, clearing his throat in a pained way. Is anything wrong, wrong, wrong? They observed him, their sides aching.

"No," gasped Linda, licking the Parmesan from her chin. "Everything's right, right, right!"

"What was that about your mother?" Rick asked.

It was a time of giving and accepting.

It was scary.

They put down their shields, they took off their armor, they forgot the war between men and women. Defenseless, shorn of protection, they exchanged vulnerabilities.

Confidences, truths poured out unbidden, secret resentments, hurts nurtured since childhood. Each stripped his soul and laid offerings of revealment on the other's altar. It was a time of tenderness, of difference, and out of it came the sweet emergence of trust.

Linda Allenby, the girl who always had had everything—excepting a best friend—found she had many things to tell.

". . . Then that summer after ninth grade, right after they'd shot my horse Soldier . . ." her voice quavered ". . . they had to hustle me off to Europe . . ."

"Why was that?"

"They said it would make me forget. As if I could ever forget! I've never forgotten, from that day to this."

For answer Rick held her close.

"They kept telling me he was only a horse. That was the most stupid thing anybody could say." Rick kissed her forehead. "*I* knew he was a horse, for goodness' sake! But why did they have to shoot him? What was the matter with those crummy doctors? Couldn't they have set his leg?"

"It's hard to control an animal." Rick's voice spoke of comfort. "One time when I was delivering for the pharmacy I heard about a horse who broke his leg at Santa Anita. They tried to operate, but when he came out of the anesthetic they couldn't hold him still. In the end, they had to destroy him."

"It was so cruel!" said Linda. Her voice broke. Tears, the same tears, the continuation of tears long ago, flooded her eyes. "I used to lie awake in that pension in Paris, wishing it had been my leg, instead of Soldier's. At least they would have set my leg. At least they wouldn't have shot me!"

"I'm glad your leg is all right," said Rick.

"I've never forgiven them," said Linda.

"You've got to be fair," Rick said gently. "It wasn't their fault."

SEVENTEEN

For several weeks after Rick and Linda gave themselves each to the other, their lives burned like a single flame. It was a period unlike any either one had known—a sojourn into security, into fulfillment.

But one night, alone in his own bed in the men's dorm, Rick wakened out of a sound sleep in a cold sweat. The dream, whatever it had been, was gone, but the old, familiar, desperate sense of loss remained. Unnerved, uneasy, he arose and padded down the hall to take a shower, alternating the water, first scalding hot, then icy cold. At length he returned to bed to lic immobilized, listening to noises: Kemp's shallow snores, a plane, or dried palm fronds scraping the window screens. He fought against remembering the dream, clanging the doors of his subconscious one outside the other, but in his heart he knew that nothing would erase the frightening sense of sudden deprivation. He'd thought that he'd made it beyond all that. He'd thought the wounds were healed, but now he knew that once again he'd become vulnerable.

Three years before, in his freshman year, Rick had roomed not with Kempie Conway, but with Darter Evans, destined to be the great Bruin quarterback, but then only a rookie like Rick himself.

Darter, a black, had been brought to UCLA from Alabama. He was a fierce militant, but once the protective crust of his personality was penetrated, it developed he was the kind of guy who would give you his last pair of clean socks.

One evening in November Darter was taken ill. He vomited, he had diarrhea, he vomited again in unending heaves. Rick had never seen anyone that sick.

"I'd better get a doctor."

Darter, the great Darter, lay on his bed, so weak he couldn't move.

"Nah! It's the twenty-four-hour flu."

He made another rush down the hall for the bathroom.

When he returned, wavering, Rick had his bed turned back, and Darter fell upon it headlong. Rick undressed him, and covered him gently. Darter's eyes were closed. Rick pulled the telephone cord from the jack.

"Maybe you can get some rest," he said, but Darter had already passed out.

Hours later, Rick was awakened by a pounding on their door. Half asleep, he groped across the room and turned the knob. A pair of uniformed policemen stood in the hall.

"You Rick Dublin?"

"Yeah?" said Rick.

His brain was soggy from sleep. His eyes hadn't adjusted to the light. He was naked.

"You come with us," said one.

They hadn't counted on Darter. Roused from unconsciousness, running a fever and delirious, Darter heard, saw, and reacted. He sprang to the door and barred the way, protecting Rick.

"Get back, man!" he hissed. "It's the fuzz!"

He lunged toward the first policeman. Rick grabbed his arm. Darter struggled. He was a wild man.

"You can't come in here," he yelled, his words barely coherent, "come in here and haul a guy off in the middle of the night!"

"It's an emergency!" shouted one of the officers.

Rick wrestled with Darter, who was thrashing, cursing, and shouting.

"You can't take him! Man, you take him over my dead body!"

"Your phone's off the hook!"

Rick's irrelevant thought was that the phone company had gone to a lot of flap.

"Like the Gestapo!" screamed Darter, the maniac.

"Darter!" Rick bellowed, getting his friend's arm in a hammer lock. "Knock it off!"

They were both grunting. Sweat poured off Darter, making him slippery.

One officer was handing Rick a piece of paper, a sheet

torn from a small notebook. As if in slow motion, the officer folded the notebook, which had a black plastic cover, and put it back in his pocket.

"It's an emergency," said the second officer. His voice held pity. The words made no sense. "It's your mother."

"My mom?"

Rick relaxed his hold on Darter. Unexpectedly, Darter bolted down the hall toward the bathroom, holding his mouth. Other doors opened and four or five guys poked their heads out, bleary from sleep.

"She's sick," said the first officer.

"Sick, why didn't you tell me?"

"We tried to tell you, but that big gorilla . . ."

"How sick?"

"Sick, or we wouldn't be here."

"They tried to call you."

"They couldn't get through."

"That's the hospital."

The policeman gestured at the paper. Rick tried to read it. His eyes wouldn't focus. He had to get hold of himself. He had to make sense of this thing.

"You got a car?" the men were saying. "You want us to take you?"

Rick shook his head.

"I have a car." He was dazed. "What's the matter? What is it?"

"We don't know, son. All we know is what's written down right there."

Running through the deserted night toward the parking lot, shrugging into his windbreaker, Rick tried to think of the fastest way. The fastest way would be the freeway even though it was longer. Wilshire to the San Diego, San Diego to the Santa Monica, Santa Monica to the San Bernardino, straight out Ten. The yellow VW churned along, making noise. The tappets. He needed new tappets. He needed a valve job. He needed a new muffler. That can wait. Just get me there, baby!

The freeways were black causeways from nowhere to nowhere; they were rivers, glassy and deep; they were routes in space, marked by stars, stretching forever.

How could she be sick? He reverted to that. She had

never been sick. Fragile, tired, but never sick. He thought of the last time he'd been home, two weeks, no, three weeks ago. She'd seemed fine. He told himself she'd been fine. He heard himself say it out loud, in an argumentative tone. She was fine.

The middle of the night in Los Angeles is different and strange. Instead of thousands of cars there are three or four. Each of them, abroad probably because of some personal disaster, streaks over the black surface with an air of foreboding. Suddenly the void ahead is punctuated by moving arrows, pinpoints of light, signaling danger. The driver swerves to another lane, and avoids crashing into the orange, box-shaped equipment and repair trucks. As he swoops by he has a split-second image of the workers in their hard hats and orange coveralls, pouring and patching, erasing the clawmarks of tragedy.

Rick knew Mercy Hospital. Sometimes when he worked at the drug store he delivered supplies to the hospital pharmacy. He knew where to park without blocking the emergency entrance.

An aide came running, her white oxfords with their white rubber soles making hollow plops on the green rubber tile.

She didn't know about Mrs. Dublin. She'd only come on duty at eleven. He'd have to go to the front desk. Down this hall, then left, then down the next hall, then past the nurses' station . . .

Rick hurried, but he was running in slow motion, like the instant replays on TV. He saw himself in color, Big Rick Dublin, running after the Husky tailback, taking great, slow, giant strides, feathery bounds of motion, like on the moon, man, the moon, the moon . . .

No one was on duty at the information desk. In the corner a cleaning woman ran a wet mop over the tile.

Melba DeLaney materialized. Melba was crying. She took Rick in her arms, buried her cheek against his T-shirt.

"Thank God you've come!" She said it over and over. "Thank God you've come. Thank God you've come. Thank God you've . . ."

"Melba, what is it? Is it bad?"

She nodded.

"It's her lung." He'd never seen Melba cry. The Melba he knew was bright and flip, on the lookout for jokers. "She's in surgery."

"In surgery?"

She'd drawn him aside, away from the vacant information desk, away from the cleaning woman, mopping.

"They had to operate. On her lung."

"What for?"

"Her lung collapsed."

"Collapsed?" All he could do was parrot her words. "How did it collapse?"

"I don't know how. I don't know anything about lungs. All I know is, we were sitting there talking . . ."

"You were with her?"

"We were sitting there same as always, chewing the fat . . ."

"Where?" Why did he ask that? It seemed important. Get to the point, the point . . .

"In your kitchen. Your mom started to cough . . ."

Rick couldn't wait for all that.

"Can I see her?"

"No, you can't see her. Not now."

"When can I see her?"

"As soon as she comes out of surgery."

He felt choked with impatience. He stood, putting his hands in his pockets, to quiet them. He paced back and forth in front of Melba. He remembered she had been telling him . . .

"She started to cough?"

"Yes."

"Then what happened?"

"She couldn't stop. She went on coughing and choking and coughing."

He glared down at her, accusing.

"Didn't you do something? Didn't you get her a drink? Didn't you pat her on the back?"

Melba looked hurt.

" 'Course I did. Ricky. What do you think I am? I got her a drink. I patted her on the back. I did everything . . . we both did everything we could think of. We couldn't get the coughing stopped. She kept on coughing, worse and worse. And then . . ." Melba shivered. "She started coughing up blood. Not dried blood. Fresh blood, bright red. That was when I knew something was . . ."

Abruptly, Rick strode away, terminating the recital. The cleaning woman had finished the waiting room and was mopping her way down the hall. He went around the corner. A sign over an archway said Admittance. He tried the door. Admittance was locked up, tighter than a drum. He went back to Melba.

"Melba, I want to see her!"

"You can, Ricky, you can. Just as soon as she comes out of surgery."

"But how long is it going to take, for God's sake?"

"I don't know," said Melba, irritably. "I'm as worried as you are."

She picked up a magazine, leafed through it without seeing the pages. Rick couldn't sit, he couldn't stand. He walked around. He looked at the goldfish in the aquarium.

A middle-aged couple wandered out of the labyrinth of the hospital into the waiting room, and perched on the front edges of the overstuffed chairs. They talked in whispers. Both of them looked gray and haggard. The woman clasped and unclasped her purse. The muscle under her left eye had developed a tic, so that her left eye winked, irrationally, lewdly, while the right eye remained focused and sober.

Rick went back to Melba.

"How long have you been here?" he asked harshly.

"I don't know," said Melba. She seemed startled at the tone of his voice.

"Think, Melba. Think!"

"It was around nine when I called the doctor. That was it. I tried to call you from my place, and after we got here, too. I didn't think you'd have gone to bed yet."

"Okay," said Rick, trying to be logical. Take things one at a time. "You got here about nine-thirty."

"Probably."

"And what happened?"

"They took her into emergency. The doctor came. After a while he came out and said he'd sent for another doctor. Then they took her upstairs. Then they came down after a while and said they had to operate."

"So when was that?"

"It might have been ten . . ."

Melba was restless. She dabbed at her face with a twisted Kleenex. Her mascara had run, making a black smudge under each eye.

"Did you see her?"

"No, Ricky." Melba's voice was gentle. "The last I saw of her was after I'd brought her over in my car. They told me on the phone to come to the emergency entrance. I ran in and got a nurse, and they came out and took your mom in with a wheelchair. She kept talking about you, Ricky—when she could talk, that is. In between the coughs."

"Did she wonder why I wasn't here?" blurted Rick. He was choked up with guilt. He felt he had failed his mom.

Melba was kind. Rick wondered why he had never noticed she was kind. He'd always thought of her as a nutty friend of his mother's, trying to get herself a man.

"She knew why you weren't here," Melba said. "She was worried because she knew you'd be worried. What she said was, 'Tell Ricky everything's going to be all right.' "

Rick's mind seized upon this, evaluated it, memorized it, filed it.

Everything's going to be all right.

He returned to the goldfish.

In fifty seconds he was back, his palms clammy.

"Melba," he demanded, "isn't that a heck of a long time? Any way you look at it? It's ten minutes after four. That's six hours, Melba, six hours!"

Melba twisted the Kleenex into a little ball. Then she lit a cigarette. She offered one to Rick, but he shook his head.

The gray, haggard couple had disappeared. Rick hadn't seen them go. Now another middle-aged man in slacks and a sports jacket came out of the elevator. He was wearing a white shirt but no tie, and he needed a shave. Rick watched him cross the hall and enter the waiting room. He looked around as if in a daze. Poor guy. He too, had someone sick. The man crossed to where Melba was sitting, and started to speak. In two strides, Rick was beside them.

"Is this the son?"

Melba nodded, getting awkwardly to her feet.

"This is Dr. Birney, Rick."

Doctor! This bleary, unshaven man a *doctor*?

Dr. Birney put his hand on Rick's arm.

"It's a hard go," he said.

Rick looked at him narrowly. The man spoke gibberish.

"My mom . . ."

"She didn't make it, son."

Rick stared at him in stupidity. What was he saying?

"We did everything we could. When we got in there . . ." he cleared his throat, "we didn't have a damn thing to work on. Tissue all shot to hell. Both lungs."

Time had ground down to a walk. Everything Rick looked at was startlingly clear—the books in the shelves, the reading lamps, the dial above the elevator . . .

Melba was crying. The long ash from her cigarette dropped onto the floor. Rick glued his eyes on Dr. Birney. Dr. Birney's lips continued to move, but in some way the sound track no longer synchronized with the film. Words and syllables exploded into the silence like intermittent static . . . *collapsed* . . . *tried* . . . *edema* . . . *fusion* . . . *better this way* . . . *wouldn't want* . . .

Terror, long buried, terror out of Rick's forgotten first years swept over him in black suffocation. He knew, too late, he was going to be sick. He ran, looking for the men's room, past the elevators, past the gift shop, past the lab, but he didn't make it. He vomited in the freshly mopped hall.

EIGHTEEN

Neither of them had a car (Rick's old yellow Volkswagen had long since worn out) so they borrowed Darter's van and went to the beach. They rolled up their jeans and walked barefoot on the wet sand, the cold waves sloshing around their ankles.

Rick told Linda about his mother.

He told her about the hospital, about Melba, about the doctor looking gray and spent.

"I couldn't get it," Rick told Linda, his voice low, hidden in the wave sound, in the seagull cries. "I couldn't get the gist of what he was saying. It didn't sink in. I couldn't understand she was . . . that I'd never . . ."

Linda waited, but nothing more came out. Rick stopped, looking past the ocean to the gray sky. She could see the muscles in his chin tremble. Standing tiptoe in the water, she drew him to her, and kissed him.

"I'm sorry," Linda whispered.

He tried to talk, but no words formed. She held him close, her face pressed against his chest. She could hear his heart pounding through his sweatshirt.

"If I'd only . . ." he burst out. "If I could have gotten there! If I could have told her good-by!"

Tenderly she held him, while the waves broke against their mid-calves, then retreated, sucking the sand from under their feet like quicksilver.

"Don't," she said softly. "My dearest! My darling! Don't. It won't do any good."

They had different places to meet, depending on the day and their schedules. This second quarter Linda was taking eighteen units and Rick was helping coach spring practice. Sometimes, the way things were, they wouldn't

114

see each other for a day, or two days, and once it went
for three.

"I hated it!" said Linda vehemently. It was night. She
had been holed up in the reference library until ten and
they'd decided to walk to clear the cobwebs. "I can't stand
to go so long without you. I hate being alone!"

Rick put his arm around her. "What about your friends?"

"What friends?"

"Delcie, those Women's Libbers."

"I don't see them any more. I'm alone when I don't
have you."

He tightened his grip. "Let's go up to your room."

"In a minute. I need to walk. Only I need to walk with
you. I can't stand to be by myself."

"Me neither. So let's . . ."

In the dark, when they lay together resting, Linda asked
him, "What did you mean by 'me neither'?"

"I mean I don't dig being alone, any more than you do."

"But you've never been alone! You've always been on a
team or something."

"You can have a million guys around you and still be
alone."

"Yes . . . yes, I guess that could be."

"Believe me. It is."

"With me," said Linda, "with me, I was always alone.
Except for a dog or a horse. It used to bug my mother.
She was forever after me to make friends. Only I don't
know, the ones she liked, the ones she thought suitable,
even the boys at Cotillion . . ."

Rick grabbed her fiercely by the shoulders.

"What boys?" he scowled.

"I'm telling you. I couldn't relate."

"You're sure?"

"Stack of bibles!"

He released her.

"I don't think it's just us," said Linda, somewhat later.
"I think everybody's scared of being alone."

"Like being scared of the dark."

"It *is* being scared of the dark. It's being scared of that
big black void out there with a million trillion stars, all
thousands of light years away, and me nothing, nothing, no
more than a grain of sand."

"That's a hell of a way to feel."

She waited.

"Rick?"

"Yeah?"

"Have you ever felt that way?"

She waited again.

"Yeah," he said, after a long while.

Linda flung her arms around his neck and clung to him passionately.

"I never want to be alone again! Never!"

"Cool it, baby," said Rick. "That's something I'm going to take care of right now."

Linda wasn't aware of it, and Rick wasn't aware of it, but they both had changed. In an inexplicable way, each had become what the other saw. Rick was taller. Rick was stronger. Rick was able to leap tall buildings at a single bound. Rick could make love every fifteen minutes. At the workouts, Rick assumed command. He was at once good-natured and decisive. The frosh players growled and blossomed.

"What are you, some kind of miracle man?" the line coach asked. "You're actually getting it on with those dudes!"

"No sweat," Rick assured him.

"I can't understand it," Rick later confided to Linda. "All of a sudden everything comes easy—things that used to get me so up-tight I was a basket case—now it's no problem. Anything I want to do, I can do. It's that simple."

"It's cause you're so wonderful," said Linda.

"It's cause you're so beautiful," said Rick.

"It's cause we're so mushy," said Linda. "It's sickening."

"Sometimes I wish you weren't quite . . . such a classy looker," said Rick after a time. "It scares me."

"What's that supposed to mean?"

"Some asshole came up to me in the locker room and asked if I'd mind if he took some pictures of you. Nude."

Linda was both shocked and intrigued. "What did you say?"

"I nearly busted him in the mouth. I would have if I hadn't been in the cage. As it was, Darter had to hold me down."

"Lucky for you. I'd hate to have to bail you out of the clink."

"It's all over school," said Rick.

"What is?"

"That you're X-rated. That you're mine. That every upstanding dude is biding his time, looking for a chance to cut in on the action."

Linda digested this. "You're kidding."

"I'm giving it to you straight."

"All I have to say is, men sure are different from girls."

"You better believe it."

"It's funny," Linda said. "People used to tell me I was very pretty, but I thought they were insincere. I thought they were trying to make Brownie points. I knew I was all right, but since you and I . . . I mean, since we've had a thing going, and I started to believe you meant it . . . well, it's weird. I've begun to think I actually am okay—for looks, anyhow."

"Okay? My God, you're . . ."

"I mean, if I'm okay to you, why then maybe I . . ."

"Listen, as far as I'm concerned, you are the most gorgeous chick that ever drew breath!"

"Chick!" reproached Linda, her eyes closed. "How soon they forget! That's a no-no."

"Sexy, too."

"Sexy," agreed Linda dreamily. "I love it. I must be out of my skull."

NINETEEN

It was inevitable, sooner or later, that the world would intrude into the glass bubble.

Kemp was the first to know, not because Rick told him, but because Kemp had the nose of a back yard gossip.

"My Gawd!" Kemp bawled, after he'd seen Linda and Rick together. "She talks! She laughs! She holds hands!"

Rick scowled at him. "Can it!"

"The hell I will. I want to know how come the ice queen started to melt."

Rick could feel the hackles bristle on the back of his neck.

"What's the matter?" said Kemp. "You taking the fifth?"

"Will you shut up?"

"The least you could do is thank me."

"For what?"

"The time I put in softening up her fat friend—on your behalf, I might add."

"You didn't!"

"I sure as hell did. How do you think you got where you are?"

Rick struggled to hold on to himself. "That had nothing to do with it."

"Want to bet?"

"Shove it!"

Kemp selected a shirt from Rick's closet and pulled it over his head.

"How sharper than a serpent's tooth, is an ungrateful . . ."

Before he knew what he was doing, Rick shot out of his chair and placed himself facing Kemp, their eyes inches apart.

"You can take your serpent's tooth, and shove it right up your . . ."

"Okay, okay! Back off! I said, Okay, damn you!"

Linda's confrontations came later, probably because she went to great pains to avoid everyone she knew.

"How are things working out?" said Janet, the girl in advanced social behavior. Linda looked blank. "The pill! How are you doing with the pill?"

"Oh, uh . . . okay, I guess. Thanks."

"No side effects?"

"No."

"No front effects, either, ha ha!"

Linda forced herself to smile.

"Sometimes there are side effects. They say even cancer."

Linda could feel her smile wearing thin, but she held on to it.

"So let me know if you run out."

"I will." It was nothing but ghastly luck that she was in debt to a person like Janet. Was this destined to go on? Would Janet have a claim on her—maybe bug her for years? Linda strained to be polite. "Thanks. That's nice of you."

"My old man's coming home from London next week."

"How great."

Janet shrugged. "London, Beverly Hills, same difference. I don't see him that much."

"Oh," said Linda. She racked her brain. Even being polite, she could dredge up absolutely nothing more to say. She gathered up her books.

"I mentioned it in case you still wanted an appointment."

"I don't think it's necessary."

"Well, you know, for whatever . . ."

"Thanks," said Linda, backing out of the room as fast as she could. "I'll keep it in mind."

Linda couldn't walk away from Delcie because Delcie came to her room and knocked. Linda was in her short nightie and opened the door. Delcie pushed herself inside before Linda could do anything about it.

"Where in heaven's name have you been?" Delcie's tone was accusing.

"Nowhere." Now that she saw Delcie she felt guilty.

"I've been trying to see you for a month."

"It hasn't been that long."

"That's what comes of your not having a phone. Why don't you get a phone put in?"

Linda was sorry she'd neglected Delcie, but she disliked being put on the defensive.

"Never seemed to need it."

"My gosh, for an emergency, suppose there was an emergency! Don't you ever pick up your messages downstairs?"

"No."

"I even Scotch taped one to the door. Didn't you see it?"

She remembered. It had been one of their nights. They'd gone to a movie. Rick had tiptoed up the back stairs with her, both of them giggling under their breath. He'd taken the slip of paper off the door, read it and said, Want me to call Delcie?

"Maybe it fell off."

Delcie looked at her in sudden suspicion. "You're not trying to avoid me?"

Linda forced herself to smile. She hated herself for being a hypocrite, and hated Delcie for making her be one.

"Of course not. What a thing to say."

"If you are, say the word. I'll leave right now."

"Don't be silly."

"That's good." Delcie sighed. She seemed satisfied. "Because I've got to talk with you. It's crucial!"

Instinctively, Linda dreaded what was coming next. How much did Delcie know?

"So okay, talk."

"I don't know where to begin. Do you know what Aggie told me?"

"No."

"That she saw you with that big jock friend of Kemp Conway's."

Linda said nothing.

"And what's more, that you were so wrapped up in each other you couldn't tell the time of day!"

Linda feigned interest in the cuticle of her thumbnail. It was none of their business. It was none of anybody's business.

"Aggie said you looked right through her and didn't speak."

"I don't remember seeing her."

"So it's true!"

"What is?"

"About what's his name."

"His name is Rick."

"My God!" said Delcie. "It *is* true! Do you . . . Is he . . . I mean, is it serious?"

What was she getting so up-tight about? There was nothing wrong. Linda looked straight at her. "Yes," she said evenly, "it is."

"What do you know!" said Delcie. She seemed agitated. "No wonder Sadie's having kittens."

"What's this got to do with Sadie?"

"First you and then me. I've never seen anybody so mad."

"Who's mad?"

"Sadie's mad."

"What about?"

"Because she considers us traitors. Traitors to the movement."

"That's ridiculous. I believe in the movement as much as I ever did. There's no reason why I can't believe in equal pay and equal opportunity—or why I can't believe in freedom—and still have a—a relationship . . ."

"With a man? With the enemy? Not in Sadie's book."

"I fail to see that it's any of Sadie's business."

"Try to tell that to her."

"I don't intend to tell her anything. I don't intend to see Sadie."

"You'll see her. She's not about to let you off the hook." Delcie took out a cigarette and lit it with trembling fingers.

"I didn't know you smoked."

"I didn't. I just started. I'm trying to keep my weight down, for Kemp."

Relieved that the conversation had shifted momentarily from her affair with Rick, Linda, with an effort, called to mind a picture of Delcie's room papered with larger-than-life posters of Kemp. Then she remembered the girls at Sadie's turning on Delcie.

"You have to help me!" Delcie burst out.

"Why? What's . . ."

"With Kemp!" Delcie's tone was pure anguish. "He's . . . Oh, Linda, something's gone wrong! Something's terribly, tragically wrong!" She looked around wildly. "Don't you have an ash tray in this crummy joint?"

"No."

Delcie ground out her cigarette on the window sill, then lit another.

"He's . . . I don't know what I've done wrong, what I've done to offend him. That's what I told him the last time I talked to him. 'If you'll just tell me what I've done to offend you, why then I can take steps to . . .'" She broke off in mid-sentence and walked up and down in a distraught manner. "He liked me in the beginning," Delcie said, trying to start again in a reasonable tone. "I know he did. Why else would he have sought me out? I ask you?"

"I don't know," said Linda.

"He came to me, mind you. I didn't make a pass at him. Oh, no. He wined me and dined me—if you can call hamburgers wining and dining. It couldn't have been because I helped him with his geology notes, because I'm positive he didn't know I'd taken that class."

Linda felt herself frowning. She tried to resist being dragged into this maelstrom but it was no use. Delcie picked up Rick's Mexican belt, which was draped over the bookshelf. Her jaw dropped as she realized what it was.

"You mean Rick's been . . . that he took off . . . My God! No wonder Sadie's mad!"

"Sadie doesn't know a thing about it."

"Want to bet?"

"She won't, if you don't tell her."

"Want to keep it a secret, huh?"

"It's none of her business."

"A secret affair," intoned Delcie, as if she were reading a title from a movie marquee. The envy in her voice was unmistakable.

"Look," said Linda. The whole conversation had gotten out of bounds. "If you . . ."

"Please," said Delcie, suddenly nice, suddenly contrite. "Tell me. Tell me. How . . . how was it?"

"How . . . what?" Linda felt the blood suffuse her face.

"You know. You know what I'm talking about. Tell me!" Her voice burned in its intensity. "I have to know! Was it worth it?"

"Why . . . ah . . ." said Linda. Damn Delcie! She hated

her and pitied her at the same time. But she felt she had to answer. "It was all right."

"Better than just all right?"

"Yes," admitted Linda. "Considerably."

"What am I going to do!" screamed Delcie. She plopped herself on the bed beside Linda and grabbed Linda's wrist, her nails digging into the skin. "Tell me what you did? How did you get him to . . ."

"To what?"

"Make out?"

"I didn't do anything."

"You won't tell me!" The sentence wrung itself from her, almost a dirge of despair. The long ash from her cigarette fell on the bedspread. Delcie brushed at it impatiently with her palm, making a sooty streak. "He won't even talk to me, anymore. When he knows who it is he hangs up the phone!"

Linda stared at the streak on the bedspread, embarrassed. When at last she looked up, Delcie was crying.

Linda had gone to bed when the telegram came. Mrs. Gugen, the hall manager, climbed the three flights to deliver it personally.

"I didn't know if you were still in school or not," she told Linda. "You got a stack of messages down in your call box a mile high."

URGENT YOU CALL US WHEN YOU RECEIVE THIS DAY OR NIGHT MOTHER

Linda put on her robe and slippers and walked downstairs to the booth. She didn't have the right coins and had to ask Mrs. Gugen to make change for a dollar. She returned with the sheaf of messages to the booth and looked at them while she dialed.

> Allenby Call your Mother
> Allenb. Call home
> Linda A. Call your folks
> Linda, Urgent you telephone
> your parents. *Today*.

Linda was discomfited to notice the *Today* note was dated two weeks previous.

"Mother?"

"Linda!"

"Mother? What's up?"

"What's up!" There was a pause, punctuated by a snuffling on the other end of the line. With dismay Linda realized her mother, who was always elegant, always controlled, was crying. "Mother, are you all right? I mean, there isn't anything wrong, is there?" She waited. She could barely detect her mother's weeping, then voices away from the phone. I can't . . . What'd she say . . . You'll have to talk to her . . .

"Linda?" Her father was brisk and strong.

"Daddy!" Linda almost sobbed in relief. "You're all right! I was beginning to think something terrible had happened."

"The terrible thing is that your mother's upset because we haven't heard from you in a month."

Linda felt disconcerted. "A month! It hasn't been that long."

"Your mother says it'll be five weeks tomorrow."

"Daddy! I'm sorry! Really I am! I don't know where the time has gone."

"I don't think you appreciate, Linda, that your mother is in delicate health."

"Mother?"

"She's practically on the verge of a nervous breakdown from worry."

"Oh, no! I . . . gee, I am sorry. It's just that . . ."

"What?"

"I've been busy."

"I don't see how anyone can be too busy to pick up a telephone for three minutes once a week."

Linda heard her father's words and at the same time she heard other words, other words but the same voice, spoken when she had been a child, when he was twice her height, when he had scolded her for breaking the china teapot, for leaving the window open so that the rain ruined the carpet, for tipping her milk over onto the lace tablecloth. Without realizing what was happening to her, Linda fell into the role of the sinner, the transgressor who must beg forgiveness, who must make amends.

"I'm sorry! I just . . . I'll call every week from now on."

She didn't know what to say next. She struggled to maintain her adult identity. "Can you put mother on again? Mother?"

"Linda dear . . ." Linda could tell from the inflection that Margaret was struggling for composure. "We've been out of our minds with worry!"

"Mother, please! Everything's fine! There's nothing to worry about!"

"If there's nothing to worry about, why don't you come home this weekend? I'll drive over and pick you up."

The conversation came to a dead stop.

"It isn't that I wouldn't like to," Linda said after a while, lamely, "but . . ."

Ten minutes later Linda replaced the phone, scooped up the rest of the coins, and dropped the sheaf of messages into the waste bin at the end of the corridor. She felt like a heel. The old churning feeling in her stomach that she had battled as a child had returned to plague her. She wished she had taken up smoking. She needed a cigarette, a drink, anything to relieve the pressure. She tried to analyze her distress. What was so impossible about this situation? After all, she was a grown woman, an adult. She had lived for twenty-one years. She was capable of taking charge of her own life. At the same time, there was no reason why she shouldn't treat her parents with consideration. Certainly she didn't want to upset them! Certainly she didn't want to cause them pain!

Having decided that, she put it to herself point blank. What was the big hang-up? She concluded there was none. Shivering, she gathered her robe about her and hurried up the stairs, her mules slapping against the cement treads.

She refused to recognize the basic disorder, which continued to fester in her subconscious. Yet when she awakened in the night she heard herself say it out loud in the dark, silent room.

"If they only knew! If they knew!"

She shuddered convulsively.

TWENTY

Reluctantly, Linda reached the conclusion that she had to do something about Delcie. After Delcie had made the initial contact, she fastened on to Linda like a leech, dropping by Linda's room unannounced at odd hours, even three in the morning. Linda took pains to lock the door, but it did no good. Delcie's knock was not to be denied.

"Who is it?"

"Linda, you know who it is! Open up the crappy door!"

"Delcie, I can't."

"Is he there?" This was uttered in awe.

"For heaven's sakes, keep your voice down!" Linda was reduced to a hoarse stage whisper, she who scorned melodramatics. She hated herself for stooping to it, and resented Delcie for forcing her to do so. Delcie started to pound the door again.

"Linda, for God's sake . . ."

In the end, Linda capitulated, as she suspected Delcie had known she would from the beginning. Delcie immediately ensconced herself in the middle of Linda's bed, lit a cigarette, and began her doleful litany.

The plaint was the same as before; Kemp would have nothing more to do with Delcie and Delcie was going crazy. Delcie had become a chain smoker, smoking three and four packs a day. When she wasn't smoking she was eating, which the smoking was designed to prevent but didn't. She had regained the ten pounds she had lost and was still climbing. This so upset her she was taking diet pills, which prevented her from sleeping and caused her to go to the bathroom every half hour. Because of the snacking her face had started to break out. Some of the pimples had become infected and Delcie thought she must be allergic to the salve the doctor had given her for them because her skin constantly itched. It was impossible to keep from scratching and this only spread the infection. In addition the general deterioration of her physical condition caused her eyes to water and burn, so she couldn't tolerate her contacts, and was forced to go back to wearing glasses. She looked more like an owl that ever before—a sick owl.

When Delcie wasn't pacing restlessly up and down Linda's room reciting her troubles she flung herself on the bed and cried.

"I'm a mess! I'm getting worse! Why couldn't he have looked at me when I was halfway decent? I did it all for him! Why did he drop me? It doesn't make sense! He'll never look at me now!"

"Delcie, you have to get hold of yourself!"

"Why? Give me one good reason. It's hopeless!"

Linda was impatient with Delcie, whose lamentations jarred Linda's idyllic relationship with Rick. She was reminded of an automobile trip she had once taken in the mountains. The radio had been tuned to a station playing a languorous melody. Suddenly, without warning, another frequency took over and the radio blared raucous rock and roll. The car went around a curve, and the radio switched back to the original soothing station. After that, the changes back and forth, from harmony to cacophony, occurred without rhyme or reason. This was the effect upon Linda's nerves each time Delcie barged in with her wails and complaints.

At the same time, it was impossible to look at Delcie and not see what was happening. Delcie had been an ordinary, healthy girl leading a normal, reasonably structured life. Now, in the space of little over a month she had disintegrated to the brink of ruin. Linda liked Delcie. Delcie was her friend. Linda realized she couldn't sit idly in her safe little life boat and let Delcie go under. Yet she was at a loss as to how to effect a rescue.

"Delce, it's okay to care about someone. I can understand that. I care about Rick—"

"Not as much! You couldn't care as much. Nobody can know how I feel. Nobody can know how much I love Kemp!"

Linda sighed with impatience.

"What I'm trying to get across is that you can love

someone and not lose your—well—your individuality. You can still be your own woman."

Delcie shook her head.

"I don't think that's possible—when all I do is think about him day and night."

"It has to be possible!" exclaimed Linda. She was in unfamiliar territory and she groped for logic. "That's what the movement really is about; woman becoming her own person, able to make her own decisions, do her own thing —and also to have the ability to love."

"But I don't want to do my own thing!" shrieked Delcie in despair. "You have to talk to Rick!"

Linda didn't want to talk to Rick. Not about Delcie.

Delcie wouldn't let up. "You have to get Rick to talk to Kemp, to try and get Kemp to . . ."

"To what, Delce?"

"To, to call me again. To let me stake him to a Big Mac. Just . . . to walk around the campus with me, for old times' sake." As she groped for words to express her longing, Delcie looked at once so ludicrous and pitiful that Linda's heart ached.

"Delce, it won't do any good. You have to face it. Whatever it was, it's over."

"Linda, for God's sake, please! It's a matter of life and death!"

Linda talked to Rick. It was the first favor she'd ever asked of him. Rick listened without reply. Linda waited impatiently.

"Well," she said, finally. Rick didn't speak. "I mean, will you?"

"No."

"No! Why not?"

"I'd rather not discuss anything with Kemp," Rick said stiffly.

"Rick! Why?"

"Because at the moment I don't want to talk to Kemp about your lovesick girl friend."

Linda was hurt. She had been under the illusion that Rick would have delivered the moon in a box from Bonwit's had she asked.

"But you're roommates!"

"All the more reason."

She flared up. "I think you're making a big deal out of nothing!"

He snapped back, "And I think you've got a hell of a nerve to ask!"

It was their first quarrel, and they stomped away from each other in a huff.

The next day they rushed into each other's arms, in front of Wilkins Hall, begging each other's forgiveness.

"It was wrong of me to come down so hard," said Rick.

"It was wrong of me to ask."

"The truth is . . . Oh hell, you might as well know. The reason Kemp gave that nutty dame a tumble in the first place was . . ."

"Was that?"

"To help me out with you. That was before we . . . He had some screwy idea . . . I guess I was as much of a basket case as she is . . ."

Linda stopped, trying to grasp the ins and outs.

"You mean you . . . me . . . he . . . she . . . ?"

Suddenly she threw her head back and roared with laughter. Rick joined in. They ran through the campus holding hands, laughing till their sides were sore and they fell on the grass exhausted.

The minute Linda returned to her room that afternoon Delcie materialized, pale and pimply, a cigarette in her trembling fingers.

"Did you talk to him?"

"He won't."

"Can't you make him?"

"No, I can't. I told you. He won't and that's that."

Linda was not prepared for the effect the refusal had on Delcie. Delcie crumpled, her face looked ashen.

"I guess that's it then." She spoke slowly, is if Linda weren't there. "I guess there's nothing left." Something in her tone, in her listless manner, set off a warning bell in Linda's mind.

"Of course there is!" Linda said positively. "There's everything left. You have to think about something else."

"I can't. There isn't any use. Not any more."

Linda plopped herself on the bed beside Delcie, and shook her by the shoulders.

"Delce, listen to me! You have to snap out of this! You were getting along fine before you met Kemp. Think about your life then. Remember our trip to Sacramento, how much fun we had? Think about the movement."

"I don't give a shit about the movement! I want to get married and have kids!"

"Don't be absurd. All you need is to get back in the swing of things. How long since you've been to a meeting at Sadie's?"

"Not long enough."

"Too long. It's Friday. That's where we're going tonight. I'm taking you out for a decent meal and then we're going to Sadie's."

"We won't be welcome at Sadie's . . . either one of us."

"Of course we will. Don't talk nonsense. Now go put on a clean shirt and comb your hair, and I'll meet you in ten minutes. Like old times."

A flicker of interest crossed Delcie's face.

"Beat it!" said Linda briskly. "And be thinking about what you want to eat!"

TWENTY-ONE

As they approached the Canyon Crest Apartments Linda had second thoughts. True, she felt constrained to help Delce, and this was the only way she could think of to do it. But suppose Sadie and the girls turned their venomous sarcasm upon her, because she was seeing a man? Clawlike pincers of dread grabbed Linda's stomach. She couldn't stand it if they cut her down the way she'd seen them decimate Delcie. At the same moment she was equally sure that was exactly what was going to happen. Why did it matter to her what Sadie thought? She could come up with no logical answer. It was a visceral feeling, the feeling of a child who has wet the bed and sees the mother going into the bedroom, knowing she will discover the damp sheet. Linda's apprehension was exacerbated by Delcie, whose finger was actually shaking as she rang the doorbell.

Sadie herself opened the door. Linda moistened her lips, but before she could summon up her speech Sadie threw up her arms in an extravagant gesture of surprise and delight.

"I can't believe it!" Sadie screamed. "If it isn't the prodigal sheep!"

She flung her arms about them and kissed each one in turn. "Come in! Come in! We were just talking about you!" She ushered them inside where they were surrounded by a dozen girls who hugged and kissed them in an effusive welcome, while others on the outskirts relayed Sadie's words amid the clatter of expresso cups. Did you hear what Sadie said? Linda and Delce are back, and Sadie said, "If it isn't the prodigal sheep!" The sound echoed and each cup clattered in its saucer. They hovered, disciples at the feet of the prophetess, savoring her remarks, endowing them with qualities they did not possess; epigrams to be saved for posterity, they thought. The quip about the prodigal sheep was not that funny, not funny at all. What meaning could it have? None. It was something that purported to be clever yet was not, but the girls all laughed. They were the sheep.

"You're just in time!" said Sadie. "We're having the most divine dessert!"

Linda and Delcie were given cups of thick black expresso. Coconut macaroons, squares of paper-thin layered Greek pastries swimming in honey and nuts, Napoleons with wavery lines of milk chocolate on vanilla cream were pressed upon them from all quarters. Welcome home, Linda read in every gesture. You have strayed, but all is forgiven. Yet why did Linda feel as if she had been accused, by innuendo, of some terrible crime? There was nothing she could pinpoint in Sadie's words or in Sadie's tone, but she was aware of the feeling as if it were a palpable aura of fog or dust. It was not something in Linda's mind only. She was convinced it was in the room, in every look, every gesture of the assemblage. Yet everyone was going out of her way to make them feel at home.

It was the "you have strayed" feeling that put Linda on the defensive, and once on the defensive it was almost as if, in her own mind, she admitted she had done something wrong, something not accepted by the group. Linda looked around the room, trying to focus, refusing to recognize these subliminal feelings. On the surface she was concerned only for Delcie. That was all that mattered.

Delcie was ensconced on a sofa, the center of attention. Already she had started to perk up. She loves it, marveled Linda. She's not love sick. She's attention starved.

A slender coffee-colored hand grasped Linda's arm. Aggie Jackson drew her into the bathroom and shut the door behind her.

"That poor kid!" Aggie breathed. "What's happened to her?"

Linda had never been one to tell tales. "Delcie? She's . . ." She stopped, wondering how to toss it off, but Aggie knew without being told. Aggie Jackson was old beyond her years; knowledgeable with an inborn wisdom of the ages. She knew that men had abused women from time immemorial, even before slavery. Therefore weren't all women, black and white, sisters under the skin?

"The viper!" Aggie spat. "The filthy viper!"

"Look, Ag, don't go jumping to conclusions. Delce is in a bad way, I grant you, nobody knows it better than I. That's why I brought her here—to see if you all couldn't help pull her out of it."

"The poor baby!"

"But listen!" said Linda. "It's not what you think. It's not what Kemp's done to her. It's something she's done to herself! She's built this whole thing up in her mind, out of nothing. Kemp did absolutely nothing. In fact," Linda laughed half-heartedly, "that's the trouble."

"The worm!" Aggie spat again.

Linda sighed. She was talking to a closed mind.

"Do you think you could do something? I mean, try to get her back in the groove, interested in something else?"

Agnes put her arm lightly around Linda. She was wearing a new cologne, *Charlie.*

"Honey," said Ag. "You leave it to me! That poor, poor chile!"

Now everyone crowded into the living room, sitting on every available surface of the furniture and the floor. The room had its own identity: the latexed green walls with their patina of nicotine; the white-painted wicker furniture with its bumpy black flowered cretonne cushions; the masses of plants, some in gallon cans hanging from the ceiling in rattan macramé slings, some on tables, some on the floor in clay and plastic pots. Philodendrons, caladiums, umbrellas, pileas, a bedraggled asparagus fern, all clustered together. There were also the paperbacks, leftist little magazines no one had ever heard of, the well-thumbed books by women writers—Millet, Jong, Didion, Lessing— and the stacks of underground newspapers.

Unbidden, the voice of Margaret Allenby sprang to Linda's mind—Margaret Allenby talking to Marcie, the Allenby cleaning woman, about the principles of thorough housekeeping. The first week out of every month we wash the inside windows and scour the showers with Clorox, the second week we wax the furniture in the dining room and den, the third . . .

Stimulated by the coffee, Delcie was letting it all hang

out—the passion, the pain, the pathos. Her eyes were bright and feverish. The girls absorbed her words, hypnotized by an electric current that fused Delcie and her listeners into one throbbing circuit. Delcie had been wronged, hence all had been wronged.

True (no one had said it but it was obvious everyone thought it), Delcie had committed an error in judgment by encouraging a man in the first place. But one had to take into consideration the frailty of the human body. Delcie was susceptible, Delcie erred, now Delcie was paying the penalty which the movement had warned all along would be there, but which was turning out to be more severe than anyone had imagined. You have strayed, Delcie, but all is forgiven. Come back to the fold. That, thought Linda in a sudden flash of insight, was where the sheep came in!

In any case, Linda was relieved to observe Delcie relating to the group in a reasonably rational manner. Coming here had been the solution after all. Delcie was going to be all right.

Sadie, sitting cross-legged on the floor, her back to the ottoman, rustled a sheaf of papers in her lap. As if by magic, conversations ceased. Sadie proceeded to schedule the NOW booth for the coming week.

". . . and Linda, Tuesday, two to four."

It was apparent to all Sadie was magnanimous, willing to accept Linda back—no pointing fingers, no questions asked. Linda felt Sadie's magnetism as a swimmer struggles against a rip tide.

"I'm sorry, Sadie. I'm afraid I can't."

Why did she say sorry? Why did she say afraid? Why didn't she say a forthright No?

"Not Tuesday? I thought that was your good day. Well then, we'll make it Thursday."

It was obvious Sadie was going out of her way to accommodate Linda, who was giving her unnecessary trouble.

"No, Sadie. Don't schedule me at all."

Sadie looked bemused, unwilling to trust her own ears. "You can't mean it."

"I do mean it. I'm carrying eighteen units and I . . ."

She hated herself for explaining. Why should she explain?

She didn't want to waste an iota of time sitting behind the NOW booth. Every spare moment she had was precious. Every spare moment was going to be spent with Rick, making love.

Sadie looked at her, the patient parent trying to lean over backwards to understand the motivation for the wayward child's misdeed.

"Linda dear . . ." Sadie spoke gently, deceptively gently, with scarcely a trace of Let's get this straight ". . . you are interested in the movement . . ."

"Oh yes," said Linda too quickly.

"I'm glad!" It seemed to be a genuine gladness, the happiness of a shared belief, with no hint of an encumbrance or a duty implied. "Because . . . I can't speak for the rest of the girls, but I know I personally have always felt so very, very close to you, Linda." A murmur of assent ran through the room. Sadie paused to let the full feeling of sisterly love wash back and forth. "You're . . . you're such a valuable person!" Sadie spoke with an unaffected rush of feeling, the words tumbling out spontaneously. "I know that . . . to me . . . our friendship is a very precious thing. I have the feeling that the rest of the girls feel the same way!" Again, the chorus of assent. You better believe it. That's right, baby. With you all the way.

Sadie took up her pencil and went on with her scheduling.

Linda was caught off guard. What had she expected—that she'd be called before the Grand High Tribunal and charged with crimes against the state? Relief flooded over her and she laughed inwardly. She was off the hook! She chided herself for her silly fears. What had she been worried about? All her apprehensions had been in her own head. She was as bad as Delcie, a victim of her own fantasies.

The scheduling accomplished, Sadie sorted through the papers on her lap, evidently wondering which to discuss next. "We have so much to take up tonight, you wouldn't believe!" By accident, or seemingly by accident, her eye caught Linda's, and she smiled warmly.

"It's so good to have you here!"

"It's good to be here."

"I always knew you were sincere about the movement."

"Yes. I was."

"Was?"

"Was—am. I hope I'm still sincere."

"You're one of the most—if not the most—sincere persons I know."

"Thank you." It was a compliment that meant something. Sincerity was a quality that Linda valued.

"It is so important," Sadie said, almost more to herself than to anyone else, ". . . so important that we accomplish what we've set out to gain—in our generation! We have to take advantage of the thrust, the momentum . . ." Her tone, even more than her words, held the old magic, the elixir that spurred their minds and hearts to action. Tension permeated the room. "We can't let up now," Sadie said softly, "even for a week, a day, a single second, or we'll lose the position we've already achieved! Once we stop going forward we'll start to fall back!" Sadie looked around, holding the attention of every pair of eyes, gathering up the souls of her listeners and sweeping them along with her. "That's why it's so important . . . so crucial . . . if we are sincere, if we truly believe, that we remain pure in our resolve . . . that we don't contaminate it with outside interests!"

Linda began to feel uneasy.

"We cannot," said Sadie, "if we're pushing for women's rights, if we are to achieve women's rights, we cannot fraternize with those very persons who are subordinating those rights!"

"But," said Linda, snapping the bait before she had time to consider, "if you're really going to change things, and if men hold the strings of power . . ."

"As we all know they do."

"As we all know they do, you're going to have to deal with them. If you want changes in the law, you're going to have to work with men on legislative committees; if you want changes in the media's attitude you have to have women with positions inside the media work with the men who manipulate the power strings."

"Work with," agreed Sadie, "work with."

"Yes."

"But not play with. Not socialize with."

Linda had the feeling she was a gazelle who had been

fleeing the drumbeats and cries of a posse of African beaters, and, having galloped down a leafy corridor that promised freedom, now found itself in a high-walled corral with no way out.

"Look," Linda said, struggling to keep her cool. "There's no reason why people can't be friends."

"Isn't there?" Sadie asked innocently.

"No!" Linda was close to shouting. "There's no reason why a person can't believe in certain principles without having them affect her private life!"

"And you do believe?"

"Of course I believe! I believe as much as anyone! I believe that freedom is more important than . . . than life itself, and that you can't have freedom if you don't have equality! Why shouldn't women have equal pay for equal work? Why should any door be closed to us because of sex?" She glanced about. Everyone was listening, all eyes reflected her passion. Linda plunged on. She couldn't have stopped herself had she tried. "I feel no woman should be forced to carry any burden or perform any task, simply because she happened to have been born female!"

The room exploded in applause. A dozen voices erupted in excitement. Sadie's eyes glistened. She shouted over the hubbub, "I have never, never, heard a more sincere commitment . . ."

Linda tried to go on. "But I don't see how any of this has any bearing on a person's private life . . ."

A dozen girls interrupted, each trying to interject her own ideas. Linda looked about helplessly. Why didn't they let her finish? Why couldn't they grasp the point she was trying to make—that it was possible for her to be a woman and be part of Rick's life at the same time?

Rhoda approached, gingerly picking her way through the crowded torsos, passing a plate of macaroons. Jody Jordan poured more coffee.

"I agree with you!" Aggie called to Linda over their heads. "We don't control our own bodies, we don't control nothing!"

"That's right," Linda concurred, "but that's not exactly what I . . ."

It was no use. Even Aggie turned away, holding up her cup for Jody to fill.

Linda felt frustrated. Somehow she had been manipulated back into the vanguard of the movement—on Sadie's terms. Somehow she was back in the position where Sadie and the girls took it for granted she believed exactly as they did. Linda sighed. She had no quarrel with women's rights. But at the same time, she knew she was never going to give up her lover. She had met the enemy, and she was his.

TWENTY-TWO

Linda wakened feeling sick: nauseated and exhausted. She closed her eyes, surprised. She never had so much as a cold or menstrual cramps. As a child she had been mildly asthmatic, and once had broken her arm, but for years she had sailed along in vigorous good health, which she had come to consider as normal for her. She was convinced that she would never be sick, never fall victim to accident, never grow old, or die. Vaguely she knew misfortunes happened to others, but she chalked them up to mismanagement. She, Linda, was immune, inviolate, and immortal.

And now, this. Slight as the indisposition no doubt was, she considered it an affront.

After a while she forced herself out of bed. Breakfast was out of the question, but she couldn't afford to miss her classes.

The nausea slackened before noon and she managed to down a bowl of soup, but the feeling returned, worse than ever, around five o'clock and she skipped dinner. She telephoned Rick she wouldn't meet him in the library, and went to bed early.

Next morning was no better. Linda drank a glass of water and threw up. She reasoned she had picked up the twenty-four-hour flu, and braced herself for a bout of diarrhea. It was well into February, the middle of the quarter and Linda was cramming for mid-terms.

The bug could not have hit at a more inconvenient time. She muddled along, sure she would begin to improve. She had no temperature or sore throat. She wasn't sick enough to be in bed, but she couldn't jolly herself into thinking she was well. She felt lousy.

"It's mono," said Delcie. "I knew a guy in Renaissance who got it last year. He had to drop out of school."

"Terrific."

"Better go to the health center. At least they'll give you a shot."

Linda put off going. Mono patients, she knew, were ordered to bed. She couldn't lose the whole quarter, eighteen units. She took the exam in anthropology, and had a battle staying awake. It was impossible to think.

She worried about Rick, and refused to kiss him.

"For Christ's sake!"

"It's called the kissing disease."

"I'm not going to get it, I tell you. I never get sick."

"That's what I thought."

Rick was grumpy and told her if that was the way she felt they might as well kiss off the whole evening.

Delcie gave her a bottle of Kaopectate, which tasted like chalk. She threw that up, too.

On Friday she did manage to get in to the health Center, but the doctor was out on an emergency. The nurse told her the disorder sounded more like intestinal flu than mono. She suggested Linda was studying too hard, not getting the right food or rest.

"Food!" said Linda. "Yuk!"

She had lost seven pounds.

"It's not fair!" complained Delcie. "I starve and gain, while you . . ."

Linda had been sick for two weeks before the idea, ghastly in its implications, burst upon her in the middle of a sleepless night. What if . . . could she be . . . pregnant!

She sat bolt upright in bed. Ridiculous! Monstrous! Impossible!

She knew her period was overdue, but that was the pill. The possibility was printed plainly, on the box: "For some individuals this medication may disrupt the menstrual cycle." Linda's cycle had never been accurate—sometimes it ran five days over, sometimes a week. She'd been too busy to keep track. Now she tried to think back, to remember, but she could not, not since Rick. She couldn't remember at all.

After that, her waking hours were nightmares. The idea was preposterous, she knew. She'd been faithful with the pill, never missed. But suppose the pills' potency had expired? Suppose they were old, a brand no longer available, suppose they'd been kicking around Janet's father's office?

Linda scolded herself for the feeling of being sucked into quicksand. Why did she allow herself to stew when she knew, unequivocally, that pregnancy was out of the question? Still . . . there had been . . . that first time . . . Nonsense!

The conflict raged within her, accentuated by her throwing up. It had been so long, now, since she had been able to keep much in her stomach—even water—that her vomit was for the most part dry retching, culminating in a thick brownish-green bile. The end of such a session would find her on her knees beside the toilet bowl, too exhausted to rise, gagging on the acrid taste, her face cold and clammy with perspiration. She knew she couldn't go on this way much longer. It was nearing the end of the winter quarter, and she would have a week's vacation. The thought of relaxing as an invalid, pampered and cared for until she was cured, in her own airy beautiful room at La Hacienda, was appealing beyond words. Conversely, the moment she entertained the idea, she reminded herself she might be pregnant. She decided to stay on campus.

At this point an unexpected phenomenon occurred. Although Linda continued to lose weight, so that her wrists were skeletal and her cheekbones sharp, her breasts began to swell. She had had little to do with Rick since she'd felt so miserable, yet all of a sudden her nipples were sore and tender, as if they'd been sucked and fingered. She appraised her silhouette in a T-shirt. Each breast was the size of a grapefruit. She didn't look sexy, but obscene.

At last she forced herself to face what she had known, subconsciously, for weeks. She needed medical attention desperately, but where to go? She was back to square one. She ruled out the health center, for the reason she had ruled out the health center before. The same applied to Dr. Dixon in Pasadena, and the same went for Janet's father—she couldn't stand a lifetime of Janet breathing down her private life.

She made an appointment with Planned Parenthood.

One week later she faced a doctor, a woman in her early thirties.

"So I'm afraid that's it, Mrs. Allenby—is it Mrs.?"

"No," said Linda shortly.

"Ms. Allenby," said the doctor.

Linda sat transfixed, trying to sort out the syllables, the vowels, the consonants of the doctor's pronouncement, and rearrange them in a sequence that made sense. What had the doctor said—that an atom bomb would go off in five minutes, leveling Los Angeles? No. The atom bomb was there, inside of Linda. She shifted uneasily to the edge of her chair. She had known, secretly and certainly, she had known; but until now she had tricked herself into believing there was hope, an outside chance, some other explanation, a tumor . . .

"I—I . . ." Linda tried to form words, to form thoughts. The icky feeling twisted her stomach. In her mind she measured the distance to the women's rest room. If the vomit came on suddenly, could she get there in time?

"You'll have to come to a decision," the doctor said.

Linda looked at her. She felt as if her eyes were glazed over.

"Now that abortion is legal, we can refer you to a clinic."

An abortion! Epithet of misfortune! Catastrophic word she heard on the news. A disaster that happened to others, never to Linda. Linda Allenby, the Linda Allenby who led a charmed life.

"I . . . I'd have to think . . ."

"You don't have much time to think. It should be done immediately, you've let things go so long."

An abortion. Her head was swimming. She had never felt so sick. Abortion was a way out.

"Does—does it hurt?"

The doctor laughed. "It's no Sunday School picnic, but I'll tell you one thing for sure. It's a hundred times easier than having a baby." She shrugged lightly. "It's about like having a tooth pulled."

Linda winced. She had never had so much as a cavity.

"The clinic doesn't keep patients overnight," said the doctor. "Rest for an hour and you're ready to go."

"What about the cost?" Linda heard herself say.

"It depends on what the patient can afford. Now if you're a student—"

"Yes."

"Most of our girls are." She laughed. Linda made no effort to join in. "The cost is minimal, compared to the cost of childbirth," said the doctor, who now seemed to be championing a cause. "That's risen to fifteen hundred for the hospital and five hundred for the obstetrician."

Linda stared at her, trying to make sense out of gibberish. Already the doctor was on the phone, talking to someone, setting things up.

"Tomorrow?" said the doctor, looking at Linda over the rims of her glasses. "At ten?"

"All right," whispered Linda.

Linda had borrowed Jody Jordan's VW. In less than half an hour she found herself at the beach, running on foot pell mell along the wet, hard sand at the water's edge, until her breath came in heaves and she was forced to slow down. Her problem, her immense, insoluble, catastrophic burden, was still with her. She could not outdistance it, no matter how hard she ran or how fast, not if she traveled to the ends of the earth. She could no longer ignore it, pretending it was the twenty-four-hour flu or that it didn't exist. She had to face it, she had to come to grips with it, and no matter what she decided her life would never again be the same. Her innocent, sheltered girlhood, her freedom which she so passionately cherished, her idyllic, carefree relationship with Rick, all were irrevocably shattered. As the total implication settled over her, covering her like a thick black cloud, she cried out in fury. She didn't want to have an abortion! She didn't want to have a baby! She wanted to be free of the whole messy business! Why had this happened to her? It wasn't right, it wasn't fair!

It was Rick's fault for getting her pregnant! It was her mother's fault, for not filling her in on the true facts of life, for not warning her against the inexorable power of sexual desire! It was her own fault, for being so gullible, so naive, so vulnerable, so stupid!

The day was cold and the waterfront was virtually deserted. Linda started to run again, a slow, determined jog, the steam of her anger distilling to droplets of grief. At last, exhausted, she climbed on a great boulder and sat, panting, looking at the pale sunlight on the water. Occasionally a wave rolled in, the swell starting far out and sweeping toward shore, unnoticed, until it lifted to become a crest of foam. It held itself motionless for one split second, transparent before the dying sun, then crashed with a roar into splintered prisms. In that moment of collapse Linda glimpsed the sinister, cold, black water hidden beneath the sheen. One could forget one's problems—and one's self—in that water. One could be sucked under by the riptide and carried out to sea.

Two small boys appeared and were now building a castle, scooping up shovelfuls of dripping sand, their shouts and laughter blending with the gulls' cries and the far-off helicopter's drone. Those boys, those sturdy, red-cheeked, exuberant little guys had once been babies, and that not too long ago. Linda was thinking, brooding, debating not about a clot, or a blob of mucus, but a baby! A baby was a person! A baby was a human being!

The realization crashed over her like one of the giant waves, crippling her with its impact. A boy baby would soon become a little boy, who would shout and laugh and build sand castles. Linda could feel the tension mounting inside her, but she couldn't check her train of thought. The boy would grow up, he would go to school, he would be good at sports, like Rick. He would look like Rick. He would have Rick's eyes, Rick's chin.

Rick! She hadn't considered Rick! She was deciding the fate of Rick's son! Surely Rick should have some say. Linda buried her face in her arms. She could still hear the laughter of the little boys.

On the other hand, the baby might be a girl, a girl Linda could take to dancing lessons . . .

Years before, when Linda's horse Soldier had broken his leg and the veterinarian had been forced to shoot him, Linda had blamed her parents. Now she saw she had been unfair. Basically she knew her parents revered life. They never tired of telling about how long they'd wanted to have a baby, how they'd almost given up hope, how it had been a miracle when Margaret became pregnant with Linda, a gift from God . . .

Yet here was that very Linda, now pregnant herself. Inside her, in minuscule form, existed a person, the next link in the never-ending chain of life, a human being. It was her own baby, hers and her beloved's . . . and she . . . she . . .

She was going to kill her baby.

The enormity of her decision settled upon her. The sun had set, the waves broke gray and cold.

Linda, who never cried, was sobbing. "I can't!" she moaned aloud, her voice breaking, tears running down her cheeks. The little boys had gone, the seagulls wheeled and squawked, nobody heard her, but it was a holy pledge of faith.

At last, still feeling nauseated but buoyed up by her determination, she clambered down from the rocks and walked back toward Jody Jordan's car.

TWENTY-THREE

It was one thing to decide against abortion—and, because Linda had been trained to be considerate, she telephoned the clinic early next morning and canceled her appointment. But it was another thing to decide what to do next. She considered—after not sleeping for twenty-four hours—the feasibility of bearing the child alone, a single woman. She had read that someone on the staff of *Ms.* magazine had done just that, and the child was always underfoot at the office, treated rather like a pet, an overbright German shepherd or a poodle, hardly ever getting in the way. Single movie stars had babies. A year or two ago the very idea had its shock value—a publicity man's dream—but now that idea was certainly acceptable—*I wanted a child but marriage is not in my plans*, the star had said. The telecast showed the actress, thin and sexy, departing on a transcontinental flight, accompanied by her retinue, her nursemaid holding the baby.

At the other end of the spectrum were the pitiful girls who were the subject of lectures in clinical sociology—the fifteen-year-old blacks and chicanos in the ghettos and barrios who (as the professor put it) became pregnant because they were too ignorant to use contraceptives. They had their babies because they were too unenlightened to seek an abortion; then they applied for welfare, and became, with their bastard children, a permanent drain on society. The professor never failed to point out that these illegitimate children would, in less than twenty years, be committing ninety per cent of the murders, rapes, and armed robberies of the Los Angeles area.

Brushing her hair, Linda frowned into the mirror. None of these categories seemed to apply to her. She was no drop-out of the ghetto. At the same time, she was no movie star nor magazine editor; in fact, because she had changed schools and changed majors, having a baby would mean she would fail to graduate. Even if she did graduate, the sociology majors who were getting their degrees were not being placed. They were applying for graduate school; everyone agreed that for a career in social work one needed an MA at the minimum.

Her mind skirted around the primary obstacle until she could avoid it no longer: her parents. Margaret and Robert Allenby would never countenance her having a child out of wedlock; her parents would never believe Linda could have become pregnant out of wedlock; her parents would never understand Linda having sex out of wedlock. Period.

There it was. Despite her passion for independence, she knew she loved her parents and could not intentionally cause them to grieve for the balance of their lifetime. Linda shivered slightly. It was not beyond the scope of possibility that hearing of such errant behavior on Linda's part could—directly or indirectly—actually kill her mother.

On the other hand, if she were married, having a baby would not plunge the Allenbys into social ostracism, but would be heralded as a joyous event.

Linda dressed thoughtfully. She might not be able to handle having the baby alone, but with Rick . . . together . . . She brightened at the prospect. Rick would make a wonderful father. After all, it was his baby as much as it was hers.

TWENTY-FOUR

When Linda had first been sick Rick had shrugged the matter off as inconsequential. He himself possessed a remarkable body, strong and vigorous, every muscle in prime condition because of constant exercise. His health included an immunity to most ailments; he never caught cold, never fell prey to sniffles or a sore throat. Yet because of his lifetime involvement in sports, Rick had weathered a long succession of bumps, bruises, abrasions and sprains. These he had learned to endure with a stoicism amounting to disdain. It was part of the macho tradition. It did no good to cry and complain about minor discomforts. You had to take your lumps, you had to grin and bear it, and after a while the hurt would go away.

When Linda's malaise did not disappear, and when in addition she became no longer loving and seductive, but snappish and cross, Rick began to worry. He was not seeing Linda as frequently as he had been, and now every time he did meet her she looked worse. She had become thin and drawn, and large, shadowy hollows appeared under her eyes.

What had caused the change? Linda wasn't well, that was obvious, and she wasn't herself; not the warm, sensual partner in love-making he had come to expect. Yet Linda wasn't sick, either—not really. Rick remembered his mother's battles with emphysema, and a cold dread clamped momentarily over his heart. Linda was in a lot better shape than his Mom had been, he told himself emphatically. Linda was fine. Linda would be better in no time.

Yet as the days ticked past and Linda was not better, but worse, Rick became more upset. He discounted the mono theory—Stu Jenks had had a month of a bad case of mono, and Linda didn't act the same way at all. Nevertheless, Rick had urged Linda to go to the health center.

Ultimately, it was Linda's boobs, in which Rick took a fierce proprietary interest, and which had now swollen to the size of cantaloupes, which tipped Rick off. He had knocked her up. His girlfriend was pregnant.

Startling as this deduction was, Rick accepted it with his usual stoicism. From the time he had been a junior in high school, one or another of his teammates had a girl in trouble—it was one of the commonest subjects of conversation in the locker room. As Rick and everyone else knew, when such a mishap occurred, there were two ways to go—marriage or abortion, and of these, abortion was the only sensible choice. Over the past six years, Rick's friends who had been sucked into marriage had bitterly regretted it. Without exception, every such marriage had ended up in divorce, preceded by hassles, quarreling, and legal red tape, and the ex-husband was left saddled with a court order to pay child support for eighteen years, a harsh and unfair penalty for an innocuous little romp in the hay. Abortion, on the other hand, was quick and easy, and now legal. The parties involved had made a mistake, but so what? Abortion gave them a chance to wipe the slate clean. It was as simple as that.

Several times Rick was on the point of voicing his suspicions to Linda, and then thought better of it. If she was pregnant, he'd know soon enough, and if not, if he was mistaken, why get her all upset? No use in rocking the boat. Besides, Rick had other, greater worries. For as long as he could remember he had geared his life-style, awake or asleep, with one ultimate goal in mind, that after his four years in college, he would play pro football. Now the draft selections were announced, and to Rick's disbelief and horror, he didn't make a team, any team. Only Darter Evans was chosen, for the Chicago Bears.

Rick tried to mask his disappointment and not let anyone know how much he really cared, but it ticked him off that Linda hardly accorded the matter a passing comment. It was not that she was trying to spare his feelings—that was what galled worst of all. Oh no! Linda was too wrapped up in herself to have any awareness of what was happening to Rick.

TWENTY-FIVE

On the day following Linda's pilgrimage to the beach, she wandered over to the field where the B squad was working out. Rick was in the thick of things, demonstrating shoulder blocks, urging, criticizing, praising, all in hoarse, one-syllable shouts. Linda sat on the wooden bleachers in the sun. She felt as wretched as ever, but now that she had made the decision, now that, in effect, there was a reason for her nausea, it seemed slightly more supportable. The sun soaked through her shirt and jeans, giving her sustenance and comfort. For the first time in weeks things seemed to be looking up.

At eleven Rick dismissed the squad and came over to her. He was sweaty and panting.

"Howdy!"

"Hi!"

He sat down on the bench below her.

"Feeling better?"

"Some."

"See. I knew it wasn't mono."

"It's not mono. I found out what it is. It's something else."

"Oh yeah?" He slapped at a fly. "Whatcha got—the bubonic plague?"

"I'm pregnant."

She looked at him closely. She realized that since she herself had heard the news she had been waiting for this instant, to see how Rick would take it. Now, to her disappointment, he wasn't taking it any way at all.

"Kinda thought you might be."

"You did! Why didn't you say something?"

"Didn't see how you could be—not when you were taking the pill."

"You're supposed to take the pill for a whole month in

advance," said Linda in a small voice. "Before you start doing anything. I just found out."

Rick's eyes wandered over the football field.

"Those lunkheads can't get the concept of cutting off the Double T," he said.

Linda tried to think of a sugar-coated way to phrase her mission, but she could not, so she blurted it out.

"I think we ought to get married."

Rick looked up at her, his eyes squinting against the sun. His face was a kaleidoscope of conflicting emotions—surprise, interest, dismay, fear.

"Why do you think that?"

"Well, you know," Linda forced brightness, "get married, have baby, live happily ever after . . ."

"Only it doesn't work out that way."

"What do you mean?"

"You know it. I know it."

"It'd be different with us. We love each other."

"Now. We wouldn't later on."

Linda took a breath and prayed for patience. Why was Rick being perverse? It had been a wrench to capture her own spirit, the wild, free Linda, poised, wings spread, about to take flight into the great adventure of life. It had been onerous, even in her mind, to thrust herself, pinioned, into the confining strictures of marriage. But Linda had not anticipated running into difficulty with Rick. Rick usually was amenable to everything she suggested. What was the matter with him? She hated being in the position of coaxing, pleading with him, of all things, to marry her! What had gone wrong? He should be begging her for her hand in marriage. That was the way things were supposed to be done.

She raised her eyes, playing the coquette, though she was becoming very mad very fast.

"I'd like to be married to you. I love you."

Rick looked unhappy.

"I love you, too. But hell, Linda, you know marriage isn't for us. We've discussed it. Marriage is on the skids. I've heard you say that a dozen times. As a way of life, it's over."

Linda cursed her own outspokenness, her phrases, so

glibly borrowed from the movement, returning to haunt her.

"Lots of people—"

"Lots of people louse up their lives and end up in the divorce courts."

"We wouldn't."

"We've got a good thing going the way it is. Let's keep it that way."

"Rick, there's no reason why we can't approach this in an honest, adult—"

"All right. If we're being honest, I don't want the responsibility. I don't want to be tied down. You ought to understand that. You're the one who's always yakking about freedom."

Wrath bubbled up inside Linda like boiling candy. She struggled for composure. She couldn't blow the whole thing. They couldn't have a fight, not now. Yet even as she tried to curb her temper, Linda was struck by the intrinsic injustice of the whole rotten situation. She, Linda, couldn't afford to tell Rick to go to the devil, as she felt like doing. Oh no, she was forced to grovel, to plead, to beg, to debase herself, anything to get him to marry her—and all because the fetus was growing inside her, and not him! It was so unfair!

"You're overlooking one little thing." She tried to make her voice pleasant, tried to take out the hurt, the need to strike back. "We're going to have a baby."

"You're going to have a baby."

"We are. It's your baby as much as it is mine."

At this last statement Rick became so agitated he sprang to his feet and paced up and down on the gravel in front of the bleachers. At last he flung himself on the bottom bench and looked up at her, his eyes squinting again.

"What about an abortion?" His voice was rough.

Linda bit her lip. She had hoped, somehow, that Rick would be above that, that Rick would never suggest, never consider abortion for an instant. Yet she had no right to feel holier than he. She, Linda, had actually made an appointment!

"I've . . . I've thought about it," she confessed.

"You better think about it some more," Rick said brusquely, "because that's the way it's going to be."

Linda felt herself on the verge of panic. In another second they would actually be fighting—when it was crucial they remain friends, crucial that Rick go along with her plan. She was desperate. Every other avenue of escape was blocked. For her, marriage was the only conceivable way out.

"What do you have against marriage?" Linda asked in a little voice.

Rick snorted.

"For openers, it doesn't work. Every guy I know who got married is now divorced."

"But . . ."

"Including my folks. My old man split—left my mom."

"Rick, that isn't the way it'd be—not with us! We *love* each other!"

"Listen, you chain two people together by force, they end up hating each other."

"Not us!"

"We wouldn't be any different. Look what's happening—we're quarreling right now!"

"I'm not—" Linda began. She could feel her lip tremble. "I love you," she insisted again, her voice breaking.

"And I don't want to be pushed!" shouted Rick.

"But—" She got no further. Suddenly, actuated by the impossibility of her situation, her eyes flooded with tears. She started to cry uncontrollably. "But I—I can't have an abortion!" she sobbed. "It's your baby! It's our baby! I can't kill our baby!"

Then the miracle happened. A softness crept over Rick's rugged face, a tenderness. In an instant he was beside her, enfolding her in his great strong arms, holding her close, comforting her.

"Honey, don't cry," Rick said, his voice low but no longer gruff. "Linda, honey, don't—don't cry!"

He kissed her gently, brushing her forehead with his lips, dozens of fragile butterfly kisses. Linda tried to stifle her sobs but they kept coming. After a while she managed to sandwich in a few words.

"I—can I have the baby?"

Rick tightened his arms about her till it hurt.

"You can, if that's the way you feel. Only don't cry!"

Her head was against his chest. She couldn't stop sniffling.

"We'll . . . get married?"

The reassuring pressure of his arms around her didn't slacken, but it was a while before he spoke.

"Yes," Rick said slowly, "we'll get married, too, if you have to have it that way."

That night in the men's dorm, after Kemp was asleep and snoring, Rick tried to think. He tried to remember back to early fall, when he was freaked out over Linda and Linda wouldn't give him the time of day. Damn it, he was still crazy about Linda! But marriage! He groaned aloud. What had he let himself in for? He had no money, no job prospects. His scholarship would end in June, but he'd be twelve units short. He wouldn't graduate. He'd have a tough time making it on his own, let alone trying to support a wife and baby! Rick rolled over, twisting the sheet into a rope. Baby! Admit it. He was scared of babies —Big Rick the scourge of the SC line—scared! What did you do with them? How did you keep them from crying? He knew nothing about babies, but already he resented the formless, nebulous creature who was coming to blight his life. Again he tossed. Wife, baby, responsibility—the words rolled around in his head. It was a nightmare, and he was wide awake.

TWENTY-SIX

Margaret and Robert Allenby were on the patio when the van pulled in to the drive, its motor tapping an erratic rhythm reminiscent of old-time telegraphy. Margaret, who was transplanting petunias from a flat into glazed pots, peered through the grillwork which shielded the patio from the front yard.

"Robert," she said nervously, "come here."

Robert, returned from an early eighteen holes at Fernleaf with his Saturday foursome, was sprawled on the lounge, drinking a beer and reading the sports section of the *Times*.

"What's the matter?"

"The oddest looking vehicle just drove in . . . sort of a delivery van, covered with flames."

"It's on fire?"

"Painted. In the front it has a face, with teeth."

Robert came to look over her shoulder.

"Some kind of hippie outfit."

"Maybe they're peddling something."

"More likely they're casing the place. Ring the doorbell, and then if nobody's home, they hit."

"It has a bumper sticker . . ." Margaret's voice was puzzled. "*National Sex Week. Don't Let Your Meat Loaf?*"

Robert started for the gate.

"I'll tell them to clear out."

"Wait . . ." Margaret's tone was incredulous. "It's Linda!"

In another moment Linda burst into the patio.

"Mother! Daddy!"

She threw her arms around her parents, kissing them. A spate of conversation erupted, everyone talking at once to ease the tension, the surprise: Can't believe it . . . had the urge to . . . thought you'd forgotten . . . here I am, though . . . haven't been home for . . . big as life . . . look so peaked . . .

Linda broke away, ran to where Rick lagged by the gate, grabbed his hand and jerked him forward.

"Mother, Dad, I want you to meet a friend of mine, Rick Dublin."

Her words produced a cataclysmic effect on her parents, as if she had thrown a switch, creating powerful magnetic fields beneath the patio, both positive and negative.

Margaret was the first to recover. She took off her gardening gloves, finger by finger, and extended a hand.

"Rick! It's a pleasure to meet you."

Robert hurried forward, pumped Rick's hand vigorously.

"Rick Dublin! This is an honor! Margaret, do you realize who this is?"

Margaret looked nonplused.

"No, I . . . should I?"

"This is Big Rick Dublin. He's famous!"

Margaret smiled, but was still puzzled.

"A football player! All Pac-8 tackle for the Bruins!"

"Honorable mention," corrected Rick.

"That's wonderful!" Margaret exclaimed. "I didn't know Linda liked football!"

"Oh, I do," said Linda, too quickly. "I do!"

"Please sit down!" Everyone found a seat. Margaret spied her husband's beer can on the flagstone and jumped up again. "Maybe the young man would like a—" She started forward.

"No, Mother," said Linda "don't both—I mean, I can get him one later."

"No trouble," said Margaret, hurrying to the kitchen. She returned with a beer and two glasses of Fresca. "I like football, too," she told Rick in a confidential manner, when the drinks were distributed and she had again settled to the rim of her chair. "All the cheering, and the chrysanthemums."

"Pardon?" said Rick.

"The chrysanthemums," said Margaret.

Linda looked nervous.

"Chrysanthemums have nothing to do with the game," said Robert.

"I realize that," said Margaret, offended. She turned to Rick. "What position do you play? Are you a kicker?"

"I was on the defensive line," said Rick.

"Defensive, offensive, it's all so confusing."

"It's not confusing in the least," said Robert. "The team which has the ball is on the offensive, so they send in their offensive team, while the team which doesn't have the ball is on the defensive, so they send in their defensive team."

"But I should think the team which has the ball would try to keep it."

"They do."

"So why wouldn't they be on the defensive?"

"Really, Margaret, for a college graduate . . ."

"Anyway," said Margaret, "I enjoy the card stunts."

"You'd enjoy the game, too," said Robert, "if you'd take the trouble to learn a few basic principles." He turned his attention back to Rick. "As I recall, this is your senior year."

"That's right."

"I can't remember . . . are you going into the pros?"

Rick squirmed slightly.

"No sir. I'm afraid I didn't make the grade."

"That's too bad."

"Yeah," said Rick, "that's the way the old cookie crumbles. Only one guy made it this year. We were hoping to do better."

"Let's see," said Robert, "I was trying to think who it was. Darter Evans?"

"Yeah. Darter got picked up by the Bears."

"It's his van we're borrowing," said Linda.

"Thank goodness!" said Margaret. "I'm glad it's not yours!"

"If you're not going into the pros," pursued Robert, "what are you going into?"

Rick looked uncomfortable.

"I haven't given it a lot of thought, sir. Some of us who didn't make it, we'd been scouted, and I guess we kind of took it for granted."

"Too bad," agreed Robert. "I can see that would leave you in a bind after graduation."

"I won't be graduating," said Rick.

"That so?" said Robert.

The conversation came to a dead silence.

"It's such a pleasant surprise," said Margaret, starting it up again, as if she were cranking a Model T Ford, "to have Linda bring a friend home."

"It's a surprise to have Linda come home," said Robert.

"Now, Daddy . . ." said Linda.

"First time we've seen you since Christmas, and you're not fifteen minutes away."

"You don't understand," said Linda. "I've been carrying eighteen units. I've had to study."

"Seems to me you could take the time to look in on your parents once in a while."

Linda went over and sat on the edge of Robert's lounge. She kissed him lightly on his receding hairline.

"I'm here," she pointed out. "Okay?" She looked from Robert to Margaret, and back to Robert, then took a deep breath. "In fact, the reason Rick and I are here, is to tell you something exciting." She returned to stand beside Rick, her hand on his shoulder. "We . . . we're going to get married."

She might have screamed fire! She might have drawn a gun, she might have thrown herself on the flagstones and kicked her heels in a fit. Nothing would have produced the same shock. Her parents looked at her; her father's eyes protruding slightly, like those of a fish, her mother's darting from Linda, to Rick, to Linda, to Rick again, then back to Linda, penetrating and probing Linda's very soul.

"Why . . . why, that is news," Margaret said at last. "Isn't it, Daddy?"

"It certainly is," said Robert. He swung his feet to the patio and stood, militarily erect. "When did you decide?"

"We . . . ah . . . Wednesday, as a matter of fact," said Linda. "It was Wednesday, wasn't it, Rick? Or was it Thursday?"

"I can't remember," said Rick. "One of those days." His expression was that of a trapped animal.

"Sort of a hasty decision, wasn't it?" said Robert.

"No," said Linda. "It wasn't. Not at all."

"All your father means," said Margaret, trying to smooth things over, "is that marriage is an important step."

"Mother, we know that."

"It's not something to rush into," said Robert.

"We're not rushing," said Linda.

Rick's skin had taken on the color of an unbaked pie crust.

Margaret made a valiant effort and forced a smile in Rick's direction.

"What he means is, your father and I are just starting to get acquainted with this very fine young man."

"Take my word for it, you'll love him!" said Linda. She held Rick's hand and looked up at him proudly. "Besides, you're not marrying him. I am."

"Seems to me Rick's been awfully quiet through all of this," said Robert. "How about it, Rick? Are you as dead set on getting married as she is?"

Rick looked as if he'd been tossed a pitch-out he wasn't expecting. He juggled the ball, knowing he was supposed to run.

"We thought we'd give it a try," he said.

"I hope you'll give it a lot more than that!" said Robert. "Marriage is a serious business. What do you plan to live on? Do you have a job?"

"Of course he has a job!" said Linda. "What a thing to say!"

"Now dear," said Margaret, "your father's only trying to be practical."

"Besides," went on Linda, "we believe marriage should be a fifty-fifty proposition. Rick will work and I'll work, too."

"That's highly commendable, daughter," said Robert. He sounded as if he were chairing a board of directors meeting. "Does the university place all its graduates?"

"I've been meaning to tell you, daddy," said Linda. "I won't exactly be a graduate, either. What with transferring from Mills, and changing my major . . ."

"I knew it was a mistake!" Margaret burst out. "I tried to tell you . . ."

"What about all those extra credits?" demanded Robert.

"I call that pretty slip-shod counseling," said Margaret. "If you graduate from Mills, I told you . . ."

Linda cut in, frantic.

"That has nothing to do with the real issue! I thought

you'd be pleased! You're always saying you wish I'd come home. Then when I do come home, to tell you I'm going to be married . . ."

"Darling," said Margaret, "we are pleased, aren't we, dear?"

"Pleased as punch." Robert seemed nervous, without conviction. "You caught us off guard, as you say in football." He forced a laugh. Rick managed a sickly smile.

Margaret took Linda in her arms and kissed her.

"My little girl!" She stood on tiptoes and kissed Rick. "My new son! I hope you'll be happy."

"Daddy," prodded Linda, "are you going to give us your blessing?"

Robert became activated, like a robot once its current is turned on. He kissed Linda on the forehead.

"Of course. You took us by surprise, that's all." He shook Rick's hand. "Congratulations. It isn't every day we welcome a football star into the family!"

Robert insisted on opening a bottle of champagne to celebrate.

"I can't believe it," said Margaret, settling into one of the patio chairs. "I'm still in a daze!"

"If you're in a daze," said Linda, "think how I feel!"

Rick tossed off his champagne in one gulp.

"Think how Rick feels," said Robert.

Everyone laughed, and Robert refilled the glasses.

"It's what I've dreamed of," Margaret told Linda, "since you were a baby."

"What do you mean?"

"The day you'd be married, in a white satin gown, coming down the aisle on the arm of your father."

"Mother, don't cry."

"I'm crying because I'm so happy. It will be so beautiful!"

'Mother, we didn't plan on having a big . . .'

"It doesn't have to be big," said Margaret in all reasonableness. "But you know you couldn't be married anywhere but at St. Mark's, where you were christened." She disappeared into the house and reappeared with a calendar. "What about June? A June wedding. School will be out."

"No, said Linda hoarsely. "We don't want to wait. We want to get married now."

"Well, then, April twenty-first. That's a Saturday."

"That's over a month away!"

"We couldn't do it a day sooner! Getting the invitations engraved and in the mail . . ."

"Mother, I'm telling you, if we're not having a big wedding we don't need invitations."

"Dear," said her mother patiently, as if Linda were six, and she was explaining the multiplication table, "there are certain people in this town who would never forgive us if they weren't invited to your wedding. Never!"

"Mother . . ." protested Linda, as if she were protesting the tide, the wind, the rain. She glanced covertly at Rick. He looked as if he were about to throw up.

"You'll have to choose your china pattern," said Margaret.

Linda moaned.

"I also have to study."

"That's all right." Margaret's voice was soothing. "I know your taste. You can leave everything to me . . . except picking out the dress. You'll have to be fitted for that."

"Mother, will you listen to me?"

"I wonder if we can get Fernleaf for the reception?"

"The country club?"

"We'd better call them this minute," said Robert.

"That's just what we didn't want . . . a lot of fanfare and publicity!"

"There won't be!" Margaret assured her. "A wedding can be starkly simple . . ."

Linda heard Rick mutter "Storkly simple?" under his breath.

". . . yet in exquisite taste. Sometimes the simplest affairs are the most elegant."

Rick strode to the patio table, poured himself a third glass of champagne, and tossed it off in one draught.

"How many bridesmaids will you have?" Margaret was asking Linda.

"Bridesmaids?" said Linda, wanly.

"Of course. And Rick has to pick the ushers. Whom will he have for best man?"

TWENTY-SEVEN

Once the four of them had sealed the pact with champagne, it was as if they had strapped themselves in one of the gondolas on the Matterhorn track at Disneyland; the machinery activated, there could be no indecision, no stepping off; they were irrevocably committed to a perilous ride fraught with stress at every screeching turn. As the pressure intensified through the month, Linda found herself mentally hanging on for dear life, her eyes closed, her lips compressed, praying for the strength to last out the engagement.

The first casualty was her privacy. Margaret insisted Linda install a phone. The phone rang at any hour, sometimes in the middle of lovemaking.

"Let it ring."

"It's mother."

"I know it's your mother, that's why I said let it ring."

"Then she'll worry about my being out this late and keep calling . . ."

"Oh, shit!"

"Mother? No, I wasn't doing anything."

"The hell you weren't!" Rick was pulling on his pants.

"No, I haven't had time. I'll ask them for sure tomorrow. No, I don't want Cissy Leighton!" She put her hand over the phone and mouthed, "Don't go!" but Rick was tying his shoes. "No, I know Rick has to decide. Probably a best man and two ushers." Rick scowled. He picked up his jacket. "Why won't that be enough? I thought we were going to keep things simple."

"I know one thing," growled Rick as he stalked out the door, "we're not having any goddammed telephone after we're married!"

The choice of—the necessity for—a best man and ushers were the first of many contested points which were bounced from Margaret to Linda to Rick and back to

Linda like a game of hot potato, with Linda always in the middle, getting burned, taking the gaff from both sides.

After what he considered a lot of uncalled-for hassle, Rick psyched himself to ask Kemp, Darter, and Stu Jenks to be best man and ushers respectively. Their reaction was more devastating than he had feared.

"She gotcha!" marveled Kemp. The four had finished two sets of doubles, and Kemp, though short of breath, managed to convey pity and shock at Rick's gullibility. "Lassoed and hogtied, huh, pardner?"

Rick, already overheated from the tennis, reminded himself he had to keep his cool.

"What happened to your, quote, great little set-up, close quote?" said Stu.

"That was it, he got set up!" said Kemp.

"No, man," said Darter. "This here's not something to fun around with, nohow." He clapped a hand on Rick's shoulder. "I want to know, man, is this marriage bit something you want, or is it something she wants?"

"Why ah . . ."

"I want to be sure my old buddy isn't being taken for a ride."

"He was!" guffawed Kemp. "That's the rub!"

"The rub!" guffawed Stu.

"I gotta know you aren't being conned into something, cause iffen you are, they got to answer to old Darter!" Darter assumed the stance of a fighter, sparring and jabbing at an imaginary opponent.

"I thought you wanted to be a single swinger," Stu said plaintively. "You told me one time you never were going to be tied down."

"Yeah, man," said Darter. "You-all wuz the one always saying as how you wuz going to be your own man!"

"Yeah, pardner," said Kemp, "you stay single, you got free rein to play the field."

"I don't want to play the field," Rick said stiffly. The more they laid it on, the more mortified he felt.

"Variety is the spice of life!" Stu said piously. He took a practice swing with his racquet.

"Yeah!" said Kemp. "You haven't tried it, don't knock it."

Rick found the whole conversation distasteful. He wished he'd never started it.

"Look, you meatheads," he said irritably, "I asked you a simple question. I'd appreciate a simple answer, yes or no."

"Sure, old buddy," said Kemp. "You want help to put your head in the noose, you got it."

"You want my opinion," said Stu, "you're being taken."

"I do not want your opinion!" Rick snapped.

"Point of information!" Darter had turned and was walking backward, facing them, twirling his racquet between his fingertips. "Why not keep on the way you been going? Man, I thought you had it made. Beautiful lady, all yours, putting it out . . ."

"Yeah, man!" said Stu. "I should think you'd want to continue, like, with the status quo."

"I do," said Rick before he thought, "but Linda . . ."

"You know, pardner," said Kemp, "that's the way I had it figured all along."

"You know," said Rick, "you can keep your damn mouth shut!"

"You want my opinion," offered Stu, in that same plaintive voice, "you're making a king size mistake."

"Yeah," drawled Kemp, "king size."

"No, I do not want your opinion!" blazed Rick. "You can go to hell, all of you!" He turned and strode away in a huff.

"Hey, man," complained Stu. "I thought we were going to play another set!"

The last words Rick heard were from Darter.

"Man," Darter said fervently, "I just hope you won't be sorry!"

Linda asked Delcie to be maid of honor. At first she had feared the prospect of anybody's marriage might again plunge down the shaft of depression, but she need not have worried. When Delcie learned M. Kemper Conway would stand opposite her in the role of best man, Delce went into orbit.

"It's not that big a deal," cautioned Linda, but Delcie was all smiles.

"I'll see him!" she gurgled. "I'll talk to him! I'll walk down the aisle with him, holding his elbow!" She flung her arms around Linda. "Oh, thank you, thank you for being my true friend!"

"Nothing's going to come of it!" Linda warned testily.

She made no impression. Delcie took heart. Delcie wanted to live. Delcie began to blossom like a rosebud in a hot house. She sang in the shower. She beamed on humanity. One would have thought Delcie was the bride to be, not Linda.

Linda wondered at her own attitude. Why wasn't she happy, as happy as Delcie had suddenly become? There was no doubt in Linda's mind that her love for Rick was more sincere—she hated the word—than Delcie's adolescent crush for Kemp. Linda believed—though she mistrusted abstractions—in Rick's affection for her. Why, then, why was she not wild with joy?

Linda's mother suggested she invite some of her former classmates from Marlborough to be bridesmaids, but Linda demurred. She hadn't seen those girls for years; they would have nothing in common. At last, torn by misgivings, she determined to ask Sadie and Agnes, who, next to Delce, were her closest friends. She underestimated Sadie's response.

"Now hear this!" Sadie proclaimed to the assemblage of the movement Friday night. "Linda Allenby is to be married!" There was no mistaking Sadie's inflection. Linda Allenby is to be jailed, to be hung, to be drawn and quartered.

A buzz of conversation erupted. Linda Gibson? No, Allenby. No kidding! Linda's cheeks burned.

"She has invited some of us," Sadie continued, her voice sonorous, "to participate in the ceremony . . ."

"I want all the rest of you to come," put in Linda hastily. "You'll all receive invitations."

"But before," intoned Sadie, "before we give Linda our blessing, we are duty bound, in honesty, to warn . . ."

Several of the timid stirred uneasily. Delce shot Linda a look, half encouragement, half apprehension.

"She should know, if she does not already know, that marriage as a viable convention is passé. Marriage is out. Kaput!" Sadie drew her finger across her throat. "Marriage is dead!"

"Not quite," quavered Delce.

Jody jumped into the fray. "Gloria Steinem says marriage was invented by men to keep women in chains."

"You know how it came about, don't you?" added Rhoda. "When the cave man got the connection between sex and kids, he shut up his woman so nobody else could ball her!"

"All men," said Jody, "are MCP's."

"They take you," said Aggie, "they use you, they throw you away."

"Sex," pontificated Sadie, "is no justification for prostituting yourself to slavery."

"You want to be able to drop them," said Carol. "If you get the urge, you want to be able to play the field!"

Linda's face flamed. She had heard these shibboleths a thousand times; still each one hit home.

"So why, if you'll excuse my curiosity," Sadie masked rapacity with politeness, "why are you voluntarily selling yourself into bondage?"

"She loves him!" insisted Delce, breathily. "He loves her . . ."

Sadie paid no more attention to Delce than she would have paid to a mosquito. "That's no reason!" Sadie said, "not for an intelligent girl like you, unless . . ." She clapped her hand over her mouth. "My God!" she screamed. "You're pregnant!"

The shock of having her carefully guarded secret broadcast in public was too much for Linda. She felt hot, she felt cold, she feared she would faint. Her agitation betrayed her.

"It's true!" Sadie's voice vibrated in reproach. "How could you? How could you be so stupid!"

Linda was tongue-tied. The situation was insupportable, humiliating beyond belief! Before she could marshal her thoughts a dozen girls were shouting in cacophony: You don't need to! Did I ever tell you— Have an abortion . . . Control of her body! What I'd do . . . The movement! My sister went to a neat-o doctor . . . The movement means . . . He used a suction cup . . . But what if she wants to . . . Linda, I can get you his number . . . Some people have a hang-up . . . just tell him a friend . . . Why don't you all shut up? . . . nothing to it . . . none of our God damn business . . . If you want that number . . . Even if she went ahead . . . only bad the first day . . . why get married? You mean adoption . . . Some people have strong feelings . . . If she felt that strong, she might as well hang in there . . . I vote for abortion . . . She couldn't be too far along, look how thin she is . . . If she kept it . . . zero population growth, the ecology, and all that . . . she wouldn't have to get married . . . no, but for the sake of argument . . . that's the in thing now-a-days. Look at all the movie stars . . . think about the stigma . . . don't be medieval . . . hypocritical . . . morals . . . no such thing as bastard . . .

Her head reeling, Linda tried to rise from her seat on the carpet. Her knees felt rubbery and refused to support her weight. Aggie Jackson reached for her hand.

"What d'you mean, they ain't no more bastards!" Aggie yelled in her vibrant contralto. It might have been a scene from *Porgy and Bess*. The tumult died. "You're all bastards, for my money. Hain't you got no feelings whatsoever?" She put an arm around Linda, giving her support. "Honey, you come out to the kitchen. I'm going to boil you a nice cup of tea. Don't pay attention to what nobody says. They all love you, every last one of 'em—only they got a funny way of showing it. You want to have your kid, that's great. You want to get married, that's great. I for one feel honored to think you'd ask me to be yo' bridesmaid . . ." She turned to glare at Sadie. Sadie sputtered.

"An archaic, meaningless custom—"

". . . and I accept with pleasure!" Aggie's tone was firm. "However, whether you still want Sadie, that's another kettle of fish!"

Linda hesitated, unnerved. Sadie's face was a mix of hauteur and wrath, but for a moment Linda thought she glimpsed a haunting sadness in Sadie's eyes. She had a flash recollection of a new girl at school who begged to be invited to Linda's eighth birthday party.

"I do want Sadie," Linda heard herself say. The little girl looking out of Sadie's eyes seemed relieved. "I want you all to come!" It was the height of absurdity, insisting, after what they'd said. She visualized the sandaled feet and granny skirts among the evening clothes and mink, but what else could she do? In spite of everything, she thought with sinking heart, she needed some friends there. It was her wedding, wasn't it?

TWENTY-EIGHT

In spite of her mother's promise that Linda could "leave everything to her," Margaret Allenby consulted Linda about every decision—invitations, minister, soloist, flowers, bridesmaids' dresses, champagne, menu, cake, orchestra; the pattern for the china, the sterling, and the gown, a Cahil from Magnin's. The gown was breathtaking, peau de soie with a high, demure neckline, long close-fitting sleeves, and an eight-foot train encrusted in seed pearls and bugle beads. It fitted Linda like a dream, but she had nightmares of not being able to zip it up on her wedding day. She lived in constant terror lest her parents should find out she was pregnant. The debilitating nausea never let up. Linda was thin as a rail, save for her enormous breasts.

"You're studying too much," her mother complained on one of their shopping trips. "You're skin and bone."

"Mother, will you get off my back?" Margaret swung the Mark IV off Wilshire into Robinson's parking lot. "Where are we going now?"

"I want to show you some new headpieces for the bridesmaids—they just got them in."

Linda moaned.

"Can't you do it on the way back? I'm beat."

"It will only take a minute to look."

"Why don't you decide," said Linda, petulantly. "It's your show anyhow."

She was remorseful the moment the words were out. A hurt look crossed her mother's face. Linda looked closely at her, seeing her for the first time in years. Despite the nurture of expensive creams, Margaret's once flawless skin had been invaded by a network of fine lines. Linda did not recall those grayish circles under her mother's eyes. How old was Margaret, anyway? Linda calculated quickly.

Forty-nine! Linda caught her breath. Impulsively, she threw her arms about Margaret and kissed her cheek.

"I'm sorry, Mother."

Margaret's eyes were brimming with tears.

"I've been working so hard!"

"I know you have."

"I've been under such a strain! I've been running on nervous energy."

"Mother, you have been fantastic."

"I've been taking pills—pep pills, tranquilizers, anything to keep me going."

"Mother, you're the one who has to be careful!"

"I do so want your wedding to be nice."

"It will be, Mother. It will be! It couldn't be more perfect!"

"I'm doing it all for you . . ."

"I know, dear. I know you . . ."

". . . and you don't even . . ."

"I do, Mother! I'm sorry! I don't know why I said that. I didn't mean it! I appreciate it, everything, really I do!"

Linda tried to involve Rick, to make him feel part of the wedding preparations, with zero success. Rick was no more interested in the bridesmaids' nosegays or the number of tiers on the cake then he would have been in the migration habits of Mongolian yaks. Besides, their relationship had entered a new and disturbing phase. Now that the female was impregnated, Mother Nature turned down the voltage of desire. Linda no longer cared much about sex; she was irritable and jumpy, and had developed sore, sensitive areas. Unfortunately Mother Nature forgot to clue the male in on this development. The more Linda put Rick off, the more insatiable he became.

"But I don't feel like—"

"You feel all right to me!" He ran his hand over her breast. "Come on, baby. You know I love you!"

"Love ought to be something besides sex!" Linda protested. "It ought to be—consideration—and affection!"

"Damn you, I try to be affectionate. You shut me off."

"That's not what I call affectionate. You don't care about my needs. You bulldoze in . . ."

"Talk about needs! You think I can turn off because you've suddenly got cold feet? I've done everything you've asked—gone along with you having the baby, gave in to your demand to get married . . ."

"My demand!"

"If I'm doing all this for you I damn well ought to get something out of it!"

"I told you, I don't have time. Mother's picking me up in ten minutes."

"You mean you're going shopping again? Tonight? When five minutes ago you told me you were too tired . . ."

"I am tired! I resent your attitude!"

"You don't have the strength to pass the time of day with me, yet when your mother . . ."

"You're overlooking one small thing. My mother also happens to be expending a lot of strength, and energy, and time, and money . . ."

Rick was unmoved.

"So?"

"So, she's doing it all for us."

"Are you kidding? She's doing it for herself."

"What a gross thing to say! That is cruel and uncalled for!"

"It's the truth. This is the biggest production of your mother's life. It's the Academy Awards and the Rose Parade rolled into one."

"Will you make the effort to have a modicum of understanding? I'm all they have, daddy and mother. I'm all they could have. You can't blame them if their lives are wound up in me."

"You said yourself you wanted to get out from under."

"I did. I do. But it won't hurt to go along with this one teeny thing. There's only going to be one wedding."

"Thank God for that!"

"It's a once-in-a-lifetime situation, and when it means so much to mother . . ."

"That's what I'm trying to tell you. It means so much to your mother, right?"

"Right."

"It's so important that we have this cockamamie spectacle, right?"

"Right."

"Why? Is it for us? When we could have gone to Vegas and had the whole thing wrapped up in an hour? It's not for us, it's for them, your mother and your father. It's saying to their friends, all those special people who would never forgive your mother if she didn't invite them, all those important business cats, look, here we are, the Allenbys, our beautiful daughter's getting married, and everything's out of sight!"

Linda looked at Rick as if he were a stranger.

"What exactly is so bad about that?" she said coldly. "Not that I'm beautiful, but the rest of it? I mean, everyone has his thing. Mother and Daddy have their life-style. It may seem medieval to you and I myself don't go for it, but I'm trying to respect it. With them, tradition is very big." Rick didn't speak. "And since that's the whole ball of wax, as far as they're concerned, I can't see how it will hurt us to go along with them for one little month, half of which already is over . . ."

"A month!" snorted Rick. "You're too blind to see what's happening. It isn't a month, it's going to be for life. They're not about to give you up, and I—I'm not about to give you up, and . . . and . . ."

"What?"

". . . they're not about to accept me, and . . ."

Linda was flabbergasted. "That's nonsense!"

Rick shook his head. "That's the vibes I get. Not your dad so much—he likes football—but your mom!"

Linda was agitated beyond measure. "That's not true!" she said fiercely. "You have to try to understand mother. She's had so much on her mind, with the wedding, she hasn't had time to . . ."

"With the wedding," Rick repeated. "I have the feeling she tolerates me, because for a wedding you have to have a groom, even if he is a figurehead. Down underneath . . ."

"That isn't so!"

". . . she doesn't really think I'm quite good enough . . ."

"Rick!" Linda's heart was breaking. She threw her arms around him, drew him to her, covered him with kisses on his cheeks, his chin, and his mouth. "You're the most wonderful, the finest, the sweetest, dearest, sexiest . . . You're too good, that's what you are, too good!" She kissed him again. "I love you," she told him, over and over. After a while, when she thought he was beginning to snap out of it, when she thought the insidious misapprehension had dissipated, she released him. "Wait and see," she counseled, looking into his eyes. "Wait till you actually come to know mother. You'll love her as much as I do."

But Rick didn't appear to be convinced.

TWENTY-NINE

The lichened stone walls, stained glass windows, and crenelated towers of St. Mark's belonged not in San Marino, California, on an April evening in the nineteen seventies, but to Bath or Canterbury in the fifteen hundreds. Inside, the shadowy vastness of the vaulted transept heightened the illusion of another time, steeped in tradition and changeless values.

The polished wooden pews were tightly packed with guests decked in a variety of finery. Most of the women, mature in years but slender, coifed, and lacquered, blossomed in flowered chiffon or pastel lace topped by full-length mink. Their escorts in white dinner jackets, bronzed, flat-tummied from rigorous tennis, exuded a Fred Astaire suaveness, smug yet debonair. In contrast, those people who had actually lived less than twenty-two years affected long dark calico dresses or faded denim—clothes their great-great-grandparents might have worn to cross the plains.

A hushed aura of anticipation permeated the chapel, mingling scents, sights, and sounds. French perfume and the fragrance of fresh flowers, quivering, overlapping shadow-silhouettes cast from a hundred candle flames; the intricate counterpoint of a Bach fugue played by a musician at the great organ, the subtle undercurrent of whisperings. Suddenly, as if prearranged, all comments ceased, all eyes turned toward the rear. The mother of the bride appeared, escorted by Darter Evans, the famous quarterback. It was beginning.

Although her every thought over the past month, waking or asleep, had focused on this moment, Margaret Allenby felt faint, her knees buckling beneath her, a thousand thoughts exploding in her mind. What had she forgotten? What had she left undone? From either side pale oval faces stared at her, familiar yet too blurred to recognize.

Not an empty seat! They all had come, those who had accepted and those who hadn't bothered to reply.

"*Mrs. Allenby, I tell you all along, I insist on exact reservation, forty-eight hours in advance. Exact!*"

"*Henri, I don't know how many dinners you'll be serving. Suppose I say four hundred and only three hundred show up?*"

"*You pay for four hundred. It's in the contract.*"

"*Then I'll say three hundred. But suppose four hundred come?*"

"*Only three hundred eat.*"

"*Henri! You wouldn't dare!*"

"*We're not in business for our health!*"

She floated in the overpowering fragrance—orange blossoms, stocks, carnations, lilacs, trailing jasmine.

"*Mr. Kleinschmidt! You must be colorblind! Those gladiolas are simply not the correct shade of pink! They're too salmony!*"

"*Pliz, Miz Allenby—*"

"*Why do you think I dropped off that sample of the ribbon? You've had it for two weeks! You were supposed to match—*"

"*Pliz, Miz Allenby, you can't change Mother Nature!*"

Margaret stepped forward onto the long white runner covering the aisle. Towering above her, Darter Evans tried to match his gait to hers.

"Robert! You knew! You knew all the time! Why didn't you tell me?"

"Tell you what?"

"That Darter Evans is a black?"

"My God, woman, Darter Evans was on television every Saturday all fall! Every numskull in the whole damn country knows he's black!"

Margaret pursed her lips. Every numskull in the country knew, except Margaret. Margaret had found out yesterday at the rehearsal. All right. No one could say Margaret Allenby was prejudiced. Darter Evans was famous—an All-American. That she could understand. But Agnes Jackson! Margaret had written Agnes Jackson's name a dozen times, had paid for Agnes Jackson's dress, her bouquet, her headpiece, her shoes, and never had an inkling the girl was black. The shock had been too much.

Really, that had not been fair of Linda. Margaret had made a terrible mistake. She had thought Aggie was a cleaning woman, waiting to dust the church. And after that—when the rehearsal started—the way the girl had sashayed up the aisle, wearing those too-tight jeans (yes, jeans in St. Mark's!), her midriff bare, the color of mahogany, all the men staring as if hypnotized—Stu Jenks, the Conway boy, and Rick, the groom! Darter Evans actually had licked his lips! Even Robert had looked at nothing else, his eyes popping from their sockets! Margaret pressed her lips into a stiff, determined smile.

The other bridesmaid was just as bad. What was her name? Sadie Blankenhazen. Sadie! Something was weird about Sadie, and no mistake. Imagine, interrupting the rehearsal, when Mrs. Buell was dubbing for Dr. McLeod, objecting to the wording! Actually, this twit of a nobody had the gall to want to change the wedding ceremony of the Episcopal Church! Then later, before the rehearsal dinner at L'Auberge, Margaret had seen Sadie in a corner with the black girl, Sadie's long horsey face suffused with anger. Even at a distance it was obvious Sadie was furious with Aggie, was threatening her. What had that been all about? Where had Linda dredged up these incredible misfits? Oh, if only Linda had stayed at Mills!

For that matter, where in heaven's name had Linda found Rick? Definitely, Rick was not Linda's type. He had no family background, no manners, money, prospects, nothing. Why couldn't Linda have liked the Prestons' nephew, the one from Harvard? What on earth could Linda see in Rick? Another oddity, Rick did not seem excited about getting married—quite the contrary. Margaret had never seen a less enthusiastic groom. And last night, Robert had tried to talk to his future son-in-law, had offered to make a place for him down at the plant, and Rick had turned him down point blank! That had really teed off Robert.

Margaret's step faltered, but she pulled herself together and went on, her smile fixed and bright. If only she didn't feel so tired, so anxious! Next to her own wedding to Robert and the day of Linda's birth, this day should have been the most important of her life. Since Linda was a baby, all Margaret's dreams had focused on this point—

the marriage of her daughter. Always she had vowed that it would be the most beautiful, most joyous celebration one could imagine. Now, after twenty years, the great event was taking place, exquisitely planned, no detail overlooked, no expense spared. Why, then, was Margaret so depressed?

The answer hit her like an avalanche. She and Robert were about to hand over their most precious possession—their vulnerable, innocent little girl—to a stranger. Who was this man? Would he be kind or harsh, intelligent or stupid? Margaret didn't know. This man would father Margaret's grandchildren. His genes would become theirs. Was he an incipient alcoholic? Would he beat Linda?

At the aisle's end, Darter Evans stood aside, and Margaret slipped into the left pew, her moment in the spotlight over. As she sank down on the cold wooden seat she had a feeling of foreboding. Everything was wrong about this marriage. Subconsciously she'd known it from the start.

The door to the vestry opened. Two young men clad in beige Edwardian tuxedoes entered and stood together, facing the congregation. A slight smile played over the features of the best man, M. Kemper Conway, but the face of the groom, Rick Dublin, was an expressionless mask.

Inwardly, Rick struggled to control his terror. What was happening to him? How had he let himself get into this predicament? A sense of the unknown surged through his veins causing his forehead to break out in perspiration. He had told no one, not Linda, not Kemp, that until the rehearsal yesterday Big Rick Dublin had never once been in a church. Big Rick Dublin had never once been in a country club. Nor had Big Rick ever worn a tuxedo. Worse than that, he'd never been present at a wedding—anybody's wedding.

He'd instantly disliked St. Mark's. The massive stone walls reminded him of a medieval dungeon, something he'd seen in a movie. Now that he was inside with the heavy door shut tight behind him, he felt trapped. He started to inhale rapid short shallow breaths. He wanted to escape.

His gaze zeroed in on Linda's mother, eying him from

the front row. Her smile was phony, that was obvious, the whole thing was a put-on; underneath the old broad was fighting gloom. This puzzled Rick. The entire senseless charade was this woman's private trip. "It means so much to mother!" Linda had repeated a thousand times. "I know you hate all the fuss. I hate it too. But I do want to make mother happy."

Rick groaned. Linda and Rick had given up their privacy, their love life, the spare time they used to spend together, to play-act in this out-of-date, absurd, expensive farce—for what? To make this woman happy, and it hadn't worked. Mrs. Allenby looked as if she'd been sucking on a lemon.

Strange feelings churned deep down inside Rick. He resented the possessiveness with which two strangers—the Allenbys—treated his beloved. He begrudged the attention Linda had given her mother over the past month, shopping, talking, listening to the woman's endless monologues —precious time that Linda could have spent with Rick. Worst of all—something he never in a hundred years would have admitted—he was jealous of Linda because she had a mother, and a father, at the wedding. What would it have been like if Dot Dublin had lived, if even now Dot were seated in the right hand pew all gussied up in a cute new dress, fighting back tears of pride? Or if Rick's father hadn't split, hadn't been the way he was— if, somehow, Rick's father had loved him, if, somehow, his father had been there too?

One by one, like paratroopers ejected over hostile territory, the bridesmaids were launched from the vestibule. Linda watched them go with mounting tension. Having shed her jeans, Aggie Jackson had metamorphosed into a totally different individual, an elegant yet sensuous Nubian princess in pink chiffon. Until the last possible second Sadie Blankenhazen had hovered close to Aggie, her equine face charged with emotion, while Aggie's chin shot up in sharp defiance, her brown-violet eyes exuding sparks. Some strange esoteric conflict raged between the two and Linda flinched, not wanting to know more. As Aggie stepped slowly down the aisle, Sadie's gaze was riveted upon her, as if to hold her back. Nervously, Linda realized her own father, Robert Allenby, was also watching Aggie as if mesmerized.

Now it was Sadie's turn to go. Swiftly Sadie looked at Linda, her lips framing words, her glance dark. Linda swallowed, trying to pretend she didn't understand. It was unbelievable, but Linda was being blackmailed.

Yesterday at the rehearsal Sadie's voice had interrupted, echoing through the transept.

"I object! No woman can be forced to honor and obey!"

Mrs. Buell, wedding coordinator for St. Mark's, a petty tyrant in her own domain, had inspected Sadie with the dispassion of an entomologist about to dissect a fly.

"You weren't listening." Mrs. Buell was icy. "The word is cherish."

"All right then," shouted Sadie. "What about 'man and wife'? Why not 'woman and husband'?"

With one withering glance, Mrs. Buell cut Sadie dead.

"To continue," Mrs. Buell said smoothly, as if Sadie did not exist, "the bride and groom now kneel before the altar . . ."

Linda had seen Sadie stiffen, Sadie who never overlooked a slight, real or imagined, Sadie who never forgave an insult. Later, at L'Auberge, Sadie had backed Linda in a corner.

"You ninny!" Sadie had denounced. "You have to take a stand! Insist on equality!"

"Sadie!" Linda tried to pass it off. "It's not that big a deal. Nobody listens to the words."

Sadie leaned close, forcing Linda back against the red flocked wallpaper.

"You cannot let that put-down go by, in front of all those people! You cannot swear to those words before God! You'd be committing perjury!"

"Sadie, for heaven's sake! I can't change the ritual of the Episcopal Church!"

"You have to!"

"There's no way!"

"Find a way!" hissed Sadie. Her eyes glittered, feverbright. She lowered her voice. "You wouldn't want your mother to know you're pregnant, would you?"

Linda stared at her friend. Her own pulse pounded. She

felt threatened, unprotected. With unerring instinct, Sadie had fastened on the jugular vein.

"Go to the minister," Sadie had dictated, "tomorrow. Tell him you insist . . ."

Now Linda swallowed, trying to moisten her dry scratchy throat. It was tomorrow. Linda had not gone to the minister. Subconsciously she equated Dr. McLeod with God. So what would happen? Would Sadie interrupt again, demand the wedding ceremony be changed? Woman and husband—that's all it would take for Rick to chuck the whole business. He'd been so antsy anyhow, objecting to every trifle he could think of. And what about Linda's mother! If Sadie spoiled the wedding, Margaret would have a coronary on the spot.

Delcie Green, maid of honor, paused eagerly at the beginning of the aisle, as if she were a bird about to soar off into space. Almost magically, Delcie had lost weight, and her skin had cleared. Her hair had been trimmed and frosted. Delcie looked seductive in her rose chiffon. She was delirious with joy.

Delcie blew Linda a kiss and started down the aisle.

The fool! thought Linda. Can't she see she's riding for another fall? Can't she see that for Kemp this wedding is no more than a game, a chance to exercise his charm? Can't she understand that just standing beside Kemp, walking with Kemp down the aisle, carries no significance?

Linda sighed, trying to discipline her thoughts, to get back to basics. The most basic basic was that she was pregnant. The Cahil gown was much too tight around her waist, so that her stomach ached. At least she'd zipped it up.

Yes, Linda Allenby was with child, and it was urgent that she marry, only the preparations for the wedding had in some mysterious way set in motion forces now out of her control. Her mother, father, Rick, Darter Evans, Sadie, Aggie, Dr. McLeod, Kemp, Delcie, Mrs. Buell—all were divergent forces—pulling at cross purposes, wanting different things, antagonizing one another.

The organ swelled and rolled into the opening bars of *Lohengrin*. The congregation stood, all faces turned to give the bride homage. Robert offered Linda his arm, his smile a secret blessing. It was time. Together they started forward. She felt the throbs of music through her feet. She was the bride, the bride!

Waves of numbness and awareness alternated through her psyche from cold to hot to cold. Now she was standing beside Rick. His eyes sought hers, searching for reassurance. Linda tried to smile. How could she help him when she was floundering herself? If only she could hold on ten more minutes, it would all be over.

Out of the past she heard her own voice, patronizing, telling off her mother.

"Personally, I think marriage stinks!"

She had said that. What was more, she'd meant it.

As in a vision, Dr. McLeod appeared before her, austere, omnipotent.

Unbidden and unwanted, she again heard her own voice.

"I never want to get married! Never!"

The memory echoed and re-echoed, floating upward toward the oaken beams.

What was she doing here, standing beside this stranger, this tall burly football jock about whom she knew nothing? A violent shivering seized her, shook her so that her teeth rattled.

But then, appealingly yet firmly, Rick reached out and took her hand. A charge of lightning ricocheted between them, searing the fragile bond of flesh. Out of Rick's somber eyes his soul leaped forth to greet her, causing her heart to melt. Ah, gentle giant! This was it—this was her love, her life! Before God and these witnesses they now were one.

He kissed her, and the whole world swam away.

THIRTY

One Saturday morning Margaret Allenby dropped in on the newlyweds unannounced. Luckily, Rick spotted the Mark IV out the window. In a dither they folded up the Hide-a-Bed and pulled on jeans while Margaret panted up three flights of stairs.

"Mother! What a surprise! You should have let us know!"

"How could I, when you don't have a phone?"

They sat facing one another, Margaret on the reassembled sofa, Rick and Linda on straight chairs.

"I was in the neighborhood and thought . . ."

That's a bald-faced lie.

Rick, bite your tongue! How can you say that!

She's never been in this part of the city in her life. She had a magnifying glass and street map in the car.

"So . . . How have you been?" Linda said.

Margaret seemed pleased to be asked.

"After the wedding I was suffering from total exhaustion—total! Dr. Dixon almost put me in the hospital! Instead, we went to the Mauna Kea." She looked at them archly. "We thought we might run into you!"

"In Hawaii?" Rick was incredulous.

"You never did say where you went on your honeymoon! Friends kept asking, 'Where did the happy couple go?' I said it was a secret."

"Right," said Linda. "A big, big secret."

"Only now . . ." Margaret's voice took on a playful lift. "It wouldn't have to be a secret any more!"

Linda bit her lip. She could not tell her mother they had spent their wedding night in Darter's van, parked on a public beach off Highway One, nor that the next night they'd been back in their respective rooms on campus.

"How's daddy?"

"Oh, you know your father—same as always, playing

lots of golf, trying to hang onto his tan!" Delicately, Margaret removed her white kid gloves, finger by finger. "We were so relieved to get your card, and know you're back and settled!" Her eyes took in the room like a wide-angle lens. "Well! Do I get the grand tour?"

"Pardon?" said Rick.

"I hope you're going to show me the apartment."

"You're looking at it."

Margaret rushed on, not listening.

"I've had a marvelous idea. So many people seem to think I have a gift for decorating . . . I thought perhaps you'd like to have me help . . ." She paused, expecting a response. "Uh— It does have a bedroom?"

"You're sitting on it."

"Really?" Margaret was flustered. "Oh, my goodness! Uh—what about the kitchen?"

"Behind you."

Uneasily Margaret glanced over her shoulder at the corner stove and sink, both stacked with dirty dishes.

"Oh! I see! But . . . It must have a bath?"

"There in the closet."

"Gracious! Well!" Margaret's voice strained to produce a compliment. "Well! It is compact!"

It is compact! For months to come Rick would use that phrase, first to describe anything too small, then anything too large, then anything at all. Rick, you are putrid! Truthful is the word. Mother was making conversation. The hell she was! You want a translation? You poor slobs, living in this crappy joint!

"I brought a few of your wedding gifts."

"Mother, you didn't! I thought I made it clear—"

"Now, dear, this is only your stoneware, and a set of stainless steel . . . You have to eat, don't you?"

"*Moth—*"

"I had planned to have Bekins come in to pack the china and crystal . . ."

"For heaven's sake, don't do that! Look around you! Can't you see we have no—N-O—room to put it—no cupboards, no shelves? Besides, the security around this place is absolute zero. The stuff would all get stolen the first time we went out."

"But you ought to have your wedding presents—what's

the point in owning all those lovely things if you don't use them? How can you entertain?"

"Mother, we do not plan to entertain!"

Her mother seemed to be undergoing an inner struggle.

"Well," she conceded at last, as if masking hurt feelings, "what do you suggest we do with them?"

"I don't care what you do with them! Do what you want!" Linda knew she was being cruel, and she hated herself for it. "Leave them in my room at home, where they are now."

"But then there won't be any room when you come home to—"

"I won't be coming home, not to stay overnight. I'm married, remember?"

Linda loathed the tone in her own voice. Rick looked unhappy. Margaret appeared tired.

"Let me get you some coffee," Linda said as an appeasement.

Margaret brightened. "If you have it made . . ."

"No, instant. I'll put water to boil."

"Never mind," said Margaret.

"It's no trouble," Linda insisted, almost petulant.

Margaret turned to Rick. "Are you still working at the university?"

"The uni— uh, no ma'am."

"Oh," said Margaret.

"That was a school job." Linda filled a saucepan from the tap. "And now school's out."

"Oh, I see," said Margaret. Another pause. How long did water take to boil? "What are your plans now?"

It was a question one might ask a chance acquaintance, but Linda saw Rick stiffen.

"Right at the present, you might say I'm looking . . ."

Margaret cleared her throat. "Mr. Allenby—Linda's father—just happened to mention to me—at breakfast, I think it was—there just happens to be an opening at the billing department at the plant . . ."

Mother, don't! Don't! Don't! If you knew how Rick feels, how he has this fixation against taking . . ."

Rick's jaw stiffened in silence.

"I'm sure if you'd drop by Monday morning . . ."

Mother, didn't daddy tell you? He went through all that

with Rick after dinner at L'Auberge, the night of the rehearsal, didn't you know? He offered Rick every kind of job he could think of and Rick turned every last one of them down, and finally they both got mad? You *did* know! You've begged and pestered daddy to reconsider, and finally he did, and that's why you came alone, because you think you're more diplomatic ...

". . . I'm sure you'd have no trouble getting hired, if you're interested . . ." Margaret looked expectantly at Rick. She waited.

"No," said Rick, after considerable time. "I'm not."

"You tell daddy thank you," said Linda.

Margaret wasn't giving up. "If you don't think you'd like billing, perhaps in the plant . . ."

"No," said Rick.

"But why not, if you're looking—"

"Mother!"

"I should think if he were serious about—"

"He is! He's serious!"

"Then wouldn't it be sensible—"

Linda stole a glance at Rick. She guessed at the conflict behind those granite features. But, on the other hand, she knew her mother's fixed and reasonable mind.

"Mother, you don't understand—"

'Understand! My dear, we only want to help!"

"Rick doesn't want to feel—"

"What?"

"Obligated . . ."

"Honey, that's ridiculous! We're your family!"

Linda's eyes met Rick's which held a trapped expression.

"What he does, he wants to do on his own," she explained in a rush. She poured the water too fast, and the coffee slopped over into the saucer. "Oh, crap!"

"Linda!" Margaret was horrified.

"Rick, you want coffee?"

"Naw," said Rick. He looked intently out the window.

"Linda, I don't think you should be drinking coffee," Margaret said. Startled, Linda jostled her own cup, spilling the burning liquid on her jeans. "You seem nervous."

Oh, Lord, don't let her guess! Not now! Not yet!

"I'm not nervous. I'm recovering from finals."

Margaret's face lit up.

"I have an inspiration! Even if Rick feels the way he does about working at the plant, how he feels needn't apply to you. You wouldn't object to working for your father!"

Linda opened her mouth, then caught a warning in Rick's eye.

"Mother, let's just cool it, okay? Let us work it out."

Margaret looked dubious. "If it will make you feel better," appeased Linda, "I'll keep the stoneware. We can put the box in the corner."

Margaret appeared mollified. She took the car keys from her purse. "Rick, would you mind? The boxes in the trunk."

When he was gone, Linda moved to sit beside her mother, putting an arm around her, a peace gesture.

"You have to try to understand Rick."

"Dear, Rick may be a nice enough young man, but you don't need to live like this."

"It's all right! We live here because we like it."

"It's dirty—"

"I'll clean it up. There's lots I want to do."

Margaret's voice strained to be objective. She talked fast, trying to say it all while Rick was gone.

"It's cramped, and it's in a wretched neighborhood. You could be beaten up or raped!"

"Oh Mother, please!"

"Oh, Linda!" Margaret almost sobbed. "It breaks my heart to think of you—a girl like you—stuck in a place like this, when there's no need . . ."

The old, familiar feeling smothered Linda. Why did she let Margaret upset her this way? It wasn't good for her, nor for the baby.

"Look!" Linda talked fast, she strove to keep an even tone. "Rick has principles—"

"That's well and good, but principles do not buy groceries!"

"We haven't starved yet!"

"Starved—I should hope not!" A flash of panic tightened Margaret's face. "You mean you might—"

"Mother, forget—"

"You actually don't—"

"Mother, I said let's cool it now, okay?"

"Exactly how much money do you have?"

"Never mind!"

In haste, Margaret fumbled in her purse, found her wallet and extracted three twenty-dollar bills.

"Take this at least! It's all I have with me."

"Mother!" Linda had the absurd idea Rick would burst in upon them, and see her take a bribe. She cringed as if the currency were tainted. "Put that away!"

"Then I'll write a check!"

"No! I told you how Rick feels!"

"He wouldn't have to know."

"He'd know. I'm not going to lie."

Margaret's lip quivered. "How can you be so stubborn!"

Linda heard Rick's footsteps on the stairs.

"I'm married, remember! That wedding that so totally exhausted you, remember! That's what it was all about!"

She barely regained her composure before Rick walked in.

Linda walked with her mother down the three flights of stairs to the car. When she came back Rick had pulled on a T-shirt.

"Where're you going?"

"Out."

"To do what?"

"Nothing. Get out of this cruddy apartment."

"I thought you liked the apartment."

"Who said so?"

"You did, when you found it."

"That was before your mother came around to tell us we were living like slobs."

"Rick, she didn't mean it that way."

"Then how did she mean it? You tell me."

Linda had a sinking feeling. She remembered how difficult it had been, convincing Rick they had to find a place of their own. He'd been content to slide back into their old arrangement, staying on in his quarters with Kemp, coming to Linda's room when he chose, leaving when he chose, free as a bird.

Linda had battled morning sickness while studying for finals. Rick had had a powerful point on his side, and he won. Their rooms were paid for to the end of school. Finally, reluctantly, Rick had agreed to go with her to look for a place. When, after endless disappointments, Rick had found the Jeeter Street apartment on his own, Linda had glowed in triumph.

Now Rick strode around the room, a tiger in a too-small cage. Linda trotted beside him.

"I like the apartment."

"You don't."

"Yes, I do. You know I do."

"You don't act like it."

"I do so. Forget anything mother said."

"That would be a little hard to do. 'It must have a bath?' "

Linda giggled. "This would be funny if you weren't so mad."

"Just let her stay away."

"Rick, she can't stay away. They're my parents!"

"Away from my house and my wife—"

"We'll have to see them sometimes!"

"I will not stand meekly by and be told I live like a slob!"

"She said no such thing."

"She implied it."

"Only in your imagination."

"She implied I'm not good enough for you!"

"You're making that up!"

"And that I'm a lousy husband. That I can never be the kind of husband you should have!"

"Rick!" Linda was overcome by pity, so unexpectedly had he bared his great, gaping wound. "You know that's not true!" She threw both arms around his waist, pulled him down beside her on the sofa. She kissed his lips. He was unresponsive.

"She's never—" Again, for her, for her alone, he bared a second deep and festering wound wihch had been bandaged, camouflaged so no one could guess at it, no one could see. "She's never liked me and she never will."

Linda's arms closed around his unrelenting shoulders. She kissed his cheek gently, again and again.

"She likes you," she said in a soft voice, as if she were talking to a child, "she loves you, or she will, if you'll give her a chance. It's just that—you're both so different, you're two different people, you're a man, she's a woman, you're young, she's older. You couldn't be more different, that I can see, and now that—well, that we're together, somehow you'll have to understand each other."

"I won't have her come here and criticize—"

"She didn't mean to criticize. Believe me. The things you got so touchy about, she just said because she's concerned—"

"She's too concerned!"

"It's because she loves me."

"She can damn well stay out of my life!"

"And I love her, too, don't you understand?"

"That's it! You said you'd broken away, but you never have and you never will."

"She's my mother! I can't help loving my mother!"

"And I'm your husband, or have you forgotten!"

"You're not jealous—"

"If you cared half as much about me as you do about her—"

"I do, Rick, I do!"

"You don't." Rick clasped his hands in front of him, and stared at the threadbare carpet. "You don't at all."

Linda felt at her wits' end. The day, which had begun happily with making love, was quickly deteriorating into a nightmare. What had come over Rick? This was a side of his personality she'd never seen, never guessed at. No matter what she said, their relationship got worse, yet she didn't dare break off the dialogue, not the way things stood now. She had to win him back, cure the breach, make it better.

"I love you more than anybody in the world," she said, taking his hand and holding it in both of hers. "That doesn't mean I have to stop caring about anyone else. I couldn't, even if I tried. My parents have their faults, granted—"

"You can say that again."

"They have money—"

"And they don't know what it's like not to have money."

"They're sort of used to having their own way—"

"Sort of!"

"—They live in what you might call an ivory tower—"

"—and only know other ivory tower–type people!"

"Right. But what's so bad about all that?"

"You don't know?"

"So it's a difficult life-style. They're still my parents. They love me."

"It seems to me I remember you called it suffocation."

"I know I did, and some things still bug me, but now I've been out in the real world—"

"Now you're feeling sorry—cause you took up with me—"

"I'm not. I'm only saying the real world is . . . different. All right. That's how they are. If you'll make some kind of effort to accept their world—"

"Why should I make all the effort? I don't notice them breaking their necks accepting me!"

"Oooh!" Linda jumped up, beside herself in frustration. "If you weren't so spoiled!"

"I'm spoiled! Look who's talking!"

"If only I hadn't got pregnant!"

"That's right!"

"If you could have gotten acquainted gradually—they'd have fallen in love with you, they will, yet . . ."

"Fat chance."

"Especially if . . ."

Rick looked at her suspiciously. "If what?"

"If you'd give in a little. What would be so bad about taking that job at the plant?"

"Are you crazy? If you don't know, it's no use to tell you."

"You have to get a job somewhere!"

"You think I'd let your old man put the screws on me, tell me what to do, what not to do, dangle a raise in front of me like a fucking carrot! No way!"

"He wouldn't do that."

"The hell he wouldn't! Do you know what he told me that night? 'If you play your cards right, come up to our expectations—' "

"That's just daddy's way."

"His way of saying if you'll be our puppet, dance when we tell you to—"

"That's a misconstruction, the same way you misconstrue mother."

"Your mother! You want to know why she came here? The real reason? To use you to talk me into taking that goddammed job!"

"Rick, she did no such—"

"She did, and you know it, and you want to know why? Just so they'd have control, just so we'd be in their debt, just so they could interior decorate our lives and give us a john that's not in a closet!'

Linda giggled. Suddenly, she sensed that the *brouhaha* was over. His anger, which had blazed out white-hot, had wrought a miracle. The cobwebs of resentment and self-doubt had vanished, purged in the flame. The crisis was past. Rick looked at her, grinning.

"Back to square one?" he suggested.

Together, they struggled with the Hide-a-Bed.

Later, Linda asked the final question lingering in her mind.

"Speaking of square one?"

"Yes?"

"If you can't get a job, and I can't get a job—what do we do for eats?"

"If-if-if," said Rick. "That's easy. Food stamps!"

Before she could burst out laughing, he kissed her again.

THIRTY-ONE

The Dublins' game plan was to get jobs, work, save money and have the baby. It came as an unpalatable surprise that no employer in metropolitan Los Angeles wished to hire them. Night after night they straggled back to Jeeter Street to lick their wounds and eat their skimpy TV dinners. Then, after two ego-eroding weeks, Linda landed a position as receptionist for Lifelong Insurance on Wilshire. She brought home steaks and a bottle of Chablis to celebrate.

"He said, 'Can you type?' and I said, 'Yes—not too well,' but then he looked me over—from all angles . . .'"

"Now wait a minute!"

"Don't get shook. He said, 'With you, baby, it doesn't matter!'"

"The bastard!"

"Keep cool. He asked if I had a sweater."

"In *June?*"

"I said I used to have, I guessed I still did, somewhere, and he said what about miniskirts, and I said I'd had a few, they might be still around if my mother hadn't given them to Goodwill Industries. I said I thought all that stuff was out of date, and he said it wasn't in their office!"

"You're not taking it!"

"I took it."

"I'm not letting my wife—"

Linda put her arms around Rick's neck.

"I can handle it! But what a gas! I only half-believed all that sex-object crap in the NOW tracts! Turns out to be true!"

Through the next week Rick continued to bomb out. His bad temper increased nightly when Linda, arriving home from work to find the Hide-a-Bed unmade and the sink stacked high with dirty dishes, demanded to know what he had done all day. Finally Rick was hired at two-fifty per hour by a church-sponsored children's day camp which met in Grundon Park. His take-home pay was less than half of Linda's.

Now that they had what they wanted—they were both working—they should have been happy. To some extent they were, but fatigue and the cramped quarters of a one room apartment extracted its toll. They had no newspapers, no television, nothing to do after dinner. Rick wanted to make love. Linda complained she was sick to her stomach.

"There's this guy works for the park, Manuel, about my age but he's got three kids, another one on the way— he says his wife never gets sick."

"Goodie for her."

"Only once or twice maybe right at first. Manuel says it could be in your head."

"Manuel can drop dead."

"So how's about it, baby?"

"You can drop dead, too."

"I need relaxation."

"After your hard day in the park."

"Yeah! Can you think of anything better to do?"

"Why can't we simply sit and talk?"

"Talk! What about?"

"Politics or something."

"Politics!" Rick was aghast.

"It doesn't have to be politics. World affairs. The situation in Mozambique."

"You've got to be kidding."

"Well, then, something closer to home. Did you notice that duplex down on the corner? They're fumigating it for termites."

"Who the hell wants to talk about termites when we could be doing something constructive?"

His great arms closed in on her. Linda struggled.

"Rick, all I'm saying is why, for once, can't we base our relationship on something besides sex?"

Rick tightened his grip, holding her arms still.

"Wouldn't wash."

"Why not?"

" 'Cause whenever I'm with you, I get that old feeling."

"That's all you think about! Sex, sex, sex."

"That's right, baby." He kissed her, and stopped to taste the flavor, as if she were a peach parfait. "That's right!"

They had purposely not told friends their address, but before long everyone was dropping in.

"Quite a place you got here!" Thoughtfully, Kemp had arrived with two cold six-packs of beer. "You should see the pad I got! Talk about Shangri La!"

"What's it called?"

"That's it. Shangri La. For swinging singles, and man, do they swing! Airline hostesses, models, you name it! It's one long party time." He leaned confidentially toward Rick, "You should have kept the old neck out of the noose a little bit longer. No offense, Linda."

"No offense," echoed Linda, her tone more offended than not. She withdrew behind the kitchen counter and began to clean the oven.

"I'm in real estate, working for a friend of my dad's. Man, it is a piece of cake!"

"Made lots of sales, huh?"

"Not yet. I'm studying for my license. Meanwhile, I'm making contacts. Talk about a fertile field!"

"I'll bet," said Linda.

"You mean at your apartment?" said Rick.

"There, at the club house—it's all part of the complex— at the marina, the courts. Tennis is the name of the game." He swung a phantom racquet. "Money—I'm here to tell you, is rampant. Every one of those guys has a Porsche or a Hobie Cat or both." He took another swing. "I've been sharpening up my backhand." He opened the refrigerator and took out two more beers. "Man, you ought to come in with me. I could get Morton to take you on."

Rick looked tempted.

"I'm going to rent a sailboat," Kemp told them. "A guy's being transferred to New York and giving up his slip. To make money you got to be with money. That's the name of the game."

"I thought it was tennis," said Linda.

"What's with her?" Kemp inquired of Rick.

After Kemp left, his presence lingered in the air between them.

"So go ahead," said Linda. "I'm not stopping you."

"I didn't say I wanted to."

"No, but that's what you're thinking."

"Come off it, Linda! Don't be an old crab. Even Kemp noticed—"

"I noticed Kemp's father's underwriting him a thou a month. That came out in passing."

"Well—"

"That's a lot of airline stewardesses."

"You know I couldn't go for anybody else—"

"No?" Linda sensed the conversation already had overstepped its limits, yet something perverse inside her kept it alive. "Suppose you weren't married. Suppose you'd never heard of me, and this chance of a lifetime, shall we say, came up. Would you go?"

Rick shrugged. "How do I know what I'd do?"

"Possibly?"

"Who knows? Sounds like a great little set up."

"You'd move in with Kemp in his swinging apartment?"

"Why not? You said suppose I'd never heard of you. Maybe."

"And tell me how, exactly how, you'd foot your share of the bill."

"Listen, this is all a supposition. Maybe I'd make a few sales."

"But before that? Till you got going? You wouldn't mind accepting board and room?"

"Why should I? He's my old buddy. He'd accept the same thing from me."

"There must be some distinction I've overlooked. From Kemp's father it's okay, from mine it's kaput."

"There is a helluva distinction. Kemp's not waiting to get the old pincers on me, to control my every move. Kemp's a friend!"

When Delcie came, she showed up before either of them arrived home from work, stayed for dinner, and continued to talk until Rick pointedly unfolded the Hide-a-Bed, at which time she reluctantly departed, promising to return soon and often. She was inexhaustible on the same topic: Kemp.

"I had forgotten, you're not going to believe it but u▒ that heavenly night of the rehearsal, I had actually forgotten what he looked like!"

"Don't you still have the posters?"

"Naturally, but it's not the same thing. Besides, by now I've moved, didn't I tell you? I'm in an apartment with Carol Welkins. We're going to summer school. She's working on her credential and I'm taking home economics. Don't laugh. Gourmet cooking, household management and family life behavior."

"I thought you were going to be a geologist."

"Don't you get it? I have not given up. You yourself were the one who told me I couldn't."

"I never held out any hope."

"You said I had to get hold of myself. Well, I did, or rather, it was the wedding that got my head screwed on right. Linda, that was the most beautiful, the most romantic, the most perfect wedding. I hope you thanked your mother, did you, and your father, he had to foot the bill. Was it expensive? I'd give anything to have one like it, down to the last chug-a-lug of champagne, but I don't think my folks, although they might, if I could bring it off. He's such a gorgeous hunk of man!"

"Delcie!" Linda scowled. "Try to calm down!"

"Calm, I am calm. You've never seen anyone more calm than I. I'm calmly trying to assess my chances."

"Your chances are exactly what they were two months ago, a big fat zero."

"You're not being nice."

"I'm being candid."

"Anyway, that's not so. Did you notice, or were you too wrapped up in yourselves, that at the rehearsal and at the wedding Kemp was—well, not rude."

"He was on his good behavior. I'll never know why."

"He was downright attentive—at least, agreeable—at least, showing there is hope, there is room for hope, H-O-P-E!"

"Delcie, I cannot go through this whole traumatic crack-up with you one more time. First you're on a trip to outer space, then you're ready to cut your throat, now you're back to the launching pad."

ealed Delcie, "you noticed it, didn't you? ed on about me that night? In a sexy way?"

out of this," said Rick. "I'm going for a hastily.

"Linda, don't you think any odds, even one chance out of a hundred, are worth fighting for?"

"I thought you were back working with the movement."

"I am, but only for one thing—you want to know what it is? To remind me I'm a Person who can achieve any goal in her own right."

"Oh, brother."

". . . So that's the reason I came over, to ask you. What's the best way, and don't tell me to get pregnant. Oh, I know it worked for you . . ."

"Don't say it worked for me. You act as if I did it on purpose, as if I wanted to get married."

"Didn't you?"

"Well—after I knew I was, I . . ."

"But if you hadn't been, wouldn't you—have wanted to, I mean?"

"I . . ." Linda's voice trailed off, then took on a heartiness, "of course! Now that I am, it's great, I wouldn't trade it."

Delcie put her hands on her hips in disgust.

"You know something? You are nuts! You're perched on top of a uranium mine and you're too stupid to appreciate it. You're the super-lucky cookie of all time!"

The next time, Delcie appeared before Rick got home.

"I have a new theory," she told Linda. "I am not, repeat, not going to make the same mistake all over. Oh, no! I am not going to pursue him. That didn't work before. It turned him off. I can't trap him the way you trapped Rick—"

"I resent that!"

"No, in all sincerity, I would if I could, but in this case it's not practical. What he needs is motivation. That's what I've been studying, motivation behavior. He has to want it of his own free will."

Linda, who was tired and hungry, had opened the refrigerator and was trying to figure out how to make supper out of a piece of liverwurst turned dark around the edges, and a half can of pork and beans.

"'Linda, you are so lucky! You don't realize how lucky you are. That's why I want to ask your advice. Do you think I should aim at being feminine? Or sexy? Would you consider them the same? Or different? I want your advice."

"My advice? Forget it. Forget the whole thing. Go back to geology. Concentrate on rocks."

Delcie pouted. "That's easy to say. You've always been pretty! What will work for me? I have to find the answer! Plain women marry and have children too, you know. They must have been doing it for years, with all the ugly people in the world!"

"Don't talk that way! You aren't ugly."

"It wouldn't matter anyway," said Delcie, "with Kemp's looks. He's handsome enough for both of us."

The next time Delcie showed up she had Aggie in tow. Rick took one look and bolted for the store. Linda made tea and the girls talked. Aggie said she had made it up again with Sadie after the big flap at the reception, when Sadie was drunk, and told everyone off. They were staying on at Canyon Crest, both working. Aggie modeled lingerie for a jobber in the wholesale district and Sadie was field manager for NOW.

"She's official?"

"Yeah. She finally went legit. Only . . ."

Only things were not, could never again be, as they had been. Aggie no longer felt the way she had, not about Sade, at any rate. Aggie was sick and tired of the arrangement.

"All you have to do is move."

"It's not that easy. No, ma'am! Not by a wiener's schnitzel! Sadie, she's not about to let me go."

"What could she do to stop you?"

"Put the hex on me, go to my boss and tell him I'm one of *those*, you know, not straight. That would give his business a bad name, get me fired, and blackball me so's I could never work."

"She wouldn't! That's blackmail!" As she spoke, Linda

remembered Sadie's threats to her, and her own over-whelming relief when Sadie had chickened out and had neither stopped the wedding nor told the Allenbys that Linda was pregnant.

"She'd do a lot worse'n blackmail!" Aggie shivered slightly.

The doorbell sounded, and Linda pressed the buzzer.

"Rick must have forgotten his key."

But in the space of two minutes, it was not Rick but Sadie who stood in the landing.

"Linda!" she said, throwing her arms about Linda as if they'd parted on the best of terms. "So this is where you've been hiding, your little lovenest." Her eye skimmed past Delcie. "Aggie," she said softly, "I had a hunch you might be here. I stopped by to take you home."

Aggie threw back her head, the spirited African queen.

"I'm not ready to go home. I'm going to stay for dinner."

"Well—" Sadie decided to be lenient. She was the mag-nanimous monarch, bestowing grace on her subjects. "I guess we can stay for dinner, if it's not too much trouble."

"Oh, no." Linda could say nothing else. She felt herself slipping back into the old pattern. What Sadie wanted, Sadie got. "No trouble at all. Rick's gone to get groceries."

Linda started to wash lettuce for a salad. Sadie sat on the Hide-a-Bed, and pressed her cheek to Aggie's.

"I've missed you," she said softly.

"Don't!" spat Aggie, shooting to her feet. She walked to the sink, took the lettuce out of Linda's hands. "Let me do that," she said. "You set the table."

"She's so touchy," Sadie explained to no one in par-ticular. "It's that crappy job of hers. She's nothing but a sex object."

"Linda, too," said Delcie in the confidential tone she sometimes used. "She has to wear a sweater and a mini skirt. It's the company uniform."

"Dirty old men!" sneered Sadie. "Preying on the de-fenseless. Why do you stand for it?"

"Money," said Aggie.

"It's not worth it! When will you learn? When will you ever learn?"

"It's that or not eat," said Linda.

"Men," said Sadie, "are vile, filthy, deceitful—they should be outlawed from society."

"In that case," said Aggie cheerfully, "the whole human race would go down the tubes."

"Not quite," said Sadie. "There'll always be suckers, like Linda, who get caught with their pants down . . ."

"Don't be crude," sighed Delce.

". . . who keep grinding out babies . . ."

"Sadie!" said Linda.

"It's true!" said Sadie. "You're caught, just as women have been since the dawn of time. When are you going to throw off the yoke? When, when, will you throw off the chains?"

THIRTY-TWO

It was bound to come, the insidious thickening of the waist, the perceptible bulbousness of the abdomen. Zippers stuck, and at last refused to close. Linda fastened the miniskirt with a safety pin and pulled her sweater down to hide the gap. Daily in the ladies' lounge at work, she reviewed her mirrored silhouette. No matter how she held her breath, she could no longer "suck it in." Despairingly, she adopted a posture ramrod stiff, holding her breasts and shoulders high and proud.

One Saturday when Rick had taken his day camp youngsters to the zoo, Margaret appeared unexpectedly, staggering up the stairs beneath a heavy bag of groceries.

"Mother! You shouldn't have!" Linda's reproach was perfunctory. At last, the nausea was easing off, and she was hungry as a hippopotamus. "Ooh, cherries! Peaches! Beefsteak tomatoes!"

"And beefsteak to go with the beefsteak tomatoes!"

Linda kissed her mother in a surge of love and tenderness. Margaret, too, had endured the nausea, the hunger, the protruding stomach, to bring Linda into being. Even now, Margaret was acting the role of parent, to the best of her ability. Why couldn't Rick see that? Why couldn't Rick make an effort to take Margaret as she was? Why couldn't a gift, offered in love, be accepted in love? Yet Linda knew she'd be hard put to explain the steaks. She and Rick had made a pact to buy only the cheapest grade of hamburger.

"Darling—" Margaret accepted the cup of instant coffee. (She, too, thought Linda, had made concessions.) "Don't you have something to tell me?"

At first Linda failed to recognize the moment she had dreaded for four months.

"Why Rick isn't home? He took his children to the zoo."

"No, dear, about you! You've put on weight! Are you expecting?"

Relief flooded over Linda. At last, at last, it was out in the open! But by now she was safely married! She had nothing to hide! She threw her arms around her mother and kissed her. Margaret was delirious with surprise.

"A baby! How fantastic! But I'll be a grandmother! Are you well? I was dreadfully sick—had to stay in bed the entire nine months! A grandmother! Do I look that old? Aren't you large for this early? Robert will be a grandfather! When is the baby due? You don't know? What does the doctor say? Who is your doctor? You haven't seen a doctor! Darling, that's not wise. You may have complications, with our family history, you can have no idea the trouble I had, I hope to heaven you don't run into that, of course, I'd lost an ovary! I can't wait to tell your father! Won't he be pleased! Grandparents! That puts us in a different category! Why don't you have a phone? Such an inconvenience! The first thing is to get you a doctor—"

"Mother—" Linda's protest was half-hearted, her mouth stuffed with cherries.

"For once listen to your mother," said Margaret. "You must see a doctor, today! No, today's Saturday. First thing Monday!"

"But I don't know any . . ."

"Leave it in my hands. Dr. Baumfield's retired—he's the obstetrician I had for you, he was so marvelous, I do wish he were still practicing, he saved your life, that's no exaggeration! That's why it's so important to have the best . . ."

"Mother, you're forgetting we don't . . ."

"Linda, if you bring up money at a time like this I shall never forgive you. Never. It is not only your baby we're talking about, it is my grandchild! I should have some say! You should be taking vitamins, iron, calcium! He'll check your diet. Did you know improper nutrition during pregnancy can cause mental retardation in the child?"

"We don't have a car."

"I'll find a doctor close to your office. I'll get you an appointment during lunch hour."

"But what—"

Margaret pressed a manicured finger over Linda's lips.

"Don't say it. Here's ten dollars, and I don't want to hear a word. It's for cab fare. It isn't for you and it isn't for Rick. It's for my grandchild." She set her cup down on the drainboard and now stood in the bathroom, examining her features in the wavery mirror, pulling the skin away from her eyes to erase the crows feet. "A grandmother!" Her voice was half delight, half disbelief. "At least I'll be young enough to enjoy her!"

"Her!" echoed Linda.

"Of course her," said Margaret. "Darling, I know it's going to be a girl!"

The morning arrived when, by any standards, the tight cashmere sweater looked grotesque. Instead, Linda wore a shirt, letting it hang loose. That afternoon she was summoned by Mr. Kirshberg, the man who had hired her.

"Ms. Dublin—"

"Mrs."

"Whatever. We're going to have to let you go."

Linda sputtered.

"Hasn't my work been satisfactory?"

Mr. Kirshberg's feet rested on his desk. He chewed the end of a cigar.

"Your work, as you call it, could be done by a chimpanzee. I'm firing you because you're pregnant. As far as I'm concerned you took the job under false pretenses."

"What!"

"We want our receptionist to look sexy, know what I mean? Gives our company that swinging image."

Linda felt rage sweep over her. The arrogance of the man, lounging, feet on desk (while she was standing), stating that her one use to the company had been to excite men—it was more than she could stomach! He was no better than a pimp, selling the sex image to his customers to get them to buy insurance!

"As far as I'm concerned, your company stinks!"

"Pick up your check at the controller."

Mr. Kirshberg's glance implied she was not worth a further expenditure of time or thought. Her anger flared up again. Once Mr. Kirshberg had found her interesting, but that had been because she had long blonde hair, a pretty face, big breasts, and a small waist. She still had the long blonde hair, her face remained unchanged, her breasts curved generously as before. It was her swollen stomach which had transformed Linda from asset to liability, to be dumped, to be hustled out of sight before a potential customer might catch sight of her offensive profile and cancel his order. In the market place, sex packed the greatest wallop. Yet pregnancy, the direct result of sex, was considered gross and obscene.

"That's not legal! Haven't you heard of equal rights! You can't fire me without cause!"

Mr. Kirshberg regarded her insolently, his eyes stripping the garments from her misshapen body, piece by piece.

"I can fire you for insubordination," he said, and flicked the switch of the intercom. "Send in the girls for the receptionist job. The redhead first."

It took weeks for Linda's anger to subside. The injustice of her cavalier dismissal because of pregnancy merged ultimately with the injustice of pregnancy itself, so that in Linda's subconscious they became indistinguishable.

It was fine enough for people to have babies who wanted them—people like her parents who had been out of school, married and settled down, with no money problems. Conceivably Linda and Rick might have arrived at such a stage—at a future time. Their relationship might have matured, they might have become financially stable, they might have married out of affection. Conceivably, if all that had occurred, they might then have decided to have a child.

But this way! The whole miserable experience—the vomiting, the bitter bile, the icky, ever-present nausea, the discomfort in standing, in sleeping, in going to the bathroom, the chagrin at becoming more distorted day by day—all this had been dumped upon her, the penalty for one abandoned fling of love. It wasn't fair!

She brooded.

The unfairest part of all was that the scourge did not strike both lovers—only one. The other went scot-free.

Rick had not been fired from his job because he would

become a father in three months. What could be more ridiculous! Rick remained unchanged—flat stomached and trim. Rick swam, played handball, tennis and squash. Rick did whatever he pleased. Linda felt helpless.

Linda tried to get another job. She answered ads, she cased agencies. Each time, the moment she walked through an office door and saw the expression on the interviewer's face, she could tell it was no use. Her abdomen expanded daily. She looked as if she balanced a basketball beneath her smock. All her life Linda had been accorded the favors which males reserve for beautiful females—smiles, glances, courtesies. Overnight these vanished. She was an ugly among other uglies, scrambling for her place in line, her seat on the bus. She felt degraded, worthless.

At last she gave up, applied for unemployment insurance, and settled into the apartment with nothing to do. The four walls closed in upon her like a prison. Her appetite had become like a demon that had taken up residence inside her body and demanded food at ten-minute intervals.

Linda became sluggish and depressed. Occasionally, in a flash of insight, she recognized her dejection as unhealthy and resolved to cast it off. She forced herself to go for walks. When she felt ambitious she cleaned the apartment, scrubbing half-heartedly at calcified layers of grease and grime left by uncaring predecessors. She worried about the doctor and hospital bills. She knew her father had made arrangements, but she also knew she'd have a row with Rick when he found out. Yet what else was there to do? Every minute, awake or asleep, she was conscious of the impending birth, drawing inexorably closer. She would have to tell Rick they were borrowing the money from her folks. They could sign a note, could pay it off with interest. She avoided the subject.

Her relationship with Rick went down the tubes. Sex was unthinkable and Rick couldn't understand why. Linda accused him of being unfeeling and inconsiderate; Rick accused her of being frigid and unreasonable. Linda stretched the money from Rick's check for rent and utilities; little remained for food. Her mother took to dropping in during the daytime, with groceries, and Linda took to lying to Rick about them at night. Her friends, his friends, all of them came, all of them aired their own problems, all of them stayed to eat, all of them remarked how poorly Linda looked. Linda's mother began to worry that the baby would be early. Linda made the doctor promise to swear it *was* early.

"Although," the doctor temporized, "if you keep on gaining, you'll have a horse. It's going to be hard to explain a six-month baby who weighs ten pounds!"

Of all the persons affected, Margaret and Robert Allenby were most excited about the coming child. They envisioned another Linda to love and cherish all over again. Margaret insisted on taking Linda shopping, and Linda worried about how she would explain the crib, the Pampers, the blankets, the shirts, the sleepers to Rick.

You shouldn't have taken them. Why not? The baby has to wear something! We could have bought them ourselves! With what? I could take out a loan. That's what this is, a loan. We can pay them back. Dammit, I don't want to be in their debt!

"Cheer up!" said Margaret, who oohed and aahed over everything the clerk brought out. "This is the happiest time of your life!"

Linda tried to smile.

"Aren't you glad about the baby?" said Margaret, catching her off guard.

"Of course!" Linda tried to smile again. Be honest, she said to herself. Are you glad? Of course. You could have gotten rid of him, you know. You had the chance. No! I didn't want that. I couldn't kill my baby! And now I can feel him moving, so strong, so alive, kicking—no, no, I never could have done that! I had to have him! It's only . . .

Each dialogue in her mind ended this way, the last sentence left dangling in midair, a song missing the final chord. She was glad, glad as she could be under the circumstances, and that was the best she could do.

In mid-September the children went back to school, and Rick's job ended. The church board of deacons were pleased with his work, and begged him to come back next year. The Reverend Woodbury told Rick he had a gift for working with children, and suggested Rick go back to school and get his degree and a teaching credential. He offered to investigate a scholarship, but Rick refused. "I'll get something else," he promised Linda, "something full time. A good job would solve all our problems." He went out looking every day, and didn't find a thing. They lived on unemployment insurance, and worried.

The skin on Linda's stomach stretched like balloon-thin rubber pulled over a watermelon. Beneath the epidermis, subcutaneous layers tore. She could see jagged lesions, their edges purple as the capillaries pulled apart. She could no longer lie on either side, and spent the nights laid out like a corpse on her back, staring at the ceiling.

One day Rick came home in mid-afternoon. Margaret was visiting Linda. They heard him, jubilant, running up the stairs.

"Honey! I got a job!" He sighted Margaret, and his enthusiasm subsided in mid-sentence. "Hello, Mrs. Allenby."

Why can't you call her mother? I dunno. She doesn't seem like mother to me. You could try. You could make the effort. I told you, there are some things I can't do, so don't bug me.

Linda ran to him.

"Tell me about it! What is— How did— Where?"

"The phone company."

Linda jumped up and down, forgetting her great stomach.

"Honey, that's so marvelous! Isn't it, mother? I knew it would happen! I knew you'd find one."

"Yes, Rick, that truly is good news." Margaret's voice seemed sincere. "What sort of work will you do?"

"I hope you're not going to climb those poles!" said Linda.

"No," said Rick, "I'm going to be an operator. For long distance calls."

"A telephone operator?"

Later, Linda was to hear her mother's voice. Three words, three insignificant words, how could three words change the course of history? It wasn't the meaning of the words, it was the tone in which they were uttered, in Margaret's cultivated, modulated voice. Some nights, lying awake, Linda tried to defend her mother. Margaret had spoken before she thought. She had not intentionally tried to put Rick down, she wasn't sneering, her tone was more of surprise. It was only that Margaret did not expect a man to be a telephone operator, not a big husky man like Rick, a six-foot-four giant who had played first string defensive tackle for the Bruins.

"Yeah," Rick said after a while. "I guess it's not much by your standards."

There was silence.

"Rick! I think it's wonderful!" said Linda. For some reason, which she afterwards couldn't analyze or define, her very words and sentences sounded contrived. Margaret rose to her feet, gathering up her Gucci bag.

"Yes. Well, I must be going."

"Don't rush off," said Rick. His voice was brusque, almost harsh. "Stay. Don't leave because of me. I happen to be going out again."

"Rick . . ." Linda followed him on to the landing. "Tell me about it."

"Nothing to tell. Why don't you go back to your mother?"

"Please, Rick, don't be rude," Linda pleaded.

He started running down the stairs. Linda watched him go, overwhelmed by her emotions, by rage. How could he treat her this way when she was so near to labor, when she was big as a balloon, her skin bursting, when her feelings were unpredictable and the least indiscretion made her cry? The skeins of self-pity were interwoven with resentment toward her mother. Rick had been excited, the Rick who for a month had been down on his luck, lachrymose, discouraged. Running up the stairs, he'd seemed the Rick she remembered, vital and confident, the man she had loved.

She walked back into the apartment. She didn't feel like talking to her mother.

"Well," her mother said, "what happened?"

"He had to go out again."

"What for?"

"I don't know what for!" said Linda irritably. "It's his own business!"

"He's a strange young man." Margaret checked her makeup in the bathroom mirror. "This light's terrible. You ought to get a better globe."

"We ought to get a lot of things." Linda stood in the doorway. "Why did you do it?"

Her mother looked up, startled. "Do what?"

"Talk to Rick that way. Put him down."

"Darling, what are you—"

"You did. It was the way you said it."

"Come, now, you're imagining."

"I am not!"

Margaret sighed.

"You need to get out of this place. You've been cooped up. It's not good for you. Do you think he's coming back?"

"I have no idea what he's going to do."

"Why not come with me? We're going to have dinner with the Fosters. We'd bring you back."

Linda considered, tempted. It would serve Rick right, to come home and find her gone.

"We're going to L'Auberge."

"L'Auberge!" L'Auberge—scene of the ill-fated rehearsal dinner—when everything had started to go wrong! "Count me out. I'd rather sit here alone and wait for Rick. I wouldn't set foot in L'Auberge again for a mink-lined potty chair!"

THIRTY-THREE

The fortnight preceding the birth of the baby had been punctuated by their skirmishes: Rick on one side, the Allenbys on the other, and Linda in between, sometimes as mediator, sometimes as battleground. Margaret was tense because the young couple had no phone. You could have an emergency. Your pains could start five minutes apart. Your water could break. You could start spotting. What if Rick's not home? You could hemorrhage. You're flirting with death. It's not only your baby, it's my grandchild!

Rick was adamant. "We are not having the phone ring every two minutes with your mother on the other end of the line telling us what to do."

"Rick, mother is not like that!"

"The hell she isn't."

"She's only concerned."

"We're not having any goddammed concerned phone put in. That's final."

Score: Christians, zero: lions, one.

The Allenbys begged Linda to get Rick to let them buy the Dublins an automobile—new, used, a compact, ten years old, anything on wheels. Rick declined.

"Well then borrow one of ours. For a few weeks. So you'll have some way to get to the hospital. You can take the Mark IV."

"We wouldn't have any place to put it."

"You could park it on the street."

"It would be stolen the first night. Either that or they'd lift the battery and hub caps."

Margaret shuddered.

"Oh dear! If you didn't insist on living in such a sinister neighborhood. There isn't a day goes by but you could be raped."

"Not in my condition."

"Linda, I wish you wouldn't be so flippant, not when I'm worried sick! How will you get to the hospital?"

"I don't know," confessed Linda.

"We'll get there," said Rick. It was a semi-taboo subject, and Linda was sorry the minute she brought it up.

"How?" said Linda, after weighing the pros and cons, back and forth in her own mind.

"I've been talking to Jake, the guy in the back apartment downstairs. He lives by himself. He'll take us. If things start up while I'm at work you can use his phone to call a cab."

"What if he's at work, too?"

"There's a booth in the drugstore on the corner. You ought to be able to get that far."

Lions, two.

Linda was uneasy. She would have been glad to cancel the whole thing. She packed and repacked her bag a dozen times. United Parcel delivered the crib from Bullock's, and Rick assembled it in the corner of the apartment, moving the table and chairs against the bookshelf. When the Hide-a-Bed was open there was scarcely any floor space left in the room to walk.

As it turned out, Linda went into labor on a Saturday night. Rick was home but Jake wasn't; Rick ran all the way to the drugstore and called a cab, then he ran all the way back to the apartment and ushered Linda downstairs. The two, soon to be three, stood on the curb in the half-twilight, nervous, almost snorting with anticipation, like race horses in the starting gate.

Linda survived the cab ride and the admitting process, but after she was separated from Rick she was terrified. At one time she had wanted to learn the Lamaze method for husbands and wives, and had asked Rick if they could take the course of instruction, but Rick would have no part of it. Count me out. We could do it together. No way. I don't want to think about it, let alone do it. You know what I think? I think you're being childish! I think you're immature! Rick? Rick, please! Oh, Rick, all right, I'm sorry. I didn't mean to call names. It's only—I mean, that way, you really could be a part of it. Goddammit, Linda, I don't want to be a part of it! No way!

She hadn't been conditioned for the pain. Wasn't that

a myth, an old wives' tale, that went out of date along with other myths: the clean white rags, kettles of boiling water, the midwife hurrying to the remote farmhouse in a horse-drawn buggy? Linda was in the obstetrics wing in Los Angeles' best hospital, yet the pains washed over her like giant waves. Each rolled from afar before the last was finally spent, at first only a hint, an obscene precursor of horror to come.

Each wave of pain gathered strength, intensified, then suddenly exploded inside her like a bomb, tearing her asunder, forcing from her life and breath and the will to survive until she quivered on the brink of eternity—and then, reluctantly, it lessened its grip and receded, leaving her for dead.

She was in a never-never land where shapes were grotesque, voices were distorted so that they were too loud, too apprehensive. The owners of those voices were frightened—frightened for her! *Bear down*! they screamed, but they echoed from a far, far shore. *Bear down*! Behind the voices, like an *obbligato*, thrummed the grinding sound, the hum, the churning of machinery, a harsh, abhorrent, recurring pulse. *Bear down*! Light—bright, bright light, brighter than the sun—blinded her naked eyes. *Bear down*!

She drifted in space, she had left the earth, the sun, the universe; she streaked, faster than sound, than light, than thought. Around her stretched a limitless black nullity. Now she was drawn, gathered, sucked into the void, into nothingness. She was done for. She was gone.

When Rick had seen them roll Linda from him toward the elevator in the wheelchair, he had been too nervous to think. He returned to the admitting desk and in terse phrases imparted the required information. After that he found his way to the obstetrics wing and prowled the waiting room like a caged Bengal tiger. He was tense with worry, with a sickening sensation of *déjà vu*. He recognized the polished floors of green rubber tile. He heard again the hushed voices, whispering their urgent utterances. Doors opened and shut; people passed by, none of them acknowledging Rick's presence. No one offered to tell him anything.

Why had he let her go? Why hadn't he stopped her when he had the chance? He could have grabbed her hand, forced her from the wheelchair, run with her down the hall. Together, they could have escaped! Only then . . .

Why had Linda become pregnant? Why hadn't the blasted pills worked? Why hadn't Linda known to take them sooner? Why hadn't he known to wear a condom? Why hadn't Kemp told him, Kemp, his best friend who knew so much? Why hadn't Rick insisted that Linda get an abortion? He could have borrowed the money from Kemp. He could have found a doctor. Abortions were legal; the Supreme Court said they were. A good doctor would have been safe. Nothing to it. The guys all talked about it. Girl goes home in an hour. Girl goes to school the next day. Business as usual. No interruption. That's what the guys all said.

He had known that. He had known what was best, from every angle, from every point of view, only he hadn't been insistent. He, Rick, the toughest tackle on the defensive line, hadn't been strong. He'd let Linda talk him out of it. If he'd won, their life together would have been perfect, with nothing but love, day and night. He cursed his indecision, his weakness, his surrender. He'd let Linda talk him into the whole mess—the wedding, which was, in Rick's book of records, the number one all-time disaster—the never-ending hassle with the Allenbys, whom Rick wished he'd never met and, worst of all, the blight of pregnancy, which had changed a gorgeous, passionate, sexy girl into a shapeless, nagging, frigid shrew. Now this! Somewhere, behind the bulbous stomach, swollen ankles, and complaining voice was the tantalizing woman he once so adored, the one for whom he cared most in all the world—and she was going to die.

The conviction, which had hovered in the back of Rick's mind, now settled in upon him like a cold crust of snow, shutting out the world. For the next twelve hours, through the interminable night, he alternately paced, sat, or strode down the corridor to the drinking fountain, tormented by uncertainty. After a while another harried male appeared in the obstetrics waiting room, and then a third; they seemed to want to talk, but Rick had no wish to communicate. What good was speech, when all that mattered in life was ebbing away, behind those double doors?

When the nurse appeared at last, to talk to him, Rick was in a stupor, slumped in a corner chair, legs apart, elbows on knees, hands supporting a head which had become too heavy for his neck.

"Mr. Dublin?"

The unfamiliar voice, the formal address, spread over his consciousness like water poured over dust-dry soil. At first he barely heard, then after delayed seconds, Rick returned to life, shot to his feet, unsure of his balance.

"Ma'am?"

"It's over. You're a father. It's a little girl."

It seemed to Rick the woman spoke a foreign language, a tongue only passably familiar; he recognized the words, but failed to grasp the import of the sentence. The woman giggled.

"Sometimes I think it's harder on the fathers than the mothers, no matter what they say."

"Linda." At last, after a false try, Rick managed to activate his voice. "My wife. Is she—"

Immediately the woman's expression was guarded; in the same instant, Rick's heart sank. What was she avoiding? What was it he should know? She was leading to it gently, she was cushioning the shock.

"Your wife . . . is resting."

"She's not . . . she didn't . . ."

"No, no. She's fine." Her tone lacked conviction. "She had a rough time of it, that's all. Now that I see you I can understand why."

This was no time for insult, for a slur, not when Rick stood there defenseless, stripped bare of his armor. He tried to decipher the remark. Was it cruel? What could she have against him? Why this sudden enmity? She had never seen Rick before in her life. Yet now the nurse, the hospital, the establishment were blaming him, blaming *him* for something that had gone wrong in *there*, behind their evil doors, while Rick was sitting harmless in the waiting room, head buried in his hands. The injustice, the absurdity of her remark seeped through his person like aniline dye, leaving an indelible stain.

"I want to see her!" Rick demanded, his voice blaring out, too loud. They were tricky, hospital people, tricky; they told you what they wanted you to hear, no more, no less. The only way to find out was to see for himself.

"You can see her," said the nurse, as if placating a gorilla. "She's asleep. She needs to rest. She needs to regain her strength."

Rick stood beside the bed, in the hospital room he immediately detested, in the hospital atmosphere he mistrusted, and gazed down upon his beloved, so still, so white, so waxen, it was impossible to believe she lived. After seconds of total, terrible stillness, he detected an almost imperceptible movement of the covers. Linda breathed; just barely, but she breathed! Rick felt the relief wash over him, but he remained on guard. Linda was alive, but sick. She still might . . . might . . .

The nurse beckoned, and Rick backed out awkwardly.

"She doesn't look so good."

"She looks fine!" She spoke with false heartiness. "As soon as the anesthetic wears off she'll be good as new! Don't you want to see the baby?"

Rick looked at her, distressed. Obviously, from the woman's tone, something was expected of him, something he'd overlooked.

"You're a father now," the nurse chided playfully. "The nursery's at the far end of the hall."

Rick stood before the window and observed what was for him a disturbingly alien scene, something from a sci-fi flick. The room was filled with what at first seemed to be grocery carts, but on closer inspection proved to be small plastic baskets on wheels. In each one was a baby; some asleep, some crying; their eyes were tightly shut, their faces the color of brick. The nursery was sound-proofed; observing the violence of the crying without hearing it only heightened the illusion of unreality. In the whole of his experience Rick had never been near infants. He was repulsed by their ugliness, by their mousy size, by their inhuman color.

A girl in a green smock, her hair bound by a white cloth,

her features hidden by a gauze mask, approached the glass carrying a bundle the size and shape of a loaf of French bread, wrapped in a pink blanket. The girl proffered the loaf for Rick's inspection as if she were displaying goods to lure a buyer; with one hand she moved the flap of the blanket. Rick, fascinated and terrified, looked for the first time upon his child. He saw the minuscule, magenta-colored, wizened features of an ancient crone. He was horrified. For this—they had been through all that hassle for this—?

Dazed, he wandered out of the hospital, across the parking lot, along the sidewalks, paying no attention to other passersby. He crossed with the stop lights, not noticing where he was going, not thinking about anything—Linda, the baby, or himself—just walking. After a time he saw a fast food restaurant and realized he was hungry. He bought two hamburgers and a large Coke. He was surprised at how good they tasted. He ordered a third burger, and then a large chocolate malt for dessert. After that he again walked. At last he wandered into a third-run movie house and fell asleep.

Linda woke to find Rick standing by the bed holding a bouquet of stock, asters, and chrysanthemums. She looked into Rick's eyes and could see the tenderness, the concern she yearned for. For a blissful interval she had the feeling that everything was fine, that now the birth was over she and Rick could turn the clock back to when they first knew love; that things between them would revert to how they once had been.

"Hi!"

"Hi!"

He kissed her, long and hungrily. She felt the smoothness of his cheek, freshly shaved, she smelled the brisk fragrance of Irish Spring. He sat close to the bed. They held hands.

"I was worried," he told her. "I was so worried I couldn't see straight."

"I know," said Linda. She smiled. She felt happy. She felt as if she were floating.

"I love you," Rick told her, "more than anything in the world. I was so scared you wouldn't . . . that something would . . ."

Linda held his hand, strong and large, in hers. She was tired, her eyes closed, but she continued to see his face, his eyes anxious, pleading with her to get well.

"I love you too," she said, before she drifted off.

The next day things were different. The sedatives had worn off. The pain of the lesions took over. When Rick came Linda was sitting up in bed. She felt frustrated because she had tried to nurse the baby, but the baby hadn't known what to do.

"How are you feeling?" said Rick.

"Not so great. I don't know why. The other women are out running up and down the hall. I'm the only one who feels crummy."

"Better take it easy."

Linda took a breath. "Rick," she said, "why didn't you call mother?"

"Oh my gosh!" said Rick. "I'll do it right now."

"They know," said Linda. "Mother became worried. She finally called the hospital."

"Have they been here?"

"They came, but the nurses wouldn't let them in. Only husbands are allowed in the maternity wing. I've talked to mother on the telephone."

"How does she like being a grandmother?"

"Sort of a mixture." Linda closed her eyes, remembering the torrent of her mother's emotions. "She's relieved it's over, glad I'm all right."

"You can say that again."

"She's mad at you for not calling."

"I'm sorry. I forgot. I was so excited it just left my head."

"She's glad it's a girl." A shadow crossed Rick's face. "Rick, you don't care if it's a girl, do you?"

"No—not that much."

"You do care."

"I told you I don't."

"You don't sound as if you meant it."

"No—it's all right."

"But you were disappointed? I want to know. Rick—

This is no time for phony double talk. I have to know the truth."

"Well—okay, if you insist. I was—a little disappointed."

"Why?"

"I dunno . . . because I counted on, I mean, I thought it would be a boy, I guess."

"Why had you thought that?"

Rick said with asperity. "You told me it was going to be a boy, 'way back when we decided you should keep the baby. You talked about my son."

For no reason, having pried it out of him, Linda took umbrage at this statement.

"So now you feel you've been cheated, is that it? You act as if I could control what it was going to be!"

"No," said Rick, "I know you . . ."

"For your information," said Linda, "it's the male gene that determines the sex."

"Linda . . ." said Rick.

"So the fact that you have a daughter and not a son is due entirely to you and to no one else."

"Why don't we forget it?"

"Not until we get something settled. This is important. It's not something we can just sweep under the rug. You're assuming boy babies are the best."

Rick looked uncomfortable. Linda didn't know why, but she felt she had to keep going. For some reason she felt at odds with Rick and with the world, anxious to make her own position clear, to crack the whip, to bring everyone in line.

"That's chauvinism, I suppose you know."

'For God's sake, let's not start on that crappy stuff . . ."

"I'm not starting. I just want to clear things up. Does it matter if it's a boy or girl—as long as it's a healthy baby . . . well, does it?"

"Not to you."

"But why should it to you?"

"You wouldn't understand."

"I don't understand. That's why I'm asking you to tell me. I'll bet you secretly wanted a boy!"

"With all that Women's Lib stuff, I'll bet you secretly wanted a girl!"

"Yes . . ." Linda realized it for the first time. "I did."

Rick groaned.

"What's wrong with girls?" Linda demanded fiercely. "Girls are smarter, quicker to learn! Girls are more sensitive—more aware!" Already Rick was edging toward the door. "Where are you going?"

"Gotta be getting back."

"But you just came . . ."

"I got things to do," said Rick. "See you!"

Linda turned over on her side, petulant. It was some time before she remembered Rick had not kissed her good-by.

THIRTY-FOUR

The next day Rick Dublin, one-time nemesis of the Trojan line, now long distance operator for Pacific Telephone, charged through the hospital lobby under a full head of steam. In the elevator on the way to the maternity floor he hummed *The Girl from Ipanema* through his teeth. Freshly showered and shaved, wearing a clean shirt and pair of pants, he felt fit all over, energetic, muscular, and in top condition. The old confidence throbbed through his arteries. He was up for anything. It was over, the baby was here, Linda was on the mend. Before long they'd be back together. Everything would be the way it had been, only better, because Linda would not be pregnant any more.

Once on the floor he noticed a crowd near the viewing window of the nursery and decided to go there first. The same nurse, still disguised in white gauze mask, green smock, and puckered hat, caught Rick's eye, and brought the Dublin baby to the glass.

To Rick's surprise, his daughter was neither crying nor asleep. Magically, the scarlet fever–red had disappeared; her skin now glowed like a delicate pink rose. Her eyes were open; she looked straight up at him, solemnly thoughtful. Rick returned the glance with equal intensity. For the first time he realized he was communicating with another person—a brand new individual, who had just arrived, materializing out of nowhere. The impact of the miracle engulfed him. This new human, with its mere presence, was a part of *him*, Rick Dublin! He was the father! His heart swelled with pride.

But even as he gazed a strong sense of recognition crept over him. That forehead, those candid wide-set eyes, he had seen before—and what's more—he'd known them all his life! He was looking at the eyes and forehead of his mother! Rick felt a tremor shake his powerful frame. His mother, whom he had so deeply loved, his mother, who had deeded her life to him without a second thought, who had been snatched out of existence wtih such rude abruptness—somehow his mother had miraculously reappeared, at least in part!

When Rick entered the four-bed ward the husbands of the three other mothers were visiting already. Rick crossed to Linda's bed and bent to kiss her. His heart leaped as it always did. Linda had only to be in the same room with him to turn him on. Linda returned his kiss, but her thoughts seemed elsewhere.

"I named the baby," she told him, her voice low.

"Oh yeah?"

Rick remembered their discussion the night before. Both had been edgy, out of sorts. What should we name her? The woman from the records department has been bugging me. Name her Linda. That would be confusing, having two Lindas. If you didn't want my opinion, why did you ask? I don't care. Name her anything you want.

"It's—it's Lindamargaret, not hyphenated, all one word . . ." Her eyes flashed defensively. "You said to name her Linda! You said to name her anything I wanted. You said you didn't care!" She paused, breathlessly, then let him have the clincher. ". . . And mother's so pleased!"

Rick stared at Linda. Linda appeared fragile, beautiful, appealing. Rick tried to get hold of himself, to gain control, tried to remember how he'd clamped down on his temper the time the Husky linebacker had kneed him in the gut. Margaret Allenby was pleased! What did it have to do with Mrs. Allenby? That wide-eyed, brand new person with whom he'd been communing had nothing in common with Mrs. Allenby! She was the spitting image of Dot Dublin!

"I can go home tomorrow," Linda rambled on, unaware of the maelstrom churning inside Rick's chest. "Mother wants me to come to La Hacienda for two weeks. She's hired a nurse—"

"No!" Rick heard himself bark hoarsely. "You're *my* wife! That's my baby in there! If you're coming home, you're coming home to Jeeter Street!"

As things turned out, the next morning Rick was unable to get off from work, so Margaret came to drive Linda and Lindamargaret to the apartment. It was a time of happy excitement. Plants, gifts and cards were packed, the baby was brought to the room and dressed in her own jump suit and pink sweater. Farewells were said to the other three mothers in the ward, and at last Linda and the baby were wheeled in triumph down the hall. In the corridor outside Maternity, not only Margaret waited, but beside her, Robert.

"Daddy!" Linda was so touched by this tender moment she began to cry. "What are you doing here?"

"I couldn't stay away!" Robert kissed Linda gently on the forehead. "This is my baby daughter," he told the nurse. "Prettiest little girl in the whole world!"

"Your little girl has competition," Linda said. "Look at your granddaughter!" Her arms shook from the excitement of holding the small bundle, feeling the warmth through the thickness of the blanket and her robe, knowing that the baby was alive, was actually alive, was here, was hers, to take away, to keep!

Margaret and Robert gazed fondly at the tiny, round, red face, the minuscule mouth, miniature button nose, lashless eyes closed tight.

"She's darling!" Margaret breathed.

"She's a little honey," added Robert. "Going to take after her mother, I can see that!"

Margaret stayed with Linda at the apartment and Robert went back to the office, but he returned in the early evening, bringing dinners of fried chicken, and two bottles of champagne. Rick arrived home at the same time. The four of them toasted Lindamargaret, who had slept since she had been deposited in her new crib. Relaxed, congenial because of the champagne, they sat together at the little table, eating chicken. Margaret and Robert exuded happiness, and even Rick seemed tolerant, if not overtly hospitable, toward his in-laws. Linda was so relieved and pleased at the phenomenon of her husband and parents breaking bread together that she downed several glasses of champagne.

"This is how it should be," she told them, her syllables slightly slurred. "I knew it could happen. From now on we'll have a won'erful life together, just the four of us."

"Five of us," corrected her mother.

"Five of us!" amended Linda. "How could I forget? How could I forget for one itty bitty instant?" Painfully, because of her stitches, she managed to ease herself to her feet and waddled to the crib to look down upon her daughter. "Isn't she sleeping a terribly long while?"

"Enjoy it!" counseled Margaret. "She'll be awake soon enough. You'll be pacing the floor!"

"Listen to grandma!" said Linda.

"Don't use that word!" Her mother's tone was sharp.

"Grandma? But you—"

"Look," said Margaret. Her words, too, were slurred. "Let's get one thing straight. I'm thrilled about the baby. I couldn't be more thrilled. You all know that." Robert nodded solemn confirmation. "But there's one point where I draw the line. I do not wish to be called grandma."

"Grandmother?"

"No!" said Margaret.

Linda was surprised. "But what about the baby? What will Lindamargaret call you?"

"We'll cross that bridge when Lindamargaret talks. I am stating here and now I am not ready for a rocking chair."

"Mother, for heaven's sake, nobody's going to put you in any kind of a chair!"

"I know, I know," Margaret waved her down. "It's not that I'm not delighted about the baby. I said I was and I am. But it's going to be difficult to explain—"

"What exactly are you going to have to explain?" inquired Rick. His tone was deceptively calm, but Linda detected an ominous undertone. Her heart sank. She had thought the champagne had been fun but she realized now it was a mistake.

"Why, that the baby arrived less than six months after you were married," said Margaret. "Don't you think I can count?"

Linda felt a warm flush suffuse her cheeks, not from champagne, from guilt. It had caught up with her at last. She'd had to get married—because she was pregnant! She opened her mouth, but her mother waved her hand for silence.

"I know exactly what you're going to say. 'The doctor says she's early.' I'm not here to pass judgment."

"Margaret . . ." said Robert.

"All I'm saying is, it's going to be difficult to explain . . ."

Linda's face continued to burn. She imagined her mother on the phone, parrying questions from Nita Foster. It would be ghastly to explain.

"Explain to who?" said Rick.

"To whom," said Margaret, automatically correcting him. Rick looked offended. "Why, to all the people we know, our friends and yours, all the people who were at your wedding."

"Listen," said Rick, "anybody I have to explain anything to, I don't want him for a friend."

"You know your friends," said Margaret.

Linda cringed. This was the tone in her mother's voice she'd dreaded in her imagination all these months, the tone accusing, implying . . . Without meaning to, she caught Rick's eye, fiercely defiant, and read his thoughts. Why should we let them bully us this way? We're married. We're together. We have our baby. What is there to be ashamed of?

". . . You know your friends," Margaret went on, "but I know ours. The people *we* know have moral standards!"

"Mother!" pleaded Linda.

"It's none of the people-you-know's damn business!" said Rick.

"Are you suggesting that our friends don't—" said Linda.

"All I'm saying is how can I explain—"

"Why should you feel you have to explain anything," countered Rick, "when you're so dead set against being a grandmother. Why don't you just pretend the baby never happened."

"I am not dead set!" protested Margaret heatedly. "You misunderstood me! I only . . ."

"You only meant to imply we shouldn't have had the baby." Rick was now aroused.

"She only meant to imply that your timing was off," said Robert. "It would have been more practical—"

"What?"

"—if you'd waited till your financial position . . ."

"Till you were in a bigger place," said Margaret, explaining, but making things not better but worse. "Till you could give the baby the advantages she ought to have."

Linda stopped eating, unable to swallow the half-chewed

piece of chicken in her mouth. The dinner party, launched so felicitously, had metamorphosed into a nightmare.

"I think we'll be able to give her everything she needs," Linda managed to say. She stole a look at Rick, who sat, red-faced, features hard as granite, looking ahead.

"Of course we'll pitch in and help," Margaret added, "every way we can."

"That won't be necessary," said Rick coldly. "We don't want your help."

"If you weren't so stubborn about not taking a job with the plant," said Robert, "you wouldn't need our help."

Rick jumped to his feet, pushing his chair over behind him.

"Look," he shouted. "We do not need your help. We do not want your help. Do I make myself clear?"

Robert, too, was standing.

"Oh, no? If you're so independent what about the doct—"

"Listen," said Rick. Linda had never seen him so angry. He leaned toward Robert, towering about him. "I don't know what kind of an arrangement Linda made with you, but she did it behind my back. I want you to know I'm going to pay you back, every last, sniveling red cent, with interest. In the meantime, I don't want any more help, understand?"

In the midst of the loud voices and commotion, the baby started to cry.

Margaret pulled on her coat. "I think we ought to be going." Her voice struggled for composure, but her lips were white. "I'll come tomorrow."

"Don't bother," said Linda, stiffly. "We can manage by ourselves."

"Then let me send Marcie. Or I can still get that nurse."

"Never mind."

"Dear, I am sorry you're upset—that we all are upset. That doesn't change the fact you'll need help for the next two or three weeks."

"I'm fine," said Linda, fighting to hold back the tears. "Just leave us alone. That's all I ask."

She opened the door for them and stood aside. Her father walked out without speaking. Her mother paused on the threshold, indecisive.

"Let me know if you change your mind."

"I don't think it will be likely," said Linda.

For the first time in her life she parted from her parents without kissing them. Rick made no effort to tell them good-by. He didn't even bother to get up from the table.

After they had gone, Linda sat down in a daze. What had happened? How had it all come on? The battle had erupted out of a peaceful dinner party where everyone was having a good time. It had materialized as suddenly as a tornado from a clear Kansas sky.

Not only had Rick's fury surprised her, but she herself was frighteningly angry. Rick came out of the bathroom, banging the door.

"You don't need to be so violent. You're making the baby cry."

Linda picked up Lindamargaret, who was wet. She started to change her.

"I don't like to be pushed around," said Rick.

"Nobody's pushing you around now."

"They think they can come in here, run our lives."

Linda slid away the wet Pamper, and awkwardly tried to fit the dry one through the small space between the baby's legs. Her hands shook. She was as angry as Rick.

"I knew they'd find out," she said.

"So they found out, so what's the big deal? Whether we slept together or not is nobody's business but ours."

"But they think . . ."

"I don't give a fart what they think, or their goddammed puritanical friends think . . ."

"No, but they're not your—"

"And you shouldn't give a damn either. You've got to stop feeling guilty. You haven't anything to be guilty about. You haven't done one thing to be ashamed of . . ."

"You know that, and I know that—"

"That's all that matters, isn't it?"

Unexpectedly, Linda started to cry.

"But then why did she have to say that . . . the people they know have high moral standards . . . as if . . ."

Rick savagely kicked the side of the Hide-a-Bed.

"I don't know why the hell she said it, but I wasn't going to sit there and take it—"

"I don't know why she had to drag our friends into it . . ."

"It wasn't our friends," said Rick. "That was a manner of speech. It was us, you and me. We're the ones she was putting down. We're the alley cats. We're the ones who don't have any morals. We're the ones who aren't good enough for your folks' friends, or for your folks, either one."

Linda's tears now flowed so fast she couldn't see what she was doing. She wrapped the blanket around the baby and sat down to nurse her.

"I didn't want a fight," Linda protested, sobbing. She bared her breast. The baby wouldn't take hold. "The last thing I wanted was a fight. That's what I tried to avoid all along."

"It couldn't be helped," said Rick. "It was that or let them walk all over us."

"Now they're mad, and we're mad—" Linda kept trying to tilt her breast and ease the nipple into the baby's mouth. By this time the baby was crying as hard as she.

"It was bound to come," said Rick, "sooner or later. I'd just as soon it happened. Cleared the air."

"Why doesn't she nurse?" said Linda.

"Maybe she doesn't know how."

"She did it in the hospital."

At last the baby latched on to the areola, and sucked fervently. Linda tried to force herself to relax.

"Isn't she cute?" she demanded of Rick.

"Yeah," said Rick. "Lucky stiff."

"What do you mean?"

"Sucking away."

In spite of herself, Linda felt herself blush.

"This is no time to talk about that."

"When is, I'd like to know? My God, you expect me to sit here and watch . . ."

"I do not expect you to sit there and watch. Why don't you do something useful? Why don't you clean up the kitchen?"

"I don't want to clean up the kitchen. I want to do something else."

"Are you out of your mind? My stitches are giving me fits. I can hardly sit down."

"Listen," said Rick, "I've been living like a monk for months."

"Weeks."

"It's over a month."

"I can't help it," said Linda, flaring up. "It's going to be a lot longer than that."

She might have been protesting to the wind. Rick didn't hear a word she said.

THIRTY-FIVE

Later, looking back, much as an inquiry board sifts through the charred and twisted bits of wreckage of an airplane, Linda tried to reason how the disaster could have been averted. If only Rick hadn't turned into a sex maniac that first night and ripped out all her stitches, if only Linda had had enough sense not to swill down champagne, if only they had not had that row with her parents, or if Linda had not raged furiously angry, or if she had not later let herself dissolve in tears—then, maybe then, Lindamargaret might not have developed colic. If Lindamargaret had not had colic, if Lindamargaret could have slept, just for a few hours that first night, it would have made the difference.

Linda's attention had been so engrossed in her struggle with Rick, she had been shouting, carrying on so hard herself, that when at last she was able to shift her attention from her own plight, when she first became aware of the child's screaming, she also had the impression it had been going on for an unreasonably long time. Linda managed to drag herself to the crib and found the baby yelling, her little face screwed up in anger, her legs thrust out straight and stiff, her body rigid—and nothing, nothing on heaven or earth could prevail on her to stop.

Linda had picked the child up and tried to sooth her, rock her, walk with her, but to no avail. The screaming rose in intensity. She changed the infant and attempted to feed her. The baby nuzzled at the nipple for a moment, then went back to crying. Linda tried everything again, burping, rocking, walking. Nothing worked. Rick had by now gone to bed. Linda was too furious to speak to him, let alone ask for his help. She paced the floor holding the rigid, screaming child. The neighbors upstairs pounded on the ceiling, the neighbors next door pounded on the wall. Linda herself started to weep helplessly, her sobs mingling with the baby's fierce, rhythmic cries. Again she walked back and forth, holding the stiff, determined little body against her shoulder as she had seen the nurse do, patting the wee back. The baby screamed on. It was a nightmare. Again Linda tried to get the child to nurse, and for a moment it seemed she might succeed. The tiny mouth rooted anxiously over the taut, smooth contour of the breast, searching for a hold. But by now a curious phenomenon had occurred. Both breasts had become engorged, the skin was stretched tightly over the swollen surface, the nipples had disappeared, and the baby might as well have tried to suck milk from a smooth rubber ball. Frustrated by failure, she bawled again with added frenzy. Linda, now overly alarmed and over-tense, continued to push the breast, like a heavy, too-ripe melon, into the baby's face.

At last, after two hours of clamor, the baby dropped off to sleep. Gently, scarcely daring to breathe, Linda deposited her in the crib, then gratefully eased herself into the bed beside Rick. In what seemed no more than seconds later, Rick was shaking her awake.

"The baby's crying."

"I can hear her."

"Aren't you going to get up?"

"Why don't you get up?"

"I don't know what to do."

"First, you change her."

"I don't know how."

"You know as much as I do. You take off one diaper and put on the other."

She hadn't realized it, but she must have again dropped off to sleep.

"Linda!"

"What?" Crossly.

"You have to get up. She's made a mess."

"Clean it up."

"I can't. It's all over everything. I don't know where to begin . . ."

"Linda!"

"What?"

"She's kicking in it! She's making it worse!"

That had been bad, but it was nothing compared to the pain Linda now felt in both breasts, which had become so distended she thought it possible that one or the other might actually burst in a carnage of gore and mother's milk. Between them, she and Rick managed to cleanse their child and her crib, scraping off the soft, yellow, odorus fecal matter which oozed everywhere. Numb with fatigue and determined to succeed, Linda again tried to coax the baby to nurse. By this time she was in such agony both from her swollen breasts and from the fiery pain of her stitches that she could not bear to sit, and stood or moved about the room, cradling the crying baby in one arm, futilely trying with the other hand to maneuver the globular breast into the baby's mouth. At last, almost yelping from the pain, she managed to squeeze the flesh so that the child could get hold and suck. Gradually, as the baby drank, the excruciating pressure on that side lessened, leaving Linda weak and trembling with relief. Before Linda could transfer the infant to the other breast, Lindamargaret went to sleep. Linda laid her gently back in the crib and climbed once again in bed beside the mountain of Rick's sleeping figure. Now one breast felt normal, but the other was still engorged, so tender she couldn't stand to have the sheet brush across its surface. She lay on her good side, and was just drifting into sleep, when the baby wakened and began to cry again. Linda listened in dazed disbelief as the cries, only sporadic at first, accelerated into full-throated, lusty yells. This time, Lindamargaret never stopped. At last Linda forced herself to climb out of bed and pick her up, but no matter what she did, she couldn't quiet her. There was no respite, no nursing. Whether the child was held erect, walked with, rocked, cradled, or patted, nothing would calm her, nothing would quiet her. She screamed, non-stop, until morning.

When Rick got up to get ready for work, Linda felt she was a walking zombie, a fugitive from the tomb. Her eyes barely open to slits, her expression glazed, she paced up and down, holding the baby, who, her energy and voice undiminished by her twelve-hour marathon, continued lustily to bawl.

Rick said, as he went toward the bathroom, "Crying again?"

"Still," said Linda, forcing herself to speak. Her voice was creaky, from long disassociation with humankind. "She's still crying. She's never stopped." She could hear the toilet flush. She wasn't sure Rick heard. "There isn't any food. And what about those dirty clothes?"

Rick was busy shaving. He didn't reply. Maybe he hadn't heard her, Lindamargaret was making such a racket. Linda thought she never wanted to hear a baby cry again.

"Rick—I feel funny."

He came to the doorway, half his face covered with lather, the other half smooth and pink.

"Funny, how?"

"Sort of hot and feverish . . . and my stitches . . . they're simply killing me! I told you . . ." Rick didn't answer. "And this one breast, it looks to me as if it's infected— it's gone all red and the skin's stretched so tight . . . Rick?"

"What?"

"What do you think we ought to do?"

Rick had gone back to shaving. "I don't know what the hell we ought to do. Just ride it out."

"Maybe you ought to call mother, after all."

"Are you nuts?"

"Before you go. You could use Jake's phone."

"Listen, your mother comes, I split. Take your pick."

"But what are we going to do—about groceries? And the washing?"

"I told you, forget it. I'll take care of it when I come home."

After Rick left, the day became almost supernatural. Images blurred, outlines wavered, areas of light and shadow merged into one another. Linda held, or rocked, or patted, or paced, and Lindamargaret cried, a throaty, breathless, never-ending cry. A long, tedious hour elapsed. At last, Linda somehow managed to squeeze her swollen right breast in such a way that the baby could close in upon the nipple and suck. She took the milk in eager, demanding gulps. "Poor little tyke," thought Linda, "you don't know it but you're drinking poison." By this time Linda was convinced her milk was somehow indigestible, and that its anomalous chemistry was the cause of the baby's violent screams. After five minutes of nursing the baby dropped into sound slumber. Linda halfway knew she should make the effort to burp her, but so great was the relief to have the breast emptied and the crying stopped that she put the sleeping baby into her crib and she herself dropped into the tangled bed clothes of the Hide-a-Bed and was asleep almost before her head touched the pillow.

The story was the same for the first several days and nights. Linda slept when the baby slept, which was not often, never more than an hour at a time, never enough for Linda. She remembered old spy movies on television, in which a captive was tortured by being constantly awakened, by never being allowed sleep. The first twenty-four hours were bad enough, but when the wakefulness extended forty-eight, then, seventy-two hours, Linda began to show the effects. Because of the prolonged labor and difficult birth, she had by no means recovered when she came from the hospital. Now the fatigue, the unrelieved nervous strain, the anxiety about the baby began to take its toll.

Sometimes in the night as she walked back and forth, holding the angry, pulsating bundle of life, she inquired of Providence how she had blundered into this ghastly plight. She reviewed the quarrel with her parents, played it back over and again, like a broken record. What had started the fracas? What had gone wrong? It became a fixation; she couldn't expunge the bitter altercation from her mind. She, Linda, in a cruel voice, had told her mother not to come, not to send the nurse, or even Marcie, the cleaning woman. Why? She had signed her own death warrant. How could she have been so stupid!

Rick had told her parents he did not want help, in any shape or form. That was understandable. At least Rick was consistent. But that, too, was a mistake, the error of the century! They desperately needed help. How could they have been so stubborn or so blind?

She and Rick had been furious. What about? At three o'clock in the morning, after one has had no more than a token of sleep for two and a half days, it was difficult to analyze the fine points. They had taken umbrage at Margaret's cutting remark citing moral standards. Again, even in Linda's half-rational, half-dazed state of mind, guilt engulfed her. Vainly she reminded herself of Rick's words. You have nothing to feel ashamed about. What's done is done. That was all well and good for Rick to say. He was a man. Men looked at sex in quite a different way. Rick hadn't been raised as she had. He'd never been to church until he was married. Linda tried to review her conduct, groping back through what seemed centuries to that first hour of love, that rainy Sunday when she had worn the Davidow suit. It had been fun to have an affair. She could never have stopped their coming together; it had been as preordained as the bees carrying pollen from one flower to the next, yet always, deep down, Linda knew now she had foreseen the hour of judgment, the time at last when her parents would find out.

As the ordeal wore on, Linda's physical appearance degenerated. Her skin lost its glow and acquired a gray-white tinge; her hair became stringy and dull. She tied it back with an elastic to keep it out of the way. Her eyes lost their alertness, and had a tendency to stare; beneath them were putty-colored hollows. She was nervous and cross, she snapped at Rick sarcastically, jeering at his ineptitude; her hands shook when performing simple tasks. At Lindamargaret's bath time she was terrified, fearing she would drop her. Her anxiety fed upon itself, compounding her fears. Why was the area around the stump of the baby's umbilical cord so red? It must be infected. With an infection so close to the heart, the child would die of blood poisoning before the day was out. Why was the area around Linda's stitches still excruciatingly sore? They, too, must be infected. Nothing could hurt so badly over so prolonged a period of time and not signal a serious disorder. She tried to look at them, using the mirror in her powder compact. They appeared red and puffy, and this intensified her dread. Why did her breasts fill so full? The baby must not be getting sufficient milk. Yet Linda couldn't force her to take more. The child had a will of her own, more stubborn than either Rick's or Linda's. Worst of all, why did Lindamargaret cry so much? The nurse at the hospital had said the baby would sleep most of the time the first couple of months. Linda laughed mirthlessly, remembering.

Sometimes when she was washing her hands, Linda would stare at the haggard creature who looked listlessly out of the bathroom mirror and wonder who she was. Surely this couldn't be the Linda Allenby who was always pointed out as a great-looking blonde? For the first time in her life, going as far back as she could recall, Linda didn't care how she looked. She didn't care what Rick thought. She didn't want Rick to touch her, she didn't want Rick to like her. And Rick, after that first violent night, made no advances.

They were like victims of a common tragedy; hikers, who, with their child, had fallen into a turbulent river and now struggled against increasing odds to keep their heads above the water, to survive.

Rick did what he could in his clumsy way. He shopped for groceries, he heated TV dinners in the apartment's unpredictable gas oven. He emptied trash and he walked blocks to the laundromat carrying a plastic basket piled with smelly, soiled clothes and waited patiently into the night while the washers and dryers ground out their respective cycles. Sometimes when the baby wakened in the wee hours, Rick would stumble out of bed, change her, and bring her to Linda to nurse. Though it seemed to Linda Rick was always asleep and only she was awake, Rick, too, began to complain about loss of rest; he became recalcitrant and cross.

They agreed at last that something must be wrong. Rick telephoned the pediatrician recommended by Linda's obstetrician and learned the doctor never made house calls, that he charged thirty dollars per office consultation, and that one had to make an appointment three weeks in advance. A woman at work told Rick about a baby clinic and so, summoning her last vestige of strength, Linda went there by cab. The anteroom was crowded with mothers and babies of every age, mostly black or chicano; some of the women had one or two toddlers as well. Linda was struck by the fact that all these women had gone through the same experience as her own, and had survived. Some few, in fact, could even joke and laugh.

When it was her turn, the nurse weighed and measured Lindamargaret, and recorded her statistics. The doctor then examined her swiftly but expertly, peering into every orifice, thumping, prodding, listening. For once, Lindamargaret was not crying. She seemed to enjoy the examination, her eyes wide open.

"Healthy as a horse," the doctor said.

"You mean there's nothing wrong?"

"Wrong? She's already gained two pounds. Whatever it is you're doing, you're on the right track."

"But she cries all the time."

"Maybe she's hungry. She's big boned. Look at those shoulders! If she weren't a girl I'd say you had a football player on your hands."

"You don't understand! She cries even when she's finished nursing!"

"Are you getting up the bubble?"

"Trying to."

The doctor glanced at his watch, signaled the nurse to bring in the next child.

"It's probably a touch of colic. Gas. Some babies have it. Some don't."

"But it's so bad!" said Linda desperately, trying not to be ushered out. "We can't stand the crying, day and night. We're not getting any sleep!"

The doctor shrugged. "She'll outgrow it. Only lasts three or four months."

"Three or four months! I won't last that long!"

The doctor had the temerity to laugh. "Sure you will. We haven't lost a mother from colic yet." He turned to the nurse. "Next!"

Unsatisfactory as Linda deemed it to be, the visit to the clinic proved to be the turning point; from then everything was on the upswing. Now that Linda knew nothing was wrong she relaxed. As she relaxed the child relaxed; Linda's skill at nursing then increased; the baby, older, stronger, more practiced, improved as well, so that nature's delicate balance of giving and receiving the magical life-supporting fluid was at last achieved. The terrible, griping colic lessened its hold and appeared less and less, the baby slept oftener and for longer periods. Linda slept more, she ate better, little by little her strength returned. One morning she wakened, refreshed, and realized Linda-margaret had slept from midnight to five-thirty a.m. For the first time in six weeks Linda didn't dread getting out of bed, in fact, she almost bounded to her feet. She crooned to Lindamargaret as she nursed, and after that sang as she fixed Rick's breakfast.

The terrible ordeal was over.

THIRTY-SIX

During the last month of Linda's pregnancy, the chief subject of Rick's thoughts, conscious and subconscious, was sex. As the period of his abstinence lengthened, his preoccupation with sex increased, until sex assumed obsessive proportions.

The first night Linda was home from the hospital when he forced her to submit to him in a swift, wild orgiastic scene, it was as if he were possessed, as if a savage demon had infiltrated his body and propelled him to bestiality. So furious was Linda at him, so blaming, indeed so pitiful had she been when he had withdrawn and she lay before him, spread out and bleeding, sobbing with pain and indignation, that Rick was singularly affected. It was as if he had raped her while under some strange spell, and then suddenly had regained his senses and realized he had inflicted cruel injury upon the person in the world he most wished to protect. He was beset by a self-loathing such as he never had experienced, and though, in time, he managed to seal off the guilt, it festered, undermining his confidence as a lover.

Although he never put it into words, he projected an image of himself as a virile male, able to perform well sexually. This was the essence of his existence: maleness and his pride in maleness throbbed in every surge of blood pumped from arteries to capillaries. Every muscle contraction, every perception of each nerve throughout his powerful frame, every breath reiterated that.

His thoughts of sex, both in the arid period before the birth of the baby and in the nightmare weeks beyond that one wild moment of release, centered upon Linda. Like the great gray northern goose he stayed true to his mate by instinct. His dreams were of a multiplicity of sexual acts with and upon Linda, some forgotten before he wakened, some lingering to haunt him with their bizarreness. How-

ever, in his conscious fantasizing, he ran again and again
through the same pattern, part daydream and part wish,
until it became a litany, an end to be desired above all else.
If only he and Linda could go back to that first month of
their relationship, that time of bliss and passion! With each
fantasy the long-ago occurrences became more idealized,
with disagreements and imperfections overlooked, until
the memory crystallized into a luminous perfection. Rick
became convinced that in that month, that one month, he
had, in actuality, been what he envisioned himself to be, a
macho man; strong, invincible, sexually irresistible. Linda
had been wild for him; she couldn't get enough of him;
they had done nothing but make love, with no hindrance
or restraint, over and over, again and again.

As he re-envisioned that paradise, in which he had performed so well (the magnetic, the compelling lover), and
then compared it with the months which had followed, the
contrast was chilling. Never since then had Linda been as
enthusiastic about sex or about him. Realistically, Rick
told himself this was the result of Linda's being pregnant,
yet the nagging doubt persisted that Linda had tired of
him, that she no longer loved him as much as she had, he
was no longer the macho male he once had been. This
nebulous insecurity troubled him; he never recognized it
consciously. Instead, when plagued by foul misgivings he
turned to his placebo: if only they could go back to things
as they first had been!

Rick tried not to brood upon all that had gone wrong,
yet in addition to grievances about his love life, he was
beset by a host of other aggravations. From the beginning
he had felt alienated from the Allenbys, from that first
Sunday in the patio he had sensed the Allenbys thought
he was not top quality for Linda. From that moment on he
read a "put down" in every glance that Margaret or Robert
threw in his direction. Never did Rick admit the possibility that he might be unfair, that he might be imagining
a slur where none existed. Subconsciously he knew he was
jealous. Linda had been entirely his for one halcyon
month, after that he had to share her; he begrudged each
hour Linda went shopping with her mother for the wedding
and later for the baby. In addition, there lurked a resentment that Linda should have her mother and father to care

for her and fuss over her, while Rick's mother was dead, lost to him forever, and Rick's father had abandoned him those many years ago. Though Rick never acknowledged his jealousy, he was quick to repudiate any influence Linda's parents sought to exercise upon her or him. He grew to regard his independence as sacrosanct; he resented any offer of financial aid, which implied that he lacked sufficient funds and was unworthy of the Allenbys' daughter.

When it was necessary for Robert to pay Linda's doctor and hospital bills, Rick felt abysmally degraded. It was an added mortification that Rick had been unable to leave work to bring his wife and baby home, but that Robert had easily arranged to leave his office and, with Margaret, had effected the homecoming.

It was upon this volatile mishmash of fireworks behind Rick's seemingly placid countenance that a spark had fallen; Margaret's remark about the high moral tone of the Allenbys' friends. Rick's ethics, such as they were, had resulted from his mother's upbringing (respect of others' rights and privacy); from athletics (sportsmanship and fair play); and from his association with friends (if it feels good, do it!). He had considered sleeping with Linda not only good but the greatest part of his life; he harbored no guilt, and Margaret's implication that this pure and beautiful love was shameful infuriated Rick to a feverish pitch.

Whenever Rick reviewed this quarrel with his in-laws his anger was renewed. No matter how desperately he, Linda, and the baby needed help during the nights and days that ensued, Rick stood adamant. They all three could have died before he would have thrown in the sponge and called upon the Allenbys for aid.

Nevertheless, his unsatisfactory relationship with the Allenbys exerted a deleterious effect upon his disposition. Never in his lifetime had Rick been seriously at odds with anyone. His own mother had worshiped the ground he walked on, so had her friend Melba DeLaney. He had been popular with teammates, lauded by coaches, cheered by fans, and praised by reporters. For eight years he had enjoyed the adulation of being a star. Always he had "gotten along," always people had thought of him as "okay." The hassle with Linda's folks, as he termed it, left a bad taste; whenever Linda brought it up, he refused to talk.

However, even more disturbing was the homecoming of the baby, who, in the space of a few hours, turned Rick's world upside down. It had not crossed Rick's mind to prepare himself for fatherhood; he had not wanted the child in the beginning, and during the term of pregnancy—even after he had put the crib together—his mind had shied away from any imagining what life would be like once the tiny stranger arrived.

Rick had had no younger brothers or sisters. He'd had no aunts, cousins, neighbors, or friends with babies. As he entered puberty and began to fantasize about the delights of sex, he never connected sex with babies. Since he had been raised by his mother, he had no memory of a father's love or care, no pattern in his mind of how a father should act. Before the birth he had thought of the baby as being Linda's. She had been so gung-ho to have her, he wanted no part of it. This feeling had cropped up again the day the baby actually was born. Rick had been frightened for Linda's life, and by an irrational transference blamed the baby for his sweetheart's brush with death. It might have been different if the child had been a boy, but she wasn't.

It was true that when Lindamargaret was two days old, Rick had undergone the profound experience of recognizing his mother in her tiny person, and had felt a surge of pride in his fatherhood, yet for some reason after the baby was actually home for the most part he shunned her.

Even after Lindamargaret had been in the apartment for a week, for two weeks, Rick was afraid to pick her up or handle her. The few times he allowed himself to be conned into cleansing Lindamargaret's bowel movements he was offended to the point of gagging.

Worst of all was the infant's crying, which never ceased. At the end of the first night, in spite of Linda's accusation that he had slept through everything, Rick's nerves were on edge; each successive nocturnal siege compounded the tension; the caterwauling went on, on, on; fierce, rhythmic, demanding, constantly, till Rick was ready to explode; he felt like smashing dishes, throwing chairs against the wall, snatching the screaming child and shaking her till she would stop.

Without realizing it, he seethed with resentment that this third person, however small or helpless, had entered, uninvited, and taken over their lives. Everything revolved around the baby, everyone catered to the baby. Rick was baffled. He hadn't allowed himself to be made into a second-class citizen by Linda's parents, but this small, imperious tyrant had displaced him the moment she was carried across the threshold. Linda thought of nothing but the baby. She never thought of Rick, she never praised Rick, nor told him how thoughtful, how considerate, how self-sacrificing he was. She never bothered to extend a little understanding to Rick's problems, to express appreciation for all that he did, or to encourage him to continue their macabre existence. Once, she'd smothered him with affection, showered him with love. That Linda had disappeared, replaced by a shrew, who wore no make-up, whose hair, once his delight, now hung in mop strings, whose breasts sagged and whose stomach still bulged. The shrew spoke only with sarcasm. Rick, stung to the quick, responded in kind.

When, finally, things started to improve, when the baby stopped crying, when Linda at last felt rested, when she once more looked beautiful, and even became interested in love, Rick's delirium knew no bounds. It was like returning to paradise after a sojourn in hell. What had been black was now white, what had been darkness changed to sunlight. Rick sang in the shower, he ran from the bus stop, so eager was he to get home at night. His ebullience was matched by Linda's high spirits and affection. Both were so relieved to be back to normal living they savored their new life as if it were an exotic, delicate dessert. Rick had bought an album of the twenties, which he played constantly on Linda's old portable stereo. *Just Mollie and me, and baby makes three, we're happy in my blue heaven.*

After a while Rick began to like the baby.

"Isn't she cute?" Linda kept asking. "She looks like you."

"I don't know if that's so good, for a girl," Rick said, but he was pleased.

Linda had gone again to the baby clinic.

"The doctor said she's gaining faster than any baby he's ever seen."

"Maybe you're feeding her too much."

"You can't, with breast feeding. They take what they need and then stop. Mother Nature knows best. Besides, she isn't fat. Just big."

"She would have made a helluva football player."

"Maybe she will, anyway. I read they're taking girls on some teams."

Now that she had more energy, Linda began to take an interest in preparing food. For Rick, who next to his love of sex loved to eat, this foray into the delights of home cooking was an adventure. Because Rick's mother had worked, he had grown up thinking all food was dry cereal, TV dinners, or came from cans. His years at the training table had assuaged his lively appetite, but there the food, though ample, had an institutional flavor. Now Linda experimented with lemon pie, carrot cake, rouladin and potato dumplings. Not everything succeeded; there were catastrophic failures, but Rick wolfed down the failures as well as the successes, begging for more.

Linda thought of ways to make the apartment more attractive; she bought some framed pictures at the cut-rate drugstore. One weekend she and Rick painted the dingy closet of a bathroom a brilliant yellow.

They fell into traditional roles. Rick had become the head of the household, going forth each day to work, proudly bringing home his check at the end of each fortnight, which provided shelter and sustenance for his dependents. Linda nursed and cared for the baby, cooked and cleaned and made herself beautiful. In the evenings after Rick came home they played with the baby, ate Linda's latest culinary experiments (dinner had become a memorable event), did the dishes, and then made love.

Thinking back to the horrors of a few short weeks earlier, recalling his frantic yearnings, Rick realized his prayers had in actuality been answered. It was true sometimes that even now, Lindamargaret cried or fussed, or that they had to defer or interrupt their own activities to cater to her needs, but the sweetness of her expression, the trust in her eyes more than repaid them. Rick had regained the paradise he thought he had lost forever. He considered himself a prince among men.

It was only natural that, after having in effect been isolated from human society for months, Linda now welcomed company. After all, Rick saw people every day at the telephone building; in fact, all he did was talk to people, but Linda only made an occasional trip to the grocery store or laundromat, pushing Lindamargaret in her new stroller. Delcie was their most frequent visitor; she had loved Lindamargaret from the beginning, and had taken turns rocking the screaming child to give Linda respite. Now that the little family had survived the trauma of colic, Delcie gurgled approval.

"I knew things would get better!"

"They had to," said Linda shuddering. "They couldn't have been worse."

"You're so lucky," breathed Delcie.

"You're always saying that."

"It's true, it's true. Oh, Linda, if only Kemp and I . . ." She brightened. "That's what I came to tell you. My big news! I'm taking a class with him! With Kemp, did you hear me? Kemp!"

"Geology?"

"No, silly. Real estate law. It's an extension, down at the beach. Kemp's going into real estate, did you know that?"

"He drops by," said Linda. "But how—"

"He asked me! That's what's fantastic. Well, not exactly asked. I told you I wasn't going to chase him, I wasn't going to make the same mistake twice, only I happened to run into him . . ."

"Happened?"

"Well anyway, we got to talking, and he mentioned— he said he thought I'd enjoy it, truly he did, Linda, on a stack of Bibles, so I enrolled . . ."

"Delce, that's dishonest! You don't care any more about real estate law than the man in the moon."

"No, but I care about Kemp! If Kemp cares about real estate, real estate's for me. I think it's important for a wife to understand her husband's business."

Linda, who was nursing the baby, looked closely at her friend, noticing Delce's appearance for the first time in months. Once again Delcie had changed. She had gone back to wearing contacts, she had lost weight, her skin had cleared up—but it was more than that. In spite of her enthusiasm she exhibited a self-assurance which had not been there before. She had restyled her hair, which fell into a soft pageboy short of her shoulders. Her clothes, too, conveyed an impression of chic.

"Delce," Linda said gently, "don't get your hopes up. Do you know where Kemp lives? In a swinging singles complex called Shangri La. Do you know what they do there?"

"Swing," said Delce. "I know all about it." Linda must have looked startled. "Don't get me wrong. I haven't been in on it. But Kemp explained it to me. It's a way of life."

"It's a way of life that doesn't synchronize with wedding bells," said Linda. "Why don't you forget Mr. Lover Boy and concentrate on your own life for a change?"

"That's what I'm doing!" said Delcie plaintively.

"Listen," said Linda, "I'll spell it out in black and white. Anyone who graduated from all-campus stud to king of the singles is not going to tie himself to anybody's apron strings."

"Don't be too sure," said Delcie cheerfully. "Clerks in a bakery shop get awfully sick of cream puffs. And that's another thing—marriage is the only way he'll get me. I used to think I'd go to bed with him at the drop of a whistle, but that's changed. I finally came up with all the answers."

Linda regarded her friend with tender pity.

"Which reminds me," Delcie rattled on, "apropos of nothing, or apropos of the busted romance department, guess who's left whom?"

"I haven't the foggiest."

"Aggie toddled out on Sadie!"

Linda whistled. "I don't believe it!"

"True, on a stack—"

"I never thought she'd have the nerve."

"Neither did I, but she did it. Got her a new apartment, nobody knows where, with an unlisted phone. Sadie's fit to be tied. When all else failed she tried to get Ag fired, out of revenge, but the floor manager said bra and pantie sales had jumped thirty per cent since Ag started modeling in June. He said that he didn't care if she was president of the call girls association and the gay liberation front rolled into one."

Linda had put the baby in her crib and set out leftovers for lunch.

"Who told you all this?"

"Aggie herself. We had lunch Monday. But that's not the clincher. Guess who's been calling her long distance, on that same telephone for which she will not divulge the number? The great Darter Evans!"

"Darter! But I thought . . . I thought . . ."

"Proving that you never can be too sure about anything." Delce took a mouthful of lasagna. "In case your big hunk of man hasn't told you, you're becoming a fabulous cook!" She jumped up from the table. "I just had a great idea! Why not have me and Kemp come to dinner? At the same time," she added hastily.

Linda relayed the suggestion to Rick, and he, with some trepidation, agreed. Together they had fun planning and getting ready for the party. Linda made lasagna, green salad, and lemon pie; Rick bought a half gallon of red wine. Their first planned entertaining was a smash success. Delcie had a high old time, that was to be expected. Lindamargaret, wearing her first dress, kicked and gooed and looked like a pink cherub. Linda and Rick urged food upon their guests, and everyone became a little drunk. Kemp gave his usual big-time-operator report about listings and buyers that awaited him as soon as he obtained his license, and Delcie hung on his every word. But as the evening wore on, the wine wrought a curious phenomenon. Even as he talked about himself, Kemp watched Rick and Linda; his eyes took on a kind of wistfulness. Twice he left the table and bent over the crib, talking in baby talk to Lindamargaret.

"I've never been around a baby," he explained, half-sheepishly, each time he returned. "I never knew they were so cute."

Later, while the girls did the dishes, Kemp spoke to Rick confidentially, but the apartment was so small that everybody heard every word, even Lindamargaret.

"Man," Kemp said, "I never thought I'd hear myself say it, but I can see now I was wrong and you were right. Man, you got it made!"

THIRTY-SEVEN

Although the Dublins received no mail other than advertising addressed to "Occupant" and the newsletter from Rick's union, Linda daily checked their box in the building's entry. One noon in mid-December she withdrew a large square envelope addressed in her mother's elegant hand. Linda had never admitted it to herself, but here at last was what she had been secretly expecting, hoping for, dreading, all at the same time. Tears flooded her eyes. She hurried back upstairs to the apartment before she opened the envelope with trembling fingers.

Dearest Linda—
    It has been so long since we have seen you or heard from you. Your father and I are heartsick to think that a silly misunderstanding could have come between us. I am writing this to tell you that whatever it could have been that we did or said to offend you or Rick, we are truly sorry.
    Please, please accept this apology in the spirit in which it is offered.
    You know you are, and always have been, the most important thing in our lives. It seems doubly tragic that we haven't seen our granddaughter through these first precious months.
    My darling, if you three could come to us for Christmas, it would do more for us than any medicine. Please write or call us and say that you will, and we'll all start afresh.
    Kiss the baby for me.

                                  Mother.

Linda could scarcely make out the last lines through her tears. She picked up Lindamargaret and kissed her round, firm, little cheek.

"They want us!" she sobbed to Lindamargaret. "They're willing to take us back—after I was so bitchy!" She hugged the baby tightly. "This is never going to happen to us, to you and me, never, never, never!"

The afternoon seemed endless. Linda propped the letter in plain sight, and that evening after Rick discovered it, he read it twice.

"Whatever it could have been!" Rick said. "Don't they know?"

Linda pressed a finger to his lips. She had washed and dried her hair, and it cascaded over her shoulders like cornsilk.

"Don't, please," she said. "They apologized. What more can we ask?"

Rick was truculent.

"Let's go," Linda suggested, as if on impulse. "We can't hold a grudge at Christmas."

"I refuse to get all involved again."

"Nobody's going to get involved. Christmas is a holiday! It will be fun. We'll simply go there around ten in the morning, have dinner, and then come home in the afternoon. Would that be so difficult to do?"

"Honey, you know as well as I do we can't afford to—"

"Afford! It won't cost us a cent."

"What about presents? If we go for Christmas, you'll want to take presents."

"I know! I'll think of something I can make. Please . . . Rick?"

"Well . . ."

"I'm all they have. How would we feel if LM walked out of our lives?"

"We'd have some peace of mind," said Rick, but he grinned. The issue was won.

Margaret had left nothing undone to create a beautiful Christmas. The tree, a ten-foot blue spruce, stood in the vaulted living room, a fairyland of decorations, with heaps of gorgeously wrapped presents massed at its base. Everywhere the eye feasted upon additional treasures: jeweled wise men, spun glass reindeer, a fragile porcelain madonna, a crêche carved from sandalwood imported from the Holy Land. Fresh-cut evergeen and holly festooned balustrades and mantels; mistletoe dangled from every doorway; banks of poinsettias in ceramic Mexican pots blazed in every alcove. The house glowed with candles, fragrant with pine and bayberry, while from the kitchen wafted the mingled aromas of turkey, sage, cranberry, and pumpkin. An undertone of Christmas carols emanated from a dozen hidden stereo speakers.

In the entry, Margaret held Linda close; Linda sensed she was struggling for composure, as she herself was close to tears. Margaret kissed Rick, who looked discomfited and made no effort to respond. Robert kissed Linda, and the men shook hands.

"Mother," said Linda, looking around, "you certainly went all out on the decorations!"

"This is an important occasion!" Margaret's voice seemed determined to keep its lightness. "Christmas comes but once a year!"

"Not like this it doesn't! More like once in a century!" Margaret seemed pleased. She reached for the baby.

"Come here, you little doll!"

"Big doll," said Linda. "Moose!"

"I wouldn't say that," said Robert. "An elk, maybe, but not a moose!" He waggled Lindamargaret's hand. "Look at that! She smiled at me!"

"She's starting to smile."

"Look at her eyes! She's taking in everything I say!"

"Her mouth is like yours, Linda," said Margaret.

"Yes, but the rest of her is like Rick."

"Too bad she wasn't a boy," said Robert. "We'd have had an all-American on our hands."

Rick looked pained.

It took the Dublins two hours to open their presents from the Allenbys.

It took the Allenbys two minutes to open their present from the Dublins.

Linda couldn't pinpoint it. Was it then that it started, the beginning of the single cancerous cell, sometime then?

Or was it later, after Linda and Rick were home, after they were in bed, after the effects of Robert's wassail bowl had worn off, leaving them with headaches?

"Why couldn't you have said thank you?"

"Every time?"

"Yes, every time. You could have acted pleased."

"Acted. That's what it would have been."

"You received some very lovely presents. The nicest bunch of things you've had in your life."

"And not one of them fits. 'I didn't realize you were so big, Rick!' "

"You know what I think? You're childish!"

"Yeah? And you're spoiled!"

"I can't see anything wrong with accepting nice presents in the spirit in which they are given. I like all my presents."

"Yours all fit. Besides that . . ."

"What?"

"I don't like to feel like a poor relation!"

"You're out of your skull!"

Yet why did Linda feel like a poor relation, too? Why, when she wandered upstairs to her old room, now crammed with wedding presents she had never unpacked, did she envy the girl who used to live there? Why, during dinner, did Linda calculate the cost of each item at the Safeway on Jeeter Street? Why was it hard for Linda to be enthusiastic when she unwrapped the tennis dress she would never wear, the racquet which would never hit a ball, the ski pants which would never see snow?

Linda stumbled crossly to the bathroom and swallowed two aspirins. The point was, they didn't need to feel poor, act poor, or be poor. The point was, Linda was not poor. All that Linda was missing she didn't need to miss. All that she was doing without she could have for the asking. There was no reason why Linda shouldn't play tennis at Fernleaf as often as she liked, or accept a personal allowance instead of scrimping along on Rick's meager salary. There was no reason why her parents shouldn't stake them to a better apartment, or why Rick shouldn't work as a junior executive at her father's plastics plant.

There was no reason save for a hang-up in Rick's thick head.

After Margaret started dropping in again, Linda began

to see the apartment on Jeeter Street as it really was—the stained carpet, the water mark on the ceiling, the cigarette burns on the counter, the toilet that perpetually ran. In addition the faucet dripped, the sink stopped up, the refrigerator rattled at night and there was algae in the shower. It wasn't anything Margaret did, nor anything she said. It was Margaret's being there in her full-length ranch mink, her fifty-dollar shoes, her twenty-dollar hair-set, her fresh manicure; it was a feeling Linda had, a feeling she had let her mother down.

At last the Dublins managed a down payment on a used Toyota, but mid-January brought heavy rains, and Rick wrecked the car. He explained to Linda it hadn't been his fault. In a blinding downpour, a newly licensed driver had skidded through a red light and ploughed into the side of the little Toyota; there was nothing Rick could have done to avoid the crash, and Linda could only say she was thankful Rick wasn't hurt. The teenager had no insurance; the Dublins' insurance paid for the Toyota repair, excepting the hundred-dollar deductible Rick had to fork out in cash. The next day Lindamargaret's stroller was stolen, and after that Linda came down with a bad cold and fever, and the baby took sick with diarrhea. The car license came due. Linda developed a toothache and made an emergency trip to the dentist she had always gone to in Pasadena. The bill came to sixty dollars. No matter how they tried to manage, they were always strapped for cash.

Linda went from Pampers to cloth diapers and started washing them by hand in the kitchen sink; she hung them on a makeshift clothesline stretched from corner to corner of the apartment. She felt closed in. The cold weather continued, alternating with rain. Linda longed for a television, anything to break the monotony. She listened to her old transistor and heard the disc jockey babble on about the snow pack at Mammoth. In her imagination, Linda pictured herself approaching the top of the run, glancing momentarily at the panorama of white mountains and blue sky, inhaling the crisp, cold air, then pushing herself off to begin the wild, exhilarating plunge downhill. A tear of self-pity rolled down her cheek. She loved to ski.

Rick had once told her he, too, was crazy about skiing. He had gone to the mountains other years with Kemp. Now they would never ski, not Linda, and not Rick—never while they were young enough to enjoy it . . .

"I think we ought to talk about money," Linda told Rick.

"What's there to talk about?" grumbled Rick. He had caught Linda's cold and was out of sorts.

"We don't have enough."

"Linda, for the love of Mike, are you getting on that tired old kick again?"

"I'm serious. It's time we sat down and had a sensible discussion. We do not have enough money to live."

"Sure we do."

"Not in a decent way."

"What's indecent about it?"

"This," said Linda, gesturing at the diapers hanging from the line. "All of it."

Rick blew his nose.

"You were the one who used to say money wasn't everything. Remember? That was your by-line."

Linda sighed, compressing her lips. "It isn't, only to a certain extent."

". . . And that material things don't matter?"

"They don't. Only you have to have a minimum."

"We haven't yet gone hungry, have we? You tell me I should lose weight."

"Rick, if you'd change jobs— If you'd talk to daddy . . ."

Rick's expression hardened. "I told you never to—"

"All right, all right! But if you'd get a different job . . ."

"Just where? Just where would I get a different job? Remember how hard it was for me to get this one? Right now they're not taking on anybody, in fact, they're letting people go. Do you know what the unemployment rate in Los Angeles is right now? Ten point eight. Besides, I like my job. I like the people I work with."

"Then why not ask for a raise?"

"You don't know the set-up. Those salaries are fixed. The union has a contract. The only way I could make more is to work nights. That's ten cents more per hour."

"Rick, can't you see it? You're locked in."

"No, I'm not. There's lots of chance for advancement."

"When?"

"After the first year. They rate you all during the first year—performance, capability, all kinds of things. Then you can maybe train to be a linesman, or a warehouseman, or an installer. An installer really makes good money. An installer makes up to eighteen thousand a year."

"Yes, but how long is that going to take?"

"I don't know. Maybe five, ten years. It takes a while to learn that stuff. You have to pass exams, aptitude tests."

"And meanwhile we—I—we're doomed to stay cooped up in this miserable little . . ."

Rick put his arm around her.

"Why don't we forget about all that junk and go to bed?"

In a fit of pique Linda brushed his arm away.

"That's your answer to everything, isn't it? No matter what might be wrong, you have the magic cure-all. Sex! Sex! Sex!"

Rick bent to unfold the Hide-a-Bed. "What's the matter with that?" he wanted to know.

THIRTY-EIGHT

If Linda had not been suffering from an acute case of cabin fever she might not have greeted Sadie with such enthusiasm.

"I've been dying to see you and darling sweetikums," said Sadie, accepting instant coffee, but it was soon evident that she had come to talk not about Linda or Linda-margaret, but about herself. Sadie needed Aggie, longed for Aggie, thought of nothing else but Aggie, day and night, and Aggie, the bitch, the ingrate, the floozie, the tramp, the dog—Aggie refused to come back.

Linda, who had been languishing from boredom, listened greedily to Sadie's soap opera descriptions—first of the cold, calculating stares of male buyers who saw Aggie parade down the runway wearing nothing but panties and a skimpy bra; then of Lou Ann, Sadie's mother, now a disheveled, emaciated recluse who demanded more and more of Sadie's time. In months past Linda had gone several times with Sadie to visit Mrs. Blankenhazen. Even as she had been repelled by Lou Ann's maniacal diatribes against the entire male sex, she pitied the poor woman and sympathized with Sadie, stuck with such a burden. Now, listening to Sadie's unending problems and complaints, Linda wondered how Sadie once could have exerted so powerful an influence over her, yet as Sadie turned her attention from Lou Ann's difficulties to the women's movement, Linda found herself nodding and agreeing with her every premise.

Sadie got up to go to the bathroom, and the line of hanging diapers brushed against her face.

"Diapers!" she exclaimed. "I didn't think anybody used diapers any more!"

"Babies still wet," said Linda.

"But I thought everything nowadays was disposable."

"We used disposables at first. They cost too much."

"And now you're back to good old basics, eh? But where's your washing machine? Down in the basement?"

"We don't have one. I wash them out here in the sink."

"*You wash diapers by hand!*" Sadie uttered the words in the same tone an anthropologist might have used as he uncovered the skull of a second Peking man. "I do not believe it."

"What's so bad about that?"

"What's so bad—you, of all people! Let me see your hands!" She seized Linda's wrists, and looked at them closely. Linda became uncomfortably aware of broken nails, the ragged remnants of red polish, the rough and scaly knuckles. "I suppose you scrub the floor."

"It's carpeted."

"What about the bathroom?"

"Of course I clean the bathroom. Don't you clean yours?"

"I have maid service in the new place. That's what you ought to have. You ought to be out in the world, doing some glamorous job, using your mind. Why don't you come back with me to the office this afternoon?"

"I can't leave LM."

"Don't you have a neighbor who can babysit?"

"No. Besides, I'm nursing."

"You don't mean you're tied down to that? What? Every three hours?"

"Four, now."

"At night, too?"

"She sleeps from ten to six."

"I don't believe it!" Sadie was so agitated she strode up and down, pushing the diapers aside as she passed through. "Didn't you learn anything? Anything? Why don't you let him do some of this? He's a parent, too!"

"Rick? Next you'll be saying he should nurse the baby."

"Haven't you heard of bottles? How can you let yourself be chained this way, imposed upon? Don't you believe in equal rights?"

"Of course, but that has nothing to do—"

"That has everything to do! That's what equal rights is! Remember when you first joined the movement, all the talks we had? Remember what you used to say about independence, how you'd found your independence, your freedom; that independence was the most important thing in life and you'd never give it up! What happened to that? You don't believe that any more?"

Linda swallowed. "No, I believe in independence, only . . ."

"My God, girl, stand up on your two hind feet and fight! You owe it to yourself to find yourself—find your identity! Who are you? Who is Linda? Do you realize you're operating at about five per cent of your capacity? Scrubbing bathrooms, washing diapers, any moron could do that! Here you are, a hundred and forty-five IQ, a top-notch education, plus extras in language, music, travel that ninety-nine per cent of people never even know about—you could contribute to society! You have so much to give—you could do so much good! Remember, you only live once, once, that's all, once—you're only young once, too. These precious years will slip away, and you'll have done nothing with your life, nothing that counts! Your whole life will add up to nothing, nothing but a big, fat blank!"

Linda didn't mention Sadie's visit to Rick that night, partly because Rick didn't get home until after eleven. His supervisor had told him about an adult education class in electrical circuits, held three nights a week, and Rick had enrolled.

By the next evening at dinner, Linda had had thirty hours to think. She discounted Sadie's diatribes about Lou Ann and about Aggie, but the impassioned oratory about women's rights had recorded itself permanently on Linda's mind and now played back to her whether Linda wished to think of it or not, with such fidelity that Sadie herself might have been in the room.

You owe it to yourself to find yourself . . .

All day it rained. Linda looked out the window at the telephone pole, the alley, the neighbor's wet board fence, the battered yellow trash bin, full of soggy newspapers and garbage.

. . . find your identity . . .

Inept as Sadie was at managing her own life, she had an uncanny knack of smelling out the weaknesses of others, of zeroing in for the kill.

Who was Linda?

So she was back to that again. Who, indeed? Linda tried to think objectively. As a child, she had been Linda Allenby, who lived in the biggest house on the street. Her parents were careful with whom she played. She went across town to private school, took piano lessons and memorized Chopin. When they thought Linda was out of earshot, her parents' friends told Margaret and Robert that Linda was the prettiest little girl they'd seen since Shirley Temple, and if the Allenbys didn't watch out, they'd have a beauty on their hands. Linda's mother seemed pleased with their remarks, but she always reminded Linda that handsome is as handsome does.

As a teenager, she had been *the* Linda Allenby, who always had the right sweaters, the right sunglasses, even the right worn and faded denim bib overalls when they appeared in the boutiques. Whenever anyone was going on a trip, Linda Allenby had already been there, though she learned early not to bring this up. Linda could do a perfect half gainer, and could beat anyone at school playing singles; she knew who everybody was and everyone knew her, but oddly enough she never had truly close friends.

Linda had started to get an inkling of who she was when she was a debutante, and later when she was at Mills and in Italy, but that was when she had decided to change.

Linda had been positive who she was when she crusaded for the women's movement with Delcie, loyal and owl-like, at her side. For four months, things had become clear; the good guys (female), versus the bad guys (male). She had liked that, values were simple, sharp and clear; but then those outlines, too, went out of focus, and began to blur.

As a lover Linda had known exactly who she was, for a brief, illuminating time, like the explosion of a star. She closed her eyes, straining to remember the ardor, the tenderness of that first love, the honeymoon with Rick as Rick was then, and Linda, the fairy story princess with golden hair, the Linda of long ago. But that identity was lost to her almost before it began, replaced by the pregnant girl with morning sickness, the girl who had to get married, the girl whose morals were a trifle shot; who was replaced in turn, by the mother, the wife, the household drudge—cooped up in this two-by-four apartment with no chance of escape.

Which one, when it came down to the wire, was the real Linda?

More important, what was that Linda's "*possible*"? What could she do with her aptitudes, her talents, her mind? What did she have the potential to become?

"Rick," Linda said, "I'm going to get a job."

Rick pushed his chair back from the table and stared at her.

"What brought this on?"

"We need the money."

"We don't need it that bad."

"I feel trapped."

"Hah!" he snorted in derision. "That's a laugh, coming from you."

"Why?"

"Don't you think I feel trapped, too?"

Linda went into the bathroom and looked in the mirror. The face she saw appeared haunted. She came back to the table.

"Rick, do you know who you are?"

He looked at her.

"I think so."

"Who?"

"I'm your husband, I'm LM's father. I work for the phone company. I'm going to night school three days a week."

Linda considered this.

"Have you always known—I mean, like when you were a little boy?"

"I was a kid who was good at sports, is that what you mean?"

"And later you were a football star."

"I guess you could call it that."

"But—did you mind changing, from being a star, after you'd had all that attention?"

Rick shrugged.

"You can't be Joe College forever. After all, I married the most beautiful girl in the world."

"No, Rick, I have to find out."

"Sooner or later, everybody seems to find his niche."

"And you've found yours."

"Looks that way."

Linda got up from the table and began to take down the diapers.

"I wish I could feel—as sure as you. I don't believe I've found my niche at all."

"What kind of talk is that?"

"I feel as if I should be out there in the world, doing something important . . ."

"You don't call taking care of LM important?"

"Using my mind . . ."

"Oh for Christ's sake!" said Rick. "I thought you got all that crap out of your system."

"Why shouldn't I leave the house every day, too, for a glamorous job?"

"Look," said Rick, "in case you've forgotten, the world out there, as you call it, is nothing but a bunch of cut-throats trying to rip out each other's guts . . ."

"Why should I be the one stuck in this cubbyhole to do the menial labor?"

"Be glad you can be here where it's safe, with our cute little baby!"

"Why can't our marriage be a team?"

"I'll buy that. On a team different people do different things. One guy's the center, one guy's the tight end. You run the home and take care of the baby, I go out and bring in the bread."

"Why can't we both run the home and take care of the baby, and both go out and bring in the bread?"

"Because that's not the way it's supposed to be, dammit!"

"Why was I assigned the role of taking care of the baby?"

"Because you're the mother! It was you had the baby, remember?"

"And you're the father! Isn't that important?"

"Fathers do different things."

"Like what?"

"Take kids fishing. Teach them to play ball."

"How do you know? You never had a father."

It was a cruel, unforgivable remark. It slipped out, in the heat of battle. The minute Linda said it she was sorry, but there was no getting it back. Rick's face reddened slowly. His features hardened and he looked like gray slate.

"What exactly did your father do for you?"

"He played tennis, he—"

"He didn't stay home and wash diapers, that's for sure."

"Nobody had to wash diapers in my house. They hired someone to do it."

"You're always holding it up to me that your folks were so great. Your dad worked, didn't he? Your mother stayed home and took care of you."

Linda hesitated, remembering the mother who had endlessly, devotedly, chauffeured her to music lessons and ballet classes.

"Mother was free to do whatever she liked. She played bridge. She worked on charities."

"If that's what you wanted, you married the wrong guy!"

"Ooooh!" screamed Linda in exasperation.

Rick read the paper and Linda did the dishes. An hour passed without their speaking.

"Why can't I get a job," said Linda. "Give me one good reason."

"The baby."

"Besides that."

"I don't want to be indebted to your folks in any shape or form."

"I suppose you think that's the only way I could get a job."

"Either that or your looks. I don't want a bunch of other studs making passes at my wife."

"Look, if I get a job, it would be because of my mind and my ability. It would not be because of who my father is or my looks. I refuse to be a sex symbol again."

"Why don't you just stay home and be a sex symbol to me?" He started to unfold the bed.

"I'd be a lot more contented sex symbol if I were fulfilled."

"You mean I don't fulfill you?" He grabbed her. "I haven't been trying hard enough."

"You do! You do! It's only . . ."

Late that night after she'd given LM her ten o'clock feeding, Linda nestled beside Rick.

"I do have a mind."

He didn't reply.

"Rick—"

"What?"

"Are you asleep?"

"Yes."

"I do have an education . . . I do need a mental challenge . . ." She turned over on her stomach. If she ever were called upon to invent a torture rack, she would employ the Hide-a-Bed designers. "Rick . . ."

"What?"

"I do think self-realization is important . . . I do think one should make the most of one's potential . . . And that women are equal to men . . ."

Rick rolled over, taking the sheet and blankets with him.

"For God's sake, will you knock it off! How much more of that confounded yakking do you think I can take?"

THIRTY-NINE

As long as Rick was so stubborn, Linda could see it would be pointless to discuss the matter of her working until she actually had a position nailed down. Accordingly, she arranged for Delcie to come and take care of Linda-margaret while she went job hunting, borrowing Delcie's car for the purpose. Delcie had ambivalent views about the transaction. She was enchanted at the prospect of tending LM, but she disapproved of Linda's resolve to work.

"You have to be out of your tree!"

"How so? Remember all those leaflets we passed out? Remember what they said?"

"That's not how it is in real life."

"That's how it can be in real life. That's how we can make it be."

Delcie shook her head.

"Not this little bundle of feathers. When I marry Kemp . . ."

Linda no longer put herself through the paces of trying to instruct Delce about the facts of life. She still thought the idea absurd that Kemp would fall for Delcie, but she had reached the point where nothing surprised her. If Delce was so hell-bent to put her neck in the noose it was no skin off Linda's back.

"What's happening between you and lover boy?"

"Slow but steady. It's like reeling in an albacore. Takes time."

"Here's LM's bottle."

"Has she ever had a bottle before?"

"No, but there has to be a first."

"Oh brother. I hope you know what you're doing."

"I do," said Linda tartly. She picked up Delcie's keys.

"I won't say I wish you luck," said Delce. "Rick's going to flip a gasket."

Linda struggled not to let Delcie get on her nerves. "Why should he? I think he'll go for it. Money talks!"

"Sometimes it uses ba-ad language!" said Delcie, picking up LM. "Come on, honey, come to your Auntie Delcie. See! She knows me. She remembers who I am!" She looked at Linda, who had opened the door. "You know what I said about—about how hard it is to reel in a husband? From all I hear, it's just as hard to keep him, after the knot is tied."

"There's another bottle in the refrigerator," said Linda, and shut the door.

For once, after close to a year of bad breaks, everything came Linda's way. A friend of Sadie's, Jill Bryant, had told Sadie of an opening with Los Angeles County, a job processing the hundreds of delinquents who streamed through the juvenile justice system. Jill herself interviewed Linda, then arranged for her to talk to the supervisor, Dr. Steinberg. Linda's major in sociology was taken into account; she was hired on a temporary basis with the understanding that she would complete the work for her degree as soon as possible.

"It will be part custodial, part counseling," said Dr. Steinberg. "We get some mean little characters in here—assault, stabbings, some things you wouldn't believe, even if they are children. The idea is, we're not just babysitters. We're trying to turn them around, make them stop hating the world, so they'll be useful members of society. Meanwhile, we try to prevent them from killing each other, and us."

Because Linda did not have her degree, because it was the last half of the fiscal year and the department was running out of funds, because no one had anticipated the steep increase in juvenile criminals and the new position was therefore unbudgeted, Linda was hired at two thirds of what the job description called for in the county employees' contract. Nevertheless, the take-home pay amounted to almost double what Rick received from the phone company. Linda drove home in excitement, thanked Delcie (who babbled on, predicting disaster), and spent the rest of the afternoon preparing dinner—lasagna, lemon refrigerator pie, all Rick's favorites.

Linda waited until Rick had eaten the last crumb of his

second piece of pie before she told him. He made no comment. To fill the gap, to keep the conversation on the upswing, as it had been during dinner, Linda kept talking. She told Rick she would at last be putting all those years of schooling to some use, she told him about Jill Bryant and the county budget, she told him about the pathetic misfits who somehow had to be reclaimed.

He sat across the table and watched her. Linda had the feeling he was only registering part of what she said, the remainder was washing about his ears like waves against a cliff. After she'd told him everything about the new job she could think of, and repeated the parts about social significance several times, her voice petered out. A great stillness settled in the room, relieved only by the gurgles of Lindamargaret, who was lying on her back, playing with her toes.

"I thought we discussed your working," Rick said at last, "and decided against it."

Linda reminded herself to keep her voice poised and light at the same time.

"We discussed it, yes."

"But we didn't decide you could."

Careful, thought Linda, careful!

"Who's to decide? I'm a free entity, am I not? I should decide what I do with my body. I should decide what I do with my life."

In an absent-minded fashion Rick wandered to the refrigerator and cut himself a third piece of pie, which he brought back to the table and began to eat thoughtfully.

"Honesty," he said. "That's what you used to say. You set a store by honesty."

Linda felt herself becoming nervous. "I still do. As much as ever."

Rick shook his head. "You tricked me. You did it behind my back."

Linda was outraged at the accusation, the more so because it was true.

"That's a crappy thing to say."

"Let's get this straight," said Rick. "I believe we're married, right? All that falderal at the church, right?"

"Right."

"Marriage means a family, right?"

"Right."

"So we should make joint decisions."

"We never could have reached a decision. It would have been a tie vote, one to one."

"You're forgetting LM. She would have voted to have her mother home."

"She wouldn't have voted to have her mother stagnate into a lifeless, useless clod, a vegetable!"

"How can you nurse her?"

"I can't. She'll have to go on the bottle."

Rick leaned back. "You'd do that—to your own baby—to spend your time with a bunch of hoodlums who aren't worth the time of day?"

Linda sighed. "Think of the money. I'll be making—" She stopped herself before she added, twice as much as you. She didn't need to. The words hung in the air between them.

"I can see the dollar signs in your eyes."

"We'll be filthy rich!"

"Don't forget the deductions."

"Even so, think what we can do. We can pay off my parents—"

"I wanted to do that myself."

Linda, not recognizing the significance of that statement, brushed it aside. "We can eat better. We can get a better apartment."

"Now hold on," said Rick. "Don't you know where most of it is going to go? To get someone to take care of LM—to hire someone to do what you ought to be home doing yourself. And take it from me, that's a hell of a life for the kid."

"You're missing the whole point!" said Linda. "That's what I'm trying to tell you. I'll work days, and you can work nights!"

"What?"

"You can go on the night shift. You said yourself they were begging people to do it. And you'd be making ten cents an hour more."

"Linda, I do not want to work the night shift!"

"Listen," said Linda eagerly, coming to sit on his lap, "we'd be a real partnership, a real team. Lindamargaret would always have one of us, one of her own parents, home. We'd share the household tasks, and the cooking, and because we'd have more money we could go back to Pampers and . . ."

"Got it all figured out, haven't you?"

Linda kissed him.

"It's going to be perfect. You'll see. For both of us."

Rick didn't kiss her back.

"It isn't going to work."

"Yes it is. Give it a chance. We're free, modern, emancipated people."

Rick cupped her face in his great hands and looked deep into her eyes, as if he were searching for someone.

"Why couldn't we go on the way things are? Everything's all right."

"That's the point. Everything is not all right."

"I was happy. I thought you were happy."

"I was. I am. But this will be better."

Rick didn't look convinced.

"You'll see, you'll see," said Linda. "Everything's going to be great!"

FORTY

Rick Dublin struggled back from sleep to wakefulness. He had been dreaming, and the images refused to fade.

He had been walking with Linda on an ice floe, holding her hand. The cold was glacial, the sky low and steely, merging at the horizon with the ice so it was impossible to tell where one ended and the other began. As he and Linda walked, talking, sometimes laughing, a crack developed in the ice between them, at first barely noticeable, then gradually widening until the ice actually split apart and they could peer down thirty feet to the black water. Even then, one or the other could have jumped across, but with the inertia of characters in a dream, neither did; each saw the danger but thought the other would make the leap, which each moment became more hazardous until it was impossible. They had been holding hands but in the end they had to let go. It was then that they heard their baby cry heartbreakingly from somewhere faroff.

Rick rolled to his feet and staggered to the bathroom. The apartment was hot and airless, faintly foul with minglings of odors: soiled Pampers, coffee grounds, a rotting orange in the overflowing trash, mildew from the shower curtain, menthol shaving cream, stale cigarette smoke imbedded in the drapes. Lindamargaret was crying, standing in her crib after her nap. Automatically Rick changed her, then laid her on her back and gave her a bottle, cold from the refrigerator. At least, she'd learned to hold it by herself. She drank greedily, observing her father out of her serious, wide-set eyes.

Rick began listlessly to wash the dirty dishes stacked in the sink, not paying attention, getting none of them quite clean. He was groggy as he always was when he slept in the afternoon; he was a day person, nothing could change that, it was in his genes. He never would adjust to working nights if he lived to be a hundred. Night after night he was sleepy on the job, not alert, not with it. He made mistakes and was earning a poor rating.

The dishes now stacked precariously in the rack, Rick pulled the bedclothes half-way straight and folded up the Hide-a-Bed. The dream was forgotten, lapsing into nothingness, but the feeling of depression lingered on. Vaguely, opening a can of pork and beans, Rick wondered what the hell could be the matter. He wasn't ill, he had no symptoms, no sore throat, but for weeks now he'd felt miserable. He was sick in spirit. His life was going down the drain. Nothing seemed valid any more, nothing gave him pleasure, everything was rush, rush, rush! Sure, he was living with Linda, his dream girl, his goddess, but she had changed. Their love life, once top priority, had been relegated to last in order of importance. They scarcely saw each other, only exchanged thier joint responsibility as relay runners exchange their baton, hello, good-by, take out the trash, your dinner's in the oven, I think LM is cutting her first tooth. Where was the order in this arrangement? Where was the sense of being in control? Rick felt like a hamster running on a wheel. Whenever he protested (usually as Linda arrived, beat from her sojourn on the freeway, and Rick was going out the door), she had a logical if tart reply.

Rick felt trapped. Worse, he felt mired in quicksand, sloughing in mud, unable to lift one foot after the other to get out, sinking deeper with every step.

The baby had finished her bottle and filled her diaper. Rick changed her again. She smiled up at him, sweetly, out of his mother's eyes.

"You're a little honey, that's what you are," he told her, his voice soft so only she could hear.

He folded the soiled Pamper together and set it on the rug beneath the crib, then lifted Lindamargaret and held her close to him, her cheek against his. He felt a lump in his throat. Once more he tried to stave off the melancholia. It wasn't proper, wasn't the macho way. Whoever had heard of a football player suffering, especially a tackle? Jocks were supposed to be hard-nosed, simplistic, and direct. They barreled through, they got the job done, they took their lumps.

"I love you, LM," Rick told the baby softly. "Always remember that—you hear, now? Always remember that!"

Several weeks later, driving home from work, Linda was caught in a freeway tie-up. The bumper-to-bumper traffic had been moving slowly but steadily when *bingo!*—a hundred brakes ahead of her flashed red, and every vehicle stopped dead. The freeway was packed solid, cars on either side of Linda, ahead of her, behind. There was no escape. At first she let the motor idle, but then she turned it off, resting her new short haircut against the seatback. It had been a difficult day.

Oh, she still loved her job, she told herself defensively. Certainly her "possible" was being explored, strained to its utmost capacity. Her work was a challenge—even scary in its implications. Every child or teenager she interviewed was a complex mechanism first to be understood, then somehow made to synchronize with the world around him. Some youngsters were frightened, some belligerent, some rebellious, some venomous in their hate, which, to Linda's shocked surprise, zeroed in on her. All were out of step, all patronizing, resisting Linda's efforts to get them back on the right track. They were human beings, Linda kept reminding herself, who must be retrieved. Not one of her junior criminals evinced the smallest shred of conscience.

It was hot in the stalled car. Linda rolled down the window and leaned out to try to see farther ahead. What could have happened to block all four lanes? Dimly she heard the wail of sirens, approaching from the opposite direction. Perhaps a semi had tipped over on the curve. She sighed. Tonight was the exam in Rick's electronics class. If he was late again he'd go into orbit.

Linda turned on the radio. Hard rock ricocheted around inside the confines of the tiny car. She twisted the volume down and tried not to think. Rick had been so grouchy anyway—for weeks, for months, ever since she'd started the county job. In some peculiar way he'd taken her working as a personal affront. After much trial and error they'd arrived at a semi-workable sharing of responsibilities—with no thanks to Rick. Linda had had to push, shove, and cajole Rick every millimeter of the way.

Linda's stomach growled. Lord, she wished the highway patrol would get things moving. She wondered what Rick would have fixed tonight for dinner. She hoped it wasn't hot dogs again. Rick kept complaining he didn't know how to cook. Linda had tried to teach him a few things even a moron could prepare. She reminded him that until they got married, she had never cooked or kept house either.

It was so stuffy in the car! She reached over and rolled down the right-hand window.

Unfortunately, Rick's opposition wasn't all she'd had to buck. Delcie kept telling her she was cutting her own throat. Her parents had been horrified. Linda smiled wryly. Imagine Margaret and Robert Allenby on the same side of an argument as Rick! She could hear them now. If Linda needed money, all she had to do was ask. It was dangerous to gamble with Lindamargaret's health. Rick was too rough to be trusted with the child. He almost pulled the baby's arms out of their sockets. Besides, he didn't keep her clean. The apartment smelled of ammonia, and worse— in fact, the crowded room was nothing better than a pig sty! One Saturday morning Margaret had come to call. Rick was out and Linda lying down, trying to get a little rest. Margaret, in spite of her nails, puttered around the kitchen. When she opened the cupboard under the sink to get the cleanser, a three-inch cockroach scuttled out. Margaret had screamed, waking the baby. It had taken half an hour to calm the child.

Linda switched stations, but could find nothing but commercials and at last snapped the radio off. Yes, she'd had opposition, but she'd stuck to her guns. After all, right was right, and she had no intention of giving up the ground she'd gained. How else could she maintain her precious, hard-won independence?

The puzzling part was, she didn't know what to expect from Rick any more. Take the matter of her hair. Both she and Rick had been dragging their tails from lack of sleep, using their days off to buy groceries, to get the car serviced, to take the washing to the Laundromat. It was obvious they had to simplify, to cut out nonessentials. One item taking up more time than it was worth was Linda's beautiful long hair, which had to be washed every other day at least, and took an hour to blow dry.

One noon on an impulse Linda went to a beauty shop close to the office, and ordered her hair scissored in a short, straight pixie cut, no longer than two inches all around.

"You can blow it dry in just a few minutes," the operator told her.

"It'll save me hours each week!" Linda affirmed, but she was startled at her reflection. She looked older, more nervous, less sexy. A stranger's first reaction no longer would be, "What a pretty girl!" Had her looks, then, been no more than her hair? At least, she appeared intelligent and competent. She tipped the hairdresser and went back to work.

When Linda had arrived home that night, Rick had been holding Lindamargaret. She had been braced for a row, had expected shouts of outrage and recriminations. Instead, Rick said nothing. His face seemed drained of color. Linda went about setting the table, and after a while Rick put LM in her crib and they sat down to eat. In the middle of the meal, Rick excused himself abruptly and went into the bathroom, slamming the door.

Linda went on eating, her mind straying to the staff meeting that afternoon. At first she was not aware of the sound, the strange, eerie, unaccustomed sound. It was muffled and smothered. It was only later that she realized what it was, but even then she couldn't believe what she was hearing. The sound was someone sobbing. Big Rick was crying.

At last traffic started moving, routed in single file around a massive produce truck which lay grotesquely on its side. When she finally reached Jeeter Street, Linda ran up the three flights without a pause for breath.

"I'm sorry!" She burst through the door. "If you leave now you'll only be a half hour late!"

Rick didn't answer. He strode out of the bathroom wearing jacket, slacks, and tie, carrying his toothbrush and razor. Lindamargaret stood in her crib, crying. Linda sniffed.

"Rick!" she reproached. "You've let her go again! How many times do I have to tell you, you have to change her as soon as it happens! No wonder she gets that awful rash!"

It was not till after she'd cleaned up Lindamargaret and washed her hands that Linda noticed the suitcase on the table. Rick emptied shorts and T-shirts from his drawer.

"Aren't you going to your class? Rick? What are you doing?"

"Packing."

"Yes, I can see that. Where did you get the suitcase?"

"It's Stu's."

"Why are you putting your clothes into Stu's suitcase?"

"I don't have a suitcase. I'm borrowing his."

"I have a suitcase. I have six or eight. All we have to do is run over to mother's."

No reply.

"You mean you're going somewhere? Where? Where are you going?"

"To Chicago."

"To Chicago! For the phone company? Why Chicago?"

No reply.

"How long are you going to be?"

"Don't know."

"Rick, will you tell me what's happening! You don't have—it isn't that—somebody didn't die or something?"

"No."

"Well then, why in heaven's name are they sending a long distance operator to Chicago in the middle of the week?"

"They're not sending me."

"They're not? Then how can you take off work?"

"I didn't."

"Rick, will you stop playing games! You're always yakking about how strict they are, they dock you if you're fifteen minutes late. You'll get fired!"

Silence.

"You were fired!"

"I wasn't fired."

"What then?"

"I quit."

"You quit! And let that precious seniority go down the tubes? I don't believe it."

He went on packing.

"Rick, listen to me. Stop fiddling around for a minute and tell me what you're doing."

"I told you. I quit work. I'm going to Chicago. I'm going to be working out with the Bears."

"With the Bears!" Linda's voice was a mixture of surprise and alarm. "You got a job with the Bears after they turned you down last spring?" She tried to assemble her thoughts. "You must have lost your mind! I can't pick up and go to Chicago! Not now!"

Silence.

"Rick, I said I am not going to Chicago!"

"I didn't expect you would."

"You didn't—then how come—" She had a sudden flash of insight. "What are they paying you?"

"Nothing."

"Nothing!"

"I won't be on the payroll. It's just a chance to mess around with the team."

A flicker of horror began to grow in Linda's mind.

"Rick, are you all right? I mean, you haven't—flipped out or—anything?" Even to Linda, her words sounded slow and dry. Rick seemed not to have heard. Linda skirted about him, nervously. "You're going to Chicago, alone, you're going to mess around with the Bears—where will you stay?"

"With Darter."

"Darter's in on it!"

"Don't blame Darter. I called and asked him."

She made a quick decision. "You can't go!" He went on packing. "You're not well!"

"I'm fine."

"You're not thinking straight! Rick! Rick?" She grabbed his arm. He pushed her hand aside. "It doesn't make sense. How will—you get to the airport?"

"Cab. It's out there now."

"At least tell me when you're coming back."

He flicked the latch on Stu's suitcase and straightened up.

"Don't you get it yet?" He looked at her steadily, soberly. "I'm not coming back."

"But that means . . ." A sense of terror hovered over her but she could not yet comprehend. ". . . You're . . . leaving me?"

He nodded. He picked up the case and started for the door.

Linda tried to think, to think fast, but her reasoning collapsed. She gasped, wildly trying to collect her words.

"But I thought . . . you meant it . . . when you said you loved me?"

Momentarily Rick paused by Lindamargaret's crib, and grasped one fat, small foot in his great hand. Then without speaking he went out the door and started down the stairs.

FORTY-ONE

Through the window Linda looked down at the street. She saw Rick get into the cab and drive away. It was like watching a puppet show from a dizzying height, trying to make sense of the characters. For a long interval she stood motionless, staring down at the toy cars traveling along Jeeter Street in both directions.

Later she could remember nothing of the evening—not prying the lid from the glass jar of Gerber's strained beef and barley, not bathing Lindamargaret and thrusting the baby's fat legs into her sleepers, not gathering up the trash and carrying it downstairs to dump. She was in shock, she was a plane flying on automatic pilot, she was numb from a thousand injections of Novocain.

She lay alone in the dark in the middle of the Hide-a-Bed, with plenty of room and no one to roll over, taking all the covers. Sleep refused to come. Eyes open and glassy, she concentrated on the faint geometric patterns of light which crossed the ceiling as the cars glided past on the street below. About three, the Novocain feeling began to wear off, and the ache, the terrible, relentless, uncompromising rolling and churning in her stomach, set in.

Ineffectually, she tried to reassure herself.

This isn't for real, she heard herself say stoutly, not once but over and over, a litany. Rick would not do this. Her tone became indignant. The idea was preposterous. Rick loves me!

Of course he loved her. He had idolized her from the first moment they met, even when she gave him the brush-off. Rick had told her he worshiped her a hundred times, a hundred hundred times! Rick loves the baby! He does, he did! Maybe he hadn't been too crazy about being a father in the beginning, but now that Lindamargaret was so cute, now that she had four teeth and could pull herself up and laugh aloud and almost talk . . .

Exhausted, Linda drifted off to sleep, to be wakened, later, by a far-away familiar sound, the door of the Toyota. It was morning. Rick was home from work! Gasping with relief, Linda brushed away the cobwebs of her nightmare. It had been a dream, a dream! She noted the slam of the front door, downstairs, then waited for the sound of Rick's footsteps, bounding upstairs two steps at a time. They never came. Slowly, like layers of thick, chilling fog, the realization settled over her. This was no dream. Rick had left her.

Two weeks after she had started the new job, Linda had been given her own office. At first this had been a source of pride. My office, she had called it not once but dozens of times to Rick. Naturally I have my own office. She tossed that off in casual conversations with her mother, as one would flick the ash from a cigarette. On this day, however, the morning after the night Rick had left her, Linda perceived that her office was nothing more than a cubbyhole, the walls flimsy partitions of plywood which stopped three feet short of the ceiling and made a mockery of privacy. All the furnishings were metal—desk, IBM Selectric, typewriter table, file cabinet, bookshelf, chairs—metal-beige, metal-gray, metal-olive drab, nothing matched. Everything had been bought by the county in wholesale lots; everything was sturdy and depressing. The desk was scarred by kicks from rebellious children.

Linda plunged into her work gratefully and fiercely, as one might, in a frenzy, stagger into the sanctuary of a churchyard's hallowed ground after fleeing from demons. She had the idea if she worked non-stop at twice her usual speed she wouldn't be able to think, and if she didn't think the hurt would go away. Work, she thought, would prove an anesthetic. It turned out to be untrue. From the beginning the day was a bummer. In the first place she was an hour late. It had taken that long to locate a day nursery that would take Lindamargaret on such short notice. The baby had sensed her mother's agitation from the moment she had wakened, and she became cranky and fussy. When she had been dumped into the arms of a total stranger she had begun to cry from fright, her screams mounting as she realized her mother was going out the door and leaving her. All day long Linda could hear those screams in the back of her mind; all day long she could see the frantic look of terror in her child's eyes, the look of abandonment. Linda understood that look. Linda herself had been abandoned. Rick didn't want her any more.

Linda had been hired to ease the department's caseload, but in the few months she'd been working, the cases to be processed had nearly doubled. Juvenile crime was on the rampage, a fire out of control. Paperwork was staggering, and all forms had to be filled out in triplicate. Linda stacked the backlog of manila files on her desk, determined to catch up before her next batch of interviews, and opened the first folder. What should she recommend the county do about Jose Alvarez, age ten, who had stabbed his six-year-old sister with a switchblade? The girl now languished in County-USC Hospital, her left lung hemorrhaging internally. Linda tried to concentrate. Jose had shown no signs of remorse or regret. All Linda had been able to pry out of him was, "I told the little snot not to bug me!" As far as Linda could discover the boy had no feelings, no vestige of kindness, nothing to reach, nothing to rehabilitate. He was a hardened criminal at ten. That was the trouble. People today had forgotten how to love. Love—the word tripped open the floodgate. The memory and the horror of her own situation washed over her. She, Mrs. Dublin, who played God with the likes of Jose Alvarez, was no longer loved. She had been deserted.

In the restroom mirror Linda examined her face—pasty and pale, with puffs of fatigue under each eye. The eye whites were marbled with a network of thread-like red veins. Her short, easy-care hair stuck forward, stiff and bristly, like that of the strawman in the Wizard of Oz. She was a mess. No wonder Rick had gone! What man would want her? She stood back, appraising her figure. Her breasts had diminished in size since she'd stopped nursing, but now they had a slight sag, in spite of the Cross-Your-Heart bra. Her waistline had never quite thinned down to its pre-pregnancy litheness, and unless she remembered to suck in her stomach she had a tummy bulge. The thought flashed through her mind that this was the tragedy of being female. As a part of birth process, something intangible dies. The woman is no longer quite as beautiful, quite as desirable—she is no longer her old alluring self—

ever again. Instead, she becomes a service organism. Henceforth all her energy must be directed to raising the young. She loses her identity, just as she has found it. She knows who she is for a moment only, with eternity stretching endlessly beyond.

One of the secretaries, Marcia Benson, emerged from a stall and began to wash her hands, her eyes meeting Linda's in the mirror.

"My God, what's the matter with you?" Marcia blurted. "You look like something the cat dragged in!"

"Nothing," insisted Linda. "Nothing's wrong."

She panicked. She didn't want Marcia to know, didn't want anybody at work to know, didn't want her parents to know. It was too humiliating—to be cast aside like a broken chair or a worn-out shoe. Standing there on the tile floor in the ladies' restroom she felt her confidence drain from her, as if she had cut a vein in her wrist and was bleeding to death.

The days that followed were no better. Linda had the unshakable conviction that she was inferior, therefore incompetent, therefore unworthy. She could see now she had obtained her position as a juvenile caseworker under false pretenses; she had neither the training nor the objectivity it required. Who was she to manipulate other people's lives, when she couldn't control her own? Even more devastating was the knowledge she was no longer attractive to men. She avoided Dr. Steinberg and the other males on the floor, and when communication became imperative she spoke in terse monosyllables. At night after she went to bed she cried herself to sleep.

The pain in the bottom of her stomach never eased up, and finally, goaded by its nerve-searing persistence, Linda began to lash back. The fury exploded one evening in Ralph's Supermarket, where, bone tired, she had stopped to purchase a few groceries before picking up the baby. What a rat-race this was, what a drag! Who did Rick think he was, that he could treat her this way and get away with it? If you wanted the truth, Rick was a nothing, a nobody, the son of a sickly, uneducated mother and a nonexistent father. Savagely, Linda pawed through the pyramid of iceberg lettuce, wincing at the price. Any way you looked at it, Rick had been selfish. He'd wanted everything his own way, and when he couldn't have it, he'd split. Talk about being childish and self-centered! That was what came from ten years of being adulated as a football star! Linda reached for a carton of milk and glared at a middle-aged man who stood in her way.

"Spoiled rotten!" she muttered under her breath.

The man stared as if she were some kind of kook. Linda turned away coldly, off on her own miserable thoughts. Rick was so immature it made her want to puke. He couldn't take responsibility—he didn't know the meaning of the word. If anybody had cause for complaint, it was Linda. She should have left him! After all, things hadn't been so peachy-easy for her. She was the one who'd had to have the baby, remember? Rick had no idea of the suffering she'd gone through. She'd tried her best to make a go of it, to build some kind of a life together, and then he'd had the effrontery to walk out. It made her so mad she could scream. She reached the checkout stand and slammed her groceries on the turntable item by item. What she wouldn't do to get even! What she wouldn't give to punish Rick, to hurt him as he'd hurt her!

The box boy stacked the heavy sacks in Linda's cart but instead of offering to help her out with them he turned to the next order. It figured. Indignantly, Linda pushed the cart toward the door. All men were the same, when you came down to it—lazy, self-centered slobs who wanted only one thing—sex!

Linda's burst of anger had not obliterated the terrible gnawing ache of hurt, but it provided temporary relief by allowing her to vent her pent-up feelings. She seized on hatred as her placebo, repeating her complaints and name-calling, over and over, each time with greater conviction, until she only needed to think about Rick at all, to set in motion the entire sound track in her brain, which then played automatically, and ended with the shibboleth that all men were lazy, self-centered slobs.

One night as Linda muttered her incantations while brushing her teeth in the buttercup-yellow bathroom she and Rick had painted together, she looked in the mirror and beheld not her own face, but the twisted, spiteful features of Lou Ann Blankenhazen. She recoiled in horror. The vision of herself as Sadie Blankenhazen's chronically complaining, paranoid mother brought Linda up short. Was it possible if she let herself carry on this way she could end up like Mrs. Blankenhazen? She shuddered at the thought. The next morning, which was Saturday, she gave herself a pep talk. She had to get hold of herself, she told herself fiercely. Rick was gone, he'd been gone two weeks, he hadn't changed his mind, he hadn't written, he hadn't phoned. She might as well face it. It wasn't the end of the world. It happened to almost everybody, sooner or later. California had more divorces than marriages. Today millions of women supported themselves, lived by themselves, and raised children by themselves. That was part of the message of Women's Lib. If millions could do it, she could do it, too. She'd get along just as well—maybe better. Probably she'd go farther in her career without Rick to slow her down. No more flak about her working, no more hassle about her folks, no more arguments, period. From here on out Linda could have everything her own way, do everything her own way, make all the decisions, live her own life. Freedom had always been her goal, and now, excepting for caring for Lindamargaret, she was at last truly free.

As part of her new course of positive action, she decided to make the announcement that she had thus far taken such pains to keep hidden—her secret shame. In a light, casual tone she mentioned to everybody that she and Rick had separated, implying that the event was of minor significance. She was unprepared for the spectrum of reactions.

Sadie was pleased—too pleased. Her long horsey face crinkled into a grin.

"I was wondering when you'd come to your senses," she said slyly. "You and that oversized jock had absolutely zilch in common."

"Really, Sadie—"

"Wait and see, this will be a divorce that was made in heaven. That marriage was doomed from the beginning. Everyone could see it but you. It was only a matter of time."

Linda found herself furiously resenting Sadie's glibness.

"Sadie, as usual, you're making a mountain—"

"Men!" exclaimed Sadie, "Who needs the creeps! Mark

my words, you and Lindamargaret will be better off. It's lucky it happened as early as it did, so she won't remember him. Thank God she's a girl!"

Aggie was different. Out of the depths of Aggie's limpid, violet-brown eyes, Linda saw a blend of sorrow, compassion, and acceptance of the inevitable.

"Bound to happen," Aggie said softly, the eternal Eve. She seemed singularly unsurprised. Did she still talk to Darter Evans on the telephone?

"Aggie!" accused Linda. "You knew!"

"Only knew what's in the stars," countered Aggie mildly. "Ain't no use fighting fate!"

But Delcie.

Telling Delcie was like tossing a lighted match into a gas tank. Delcie exploded and kept on burning. The ferocity of her wrath prevented Linda from getting a word in edgewise.

"You can't mean it! You're joking! It isn't true! You *do* mean it! You're crazy, I'm telling you right now you ought to see a psychiatrist. You have to be nuts! How else could you do this to my precious godchild?" Delcie insisted on calling Lindamargaret her godchild, even though she wasn't. "Great holy Lucifer! You're married, married to your one and only, and you don't have the horse sense to appreciate it! You have the hottest love match on record since Romeo and Juliet, and you bust it up! You dumb-kopf!"

"*I* didn't bust it up." Linda hadn't intended to say that, but Delcie had jabbed an exposed nerve. "He was the one who left."

"Why didn't you stop him?" Delcie demanded in shrill accusation. "Why didn't you block the door? Why didn't you throw your arms around his knees and drag your heels and beg him to stay?"

Linda had put off telling her parents, making one excuse after another as to Rick's whereabouts, but at last one Sunday when she and Lindamargaret arrived for dinner, she spit the news out in a rush, before Margaret could remark on Rick's absence. To Linda's discomfiture, her mother burst into tears.

"Mother—"

They had drifted into the living room, where Margaret

now sank into the down pillows of the blue velvet sofa, casting about for a handkerchief, which Robert supplied.

"Mother, for heaven's sake! It's not that bad!"

"Not that bad!" Her mother looked at her daughter as if Linda had just snatched the purse from a ninety-year-old cripple to support her dope habit. "How could you do this to us?"

"To you!" Linda was edgy these days and didn't let unimportant things slip by. "I was under the impression it was happening to me."

"How can we ever explain it?"

"Who do you have to explain it to?"

"Whom!"

"Whom."

Her mother was at once indignant and accusing.

"You can say that, when you have ten thousand dollars worth of wedding presents still in their boxes!"

Linda moaned.

"That has no bearing whatsoever—"

"You seem to be determined to disgrace us!"

"Muth-er!"

Lindamargaret, radar-sensitive to the emotions crackling through the room, began to cry, and Linda hoisted the heavy baby upright against her shoulder and rocked back and forth on the balls of her feet, trying to calm the child.

"I should think for once you'd think about how your actions affect other people," complained Margaret, her face muffled in the handkerchief.

"Mother, what I do affects me and me alone!"

"You're overlooking the fact that your mother spent a good deal of time and money on your wedding," reminded Robert, his voice stern.

"Oh for cripes sake, are we back to that old wedding syndrome again?"

The baby continued to scream.

"Not to mention Lindamargaret!" said Margaret. "You haven't even considered how this is going to affect her!"

Linda left without having dinner. She couldn't have choked down a grain of salt. She was up-tight, her mother was still sobbing into the moist handkerchief, her father bristled. Lindamargaret was yelling her lungs out. How ironic, Linda thought as she gunned down Huntington

Drive in the Toyota, clenching the steering wheel so tightly her knuckles turned white. How utterly ironic! Her parents had done everything possible to break up her marriage, yet now it had happened they acted as if it was the end of the world!

Word of Mrs. Dublin's separation spread through the department like the odor of a pungent cigar, its chemistry evoking a subtle change in the attitude of her male co-workers toward Linda. Whether standing by her in an elevator or beside the watercooler, the men took to companionably draping an arm about Linda's shoulder, or her waist, or dropping one hand down her back so that the palm accidentally brushed her fanny.

Super-sensitive, Linda took offense at everyone's reaction, no matter what it was. To hell with all of them! Her separation was nobody's business but her own. She decided to avoid the whole bunch—acquaintances, friends, family, keeping to herself as much as possible. She was determined to be brave, make a go of it, lead her own life, do her own thing. She reminded herself her job was true intellectual fulfillment.

Time went by and her days were filled with cruddy kids and cruddy adults who had perpetrated cruddy acts upon each other, who had cheated, stolen, pimped, solicited, fucked, raped, beaten, stabbed. Sex was all over the place, but where was love? Didn't kids fall in love any more? One night, going home on the freeway, it hit her. She knew what love was, but not many people did. What she'd had—she and Rick—hardly ever happened any more.

By now she had settled into a routine. She had everything reasoned out, apportioned into neat pigeonholes in her mind. So why did she feel so blue? Why did she feel herself a solitary wayfarer in a Dali wasteland of loneliness? The deep, terrible, grinding pain built up inside her viscera till she could scarcely function. She longed for Rick, longed for his warm, firm touch, his arms around her, crushing her ribcage, his fresh-shaved cheek pressed against hers, his sweet mouth closing over hers. She wakened in the morning feeling the salt dried on her cheeks, knowing she had cried in her dreams. She was sarcastic to the secretaries, she was vindictive with her parents on the phone, she snapped at Lindamargaret and once she shook the baby roughly till she cried. Ahead, stretching to infinity, she had visions of the midnight earaches, the onslaught of intestinal flu, the fall from the tricycle, the tonsillitis, the broken arm, the orthodontia, the chicken pox, the hives—all the problems of parenthood which she would have to solve by herself. Lying in bed alone at three a.m., the agony that came over her left her so cold she was overwhelmed. She felt as if she was being swept away, as if she would drown in her own sorrow.

Vaguely, as if it were happening to someone else, Linda realized her depression had passed its normal bounds and verged on the pathological. Sometimes she felt she couldn't go on, not another day, not another hour. She sensed she needed help, but was too proud to seek it. What was the matter with her? Why couldn't she get her head on straight, get it all together? Finally one sunny Sunday morning Linda took Lindamargaret to the park. She was supposed to be the counselor, the solver of others' problems. Why shouldn't she solve her own? While the baby crawled on the grass, Linda sat on a blanket, determined to find out what was bugging her, and to try to put a stop to it once and for all.

One would think that when two people started out loving each other, really loving each other, they could make it work. Wasn't that the American dream?

He'd given her no advance warning—none! There was no reason, absolutely not one shred of reason for him to split. There had never been another man. He had nothing to be jealous about, nothing.

But there must have been some reason . . .

She'd gone over the reasons a hundred times. Obviously, it was Rick's fault. Rick couldn't take the hassle, couldn't take the responsibility. Rick was selfish, he chickened out, he came from a disadvantaged background, his father had been a crum.

In the pellucid yellow-green sunlight, Linda perceived these were not truths, but mere accusations. She ran to pick up the baby who in her explorations had crawled far afield, and carried her back to the blanket.

What were the real reasons?

Linda frowned, dredging them up one by one from the tarpit of her subconscious, where they had purposely been buried. We never get to sleep together! We never have time to make love! (But that wasn't *her* fault!) You don't love me any more! (There ought to be more to a relationship than sex!) You care more about your job than about me! (What an immature remark! But was it true?) Sure I love the baby, but you never have time for me! (My God, he was a father, and he still saw himself in the role of a child!) All right, so I resent your parents! (Why couldn't he have been mature enough to accept them as they were?)

The trouble was, people were either givers or takers. She and Rick had both been takers.

Let's face it, I just don't want to get married! She'd felt that way, too—till she got pregnant. So did all their friends. Songwriters, talk shows, everybody was down on marriage these days. Nobody wanted to get married, nobody expected marriage to work. A generation ago, everyone expected to get married. Marriage was the In Thing. Now marriage was the Out Thing. She'd had to work so hard to sell Rick on the idea of marriage, she never considered the possibility the marriage might not work, never guessed she would have to *continue* selling him on marriage, all along! She took it for granted that once the knot was tied they'd live happily ever after. Foolishly, she'd sat back on her oars and let the boat drift toward the cataract.

On her present crawling expedition, Lindamargaret had arrived at the edge of a flower bed and now paused like a pointer, on pink, plump knees and hands, observing the miracle of a petunia.

"Flower," said her mother. "Pretty flower! Ooh no, don't touch it! It's so delicate!"

That was it. Linda hadn't realized how delicate love was, or that it could die of neglect.

Lindamargaret was growing sleepy. Linda took the baby on her lap and offered her a bottle. The child sucked contentedly, looking up at her mother with trusting gray eyes —Rick's eyes. Linda sighed. She'd been so concerned with fulfilling her "possible" she'd never once thought about Rick's. What about Rick's aspirations, his dreams? Rick was meant to play football, coach football, not sit behind a telephone switchboard on the graveyard shift.

Together, she and Rick had had a unique, precious love. They had brought a love child into being—and then they'd smashed the whole thing to smithereens! If Rick was guilty, she was guilty, too.

Slowly, Linda stuffed the rattle and bottle in the diaper bag and gathered up the blanket to go home. At last she'd figured out the whys, but none of the whys had answers.

On Monday morning Linda tried to figure out how to rehab Debbie, a thirteen-year-old who'd been booked for prostitution, who was mainlining heroin; who had VD and was four months pregnant.

Dr. Steinberg said, "But you know what the problem *is*, don't you, Mrs. Dublin?"

"No," said Linda, stupidly as it turned out.

"The child reared in a one-parent home is unable to pattern after a loving man-woman relationship."

"Doctor," Linda said, "that's a psychological cop-out."

"Read the cum file," he said. "Debbie's been on an emotional see-saw since she was two. Debbie's mother has been like a bitch in heat. She's gone through one boyfriend after another."

Linda started to argue. The air conditioning had gone on the blink and it was hot and smelly, even in the conference room.

"Let's be objective," Linda said. "What Debbie's mother did—"

"Debbie's been deprived of the masculine half of parenting."

"Next I suppose you'll say that's responsible—"

Dr. Steinberg could be so damned pedantic!

"Debbie has been subjected to a *sub rosa* disdain of men, devaluing of men, hatred of men—"

That got Linda's hackles up.

"It seems to me—" she began.

"Did you know there had been a marriage?"

"Look," Linda said, "a million factors enter in to what happened to Debbie—bad companions, bad grades at school, a crowd hooked on drugs . . ."

"We followed up on the father," Dr. Steinberg said.

That was when the whole mess started to get to Linda.

"Look," she said, "that couple was divorced when

Debbie was two. The father has as much to do with this case as the man in the moon."

"Would it interest you to know that the father, like the mother, has never since been able to maintain a lasting relationship with a person of the opposite sex?"

"It wouldn't interest me at all," Linda told him. "Let's stop playing this sociological tic tac toe and figure out a positive program to help Debbie."

At this point Dr. Steinberg leaned across the desk. He seemed to be peering down inside the scoop neckline of Linda's blouse.

"Why don't we go somewhere after work," he suggested, "and figure it out over a tall cold vodka collins? I know a nice motel out in the valley . . ."

He reached out and brushed her bare arm. There was no mistaking his meaning. Linda shuddered involuntarily. She admired Dr. Steinberg, he was her superior, he was the person who would critique her master's thesis, but he had the clammy touch of a lizard. That was when she knew, fervently and unequivocally, that she was still in love with Rick, that she probably always would be, that the thought of doing it with any other man made her physically ill.

Now that she had made a few discoveries and settled down to try to live with them, Linda felt more miserable than before, her despondency exacerbated by guilt. Not only had she ruined her own life, she had deprived her baby of a father.

Yet the more she thought of it, she found that she was impaled on the horns of a cruel dilemma. Her heart and body yearned for, agonized for Rick. She didn't want to live her life alone. She needed love as she needed air. She couldn't go on without love. Bereft of love she would assuredly languish and die. Nevertheless, she could not relinquish her self-determination. Now she'd had a taste of freedom she could never give it up! She had to continue to explore her "possible," to make the most of what she had inside her. That, she realized slowly, was not her problem alone. It was the crisis which was tearing apart every woman of her generation. No wonder tradition was turned upside down! No wonder California had more divorces than marriages! It was the pressing question of her time— so far, without a viable solution!

At night, Linda's heart cried out for love. How could love cause such pain? But then, out of the night, the black, quiet, all-enveloping dark in which her mind burned and flickered like a candle, the answers began to come. Love, she began to see, to reason—love didn't cause the pain. Love was not the culprit. The difficulty was in grafting together two unrelated lives. Love in and of itself did not destroy one's individuality. On the contrary, she remembered the first month she had loved Rick—never had she looked prettier, felt more alive, been smarter. That, too, had been true of Rick. He'd been terrific with the freshman squad! He'd told her since he'd started loving her he could jump higher, run faster, do anything he tried!

Linda held her breath. Could that mean that if a person loved unreservedly—and was so loved in return—that person's abilities exploded? Feverishly, Linda jumped up and started pacing the worn carpet between the crib and the Hide-a-Bed. Could love be a source of energy? Her thoughts flew back to what she classified as their "other good period"—the months after Lindamargaret recovered from the colic. How happy Linda and Rick had both been then! How well they'd felt! They'd had the world by the tail—they could have moved mountains! Linda stopped by the window and looked down at the deserted street, a canyon of charcoal shadows. How desperately she longed to recapture those bright, cheerful days of happiness!

What had gone wrong? She'd wanted to achieve her "possible"—but wait! Didn't her "possible" include her capacity to love?

If she was right—if love was a wellspring of power—if she truly loved Rick, as she now knew she did, and if Rick still loved her—*anything was possible*! Whatever potential either of them had, love would increase it. So many ifs! But, like a scientist on the brink of earth-shaking discovery, Linda by instinct knew this was the answer!

Love was energy. Love was unending power. If they could throw away their hang-ups, their reservations, their hurt feelings, their imagined slights, and depend on the energy of love, they'd have it made! The mere mechanics of meshing their two—no, their three—lives would solve themselves.

Awakened by her mother's footsteps, Lindamargaret stood up questioningly. Linda lifted her, reveling in the fresh, cool, exquisite newness of the baby's skin. An outpouring of tenderness toward her child, toward Rick—and toward herself—flowed through her body. How is it I exist? she whispered. The answer came as if she heard it spoken: a person exists in his or her own self-liking, self-assertiveness—(that much she knew, that much was true enough, but there was more)—*that person can grow and blossom, can achieve unguessed-at heights of "possible" in the radiant, life-giving climate of love!*

At last, she had the solution she had sought so long! At last, at long last, she had discovered her identity! Surprisingly, that identity was three-faceted: the competent, decisive Linda who used her mind and education to the fullest, the Linda who nurtured Lindamargaret, and the Linda who loved Rick, and who needed Rick to love her in return.

FORTY-TWO

United Flight 100 had been stacked over Chicago's O'Hare Airport for forty minutes, but at last the control tower called it in. After certain maneuverings (the giant 747 was as clumsy on the ground as it was graceful in the air) it nestled up to its accordion-pleated corridors and disgorged its three hundred and seventy-four passengers.

Linda Dublin was neither first nor last to disembark, but somewhere in the amorphous middle of the slowly moving crowd. Once she emerged into the brightly lighted lounge she paused uncertainly, clutching her heavy child. Her fellow passengers and their welcoming relatives jostled about her. Everyone else was being met, Linda noted with a pang of envy. She had been so preoccupied with the mechanics of packing and storing her possessions, transporting herself to Los Angeles Airport and boarding the flight that she had neglected to think about what would happen at the other end. At least she'd done it!

The previous morning Linda had been waiting for Dr. Steinberg in his private office when he arrived at eight. His pleasure at encountering her—alone—had changed to indignation when Linda told him she wanted to resign—that afternoon. Dr. Steinberg threatened, bluffed, pleaded, and in the end wrote her a flowery recommendation, in triplicate.

Linda's parents had been more intractable, alternating between ranting and crying, each on an extension phone. They were nervous about their grandchild's safety on this manic goosechase, they feared Linda wouldn't find Rick, they predicted Rick would not want Linda back. Energized by her new-found inner source of strength, Linda had been neither patronizing nor snotty. She parried their objections with detachment. It was amazing! For the first time in her life she was able to view Margaret and Robert Allenby not as her parents but as human beings, beset by frailties and shortcomings as were all humans, but persons in their own right nonetheless, beautiful persons, persons who loved her. As one adult to another she had answered them calmly and truthfully, but nothing they said could swerve her from her course. She was like an intercontinental missile, locked on target.

At least she hadn't had to explain her motivations to Delcie. Delcie had come over all-a-flutter as soon as she could get there after work, to give Linda moral support, to help her pack, to tend Lindamargaret. Delcie had been delirious with approval. But Sadie! On no account would Linda have told Sadie Blankenhazen she was going to Chicago, but Sadie had found out through Jill Bryant. The phone jangled a few minutes before midnight, and Sadie's shrill voice had screamed, "Traitor! You'll be sorry!"

Remembering, Linda shivered. Throughout the last thirty-six hours since her miraculous discovery she had remained steadfast in her resolve, drawing sustenance from her new fount of strength, certain she was doing the right thing. But now she was actually in Chicago, what did she do next? The crowd milled about her. She had forgotten how disorienting such a mob could be. She had no phone number to reach Rick, no address. Should she telephone the ball club? How would they be listed—Bears? It was all too ludicrous. How would she ask for Rick? He wasn't a member of the team, he wasn't on the payroll. He was a hanger-on. I want to speak to my husband, he's been hanging around with the Bears. For all she knew, the Bears might have dozens of hangers-on. Would the girl at the switchboard know which hanger-on was Rick?

Or suppose Rick was no longer here. Linda should have telephoned Darter Evans before she started out. Suppose Rick had stopped hanging out with the Bears and had latched onto a job somewhere else? He might have left Chicago, left the state. He could be anywhere.

Or, even worse, the possibility Linda had shut out of her mind but which now came storming the barricades— suppose Rick was living with another woman?

A stout old lady carrying a wig case crashed into Linda from behind, mumbling a prefunctory "Sorry." Linda shifted Lindamargaret to the other hip. Maybe the whole trip had been a mistake. It had seemed right at the time but now she could see the proposed reunion was a fantasy, something she'd fabricated in her own mind, something that couldn't happen in real life. Supposing Linda found out where Rick was living, and went to the apartment, and a girlfriend opened the door?

Linda felt her eyes fill with tears. She couldn't stand here all day. She had to do something. Go back? Trouble was, she'd burned all her bridges. The baby seemed to weigh more by the second. Linda's back began to ache. At least, she'd go and get her suitcase, and then she'd make some kind of a decision.

It was at this point, over the hubbub, she heard her name called, harshly, incredulously.

"Linda?"

Thoughts flashed through Linda's head with the speed of electricity. Se knew no one in Chicago. Linda was a common name. This had to be some other Linda. Someone was calling some other Linda—but oh, dear God, *that someone had Rick's voice!*

She turned, not believing, not daring to believe, and saw him, head and shoulders above the crowd, bulldozing toward her, jostling passengers aside right and left like so many attacking Trojans.

"Rick!" Linda heard her own voice, squeaky with surprise. "What are you doing here?"

He was upon her then, his great arms enfolding her and the baby in a giant bear hug, his lips on Linda's, hungrily, greedily sweet, for one long suspended slice of heaven. At last he released her, held her at arm's length, drank in her image with his eyes.

"You came!" Rick managed to say. He was crying. Big Rick was crying, but Linda didn't care. Linda was crying too. "I couldn't stand it," Rick confessed, "that's why I'm here, I couldn't take it any longer, not without you! I just bought my ticket. I was coming back!"

For no reason, for every reason, they went on crying, tears sliding down their cheeks. Only Lindamargaret smiled. Lindamargaret reached out one plump, pink hand to touch Rick's chest.

"Da." said Lindamargaret. "Da-da-da-da!"

Tenderly Lindamargaret's father took her from her mother and tucked her in the crook of his elbow, like a football. Then, his other arm around Linda, the three of them went forth to claim the baggage.

IN HOLLYWOOD, WHERE DREAMS DIE QUICKLY, ONE LOVE LASTS FOREVER . . .

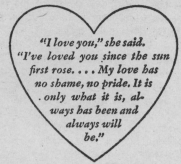

"I love you," she said. "I've loved you since the sun first rose. . . . My love has no shame, no pride. It is only what it is, always has been and always will be."

The words are spoken by Brooke Ashley, a beautiful forties film star, in the last movie she ever made. She died in a tragic fire in 1947.

A young screenwriter in a theater in Los Angeles today hears those words, sees her face, and is moved to tears. Later he discovers that he wrote those words, long ago; that he has been born again—as she has.

What will she look like? Who could she be? He begins to look for her in every woman he sees . . .

A Romantic Thriller
by
TREVOR MELDAL-JOHNSEN

AVON

41897
$2.50

THE BIG BESTSELLERS
ARE AVON BOOKS

A Woman of Independent Means

A Novel by
Elizabeth
Forsythe
Hailey

THE SPLENDID
NATIONAL BESTSELLER

"Nothing about it is ordinary . . . irresistible."
Los Angeles Times

"Bares the soul of an independent American housewife . . .
a woman to respect . . . a writer to remember."
John Barkham Reviews

AVON $2.50

AVON ◆ THE BEST IN BESTSELLING ENTERTAINMENT

Available at better bookstores everywhere, or order direct from the publisher.

He is happily married to another woman.
She is happily married to another man.

ADJACENT LIVES

How do you
choose between
the love of
your life and
the passion of
a lifetime?

Find out in
one of the most
beautifully
written love
stories in years.

"FINE AND
PASSIONATE....
Her gift is for
evoking desire...
a serious and
important writer."
The New Republic

ELLEN SCHWAMM

ADJ-9/79